SUZANNAH DUNN is t̶h̶e̶ ̶a̶u̶t̶h̶o̶r̶ ... h
have been critically ac... ls
include *The Sixth Wife*, *The Queen's* ... st
recent success, *The Confession of Katherine Howard*.

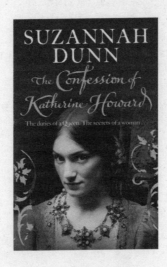

The Queen of Subtleties

❀ ❀ ❀

SUZANNAH DUNN

Harper
Press

HarperPress
An imprint of HarperCollins*Publishers*
77–85 Fulham Palace Road, Hammersmith, London W6 8JB

This Harper*Press* paperback edition published 2011

1

First published by Flamingo 2004

Copyright © Suzannah Dunn 2004

Suzannah Dunn asserts the moral right to
be identified as the author of this work

A catalogue record for this book is available from the British Library

ISBN: 978-0-00-790774-8

Set in Sabon by
Palimpsest Book Production Limited, Falkirk, Stirlingshire

Printed and bound in Great Britain by Clays Ltd, St Ives plc

MIX
Paper from
responsible sources
FSC **FSC˚ C007454**
www.fsc.org

FSC™ is a non-profit international organisation established to promote
the responsible management of the world's forests. Products carrying the
FSC label are independently certified to assure consumers that they come
from forests that are managed to meet the social, economic and
ecological needs of present and future generations,
and other controlled sources.

Find out more about HarperCollins and the environment at
www.harpercollins.co.uk/green

Contents

❀ ❀ ❀

For my own little
Tudor-redheaded heir,
Vincent

Notes

❀ ❀ ❀

A 'Mrs Cornwallis' is recorded as having been Henry VIII's confectioner, and the only woman in the household's two hundred kitchen staff. All that is known of her, apart from her surname and job, is that the king eventually gave her a fine house in Aldgate in recognition of her services. All other aspects of the Lucy Cornwallis character and her story in this novel are fictional, as are those of her close colleagues. Names and job titles of other household staff aim to be historically accurate, as is the itinerary for the summer 'progress' (royal tour) of 1535.

All events recorded or referred to in the 'Anne Boleyn' sections of the novel aim to be historically accurate, with three small exceptions: the motto embroidered on the king's jousting costume for Shrove Tuesday, 1526, was not in fact 'No Comment' but 'Declare je nos' ('Declare I dare not'); Anne's uncle, the Duke of Norfolk, not Sir Henry Norris, broke the news to her of Henry's serious fall in the spring of 1536; and the aunt with Anne in the Tower was not the Elizabeth who had been Duchess of Norfolk, but another one.

Diminutives of names have been used to avoid confusion (between, for example, the many Henrys and Francises, Marys and Elizabeths) or to avoid a dated version (Meg Shelton was in fact known as Madge, and Betsy Blount as Bessie). Anne Boleyn's dog was in fact named 'Purkoy' (believed to be from the French 'pourqois', because of his enquiring expression) and not, as here, 'Pixie'.

THE QUEEN OF SUBTLETIES

Anne Boleyn

❀ ❀ ❀

Elizabeth, you'll be told lies about me, or perhaps even nothing at all. I don't know which is worse. You, too, my only baby: your own lifestory is being re-written. You're no longer the king's legitimate daughter and heir. Yesterday, with a few pen-strokes, you were bastardized. Tomorrow, for good measure, a sword-stroke will leave you motherless.

There are people who'd have liked to have claimed that you're not your father's daughter at all, but you've confounded them. You're a Tudor rose, a pale redhead, whereas I'm a black-haired, olive-skinned, coal-eyed Englishwoman as dark as a Spaniard. No one has felt able to suggest that you're other than your father's flesh and blood.

You won't remember how I look, and I don't suppose you'll ever come across my likeness. Portraits of me will be burned. You'll probably never even come across my handwriting, because my letters and diaries will go the same way. Even my initial will be chiselled from your father's on carvings and masonry all around the country. And it starts tomorrow, with the thud of the sword to my bared neck in time for my husband's public announcement of his forthcoming marriage. As his current wife, I pose a problem. Not such a big one, though, that the thinnest of blades can't solve it.

I want you to know about me, Elizabeth. So, let's start at the beginning. I was born at the turn of the century. And what a turn, what a century: the sixteenth, so different from every one before it. The changes I've seen. Gone, quite suddenly, is the old England, the old order of knights and priests. England used to be made of old men. Men born to their place, knowing their place. We Boleyns have always prided ourselves on knowing just

1

about everything there is to know about anything, with the exception of our place.

I was born in Norfolk. My mother is a Howard. Her brother is the Duke of Norfolk. I was born in Blickling Hall. I've no memories of Norfolk, but I'm told that the land is flat, the sky high and wide. So, from the beginning, it seems, I've had my sights on the horizon. The climate, in Norfolk, is something I've heard about: blanketed summers and bare, bone-cracking winters. Inhospitable and uncompromising, like the Howards. If the world had never changed, that would have suited the Howards.

Something else I've heard about the Howards: that the Duke, my Uncle Norfolk, has the common touch. At first, it seems a strange thing to hear about the last man in England to have owned serfs; but in a way, it's true, because, for him, business is everything and he's unafraid to get his hands dirty. No airs and graces. Land and money: that's what matters to a Howard. My uncle has never read a book, and he's proud of the fact. Ruthlessness and efficiency: that's what matters. He'll clap you on the back, one day; stab you in it, the next. No hard feelings, just business as usual. Never trust a Howard, Elizabeth, not even if you are one. Look where it got me, sent here to the Tower by my own uncle.

But I'm a Boleyn first and foremost. My father didn't have the Howard privileges; he's had to make his own way in the world. And he has; oh, he has: cultured, clever, cool-eyed Thomas Boleyn. England has never seen the likes of him. For a start, he has a talent almost unknown here: he speaks French like a Frenchman. Which has made him indispensable to the king.

We Boleyns have lived a very different life from everyone else, in this country; from everyone else under these heavy English skies, in their musty old robes and gowns, slowly digesting their stews. I lived in France from when I was twelve until I was twenty. I grew up to be a Frenchwoman, I came back to England as a Frenchwoman. There are women in France who are strong, Elizabeth, because they're educated. Unlike here, where the only way to be a strong woman is to be a harridan. Imagine how it was, for me, to come back. For years, I'd been thinking in French. In France, anything seems possible, and life is to be lived. Even now, stuck in the Tower, a day away from death, I'm alive, Elizabeth, in a way that most people here haven't ever been and won't ever be. I pity their bleak, grovelling little lives.

Forget Norfolk, Elizabeth; forget the Howards, and old England and Catholicism and creaky Blickling Hall. Think Hever: the castle which we, the Boleyn family, made our home. Mellowcoloured, grand and assured. Perhaps you'll go there, one day. I grew up there.

I was a commoner, but I became queen. No one thought it possible, but I did it. I supplanted the woman who'd been England's queen for nineteen years, a woman who'd been born 'the daughter of the Catholic Kings'. Her royal blood, her regal bearing, her famed grace and benevolence were nothing against me, in the end. She was a fat old pious woman when I'd finished with her. And England was changed for ever. It had to be done. I got old England by the throat, and shook it until it died.

Forget the ex-wife, for now, and let's start instead with men. Because the story of my life – and now, it seems, my death – is largely a story of me and men. I like them. They're easy to impress. I like male openness, eagerness. When I came to the English court, twenty and fresh from France, I fell in love with Harry, Lord Percy. Nothing particularly unusual in that. Women did it all the time. What made the difference was that Harry was in love with me. Twenty-two-year-old Harry Percy: that lazy smile; the big, kissable mouth. He dressed beautifully, but with none of the awful, old-fashioned flamboyance of his fellow-Englishmen. He was stylish. He could afford to be: he was one of the wealthiest heirs in the country. Which was another point in his favour.

Too easy-going for the saddle, and clearly bored by the prospect of tennis, he managed to be surprisingly popular with the men. He was a drinker, though, even then, which might explain it. He was somehow in the thick of things yet an outsider, an observer; and that appealed to me, newly arrived at court. Women loved him because he loved women: loved women's company, women's bodies. That was obvious, or at least to women. Men, clueless, probably didn't see him for the competition that he was. We women instinctively understood that Harry was a pleasure-seeker and that if we granted him his pleasures, he'd savour them. Nevertheless, as far as I could discover, he had no reputation for sleeping around. On the contrary, it seemed that he was choosy, and unwilling to play the game of big romances. There was a take-it-or-leave-it air to him, a clarity of purpose and refusal to compromise that intrigued me and which I admired.

We circled each other for a couple of weeks, if 'circled' isn't too active a word for Harry. I knew he'd noticed me. How could he not? – I was the new girl at court, wearing the latest French fashions. One late afternoon, when I was sauntering down a passageway, he stepped from behind a door to stop me in my tracks.

'Walk with me,' he said.

I said nothing – biding my time – and simply did as he requested, moving ahead of him through the doorway into a courtyard. The air was warmer than I'd anticipated. All day long, I'd been stuck indoors, doing my lady-in-waiting duties: playing cards, playing music. Outside, my eyes seemed to open properly, wide, and I felt my shoulders drop. I wondered, briefly, why I didn't do this more often: get away, walk away.

We went towards the rose garden. 'Back home,' he said, breaking the silence, 'in our gardens, we can smell the sea. I miss it. I feel so hemmed in, here.'

'Oh, so, we're walking and talking, are we?'

That shut him up. Good. *Walk with me*, indeed.

I had a question for him: 'What did you think of the play, last night?'

He looked about to offer up a platitude, but caught himself in time. His shrug was pitched somewhere between non-committal and despondent.

I said, 'Yes, but you laughed all through it.'

He was defensive. 'We're at court.' Court: eat, drink, and be merry. Then came that smile of his: 'And, anyway, so were you; you were laughing.'

My turn to shrug. 'We're at court.'

'You were probably laughing the most of anyone. You're very good at it, aren't you.'

'At laughing?'

'At being at court.'

I said, 'I don't do anything by halves.'

In the garden, we sat on a bench, and I said, 'Do you want to know what I really think, Harry Percy, about that play? And all the plays, here? And the music, the poetry, the food, clothes, manners?' I sat back, crossed my ankles. 'The gardens, even?'

Elbows on thighs, he stared at the ground. 'You miss France.'

I snatched a petal, rolled it between my fingertips. 'Don't get me started. I mean it. Tell me about where *you* miss. Tell me about that home of yours.'

So, we started with the places we'd come from, and ended, hours later, with the books that were changing our lives. I remember asking him how he'd got hold of one of them, still banned in England, and him replying that he had his sources. I said that was a secret I'd like him to let me in on, when he felt able.

He took the fragment of petal from me and said, 'Oh, I don't envisage keeping any secrets from you.'

Dusk had closed over us. The palace was emerging as a constellation of lit porches, lit windows. Passers-by, spellbound by the half-light, talked less guardedly than usual. Harry and I were adrift from the rest of the world, yet right at the heart of it. On dark water, but in the shallows.

'Anne?' He sounded almost weary. The kiss was the barest brush of his lips, very slowly, over mine. And mine over his.

From that moment onwards, all that mattered to us was being together. Whenever I saw him across a room being sweet and attentive to some woman, I'd smile to think how, a little later, he'd have his mouth jammed against mine and I'd have him helpless. I lived in a permanent state of offering silent thanks to God for Harry's existence. I couldn't believe my luck; I couldn't believe how close I'd come, unknowingly, to a living death of never having known him.

But I'd reckoned without the man who, in England, at that time, played God: Cardinal Wolsey. Wolsey had other plans for Harry, for various political reasons. He had plans for Harry's family which didn't include a Boleyn. He contacted Harry's father, who came and gave him hell before dragging him home and marrying him to a woman he didn't know and grew to hate. And he's still there: up there in Northumberland, rattling around his ancestral home, childless and drunk.

The worst that happened to me was that I was sent home to Hever for the summer; but, of course, at the time, it felt like a fate worse than death. I spent that summer railing against Wolsey. It wasn't long before I was joined in that by the rest of my family, because that was the summer when my father was made a peer – Lord Rochford – and it looked as if all his hard work was paying off until Wolsey forced his resignation as Lord Treasurer. Some rubbish about a conflict of interests. We Boleyns lost a salary, and Wolsey gained considerably in our animosity.

My father hadn't been alone, kneeling to be honoured in that crowded and unbearably hot Presence Chamber. In front of him was six-year-old Fitz, the king's bastard son. Dimple-faced, apricot-haired Fitz, brought from his nursery in Durham House on the Strand. He was made Duke of Richmond, then he sat for the rest of the ceremony on the royal dais at his father's right hand. Officially welcomed to court. A month later, he was sent away again, but only because of the sweating sickness that drove into London's population. Suddenly he was the owner of a castle up north, and recipient of an income from eighty manor houses. Travelling up there with him was a staff of three hundred, including a retinue of the very best tutors. My point is that he left court not as he'd arrived – as Betsy Blount's lovely little boy, the king's adored bastard boy – but as a kind of prince.

Of course, something similar had to be seen to be done for the princess. Ludlow, for her, in August. I didn't see Fitz's departure but I was there in the courtyard for Mary's; I remember the vivid livery of those two hundred servants: blue and green. I was one of the queen's ladies-in-waiting. The queen was snivelling; she snivelled not only when the princess was taken away through the gates but for days afterwards. She was already becoming hard to please. Certainly the pomp of her daughter's departure for Ludlow wasn't enough to mollify her. She'd sat through little Fitz becoming a knight of the garter in April, but his peerage in June and the northern palace in July was, in her view, going too far. Wolsey dismissed three of her women for moaning about Fitz's fortunes, and, worse, when she appealed, he refused to reinstate them. He had his uses, he had his moments. This was quite a shot across Catherine's bows. And at a bad time, for her, too: the previously talked-of Spanish betrothal for her under-sized brat having been scuppered. My point is that quite suddenly, that summer, no one of any standing was taking Catherine seriously, nor did they look set to.

The story that everyone tells is that Henry divorced his long-suffering, sweet-natured, middle-aged queen for me, a younger woman, a dark-eyed, gold-digging, devil-may-care temptress. The truth is more complicated. Take my age. I was twenty-six when Henry fell for me. No girl, then. At that age, I really should have been married (and would have been – I'd have been Countess of Northumberland – but for Wolsey). I should have had children. At twenty-six, I was worldly, educated, ambitious. No wide-eyed plaything. Yes, I was younger than Catherine – but who wasn't? She was forty, and seemed half as old again. It was all over, for her: the supposed bearer of heirs, she hadn't been pregnant for a decade. She was a dead weight on Henry.

And what a weight! What she lacked in stature, she made up for in girth. With all the health problems that you'd expect. And no wonder: all those failed pregnancies. And no wonder they failed, with everything that she put herself through: the ritual fasting, the rising during the small hours to pray, the arduous pilgrimages, trekking in all weathers, for weeks on end, to Walsingham. All this took a toll on her spirits, too. She retreated among her pious Spanish ladies and their Spanish priests. Ceased to live in the real world. But, then, in many ways, she never had. I'll not deny what people say, that she always had a kind word for everyone. The problem was in understanding it. Despite all her years in England, she was hopelessly foreign.

Why had Henry ever married her? Let's not forget it was his choice. His father had died. Only just died, in fact, and there's the answer: the marriage was Henry's choice, his first; the first big decision of a new, seventeen-year-old king. Marrying Catherine, he all at once made his mark and a prudent political move, an alliance with Spain. And, anyway, Henry was a chivalrous man; big-hearted, and determined to do the right thing. He wanted to end Catherine's misery: this kind, stoical, scholarly young woman, as he saw her, who was stuck in England, widowed, orphaned, and impoverished.

Anyway, there they were, years later: an odd couple. They even *looked* mismatched: she was the shortest woman at court; he, probably the tallest man in England. She waddled, whereas he was one of the best tennis players in Europe. She played cards with her ladies and then retired early to her bed. He partied until the early hours. She'd become an old lady while he was still a young man. She was looking forward to grandchildren, he was still hoping for heirs. There was, too, a fundamental difference in their attitudes to their faith. Henry's relationship with God was robust, direct. He didn't so much kneel before priests, in Catherine's manner, as clap them on the back and challenge them to debate.

By the time that I was one of her ladies-in-waiting, her life revolved around that scrappy, priest-worshipping daughter of hers. A repulsively colourless child. It was ridiculous, the idea that the dwarf daughter of an old Spaniard from a defunct lineage could ever follow in Henry's footsteps and rule England.

When Henry made his first move on me, my attention was elsewhere, albeit reluctantly. I hadn't bothered with love since Harry Percy. I didn't seem to have the heart for it. I didn't quite have the heart for Thomas Wyatt. Don't get me wrong, I was very fond of him: we'd been friends since childhood, and he was probably one of the best friends I had. But as a lover? I wasn't convinced. His feelings on this matter were unequivocal, though, and he was making them known. Easy, if you're a poet; and he was – is – one of England's finest. Everyone was reading the poems. No one could understand my reticence. The consensus among my friends was that Tommy was the ultimate catch: dashing, and clever; sensitive, and baby-blond.

Henry made his first move with a gift: a sugar rosebud. Placed on my pillow. Someone had come into my room while I was out, and placed on my pillow a bud cast in molten sugar. Glassy; rosewater-tinted. I didn't know it was from Henry until I read the tag, *HR*.

The presents that started coming were sometimes sugar, sometimes gold, and sometimes the sugary-gold of marchepane. Brooches, emblems, statuettes; stars, unicorns, Venus herself. Of course I thanked him for every one of them. But I hated it. With every ounce of sugar and gold, he must have felt that he was putting down another payment. And I wasn't for buying. Eventually I decided that something would have to be said, and asked him for a moment in private. I hated it, that I had to go and ask and he got what he wanted: word from me.

I told him, 'I don't mean to seem ungrateful – and I'm not – but you should stop giving me presents.'

He said, 'Should I?' Amused. Lofty and amused.

Which annoyed me, although of course I was careful not to show it. Careful to act the gracious girl. Everything was always easy for him, nothing could ever compromise him: king, doing just as he pleased. 'Yes,' I said.

'Oh? Why?'

The honest answer? 'Because it makes things difficult for me.'

'Oh.'

Yes. You, sailing through life, the rest of us eddying in your wake.

He switched tactics, to wheedling. 'I *like* giving you presents.'

I commanded myself, Stay gracious. 'And I like receiving them,' and I did; of course I did, 'But –'

An imperious wave of that jewelled hand, *No buts*. 'They suit you. Gold suits you. Presents suit you.' A grin. 'You're a presents sort of person.'

True. *Damn*. The hook, the reeling in.

He said, 'They're only presents.' Then, quieter, 'I *have* to give you presents.' Then, '*Please*.'

It stopped nothing, my confrontation. On the contrary ... The first letter came: *I should explain* ...

And what was it, that he explained? Oh, that he'd never known anyone like me. That kind of thing.

So then I had to go to him about the letter. 'Your letter –'

'Yes?'

Well? 'Thank you for it.'

'Oh. And?'

And? 'That's all: thank you for your letter.'

He laughed as if I'd made a joke. 'You'll write back to me?' He was still amused, but there was another look, too: his eyes clear and steady.

'Oh. Yes.' *Damn.* 'Yes, if you like.'

'If *you* like.'

I nodded while it sank in. 'I do.' But I had to, didn't I.

A week or so later, when I couldn't put if off any longer, when he'd mentioned it several times, I wrote that letter. *I can't*, I wrote. *I'm touched and honoured but I can't. It's not you, it's me. I can't be anyone's mistress, not even yours.*

He'd had mistresses; of course he had, married to Catherine. No surprise, there. The surprise was his discretion: Henry, the consummate showman, becoming low-key, cloak and dagger, keeping it all under wraps. There were times when everyone had suspected there was someone, but no one seemed to know who. A considerable achievement, such secrecy, at court. Other times, though, all was revealed and revelled in. Six or seven years before Henry wrote that first love letter to me, his mistress of the time had given birth to a baby boy. Mother of the king's only son, Betsy Blount was fêted. Little Fitz was given a grand christening, with Cardinal Wolsey, no less, named as Godfather. Catherine attended, fixed with that serene smile. Gracious, people said. Stupid, would be another way of putting it.

All my poor sister achieved was to have Henry name a battleship in her honour. Fitting, I imagine people said: *Mary Boleyn*, they probably said, has a lot of sailors in every port; *Mary Boleyn* rides the swell.

Any mistress of his known to us – my sister no exception – was of a certain type. Giggly. Fun. Fun is what a mistress is; it's what she's for. Henry loved fun, in those days; nothing was more important, to him, so nothing was more important to us at court. Court seemed to exist solely for that purpose: Henry's fun, day and night, summer and winter. Jousts, banquets, charades. Singing, hunting, gambling. And a mistress played her role. Knew her place, too. Fun while it – she – lasted. No misunderstandings. After Betsy had produced Fitz, in a residence provided for the purpose by the king, she never returned to court. Instead, she was married off to a man who was then favoured for various lucrative appointments. They've since had several children. My sister, too, in time, had had marital arrangements made on her behalf. Again, no problem: it was a happy marriage. No hard feelings, and no complications. For Henry, mistresses were mistresses, not potential wives. He *had* a wife.

I could never have been a mistress; it simply wasn't my style. Don't think that I couldn't be fun with the rest of them; more fun than the rest of them. (Remember: nothing by halves.) But I could never have been discarded, like that; passed over, married off. All good things come to an end, Henry had said to my sister. But of course she'd had no say in when.

Henry said to me, 'I don't *want* you to be my mistress.' We were sitting side by side in his private garden at Greenwich; a private moment at his request. '"Mistress",' he quoted, full of impatience, derision. 'You're not – you couldn't be.' He shook his head as if to clear it. 'I don't want a mistress; I want *you*.' A shrug, helpless. 'I want to *be with* you.'

That's all very nice, I said; noble sentiments, I said; but – face it – what I'd be is a mistress. His long, blank look was unreadable; I anticipated a berating for being hard-hearted.

But he muttered, 'I wish –' Then closed his eyes, gave up, said nothing.

Never mind: it would pass in any case, I assumed; this crush on me. I was intriguing, he was intrigued: that was all it was. When nothing happened, he'd lose interest. But I was wrong: six months later, his infatuation was worse. There was no escaping him, not even when I retreated to Hever: letters came (*Listen to me: there has never been and never will be anyone but you; I knew nothing until I met you*); presents came (clusters of jewels, sugar-shapes, and haunches of venison); and on one occasion *he* came (dining with my family and staying overnight).

I wouldn't have known those letters were from Henry but for the handwriting, the signature. They had nothing in them of the king that I or anyone else knew; our valiant, bombastic king. In these letters was someone at sea, in the dark.

Anne, yesterday you said . . .

Anne, please, may I just . . . ?

His problem was that he'd never been in love. This was unknown territory, for him. He'd lusted after women, yes. And there'd been women whose company he'd loved: he was a man who loved company, and there had been women. His marriage was testament to his chivalry, if nothing else. But in love? At someone's mercy? No, never. Not until me.

Not that this was enough, for me. Not enough to make me love him. Enough to stop me in my tracks, certainly, but to turn my head? No. All those letters, the walks in the gardens, the trysts that he requested: lovely though they were, they didn't do the trick. During those first weeks, he confided in me: his family, his horses, music, books, buildings, faith, France and Spain. I did warm to him, I'll admit, finding him mostly untouched despite the weight of the world on his shoulders. I listened, but deflected his questions. Keeping my distance, giving no ground.

It wasn't that I didn't like him. I did; by this time I liked him a lot. Funnily enough, what I liked in him was something that I loathe in everyone else: conservatism. It was understandable, in his case: part of the job. He wasn't a natural at it, though, which made him perfect prey for me to rib. And I do love to rib. And with no one but him was there ever enough danger, for me; no getting beneath the skin. He loved to *be* ribbed, perhaps because no one had ever dared do it. He was ripe for it, and I was match enough for him.

Winter came and there wasn't a single day, I don't think, when it didn't rain. Wolsey began 1526 cheerfully, though, with a spring-clean. His vision was a tidied royal household. One result was that my brother George lost his place in the Privy Chamber. Nothing personal, we were assured. He was just one of the six closest companions to the king to lose his job. Another, incidentally, was our cousin Francis. Gentlemen of the Privy Chamber down from twelve to six; just one of the cuts.

George was livid to have been so close to the centre and now be just another courtier. And – worse – guess who was in? Our brother-in-law, Mary's new husband: inoffensive William. William Carey: the name speaks for itself. And nice Harry Norris: Groom of the Stool, now, and Keeper of the Privy Purse (and who could be closer to a constipated, spendthrift king?). And cute Franky Weston, with his then not-quite-broken voice: he was taken on as a page. No one could ever have said that my brother or cousin were caring or nice or cute; theirs were different strengths. Not that it made much difference, in the end. Because they're all dead now, except Francis. Francis probably couldn't die unless a stake were driven through his heart. If he had a heart.

Not a stake through the heart, but a splinter in an eye: dashing Francis lost more than his place in the Privy Chamber, that year. It happened at the usual Shrovetide joust. Henry had ridden into the tiltyard on Govenatore, who was new to him then and perhaps even keener than him to make an impression. The horse played to the audience; and Henry, though loving the challenge and the spectacle, had his hands full. Hannibal Zinzano, the horsekeeper, was, I noticed, watchful at the side. It wasn't for Govenatore, though, that the crowd gasped; it was for what was embroidered in scarlet across the king's gold-and-silver chest: *No Comment*. Recognition rippled through the crowd as Henry cantered around and people saw it or had it translated for them. Everyone knew what it meant: there was someone; someone new. They thrilled to it; it was a game to them, a laugh. His own smile, if there was one, was behind his visor. I don't think he looked at me. He didn't need to. Me, I had no such luxury. Like everyone else, I was there to spectate.

I couldn't quite believe he'd done it. Indeed, I wasn't quite sure what it was that he'd done. Didn't know quite what to make of it. This declaring that he wouldn't declare. This being so public about his privacy. Was I in on the joke, or was the joke on me? And then, as I watched him skittering around the yard, it was as if the joke unfurled. This is what I saw: that when he'd had the idea, he would have had to go to Mr Jaspar, his tailor, and discuss design and colour; and later, he'd have had to take delivery of it, and express his appreciation. And on the morning of the joust, he'd have had to arrive at the stables in it to do his best with Govenatore. What I saw wasn't the seriousness of Henry's pursuit of me. Quite the opposite. What I saw was that it was a practicality, sometimes; and others, almost an irrelevancy. It was a fact of his life.

I saw it, and I turned away; I turned to my little cousin Maria. She and Hal, Uncle Norfolk's children, were at court for distraction from the worst of their parents' separation, and they'd come along with me to the joust. Maria was snuggled up to me and I turned to check she was wrapped tight against the cold. Behind me came a distinctive crowd-gasp: low, blunt. I snapped back to see Harry Norris sprinting across the tilt-yard. He was aiming for Henry and Francis, who were dismounted and fighting, or so it looked: Henry, trying to hold Francis's visored head; and Francis, frantic, reeling, crouching, pushing him away. The horses stood by, helpless; Govenatore, subdued. Henry's shouting was becoming words, a name: *Vicary; get Vicary*. His surgeon.

Vicary's good but he can't perform miracles. In the days after the accident, Francis's eye dried up and he never again removed the patch. It doesn't seem to have hampered him. On the contrary. Somehow he looks more dashing with it. No one knew how it had happened, that splinter into Francis's eye; not even Henry or Francis. Francis and I were good friends, back then; Francis and George and I. He was one of us. But that hasn't been true for a while now, to say the least, and I have found myself wishing that I'd seen it and could relish the memory of it: that sly, stunning blow.

No comment? But those in the know, already knew. Privacy at court is scarce; and, of course, the bigger you are, the less you have. There was all the *Dance with me, Anne*; and only so many ruby earrings that I could explain away and sugar stallions that I could get the boys to eat. I was beginning to understand that my resistance was, to a great extent, irrelevant. Word was that the king was obsessed with Anne Boleyn; and no one cared about the details, such as which favours he was or wasn't being granted. Why not play along with it, then? Go with it, get what I could from it? In a way, I didn't have a choice. Or, that wasn't the choice; the choice was not to end up as mother to some half-royal son and wife to some compliant, paid-off nonentity. That, I definitely wouldn't have. But why not have some fun, for a while? I should have been Countess Northumberland, with my own vast household, but instead I was still in the queen's rooms – all that praying and sewing – with no other suitor daring to raise his head. Why shouldn't I have a little fun, perhaps, and some jewellery?

So, I went to Henry, one evening, after a year or more of his attentions; I went changed, resolved, chancing it. He didn't register my change and was as unassumedly welcoming as usual: this king who, for my sake, was learning to live with so little of what he most wanted. I loved it, that evening: his guilelessness, openness. It dizzied me, made me tender. He was a sweet-natured man, in those days. His real nature is that of a soft-hearted man. At the end of that evening, when everyone had gone, I was still there. Me, the six weary musicians, and a whey-faced Franky Weston who was on duty to prepare Henry's bed. Outstaying my brother and the others – cousin Francis, Harry, Billy – had taken some doing, even for me. Did I say evening? The small hours, more like. The banquet table was littered with sugar lemons, oranges, figs and walnuts that had been cracked open and chiselled away at, bitten into: shells, now, on a sugary sand. I told Henry that I'd like a word. 'In private,' I said, quietly.

He leaned towards me, expectant.

'Strictly private,' I whispered.

He indicated to the others: *Skedaddle, would you?*

Six lots of strings winding to a sudden silence, seven pairs of feet released across the carpet. He turned to me, pleasant; nothing too much trouble. I felt both solemn – this was some undertaking, *this was it* – and ridiculously giggly. I kissed him, and he took up the kiss and carried it on.

Later that night, that dawn, he asked me if I'd stay, and I said no. He didn't mind; he was happy, it was a novelty, and there was everything to look forward to. Not long now, he was probably thinking. '*You*,' he chided: indulgent, familiar.

Those early days were bliss, for me. It had been a long time since someone had placed his lips on my pulse. Too long since someone's forefinger had run down my naked ring finger. Every evening, that summer, we stayed alone on the riverbank when the shadows were too blue for comfort.

But that was all we did. Every night, he asked me if I'd stay; every night, I said no. I wouldn't be his mistress. Our relationship, as far as I was concerned, was a dalliance. I even liked the word, *dalliance*. And of course I liked the jewellery. But then, one day, sometime late in 1526, something happened. All that happened was that he walked into a room, smiling, and sat down. That was all, but that was it. He didn't see me, when he came through that door. He came in with Billy Brereton, relating some tale that had Billy weak with laughter. I don't think he saw any of us in particular, merely raised a hand to the room, *Don't get up*. He strode past us all and slung himself into his throne; a long-limbed, loose-limbed man. He was grinning, pleased with himself: this king, this most kingly of kings, grinning like a boy. His hand flicked through his hair before he settled back and closed those gem-like eyes. *Look at you*, I thought, and knew, in that instant, that I'd been naive: we would have to spend our lives together. It was time, I saw, for him to move on. His marriage was over. Not that it was ever a marriage. Only ever a formality.

So, later that same evening, I asked him: 'If you love me so very much –'

'– Oh, I do, I do,' punctuated with kisses to my shoulder.

'– why don't you marry me?'

He laughed, 'Well–' Stopped. Stopped laughing.

Yes. Precisely. You're already married.

Shaken, he tried to make light of it: 'Anyway, *you* wouldn't marry *me*.'

'Wouldn't I?'

That smile was frozen; behind it, I could see, he was thinking fast. 'A clever young girl like you.'

'I thought there was no one like me.'

'There isn't.'

'Well, then.'

He sat back, the better to see my face. 'But you wouldn't, would you?'

And now I allowed him a smile. 'You asking?'

The next time he asked me to sleep with him, he tried to bolster his case by reminding me that we were going to be married.

'*When* we're married,' I said, 'I'll stay.'

I could see that he barely believed it – that I was still refusing him – and was about to laugh me down, to protest long and loud. But of course there was no denying it: when we were married, we'd sleep together.

I pressed on: 'Henry, Henry, *listen*: what you don't need is another bastard.'

He might not have liked hearing it, but it was the truth. He said nothing for a moment, and then he conceded, 'Well, it'd better be soon, anyway.'

'Yes,' I said, 'that's right, it'd better be.'

Why hadn't it happened sooner? If it was the perfect match that I claim it was, a meeting of minds, why didn't it begin as soon as we met? I've been thinking about that. I've been thinking about those six years we lived alongside each other at court before he asked his confectioner to make me that sugar rose. It wasn't as if we hadn't been well-acquainted. The Boleyns couldn't have been closer to Henry: my father was Treasurer; my brother was a Gentleman of the Privy Chamber, one of the elite attending to the king; my sister doing the same, but differently, for her year or so as royal mistress. I suspect it was for precisely that reason: Henry was always there, and he was everything; defining our lives, our lives revolving around him. Because of that, he was almost irrelevant to me. I was busy, in my early twenties, with my girl-life. Smitten with a pretty-boy. Henry was a man, in his thirties and into his second decade of marriage. Moreover, of course, he was the king. For me, he wasn't a potential lover; it never crossed my mind. And if it had, Henry wouldn't have appealed to me. Oh, he *impressed* me, yes, of course. And intrigued me. But the sheer spectacle of him ... Well, that was what it was: spectacle. He wasn't for falling in love with.

Henry didn't divorce Catherine because of me. *For* me, yes; in the end, yes. But not *because* of me. He was thinking of doing so anyway, in time, probably to marry some French princess. Wolsey was keen on that idea. He was late to catch on to what was happening, was know-all Wolsey. Even though he did know about me. Or thought he did. But what he knew – or thought he did – was that I was the king's new bit on the side. I'd been suitable to invite again and again to lavish dinners at his gorgeous Hampton Court (a thousand rooms, a thousand crimson-clad servants) on the arm of the king . . . but I was nothing more. As wife-to-be, I rather crept up on Wolsey. But that's because he'd been kept in the dark. Replaced as the king's confidant. By me, funnily enough, as it happens. Right-hand man replaced by bit on the side: no wonder he was caught off-guard.

Leviticus 20, verse 21: *And if a man shall take his brother's wife, it is an unclean thing: he hath uncovered his brother's naked-ness; they shall be childless.* Henry's wife was his – had been his – brother's wife, briefly, before his brother's death. The marriage had been deemed a non-event because, according to Catherine, Arthur hadn't been up to doing his husbandly duty. The problem was, Henry and Catherine still had no children. Well, no sons. There was of course the daughter, pathetic example though she was. A mis-translation, said Henry, turning sudden specialist in Hebrew: it should read 'sonless'. Henry and Catherine's lack of a surviving son, he decided, was God's judgement on a sinful marriage. That's what he said, and he believed it; he talked himself into believing it and from then onwards his fervour was unshake-able.

I didn't suggest Leviticus to him. Why would I? In my view, he had grounds enough to rid himself of that Spaniard: she'd proved no use at all, and now – aunt of a rampaging emperor – she was a liability. And Leviticus was no discovery for him: he'd quoted it, years before we met, in his book on Luther. As for the dubious validity of his marriage: he knew that it had been an issue at the time; and he knew, too, that for some the misgiv-ings had persisted. A French bishop, for example, had queried the brat's legitimacy during a round of marriage-brokering. None of it was news, and none of it – yet – was due to me.

Like anyone else at court, I'd heard speculation from time to time about a royal divorce: *Why doesn't he just get rid of her?* Marriage breakdown and separation happens all the time. Sometimes an annulment, or a divorce. And in this particular case? Our lovely young king married to a babbling old nun? Worse: a babbling old *Spanish* nun, when England's focus was firmly on France. Her being a Spaniard could be overlooked, though; she'd been here a long time. What really mattered was that distinct lack of live baby boys.

If Wolsey had had his way, he'd have got Henry his divorce and then shipped in some French flesh to produce princes, and to have French friends and deck up for functions. Well, I could do that. And more. And I wouldn't have to be royal; Elizabeth Woodville hadn't been, and it hadn't stopped her marrying Edward IV. And anyway I wasn't completely *un*-royal; I had that smidgeon of Plantagenet blood. (Didn't we all, though. All except Wolsey, that is.) Surely I could produce sons – my useless sister had just managed one – and I was practically French, I'd done a long stint at the French court and was liked by anyone, there, who was anyone. There was another way in which I was queen material, too: no one in England rivalled my dress sense. I dressed the part. So, I'd do. Better still, I'd be no homesick half-wit. But best of all, this was my country and I had plans for it, along with the guts to see them through. And one of those plans was going to make me very popular with just about anyone who wasn't Wolsey: I wanted rid of Wolsey.

I'd say Wolsey was too big for his boots, but let's not beat about the bush: what Wolsey was too big for was England. Never before had there been a man in England so rich and powerful who wasn't a king. Moreover, this was a man who wasn't anything at all, not originally: a nobody turned cleric, a butcher's boy become cardinal. The nobles had a thing or two to say about that, behind his back.

I suppose that's why Henry trusted him with the kingdom: no friends to favour; no claim to the throne. Henry's talent – the best talent of all – is for recognizing others' talents. I wonder, now, if I should include myself in that. Did he see that I'd flinch at nothing to rid him of that used-up wife? He recognizes talent and he trusts: he trusts absolutely; right up until when, suddenly, he doesn't. It's Thomas Cromwell whom he trusts now: Cromwell, the next and even better Wolsey. Wolsey's talent had been running the country for Henry. And serious statesman though Henry is . . . well, when he was young, his passion was for the good life. He'd do a certain amount of work, but then he'd want to go hunting or dancing. Wolsey would stay behind and pick up the pieces. And build palaces from them.

If anyone was a match for Wolsey, glorified butcher's boy, then it was me, king-favoured granddaughter of a merchant. I knew where he was coming from. He, however, didn't even know I was coming. Me being a woman, he didn't see me coming. And I was ample match for him: no chinless wonder; no Stafford, who, four or five years earlier, had assumed he could click his fingers and have the nobility collect quietly behind him while he asked the Tudors a few awkward questions about their lineage. When Stafford clicked his fingers, Henry overheard. Henry did some clicking of his own – for quill, ink, warrant – and Stafford went to the block. This, from a king not given in those days to bloodshed; a king who loved to be loved. Stafford's execution had left them all – even my Uncle Norfolk – sulking, subdued. But me, no. Stafford was history for me, I'd never known the man and wouldn't have liked him if I had. He was no loss for me: one more English aristocrat peering down his pox-eroded nose at the likes of us Boleyns. What had happened to Stafford was no warning to me. I wasn't about to lose my nerve.

Lucy Cornwallis

❀❀❀

SPRING 1535

The door's opening, and there's someone in the doorway. The someone's asking, 'Miss Cornwallis?' Male, young, not a voice I know. Bad timing: I can't take my eyes from this pan of boiling sugar, it's just about to reach the crucial point. He shouldn't be knocking at the confectionery door; he should know better. There's delicate work going on, in here; everyone knows that. What's the matter with these boys, knocking on this door all day long? 'Richard's not here,' I tell him. 'Can you shut the door, please?' I can't have the temperature drop; and it's barely spring, outside.

He obliges. But he's still here. True, I didn't actually say, *With you on the other side of it.* Swiping the pan from the flame, I glimpse him. Glossy black hair; pale-faced, kid-pale; dark eyes. I settle the pan in a basin of water; and through the hiss of steam, I hear him saying, 'You've a sore throat.' Concerned. For me, by the sound of it; not for himself, for the prospect of contagion.

'Dry,' I clarify; feel obliged to. 'Sticky. Comes of working in here.' Our confectionery kitchen is purpose-built, here, at Hampton Court: we're on the first floor above the pastry ovens. Good for sugar, not so good for me. 'And from the sugar.' Sugar, powdered, gets everywhere. In my hair and down my throat. When I glimpsed him, just now, it was through sugared eyelashes. 'Look,' I ask him, 'if you find Richard, can you tell him to get back here?'

He draws breath, as if he's about to say something, but I hear no more.

Good. I'm not passing messages.

And he goes. Gently closing the door. Not a typical Richard-visitor, in that respect.

Time to take the pan to the marble slab, to drop and settle the syrup, bit by bit, into the warmed, oiled moulds. Three dozen Tudor roses, each the size of the circle made by forefinger and thumb. Old-fashioned sugar plate, the boiled-up kind. The temperamental kind. Why isn't Richard doing this? I could be getting on with something else. It's not as if there isn't a lot else for me to do.

And lo and behold: Richard, slipping into the room as if his absence has been of no consequence. In his twenties, but acting as if he's still in his teens. An odd mix, Richard: worldly and other-worldly. Whatever he says – and whatever I feel – I'm not in fact old enough to be his mother. Yet it's as if there's not just a generation's difference between us, but a lifetime's. He steps out of his clogs and, shoeless, pads across the warm oak floor. Standing a head above me, he looks down over my shoulder at the glistening, amber roses. And keeps looking. Which makes me uneasy. I scan the roses for imperfections – bubblings, darkenings – and wonder how it happened that *he* checks up on *my* work.

Now he has his back to me, bending down, putting his leather slippers on. 'What needs doing?'

'You *know* what needs doing. Because you did *half* of it, earlier.'

We both look at it: a marchepane, an embossed disc of marzipan as big as the king's biggest dinner plates. Not long out of the mould, it's cooling. But if Richard isn't quick, it'll be too cool and the goldleaf won't stick.

'Did we get the goldleaf?' he asks.

'*I* got the goldleaf, yes. I need this pan washed – where *is* Stephen?' A glance out of the window reveals nothing but wet cobbles and a smile from the yeoman guarding the spicery office. 'Oh –' I remember – 'did he find you?'

'Stephen?' Richard's peering into Kit's abandoned mortar; shifting the pestle among the grains, his eyes closed and head cocked.

'No. That boy, just now.'

'Who?' He touches a fingertip to the inside of the mortar, then raises the hand, palm upwards, into the light, as if setting something free.

'He didn't, then.'

'*Who?*'

'*I* don't know. Someone came looking for you.'

He dabs the forefinger into the basin of water, rubs it with his thumb. 'What'd he look like?'

'Nice-looking.' Because it occurs to me that this was what he'd been.

'*Nice-looking?*' Richard regards me admiringly. He enunciated the expression as if it had never been used before. 'Well, could have been anyone,' he concludes, breezily. 'You know what I always say: if he wants me badly enough, he'll come looking again.'

'Is that –' I nod towards the mortar – 'up to it?' *Down* to it: ground sufficiently for today's purposes.

'Of course. Kit's a good man.'

True, but Richard rarely says so. He can be a hard taskmaster, even though it isn't his job to be any kind of taskmaster at all; it's mine. I say, 'You're in a good mood.'

He's browsing along the shelves of spices, doesn't look at me. 'Yeah, well,' is all he says.

And yet again I wonder: how come he's so familiar with me, and I know so little about him? I brought him up from an orphan, an under-sized urchin living on his wits. I made him who he is, now: confident, respected assistant to the king's confectioner. (Equal, really: face it. Equal, now, in skill. Rival, if he so chose.) But in so many ways he's a mystery to me. Sometimes I can barely believe that we've spent a decade living alongside each other, working together all day every day and then spending our nights in adjacent lodgings. All these years living like sister and brother. Perhaps that's why he still captivates me. I find myself watching him when he's absorbed, when a peculiar clarity comes into those river-green eyes of his and everything that is Richard dissolves away in them, leaving them with a life of their own. For all the contrived appearance to the contrary, he's deadly serious about his work. That's something I *do* know about him. Something I've learned. It's probably the only aspect of life that he's serious about. I'm probably the only person who ever gets to see beyond his flippancy.

When he arrived, a decade ago, to chance his luck in the royal kitchens, he was just one of so many boys hanging around in hope of paid work. Who could blame them? Doubtless they'd heard how there were wages to be earned as well as two meals a day and, at night, space to curl up near the massive ovens. A job in the royal household is a job for life, and it's a good life; and when we're not up to the job – sick, or old – we're *still* paid. Less, yes, of course, but enough to keep body and soul. It's hard work, in the kitchens, but worth it. If the boys couldn't find paid work, they worked anyway and made it pay: muscling in on household life, and trading in the leftovers which were supposed to go to beggars. They made lives for themselves, even if they were barely clothed. My own little kitchen had a bevy of such boys, always coming and going. I'd inherited a situation which had been gaining ground, unchecked, for years. I didn't like it; didn't like the chaos. I only managed any serious work after the boys had gone away to sleep and before they returned in the mornings. And then, inevitably, there was the filching. The sticky fingers. The Chief Clerks hold me personally accountable for the most valuable substance in all the kitchens, but how could I watch every grain? How could I supervise hordes of hungry, destitute children around sugar?

The day I came across Richard, I was doing just as I was doing a moment ago: boiling sugar syrup. One of the boys wanted my attention. *Mrs Cornwallis? Mrs Cornwallis? Mrs Cornwallis?* I was very busy; surely that was obvious. No? Well, I'd *make* it obvious, by ignoring him. Not that I had much choice – I couldn't take my attention from the sugar – but I could have spoken. I could have said, *Hang on, please, Joseph*, or whoever. *Just a moment, John. Missuscornwallismissuscornwallismissuscornwallis* – Before I knew it, I'd shot round and was glaring at him, furious with myself for having been distracted. Heat bloomed in the pan behind me, and there was a coppery flash as I whirled back to it. It was gone from the charcoal brazier; it was sinking into a basin of water. I was there, instantly, assessing the damage: none. It was saved, *it was saved*. I took a moment to appreciate that some kid had done it. Some boy had not only judged the critical point – and from across the room – but had acted without hesitation, snatching a weight of flame-hot and explosive gold from the king's own confectioner. Then he'd relinquished it, immediately; he was already busy wiping a workbench. He didn't look at me.

I asked him: 'Who are you?'

Strange eyes: green, slanted. Elfin. He could have been any age between seven and twelve. 'Richard.' He shrugged.

'Richard,' I repeated, stupidly, because I didn't know what else to say; where to start. And, anyway, he was wiping again. His mousy hair was a little matted at the back, I noticed.

Less than a fortnight later, we were visited by a representative of the Cofferer. A not unexpected visit. Word was that Cardinal Wolsey had decreed a great clean-up, a great head-count in the household: enough is enough; time's up for hangers-on, and hangers-on of hangers-on. When the representative had finished remarking on the fact that I'm the only woman working in the kitchens, which was hardly news to me or to anyone else, he explained his mission: 'When I've finished, there should be around two hundred people working in the kitchens. Not ...' he faltered. 'Well, not more.' He said, 'Basically, anybody who's not somebody has to go.' He looked at Kit. 'Obviously the yeoman here *is* somebody.' Kit smiled. Kit, in his yeoman's green. What Kit is, actually, is a pair of hands, and a very useful, capable one, at that. The man asked me. 'And you have a groom?'

Someone to wash up and run errands, yes. 'Geoffrey,' I said. (These were the days before Stephen; the days before Geoffrey moved on up in the world into the Privy Kitchen and Stephen stepped into his shoes.) 'He's at the scullery.'

'And ... these.' It might have been intended as a question but it fell flat, leaving us facing them. The boys. Seven or so of them; or ten, perhaps. They looked back, as nonchalant and calculating as cats.

I sighed. Their days were numbered, here, and they knew it. Turning so that they couldn't see me, I said so that they couldn't hear me, 'Richard has to stay.'

'Richard?' The man frowned; he wanted no difficulties.

I lied, 'He's my assistant.'

The man consulted his notes.

I came clean. 'He'll be my assistant,' I said, and folded my arms, which was, and still is, the only way I know to stand my ground. 'Confectionery is skilled work,' I proclaimed; I was trying hard, now.

He sighed. 'Richard who?'

I had to turn around and face them all; to brazen it out. I half-turned, and quietly asked Richard: 'Richard who?'

He shrugged.

I looked back at the man, and shrugged in turn.

The man sighed, frowned, and opened his mouth to say something.

'Cornwallis,' I said.

It's the nice-looking boy, again; the black-haired one who came here the other day. Luminous complexion.

'He's not here.' I roll my eyes; more biddable, today.

'Richard?'

'Yes. Richard. Not here.' Seeds scuttle beneath my fingertips – fennel, aniseed, caraway, coriander – as syrup dries around them, making sugar hailstones. 'Any message?'

'For Richard?'

'Yes.' What *is* this? '*For Richard.*' I spoon more syrup into the pan, and the stranger raises his eyes back to mine. Presumably he hasn't ever seen this before: a pan swinging on cords above a brazier. His eyes aren't dark, I see now; they're shadowed by dark eyelashes, lots of them. The eyes are blue. I nod at the pan. 'There's a good reason for it. Maintains an even heat.'

He nods, still wide-eyed.

This is no kitchen-lad: no yeoman's uniform, and his clothes are much better than a groom's. Much better than any household employee's, it occurs to me. But nor is he a courtier. He doesn't have the pristine, polished appearance. Doesn't have the strut; there's no trace of it in his stance. He's wearing battered clogs. What's his link with Richard? What on earth does Richard – fastidious Richard – make of him?

He says, 'I don't know . . . Richard.' It's a gentle voice.

'Well, he'll be back later, if you want to try again then.'

'No –' the eyes dip away into a smile, 'I mean, I'm not here to see Richard.'

'Oh. *Oh*. Sorry. It's just that . . . well, everyone always is.' We exchange smiles, now. 'Can *I* help?'

This is somehow unhelpful in itself, because he freezes, lips parted. Mute. I can wait; I've plenty to occupy me. Comfits take hours; hours and hours of this, to get them perfectly round.

'This is stupid, probably, but it's you I've come to see. I've been at the king's banquets and feasts, and I've seen . . .' He stops, shuts his eyes briefly but emphatically; a lavish blink. 'You remember the Saint Anne you made?'

Well, of course I do; it took me long enough. This man, this boy, has been at the king's banquets and feasts? He's a server, that's what he is. Must be. A privileged young man putting in his time at the tables before moving on to better things. But presumably not in those clogs.

'And that leopard? It's just that they're so . . .' He looks upwards, skyward.

So . . . ?

'Lovely.' His gaze back to mine. 'Detailed. Perfect. And I wanted to meet the person who made them. Everyone talks about you. The king –' He leaves it there: enough said.

'The king's very kind.' And it's true.

'I just wanted to meet you, and to see how you do it.'

What a strange request: everyone's very interested in the finished articles, but I've never come across anyone who cares how they're made. 'Well, I'm afraid, as you can see, it's not really happening today. Today is comfits.'

A wince of a smile from him, as if it's his fault. He glances appreciatively around the room, making the best of it now that he's here.

'If you come back on Friday, I'll be sculpting.'

'Right.' He snaps to attention. 'See you on Friday.'

I'm saying, 'Well, only if you want to,' but he's already gone.

This next time, funnily enough, they pass each other in the doorway. When he's shut the door, Richard asks me, 'What was Smeaton doing here?'

'Smeaton?'

He comes over to look at what I've been doing.

'His name's Mark.'

'Yep. Mark Smeaton.'

'How do *you* know who he is?'

He saunters away with a smirk. 'I know anyone who's anyone, Lulabel.'

'But he's a musician.' That's what he's just told me.

He stops, turns back to me. 'A musician?' He looks amused. 'Is that what he told you?'

My heart flounders: what does he mean? what's going on?

'He's *the* musician, more like. The up-and-coming musician. In the king's opinion.' He ties his apron around his waist.

'Mark?' The Mark who was in here, just now?

'Smeaton. Otherwise known as Angel-voice.'

Angel-voice? 'Is he?'

'Well, no, but he *could* be.' He's washing his hands. 'His voice is what he's famous for.'

'Famous?'

'Well, kind of. Known for.' Slant-eyes sideways. 'Let's face it, it isn't for his dress sense, is it.'

Sometimes Richard is so shallow. He has a lot to learn about what matters in life.

'Anyway,' he dries his hands on his apron, 'what was he doing in here? Ol' Angel-face.'

Angel-face. Angel-voice, Angel-face. Which is it? I don't seem able to see him, hear him, now, in my memory, as if Richard's names for him have brought me up too close. 'He wanted to see me.'

'What about?'

'Nothing. He wanted to . . . see what we do. How we do it.' It sounds ridiculous. Spoken, it's become ridiculous.

Richard is craning along a shelf of moulds. 'Thinking of becoming a confectioner, is he? Nice little sideline for when his voice breaks.'

Right, that's enough. I reach around him, on tip-toe, and swipe a tiger from the shelf: 'This one.'

He whips around, his weird eyes on mine. Amused, again. 'What *do* you get up to when I leave you in here? Do Gentlemen of the Privy Chamber *usually* drop by?'

And now he's getting carried away. 'No, but he's not a Gentleman of the Privy Chamber, is he. He's a musician.' As if *any* musicians ever come in here. As if anyone at all ever comes in here, when Richard's not around.

'*Yes, and*, Lulatrix, he's a Gentleman of the Privy Chamber.'

But this is absurd: what does Richard take me for? 'He's a *musician*. You just *said* so. Which means he *works*. Doesn't *joust*, all day long. And he's ... he's *nice*.'

'Oh, come on, Lucy. You, of all people, should know that our dear good king can be ... unconventional, shall we say, when it comes to staffing. He likes talented people. Recognizes talented people. Likes them around. And he loves music. Is there anything he loves more than music? Well, except ... well, except a lot of things.'

'Mark's *really* a Gentleman of the Privy Chamber?'

Richard's busy checking that the mould is clean, dry, undamaged. 'The king likes him; I mean, really likes him. God knows why, but he does.'

'What d'you mean, God knows why?'

'Well, he's hardly Privy Chamber material, is he.'

And isn't that good? Perhaps not in Richard's view, but certainly in mine. I lose track of who's in the Privy Chamber, but anyway they're all the same in that merry band: top-heavy with titles, too handsome to be true, too clever for their own good and a law unto themselves.

I ask him, 'How do you know all this?'

He grins. 'I have friends in high places.'

For once, I'm not going to let him get away with his usual flippancy. 'Who?'

He seems genuinely surprised; he puts the mould aside. 'In particular? At the moment?' He means it: it's a proper question. I nod.

'Silvester Parry. One of Sir Henry Norris's pages.'

'Silvester.' Unusual name.

'Silvester,' he agrees, as if I'm a clever child.

'Well, you're going up in the world.'

Something amuses him; he's about to say, but seems to think better of it.

Sir Henry Norris, I'm thinking. Isn't he the king's best friend? A Gentleman of the Privy Chamber; I do know that. And the one who is indeed a gentleman, by all accounts. Or perhaps by Richard's account; I don't remember where I heard it. Isn't he the widower? With the little boy? 'Is he a recent friend? Silvester?'

'*Very* recent. But very *good*.' Richard, gathering ingredients, laughs even as he's turning his nose up at the remains of my gum tragacanth mix.

'Good,' I say. 'Good.' And *I* made a friend, today.

He'd hesitated – Mark – as before, in the doorway, and said, 'Well, here I am.'

Presumably it seemed just as odd to him as to me that we'd made the arrangement. If 'Friday' could be said to be an arrangement. It seemed to have worked as one, though, because – as he said – here he was. And early. Calling to him to come in, I tried to make it sound as if I did this all the time: welcomed spectators. As he crossed the threshold, he took a deep, slow breath.

'The *smell* in here . . .' He sounded appreciative, and full of wonder.

I confided my suspicion that I can't smell it, any more; not really, not how it smells to an outsider.

He looked stricken, on my behalf. 'You need a stronger dose. You'll have to stroll through some sugar-and-spices orchards; perhaps that'd do the trick.'

'Yes, but first I'd have to go to sea for weeks on end.'

'Ah. Yes.' He made a show of shuddering.

That, we were agreed on. I indicated for him to draw up a stool, and he settled beside me. The scent of *him* was of outside: his lodgings' woodsmoke and the incense of chapel; and, below all that, was . . . birdsong. Birdsong? Morning air. He smells alive, I thought, and presumably I smell preserved. Even when I do manage to get outside, I'm usually only crossing the yard between my lodgings and here. The air in the yard throbs with baking bread, brewing and roasting. 'And I'm not sure about those "orchards",' I said. 'I'm not sure that sugar, when it's growing . . . well, that it's anything like what turns up at Southampton. Unless it grows in blue paper wrappers.'

'Oh.' He glanced around, expectantly, presumably looking for them, our conical sugar loaves. I broke it to him that he wouldn't find any, here. They're locked in a trunk in the spicery. Even I have to apply to the Chief Clerk for my requirements. Then he asked me about spices, about whether they grow. 'I just can't *imagine* them growing,' he said.

I explained that they're seeds, mostly.

'Yes, but that's it: I can't imagine the plants.'

I considered this. Reaching into a bowl, I took a rose-petal. With it on my palm, I said, 'I wonder, if you'd never seen a rose-bush, whether you could imagine where this came from.' I passed it to him.

He held it and then rubbed it slowly between forefinger and thumb. It kept its shape, bounced back from every fold; effectively remained untouched. 'I'd never thought of them as tough,' he said, and he was as surprised as I'd known he would be. 'They're not really delicate at all, are they.'

'Not at all,' I agreed. 'But nor is a rose-bush.'

It wasn't until then that we exchanged names: 'I'm Mark, by the way,' he said.

'Lucy,' I said. Well, why not? Richard calls me Lucy.

He thanked me for allowing him in to watch, and I asked, 'Didn't you ever watch anyone making confectionery, when you were little?' His mother, if he had a mother. If she lived until he could remember her. Few women are so grand that they don't cook, and all of them aspire to confectionery.

'I didn't have that kind of childhood,' was his cheerful answer. 'I was a choirboy.'

Oh. So, another orphan of a kind.

'Here, usually.'

'Hampton Court?' And then it sank in.

But he said it anyway: 'I was in Cardinal Wolsey's choir.'

I was careful to echo his even tone when I said, 'How things change.' Which could, of course, be taken to refer to the palace itself and not the cardinal's demise. And it partly did, because what is Hampton Court other than endless building-work? It's been five or six years, now, since the king took it over, and will he ever stop? Wine cellars are the latest addition to our kitchens; massive, vaulted wine cellars. It's said that the palace was colossal in the cardinal's time. What's the word for it now that it's twice the size?

He said, 'Some things change, others don't: I'm still singing.' He smiled. 'Rather lower, though.'

He's a chorister, still. Then I'll have heard him, in Chapel. His is one of the voices making that shining wall of sound. It's a strange feeling that those voices cause in me; coolheaded, everyday me. As if the coping that I've been doing is nothing;

as if everything I am and everything I do is nothing, a sham. And isn't that wonderful, in a way? Isn't it a kind of relief?

When he'd gone, I decided to take a break, a stroll. I don't get enough air. I walked past the chapel, but it was silent. Walked on into the rose gardens, and, there, savoured the fragrance. It's the faintest of scents, but steady. No muskiness, no headiness to it. Just a single, clean, high note.

Rose shapes, though, are anything but simple. Here in the kitchen we have stamps and flat moulds of roses that are regularly-petalled. Tudor roses. And we have one old mould of a rosebud which yields a rosebud-shaped pebble of sugar. But real roses have intricate whorls of petals as individual as fingerprints. If I were to try to make a faithful reproduction of a rose, I'd have to build it petal by petal, modelling each petal by hand; each one bowed and tapered between fingertip and thumb.

'By the way,' Richard says, 'if you want the latest royal gossip, it's that *Henri fait l'amour avec* Meg Shelston.'

'Thank you, Richard. I don't.' And I wish he wouldn't be so disrespectful. Someone will hear him, one day; someone other than me. And his ridiculous attempts at code: I should feign ignorance. He's persuaded someone to teach him a little French, over the last year or so. Regrettably, not to broaden his mind. He's aware that I know some French, but not how much. And in fact it isn't much. I trained with a French cook, and I know what people say about the French but he really didn't have much time or use for expressions like *fait l'amour*. I can work it out, though. What I don't know is, who's Meg Shelston?

'And *Le Corbeau* isn't best pleased about it, to put it very, very mildly indeed.'

Initially, *Le Corbeau* stumped me. He had to tell me that it's a translation of a name for her that's been in use for a while. According to some people, he says, it was Cardinal Wolsey's own name for her, in his time; except that the cardinal's name was The *Midnight* Crow, and although Richard can manage *minuit*, it makes it a bit much. I'm surprised to hear Richard using such a name at all; because, until recently, he was all for her. 'Richard, sometimes I think you like to make something out of nothing.'

'Yes, I know. I know that's what you *think*.' He's offended that I've rejected this titbit that I never asked for.

Which annoys me. 'Richard, why *would* he? Think about it: he turned this country upside-down and re-wrote all the rules, two years ago, just two years ago, so that he could marry –' What do I call her? I don't like calling her *the queen*. 'So that he could marry. He went through all that – took us all through that – and now they have the lovely little princess –' Say what you like, she's a treasure; born under a waning moon, so the next one's bound to be a boy. 'Why would he bother with any ... *Meg*?' I do honestly think, sometimes, that Richard lives in fairyland.

'Well ...' He stops, seems to abandon whatever point he was about to make, and merely says, pleasantly, 'You don't understand men at all, do you, Lucy.'

I knew he'd come again. Somehow, though, I'm still surprised to see him. A shock: that's how it feels; a jolt. This time, Richard's here; but absorbed, sculpting. Hungover. Choosing not to respond to the knock at the door, but now glancing up, apparently goodnatured and almost smiling. 'Morning, Mr Smeaton.' So casual, yet somehow making everything so awkward. Well, that's a Richard-speciality, and I must rise above it.

'Richard.' I indicate him to Mark: an introduction. A flicker of amusement between us: Richard seems to have become our private joke; *Ah, Richard, at last.*

'... Cornwallis,' Richard adds, with the same goodnatured near-smile that isn't either goodnatured or a smile. Never mind: no one else knows the difference.

'Mr Cornwallis.' Mark nods.

I'd like to say, He's not my son; I'm not his mother. I don't know how to address Mark, now; after all the Mister this and Mister that. Did I imagine that he ever introduced himself as Mark?

He's saying, 'I hope you don't mind; you must have a lot on your hands, this time of year.'

'You, too.'

He agrees. 'We do have a bit of a rush on, around Easter.'

I only realize we've giggled when Richard gives us an irritated flick of a glance. I indicate for Mark to sit.

He says, 'This is the warmest place I know. Chapel's freezing, and we were in there for hours.'

It *is* cold outside, and we've candles lit. His hair is catching the shine of them; he's brightening the room. 'It went well, though?' I wish I knew how to talk about his work.

'Could be better.' Cheerful, though. '*Will* be better.'

We smile at each other. 'Good,' I say. 'Good.'

He says, 'It's just that it's so comforting, in here. The royal apartments haven't been a comfortable place to be, lately.'

He could mean physically, because of all the building-works, but his demeanour suggests otherwise: he's tense, tentative. I recall what Richard said: *Le Corbeau isn't best pleased about it, to put it very, very mildly*. It's true, then? I don't look at Richard; resolutely, I don't. Not that he's looking at me: what I can feel is him listening. Perhaps this is how he does it: not jubilant, ribald exchanges of gossip, but stealth. Taking what he can, when he can. And now here's me doing the same.

Mark almost whispers, 'It's a gift, isn't it, to be so full of life. To be so sure. So *sure* of yourself.'

Ah, yes, but that's the life of a king, isn't it.

'She's –' he frowns, thinking, 'true to herself.'

She? 'Who?'

'The queen. True to herself. In this place, where everyone's saying one thing and thinking another. Where everyone's saying something to one person, and something else to the next. Which means, though, that she's very alone.'

Alone? Anne Boleyn? Whenever I've seen her, she's been the centre of attention: the king's attention, indulgent and lavish; the Gentlemen of the Privy Chamber, playing up to her. Her family: that brother, father, uncle. It's Queen Catherine who's alone. Banished to some old castle. Forbidden, even, to see her own daughter. And she's never had family, here: shipped, at sixteen, a thousand miles from her happy childhood home. Imagine: to be told, over the years, of the deaths; her mother, first, then father, big sister, little brother. Friends, though, she does have; and has always had. Proper friends. There was no playing up to Queen Catherine; no need for it. By all accounts, she made friends and kept them: a few came with her on that galleon and are locked away with her now in that castle.

Mark sighs. 'I can't understand why he's doing it.'

The king, he means. The mistress. Well, yes: that, we can agree on.

'He married for love,' he says. 'Married a fascinating woman: a clever and stunning woman. Had – has – a child by her.'

'Beautiful kid,' it has to be said.

'So, why should he need to do this? If I were him, I'd never *look* at another woman.'

He is so serious that, oddly, I can't help but smile. He's looking tired, too, though. 'Listen, Mark, I'm going to mix you a tonic.' Perhaps even risk passing him a manus christi, one of the amber roses I was making when I first saw him, one of the few to which I added rosewater and later gilded. Let's see if sugar, rosewater and gold can't work their powers to wash away that lavender tint around his eyes.

His gloom vanishes. 'Really? A potion? Later, though. I have to go.'

'Go? Already?'

'I shouldn't be here. Things to do. I only dropped by. Just wanted to –' He shrugs. 'Lucy, you're so . . .'

I'm so . . . ?

'. . . *sane.*'

Sane?

'I'll be back,' he promises.

And he's gone. I'd sort of forgotten about Richard; that he's here. But here he is; as he has been, all along. The only sound, his blade scratching at a chunk of sugarloaf. Between us, nothing; silence. It'll be me who breaks it. 'Poor Mark.' Something which means nothing at all; which simply means, *Mark was here.*

'Oh, he's always like that.' This comes back very quickly.

And it surprises me in all kinds of ways. Not least, 'Like what?' And, anyway, how does he know?

'That's what Silvester says: Smeaton's always like that. All *chivalrous.*' Said as if it's a dirty word. Which is a new one on me.

'And since when has there been anything wrong with chivalry?'

He still doesn't look up. 'Oh, come on, Lucy,' he murmurs, low-key, casual. 'He's like some fifteenth-century knight. Love and devotion. He's kidding himself. This is the real world.'

Is it?

'Of course, he'd *like* to be a knight; but he's the son of a seamstress, you know, and a Dutch father who's dead. You *won't* know, of course, because he doesn't *like* it known.'

Scrape, scrape, scrape.

He could at least look at me. If he's going to be that rude about a friend of mine, he could at least look at me when he does it. 'So? At least he *knows* who he's the son of.'

Richard's expression as he does look up isn't the one I'm already cringing from. It's one of surprise. 'Oh, Lucy.' And disappointment has softened his voice. 'That was a bit close to the bone.'

But he deserved it; he deserved it, didn't he? 'Well, don't be so quick to judge people!'

How on earth did I bring him up to be so shallow? Why have I always let him get away with it?

He makes a small show of giving in gracefully. Resumes his work. Says nothing.

Me, likewise.

So, we're not speaking. Which has never happened before.

Anne Boleyn

❀❀❀

We moved into 1527 and it seemed that the rain that'd started a year earlier still didn't let up. Spring was slow off the ground. Our rooms were choked with woodsmoke, our clothes bitter-smelling with it. I remember my brother's wife at a window, wondering, 'When will this weather break?' I remember the longing in her voice. The weather didn't bother me greatly; I was happy and had so much to look forward to. Henry would be divorced, that year, and he'd marry me. I'd be queen, we'd have a baby prince, and there would be a long-overdue new beginning: a young, strong monarchy, busy and respected in Europe. There'd be reform, if I had my way, and of course I *would* have my way. I wasn't interested in looking out of windows at monotonous, drenching rain.

Mid-May, when summer should have been peeking from the trees but was in fact still slithering in the mud, Henry asked for an ecclesiastical court to meet in secret to rule his marriage invalid. Wolsey, Warham – the old archbishop – and the other bishops, and a lot of church lawyers, they were all there: the great and the good, in most people's view, although I can think of other ways to describe them. They informed Henry that he'd be called to give evidence. He did his homework. He was nervous, and asked me to listen to him rehearsing his case. As far as I could see, there was no case to answer; it was open and shut: she was no wife to him. And anyway, why answer to them? 'Who's king?' I'd complain. It infuriated me that he had to go scraping and bowing to those old men in their dingy robes.

I was right not to have held them in any esteem. They heard him out (which was big of them), then met twice more (to avail themselves of Henry's ample hospitality), before announcing on the very last day of May that they weren't men enough to give a ruling without the blessing of the Pope. Well, there was one problem with that: three weeks earlier, Rome and the Pope had been taken by the Imperial Army. Catherine's own nephew, the emperor, was holding the Pope captive. How likely was it that the Pope could rule unfavourably for his captor's aunt?

Nevertheless, that was what Wolsey reckoned we had to have: the Pope's permission. But then off he went to France – with boatloads of servants – on some vague, alliance-building, anti-Spanish mission. I can't say I missed him, but I was annoyed by the delay he was causing us. Although Henry knew, by now, not to bother asking me to spend the nights with him, there were evenings now when I made a point of retiring early. *You know the deal*, my sour glance said; *sort it out*.

I didn't have all that many opportunities for sweeping exits, though, because Henry insisted I spend much of my time back at Hever. Something I hadn't foreseen was that Henry now had to look respectable. He was a king anxious about his sinful marriage; not an adulterer. No one should know about me; although of course everyone did. Or, they knew something; but perhaps, like Wolsey, they assumed I was a distraction for Henry before the next royal marriage. Nevertheless, they were to see no distractions. Just a distraught, godly king.

So, back to Hever for me while a lot of incompetent, Pope-obsessed old men mishandled Henry's case for him. Although I love Hever, I'd have put up more of a fight if I'd known that I'd end up spending the best part of two years of the prime of my life holed up there. Back and forth to Hever, where I had only my mother and our maids for daily company. Visiting the parish sick and giving to the parish poor. Lacemaking and lute-playing. Looking at the view. Looking into the moat. Hoping hard for visitors – as long as they didn't include Auntie Liz, who came regularly to treat us to complaints about her estranged husband – my Uncle Norfolk – and his new girlfriend. No matter that he was my mother's brother and my uncle; we were a captive audience, so we'd do. She'd exhausted everyone else's goodwill with her lies about Beth (a *washerwoman*? She'd worked in their house-hold, yes, but as nanny, and the children adored her). Every visit, she pressed us for our support, and I suppose we let her think she had it – raising our eyebrows, sighing indignantly – just to get rid of her. The truth is that the one human move Uncle Norfolk has ever made, in his whole life, was to leave that thin-lipped, bile-sodden Stafford-daughter, to take his children with him away from their slap-happy mother, and set up home with Beth.

I'd sit there, across from Auntie Liz, thinking how there'd bound to be this kind of carry-on from Fat Cath once she knew about me. But at least I wouldn't be the one to have to hear it. Indeed, as few people as possible should hear anything of it. To contain her protests, I decided, Henry should present their separation as a fait accompli.

Tell her nothing, I'd say.

And he'd look lily-livered.

'*Henry* . . .'

And he'd smile, but look away.

Mid-June, while I was stuck at Hever and unable to stop him, he did it: he went to her, told her that their marriage seemed to be invalid and would have to be annulled. Imagine a female version of the Pope being told that she'd been living in sin for nearly twenty years. She reacted as you'd expect: cried. A lot. And he – stupid sod – did what you'd predict: got flustered. Giving her time to dry those tears and insist that what she'd said at the time was true: she'd never slept with his brother; so, that first marriage was no marriage at all. She seemed to be blaming it all on Wolsey; she couldn't believe it of Henry.

Henry has never been any good at secrets. He'd told my father our plans back before those ineffectual meetings of the bishops in May.

'I've told your father,' he'd owned up, somehow both shamefaced and proud.

'*You've* told *my* father?'

When I next saw my father, the next day, on our way into the council chamber to dine, I didn't quite know what to say. 'You've heard,' was what I managed. My mother wouldn't yet know: she was at Hever, and my father hadn't been back there for a couple of weeks. And no way would he have trusted the news to a letter, to servants' hands. I suppose I wasn't quite sure what he'd think. He's an intensely ambitious man, so of course he'd relish the prospect of his daughter as queen. But as befits the highest of achievers, he's a formidable pragmatist. He requires everything to run smoothly. No unnecessary risks. He might have been anticipating trouble that I couldn't foresee, and trouble would have been the last thing he'd want for the Boleyns. As it happened, though, he nodded appreciatively. Slightly incredulous, I thought. 'Good move,' was all he said.

He'd already told Uncle Norfolk, his brother-in-law: this I discovered when my uncle immediately left his place at his table and came over to say, 'I've heard.' That sharp-toothed smile on that pointed face. Admiration, avarice, and envy, all at once. No incredulity. 'Congratulations,' he whispered. 'This really is something.' For us, he meant; for our families. And then, 'We'll have Wolsey running for cover, won't we,' and there was that phlegmy laugh of his as he turned and was on his way.

They thought they were the first to know, those two, my father and my uncle, but of course I'd already told my brother, George. He'd been impatient at my previous reticence with Henry. He was as ambitious as my father and me; but he lacked, on the one hand, my father's caution and, on the other, my desire to play for the highest stakes. He simply took whatever – or whomever – was available. He was good at seeing what might be available to him, and making sure that it – or he, or she – then was. He couldn't appreciate what would be wrong with being Henry's mistress. 'Listen,' I'd told him, often enough: '*I* want a *proper* marriage.' We both knew what that meant: a marriage nothing like his. It had been regarded as a good marriage, the marriage between the Boleyn boy and the Parker girl, but it wasn't good for them. Not that I cared about her. They'd married at parental instigation, back when I was heartsick over Harry Percy. Three years had passed and there was no pretence now that there was anything between them. At the time, George had tried to persuade me that she perhaps wasn't all that bad, and, when I'd sceptically raised an eyebrow, admitted, 'Well, what difference does it make, anyway.' Sure enough, he'd continued womanizing and God knows what else. What he hadn't bargained for was her open, much-voiced displeasure. I don't know what she'd expected, marrying George.

Make no mistake, I had no sympathy for her and if I'd known then what I know now, I'd have wished her more than marital unhappiness. I might not have had the gift of foresight, but I did have sharp instincts and I knew from the beginning to mistrust her. She tried to be sisterly with me, at first. Well, I had one sister and I didn't need another. More importantly, I had a brother, and my allegiance was to him. And I could sense that he'd need it before long. In those early days, she'd bring me things. Posies. Do I seem like someone who has any use for posies? There was a heaviness to it, this present-giving. Ceremony, bribery: *Look, I've brought you something.*

What she wanted from me was *Thank you, thank you, thank you*, although I doubt there'd ever have been enough thanks. And she'd have liked, *Here in return is just a little something I've picked for you, cooked for you, sewn for you, grown for you.*

What she was after was attention. Conspiracy, even.

Well, no. No way.

We're friends, you and I, she'd say, *aren't we*. Desperate, pushing it, ready for the spurning which she'd wanted all along so that she could say, *That Boleyn bitch* ... which was what she'd always thought. And with that, she could claim herself some more attention, build herself some more conspiracy. In her view, George and I were in league against her and she was keen to out-do us.

When Henry agreed to go for a divorce, George was who I told. I tracked him down to Francis's room; he was playing poker with Francis, Billy and Harry Norris. The room stank of ale and I'd have liked to open the window, but I circled the table – only Harry glancing up at me, a half-smile – to whisper in my brother's ear, 'It's on.'

'Hmm?'

'The wedding,' I breathed, so that no one else could hear. 'Mine and Henry's.'

Is it possible that someone sitting completely still can turn even more so? Because that's what he did. All except the eyes – those big, dark Boleyn-eyes – which swooped up to mine.

'Anne,' this was Francis, for once oblivious, merely irritated at the interruption; he spoke without raising his one uncovered eye, 'fuck off.'

It was George who was waiting to greet me at the gatehouse at Beaulieu, that August, after Henry had finally relented and allowed me out of confinement at Hever to join him and the select few of his household spending the month there. George came up the avenue to meet us, calling, 'Well, look who it is!'

'Yes,' I said, as he helped me down, 'your future queen –' which made him laugh – 'and, would you believe, her chaperone.' I nodded towards Mum, who bridled. Poor Mum, she had been Henry's one condition, and I doubt the prospect was all that enticing for her. George kissed her, reassured her, 'You'll love it; it's lovely, here.'

She did; it was. Despite the dank weather – cloud-stuffed skies, splashy summer rain – it was an idyll. The garden's resilient lavender borders puffed scent when brushed by our skirts, and we grew as sleepy on it as if we were sitting in sunshine. Henry went hunting all day, every day. Sometimes I joined him, sometimes I chose to stay. I was among friends. One afternoon in particular I remember: cherry-picking with Harry Norris, who'd earlier had one of his headaches and missed the hunt. Also there in the orchard – also cherry-picking – was the confectioner's boy; or that's who he said he was, when we asked him. Funny little kid. All eyes. All ears, no doubt, while Harry and I gossiped. But then, quite abruptly, he seemed self-absorbed, up to something. When we challenged him, he reluctantly opened his cupped hands to reveal a scrawny fledgling.

'Something's wrong with it,' he confided, hushed, pained. 'It can't fly.'

Harry took a closer look. 'It's scared,' he said, gently. 'It's a baby. That's all. We have to let it go.'

The boy looked panic-stricken. 'But it can't fly.'

'It will,' Harry reassured him. 'Chances are, it will.'

Dear Harry, he was a favourite of my mother's, a feeling which was reciprocated. She was the oldest person at Beaulieu, a distinction which she learned to play up to and was amply rewarded for, all the boys being fond of her. Gone were the likes of Uncle Norfolk – to Beth, in his case, at Kenning Hall – and of course Wolsey was a million miles away, in France. We could be ourselves. Our meals were gloriously informal – no separate chambers – and we all dined on whatever Henry hauled home with him. Henry could eat uninterrupted by Wolsey's usual end-of-day missives: no dictating a response, his meal going cold while he did so. We ate so well; it was impossible to give credence to the occasional reports we had from London of people crushed to death around bread carts. Impossible, too, out there in the calm, empty countryside, to worry about the reportedly rampaging sweating sickness. We were safe. Henry had brought his confectioner with him and her stunning, glinting work was brought into us every evening after dinner. Silly on sugar, with specks of goldleaf between our teeth and under our fingernails, we all danced and talked for hours, laughing at Henry's fool's dry, witty commentary on us.

Even though our time at Beaulieu was almost unimaginably private, Henry and I knew that this was it: we'd gone public. And sure enough, Señor Mendoza, the Spanish ambassador, wasted no time in reporting back on us. I doubt his letter arrived in Spain long after we arrived home at Greenwich in September. Suspiciously absent from Greenwich when we returned was Henry's own sister, Mary. And, pointedly, she stayed absent. Well, *she* could talk! – what had she done, if not make an enormous fuss about marrying for love? Done her duty first time around, by marrying the old French king, but only on the understanding that she could marry Charles Brandon, Duke of Suffolk, when it was all over. Wasn't that what her brother was doing, marrying for love? True, he wasn't widowed as she'd been, but otherwise it was exactly what she'd done. Secretly, it irked me that she wasn't a supporter of mine. Like any girl, I'd been quite besotted with her when I was younger: all that flaming hair, and the fire in her eyes. But Charlie Brandon? Well, I know he was supposed to have been a heartthrob, in his day, but I just couldn't see it, couldn't imagine it. A wet fish, was my view. A close friend of my Uncle Norfolk's, which, for me, just about says it all.

Henry's attitude to some people being scandalized by us was that we should take advantage of our intentions now being known. He sent Sir William Knight to Rome for permission for him to marry again: an English girl, this time. Which, incidentally, he was granted, although he was required to be free of Catherine. En route to Rome, Sir William had dropped in to see Wolsey; and it was then that Wolsey finally, belatedly knew Henry's plans. The wording on Sir William's document didn't name me but there couldn't have been any mistaking who it meant. And Sir William would have told him that we'd been at Beaulieu. I bet it turned Wolsey cold, the thought of it: *all of that lot, there; and me, a million miles away.* When he arrived back – hurriedly, I bet – from France, we were at Greenwich. We were at dinner. He sent one of his staff to inform Henry of his arrival, expecting his usual private audience. Conceited bastard. I leaned across to the servant before Henry could say a word. 'Tell him,' I said, 'that he can come here like anyone else.'

Our cordiality was waning, mine and Wolsey's, but Wolsey put on a brave face. Two-faced, you might say.

Well, I could play him at that game. I was as nice as pie. And in the letter he sent with his envoys to the Pope, the following February, he made me out to be a paragon. It must have pained him to sing the praises of the upstart he loathed. Just as it pained me to appear interested in, and grateful for, his various, useless schemes. But I needed him, for the while, because Henry wasn't yet ready to listen to anyone else's advice. And Wolsey needed me, now, because I was the centre of Henry's world. He wasn't invited to Windsor with us in March: another idyllic month for Henry and me, nowhere near Catherine, albeit with my mother again as chaperone. A month in springtime in the country, while our two trusted envoys, bearing a letter of extravagant praise, were granted an audience with the Pope: I think I can be forgiven for thinking that everything was going very well. And for a while longer, it did.

Our two envoys, Eddie Fox and Stephen Gardiner, came ashore

at Sandwich one morning in May. Still sea-legged, they managed to ride through the afternoon to Greenwich, desperate to tell Henry their news. Having heard the gist, he immediately turned them around and sent them across the courtyard to my rooms. They arrived dusty and sweaty at my door, Eddie Fox's eyes bloodshot. The news was that they'd got what they'd gone for: the Pope would do as Wolsey had requested and send a legate to try our case in England. I laughed, and they laughed: the three of us, half-delirious. Annie, my maid, was suddenly there, her hand on my shoulder, her own laughter a hum. My mother put down her sewing. My brother appeared from my bedroom, where he'd been teaching French to Franky Weston.

'What?' he demanded.

'I think it's starting to go our way,' I told him. 'I think we're winning. Some papal lackey is coming all the way to rainy England to rule Henry's marriage over.' I shooed the two men away: 'Go and tell Wolsey, at York Place.' To be honest, they were reeking, and I reckoned Wolsey should have to see to them.

That summer, I nearly died. What would have happened if I had? Would Henry have stayed with the ridiculous Spaniard? I do think he might have done, more fool him; I doubt he'd have seen the divorce through. I suspect he'd have seen my death as God's judgement; he'd have been scared out of his wits, chastened. In his own way he's a very God-fearing man – he has good reason, doesn't he – but nothing terrifies him as much as illness. For a brave man, he's easily scared. He'd have sacrificed me – the dream of me, the memory of me – to keep himself free from sickness, I suspect. He'd have been the model husband again and no one would have ever spoken of me. That's what I think. But of course I'm cynical, these days.

That summer's awful bout of 'the sweat' started with Wolsey's report of a couple of deaths one day in his household. Immediately, Henry was on the move from Greenwich, with both Catherine and me, in pursuit of fresh air. We took few staff, for speed; the most important member of our little travelling household being Henry's apothecary, Mr Blackden. Our first stop, Waltham Abbey, was no refuge: there was a death on the evening we arrived. The next morning, Henry revised his plans and sent me home to Hever. Hever's a good place, he insisted: you're lucky. He – and Catherine – moved on to Hunsdon, that day; and kept moving, every day, chased by the disease – a death here, three deaths there – until they arrived at Wolsey's vacant manor in the back of beyond at Tittenhanger. There, Franky Weston later informed me, Henry had the walls and floors washed with vinegar, and fires burned in every room to burn up any bad air. For fresher air, he wanted his bedroom window enlarged. So, local workmen arrived, and made a lot of mess and dust. Henry's mind had turned to higher matters, though: he was busy trying to appease his disgruntled God by saying confession daily and hearing Mass – with Catherine – more than he usually would.

'Yes, yes,' I said impatiently to Franky, 'but did they … ?'

'Did they … ?'

'Him and the queen: *you* know.'

'Oh. No.'

'You sure?'

Franky assured me that he'd had the job, nightly, of sleeping in Henry's room, on hand in case of an emergency. 'And he smelt vile,' he added, 'from Mr Blackden's potions.'

Hever, in contrast, was entirely as normal – until Dad and I became ill. People say of sweating sickness, Fine at lunch, dead by supper. On the day concerned, Dad and I were fine at lunch, but by mid-afternoon it was clear that we wouldn't be showing up for supper. Not that I knew anything about Dad; I knew nothing but the ball in my throat and the fire in my joints. I now know that Mum sent one of our servants at speed to Henry, but all I knew at the time was the momentary relief of water-soaked linen strips to my forehead. She'd sent Annie from my room and was nursing me – and Dad. She'd learned from her stepmother, who had a reputation for being able to beat 'the sweat' (and indeed everything and everyone else that didn't meet with her approval; not for nothing was she the Dowager Duchess of Norfolk). Bed, my grandmother reckoned, for a day and a night; no food for a day, a night and a day; no visitors for a week; and as many spoonfuls of some herbal, treacly concoction of hers that a delirious person could be tricked into taking.

By the time that Henry's trusted Dr Butts arrived on our drawbridge, both Dad and I had survived into the 'no visitors' stage. An exception was made for one of the king's doctors, of course, and I made the most of it. He and I ended up talking about the new ideas, the changes in what we believed and how we believed. No morbid priest-lover, Dr Butts; instead, a gently sensible man with a sense of humour. It's not that I was starved of like-minded company when I was home. Quite the opposite. Nor back at court, where my brother's radical friends had become mine and I was no longer in Catherine's service. But after those few days of wild sickness and my mother's ministrations, I felt stunningly isolated. Dr Butts did me the favour of staying for I don't know how long on a stool by my bed, talking about the future while the June rain sloshed into the moat and the day's light thinned.

As it happened, Uncle Norfolk, at Kenning Hall, had also had the illness, and had also survived. Did it surprise us, our survival? Nothing much surprises a Boleyn or Norfolk; least of all, survival. None of us was surprised, though, when my sister's husband William succumbed. Except her. None of us was surprised that he'd made no provisions and, worse, had run up some nasty debts. Except her. She wrote to Dad from Richmond, desperate and destitute with her two small children. But he was in no mood for Mary. 'I said she shouldn't have married him,' was his view.

'But she *did*, dear,' Mum reasoned.

He'd always despised Mary; she embarrassed him, unmistakably Boleyn in her looks but easy-going, easily pleased. He refused to help her. Wouldn't even allow her home. She should be at Leeds Castle, he said, asking Wolsey for her due. William had been employed in the Privy Chamber by the king; so, according to my father, it was up to Wolsey to make suitable arrangements for 'the widow', as he called her. We'd had word that Wolsey was besieged by people demanding debts be repaid from the estates of deceased, and vying for their now-vacant jobs (cousin Francis getting William's).

'She should be there in the middle of it all,' Dad said, 'making a case, telling a few lies if needs be; whatever it takes to get whatever she can. Instead of acting the baby and wailing for me to do it. She didn't want my advice, before, when I offered it.'

'That's because she was in love,' my mother said. 'She has two small children, she can't be gadding to Leeds Castle. We don't even know that she has any way of getting there. She has no money, Thomas; just the coins in her purse.'

But he wouldn't budge, and I suspected that he was still far from normal after his fever. Because otherwise, I couldn't fathom it. He's a hard man, yes, a cold man, but he's a pragmatist; and his rejection of Mary seemed self-defeating, to me. I could understand that he might be more than usually sensitive to how people saw us, now that we Boleyns were so much in the public eye, but this was entirely the wrong tactic. Mary's a fact, I told him; she isn't going away because you won't see her.

'Everyone *else* will see her,' I assured him, 'rattling around the country, threadbare. Is that how you want them to see a Boleyn?' He knew I was right, but he wouldn't hear it from me. I knew someone whom he *would* take it from, though. I wrote to Henry; he'd written me the most wonderful long letter as soon as he knew that I'd survived. *You do know, don't you, that I'll do anything, anything, anything for you.*

Well, this one's easy enough, I wrote back. *Tell my father to stop being so stupid about Mary.*

Sure enough, a letter came, and my father's attitude seemed to change. Mary'd better come home, he told my mother, although she'd better keep out of my way.

I hadn't long been back at court with Henry before word came that the Pope's cardinal – Campeggio – was at last in Calais. He'd certainly taken his time. Gout, apparently, was his bugbear, had slowed him up. The future of England had hung in the balance while some fat old Italian had vacationed in various European cities. Worse: now that he was well and truly on his way to us, I had to go back home to Hever. This was so that Henry could look respectable, again, and properly conscience-racked. I accepted it for a few days, until I came to my senses, and then I returned to London. If they were to decide my future, I wasn't going to sit demurely in Kent while they did it.

Henry kept me at a discreet distance, offering me the use of Durham House on the Strand. A move there would give the wrong signals, I told him. It was a nice enough London house, but hardly the abode of a queen-in-waiting; and home not long ago to Betsy and Fitz, whereas I was no mistress and I'd be having no bastard. So he moved me to the Suffolks' house in Southwark – one of wet-fish Brandon's places. 'Have you *seen* it?' I complained. No doubt grand, once, it hadn't been decorated for decades and was particularly unappealing in a dark, damp October. Henry agreed to renovations. So, for months I had to live with the thumps and whistling of workmen as rooms were re-panelled, ceilings re-painted, windows re-glazed, tapestries hung, a gallery built and the kitchen enlarged. I had distractions enough, though, because all the boys came, most days, to keep me company. They loved it that we had a place of our own and could do as we pleased. I kept odd hours and bad company: my definition of a good time. I knew what the people of London were saying; they were saying what people love to say in such a situation: how dare he leave his dear old wife for a little tart. It rankled that I couldn't put the record straight – he'd left her long ago, she was a wily old bird, and I wasn't little nor a tart – but you can't live your life by what people think.

There was one person whose thoughts did matter. One visitor I did need. The cardinal himself. Let him come and meet me, I said to Henry; give me enough notice and he'll find someone gracious, practical, educated and well-informed.

'I'm sure he will,' Henry laughed. 'But for now he's laid up with gout.'

Again?

Again.

And when he was back on his less-gouty feet, it was Fat Cath he went to see. 'He has to,' Henry said. 'He has some options to put to her, to try to sort this out before it gets to trial.'

'Options? Such as?'

'Such as, why not do what she does best? Take up the religious life, full-time, by going into a nunnery.'

I liked it; and, better still, surely so would she. 'But that's only one,' I said; 'one option. What are the others?'

Henry looked uncomfortable. 'Well, they were for me.'

'And?'

'And I've already said no.'

'But they were ... ?'

They were that the Pope could give a fresh, unambiguous dispensation, in retrospect, for Henry's existing 'marriage' to his dead brother's wife – in other words, excuse it – or that the problem of his having no heir could be solved by the marriage of his weasel-faced daughter to his bastard son.

'They're suggesting that?' Naturally, I was aghast. 'They're suggesting that half-sister and half-brother could marry?'

Henry nodded, clearly as baffled as I was.

'Those people are *sick*.'

Henry said, 'I didn't put it quite as bluntly as that – I avoided the word "sick" – but I think I made myself clear.'

More than ever I needed that cardinal to meet me. Then he'd realize that I was far from such a bad proposition and didn't need to be thwarted by such drastic measures – or indeed thwarted at all. I can charm anyone, if necessary; even a footsore, pious old Italian. I asked Henry to keep inviting him on my behalf, and to bring some confectionery for me to store at the ready in my kitchens. He brought the confectionery but remained evasive on the subject of the cardinal's visit. I believed him that he was trying; it was the cardinal, I felt, who was saying no. Instead, I was told, he was visiting Catherine, with Wolsey, where they all spoke in the one language that they had in common: French. My language. She was having the audience that I should have been having, speaking in the language that was mine. As ever, she was insisting that she had been a virgin when she married Henry, that she'd never been a true wife to his brother. For a year now she'd been regaling anyone who would listen – and plenty who weren't so keen to – with this tale. Had she no shame? Didn't she understand that this wasn't really what it was about? Henry wanted rid of her: it was as simple as that. It was obvious. How could she still want him? But she did. She refused the nunnery, time and time again, even when it was put to her in earnest by those she trusted. Even the Pope was keen on the nunnery option; it would solve everyone's problems. Except Catherine's, in Catherine's opinion. She remained insistent that she was Henry's wife and England's queen, and would bear those responsibilities until the day she died.

Roll on, that day, I urged.

My Uncle Norfolk said to me. 'Whatever you think of her, you can't help admire her.'

'*You* can't,' I corrected.

It seemed to me, from all the visits to Catherine and snubs to me, and the talk of nunneries and incest, that our plans now weren't going well. And God knows what Wolsey was doing about it. Nothing, as far as I could see.

I raised it with Henry: 'This isn't going well, is it.'

He said nothing, but looked guilty.

I waited; I knew he had something to say.

Sure enough: 'I don't think it's going at all,' he admitted.

I still said nothing; there was more.

Now he looked miserable. 'I wonder, Anne, whether we shouldn't just accept it, and find a way around it.'

That intrigued me. 'Around it?'

'Just . . . be together.' His eyes full of pleading.

That again! 'We can't just "be together", Henry! We don't have that luxury. You're a *king*. Your *duty* is to make sure that it's *your son* who's king *after* you.' I dropped the hectoring. 'And I'm your chance,' I urged, 'And I'm here, I'm ready. Are you really going to let a few scurrying Italians and Spaniards stand in our way?'

His head was bowed, his lip bitten. 'No,' he said, quietly. 'Of course not.'

A week later, at Bridewell, he summoned everyone who was at court and read them a long statement. The gist, relayed to me by George, was that he was sick of gossip and wished to make clear that Catherine was a truly marvellous woman, had been an adoring wife, and theirs had been a supremely happy marriage. And impossible though he knew it was, there was nothing he'd like more than for Cardinal Campeggio to find in Catherine's favour. And, indeed, if he did so, Henry would marry her all over again.

He was doing well, George said, up to this point. The problem came as he folded up the piece of paper and could no longer avoid facing the polite, restrained but wide-eyed incredulity of his audience. 'And I'm telling you,' he suddenly yelled, 'if I don't get full cooperation on all this, there's none of you so grand your head won't fly.'

Strange to think, now, how I laughed when I heard that. But George, bless him, did a good impression, all puffed-up petulance; and I was thinking, too, I suppose, of the grandees in the audience, the suddenly rigid, po-faced Dukes of Suffolk and Norfolk. I didn't know, then, of course, how many heads would fly and how many of them would be of people I liked and loved. Nor that mine would, in the end, be joining them.

Lucy Cornwallis

❀❀❀

SUMMER 1535

'Mark! Haven't seen you for a while.' Not since Nonsuch, three or four weeks ago. One step across the threshold and he takes two backwards, aghast at the heat. 'Oh, the heat: I know,' and I'm laughing despite being aware of how awful I must look, red- and shiny-faced. But it's too late to do anything about that, and I'm just glad he's here. 'Come in.'

He glances around the preserving pans, the baskets of fruits, rows of jars. Moulds are laid to dry, and subtleties – marchepane baskets, sugar bowls, marchepane and sugar fruits – are in various states of assembly and decoration. 'You're busy,' he says, and now it's him who's laughing: 'You are *so* busy.'

'Summer needs bottling.' Hence the jars. 'And then there's *mid*summer.' The Feast of St John the Baptist: hence the subtleties.

He enthuses, 'You're so *organized*.'

No, 'I'm just used to it.' Which isn't to say that I don't think back fondly to when I was a child and the feast day meant none of this, no work, just the bonfire in the fields and the cartwheel set alight and rolled through the village. That village bonfire seemed enormous, to me, then, but I don't suppose it's a patch on the one that's built here, every year.

Inhaling deeply, Mark wants to know, 'What's cooking?'

'That'll be the cherries,' a nod towards one of the steaming cauldrons, 'with cloves and cinnamon.'

He widens his eyes, beguiled. 'I'd best leave you to it.'

'No, really: all the more need for a distraction.' But *distraction* didn't sound quite right; nor to him, to judge from his flutter of hesitation. 'Really,' I repeat quickly, striking my fruit-sticky hands down my apron.

So, he obliges. Acknowledges Richard: 'Mr Cornwallis,' with

a twitch of a smile that Richard is clearly intended to see and appreciate.

Which – miraculously – he does: 'Mr Smeaton,' he says, quite jollily, although he's straight back to work. It's close work that he's doing: casting tiny details – twigs, in brown sugar paste (cinnamon, ginger), leaves in green (spinach juice), pips in both – and sticking them to various fruits. He *is* quite jolly, today; there's been a carnival atmosphere, in here, today. One way to survive, with this much to do.

Mark says, 'You two have a lot of fun in here, don't you.'

Actually, I don't know whether that's close to the truth or couldn't be further from it, and my own bafflement makes me laugh. Richard gives me what I think is called a long look; I'm aware of it even though I've turned away. I did see, though, that he wasn't entirely unamused.

Mark sidles in but stays close to the door, leans back against the wall; hoping, I imagine, to be inconspicuous. Summertime has barely touched him, he's as pale as ever, but the heat in here is bringing a glow to his face. 'Well,' he says to me, 'I've caught up with you.'

Does he mean that one of us has been remiss? Which of us, though? It can't have been me: I can't rove around inside the various palaces, looking for him. I find myself stating the obvious: 'We've been on progress.' But has *he*? Has he been on progress, for the whole time? Has he been in all the places I've been, these past three or four weeks? Nonsuch, yes: we did meet up at Nonsuch. But the others? Does the king always take all his musicians with him? If not all, does he take his favourites?

'I've been lucky enough to have a couple of quick breaks,' he says.

'For us, it's been relentless. Poor Joseph – our pack-man: all this to pack up, every few days.' I'm babbling, but it's also true: I do feel for Joseph. It's bad enough for him in the winters, moving us between the major palaces every few weeks, but at least those kitchens are basically equipped. These moves to the smaller houses, the hunting lodges, require us to take everything, every last pan and spoon. 'And lately, he's had to deal with all these subtleties, in pieces; packing them so carefully into chests.'

I don't understand it: every previous summer, there've been occasions when we've been paid our retainers and told to stay behind in whichever palace we're in while it's being cleaned. Time off is welcome, of course, but I can never help thinking of the hard work going on around us: Mr Wilkinson, in his trademark red coat, cleaning the kitchen drains. Worse, beneath us: Poor Mr Long and his poor boys, the gong scourers, digging down alongside the latrine pits, removing bricks and climbing in to take away the mess and scrub the shafts and walls and floors.

Whether or not Richard and I go on progress depends, presumably, on the hospitality offered to the king. Perhaps, sometimes, it'd be a snub to take us. Perhaps sometimes a snub *not* to. I don't know the niceties, but someone does. It's the Knight Harbinger's job to know if we're going or not, to arrange accommodation for us if we need it. We simply follow the orders that filter down. But this summer has been different. No niceties. Everywhere the king has gone, we've gone, too. Our only orders have been to produce more, and bigger, and better.

I try to be positive. 'Nonsuch, though: that was lovely, wasn't it.' Brand new Nonsuch.

'Queen Anne's, now, of course,' he says. 'Given to her by the king.'

I don't care whose it is. 'Not the house, particularly; but the orchards. I don't suppose you went into the orchards? Then you'll not have seen these.' I take one from the basket and approach him, offering it up for inspection. He brushes a fingertip over the small fruit; it stirs on my palm.

'What is it?' he asks. 'Some kind of baby peach? A funny, little … smooth, little … egg-yolk-coloured peach?' He gives up with a half-laugh, but remains intrigued.

'It's an apricot. Mr Harris – the king's fruiterer – brought a cutting back from abroad, a couple of years ago, and he's been nursing it at Nonsuch. And here we are.'

Despite the note of triumph, I suddenly feel silly. Because it's nothing, really, is it. It's a fruit; it's a bit like a peach. I've been carried away by all the excitement: Mr Harris's, and then my own and Richard's. Why on earth would Mark be interested? And yet. It also *is* something, isn't it? It *is something*: it's new, it's alive, and we've never seen it before, and isn't that something?

He's asking, 'What are you going to do with it?' He's watchful as I replace it with the others.

'Same as I do with every other fruit. Same as I'm doing over there with the peaches. Cook them. Preserve them. Cook a very thick jam, cut it into pieces, stamp each piece and dust it with sugar.'

'No one'll eat them fresh?'

I'm back to the peaches; my knife-blade drops through slick flesh. 'Fresh fruit's indigestible, Mark.' He should know that;

should look after himself. 'It stews in your stomach.' No wonder he looks so pale.

'Seems a shame, though. To cook them.' I can barely hear him over the raps of my knife. 'To mush them up. When they're so beautiful.'

A glance, and there they are: nestled in the bowl, but each one also very *itself*. Staring me down. Looking either helpless, or supremely confident; I can't decide which. 'But they have to be eaten. That's what they're *for*.'

'Well, I suppose you can model them in sugar. That way, you can keep them intact.'

On the shelves above me are box-loads of lemons and oranges that Richard and I have cast and coloured for the coming feast. Point taken: I know very well that fruits aren't just for eating, but also for looking at. Of course I do. Much of my time is taken with preserving them or faking them in sugar and marchepane. I can't have him thinking that I don't find the apricots beautiful. The first one I ever saw was sunset-coloured; it was bowed by its cleft, and the skin was a blur however sharply I focused.

'Simple pleasures,' he says, 'in these difficult times. These dark times.'

I could ignore that; I could let it pass in respectful silence. Could I? No. No, of course not. He's right: if it isn't acknowledged – what's happened – then it waits to be acknowledged. My problem is with Richard: I really don't wish to discuss it with or in front of Richard, who's been so very keen to discuss it with me. Keen to subject me to gossip, to make me hear the details. I don't even want to think about it. There's no point; there's nothing I can do. Except think about it. And I can't bear to think about it. Mark and I didn't talk about it at Nonsuch; we could've done – everyone else was – but we didn't. By mutual consent, I presumed. Because what would we have said? If we weren't going to talk about it like everyone else was – the gossip, the details – then what would we have said? We'd have ended up saying something pointless like, The Tyburn executions – what an awful business! But now something more has happened – it's happened to Bishop Fisher – and something will have to be said. What, though?

I say, 'She put him up to it.' Well, it's the truth.

'Not true, Lucy.' He was ready for me, his response immediate. His head is tilted to one side, appraising me. 'It's the king who signs.'

'Yes, I do know who signs death warrants. As I say, she put him up to it.' Actually, I can't quite believe what I've said. Oh,

I believe *in* what I've said; just can't believe that I said it, and like that. To Mark.

Richard downs tools: the whispered clink of some utensil.

'Lucy . . .' Mark looks pained, now; the tilted-head coolness is gone.

'He wouldn't have done it, otherwise, would he. A traitor's death for Bishop Fisher? Maybe – *maybe* – the Tyburn men *were* traitors. Everyone says they were bookish, religious men, but maybe they *did* deserve to be hanged, drawn and quartered in front of that audience of male Boleyns and Boleyn-friends. If anyone ever does deserve to be butchered.'

Richard says, 'Lucy . . .' warning me that, in theory, I could join them for saying so.

'But Bishop Fisher, Mark? Because he wouldn't sign a piece of paper? Wouldn't sign his support for Princess Elizabeth as heir, rather than Princess Mary? No protest. No incitement to others. Just a missing signature from an old man. A man of the Church. And there's Sir Thomas More.'

'Sir Thomas isn't –'

'He'll go the same way, he'll have his trial but he'll go the same way.'

'*Lucy* . . .' Richard, again, and still I don't look at him. It's Mark I'm looking at; pale-faced Mark.

'And all this from a king known all over the world for his love of debate, his love of thinkers and writers? A big-hearted man. Huge-spirited. Generous to a fault. Would he order the butchering of an old bishop who declined to sign a piece of paper?'

Mark is still back against the wall but no longer leaning. Standing to attention. Expressionless, as far as I can tell. I had no idea I was so angry. No, that's untrue. I had no idea that I could go on and on, like this, at someone. But, then, it isn't 'someone', is it; it's Mark. Thank goodness it's Mark. Thank goodness for Mark.

'It's not a piece of paper.' He's still expressionless; or, the expression is one of patience. 'You know that.'

Yes, I do know. Of course I do. It was stupid of me to say so. So, why did I? Because I wish it was? Because a piece of paper really would be inconsequential and none of this horribleness would be happening.

He says, 'There's a lot that's done in her name. Others want something done, for their own reasons, and she gets the blame. Look how she gets the blame for what's happening to the religious houses. But that's never been what she's wanted. She's for reform. She's made a point of visiting nuns, talking to them –'

'Exactly: she makes *a point* of it.' Dear Mark, so keen to think the best. 'She likes show, Mark; she's good at it.' Here I am, suddenly cynical. Is this how Richard has always felt, dealing with me?

But Mark laughs, or almost: exasperation, half-amused. 'She doesn't care about appearances. I've never met anyone who cares less about impressing people –' He halts; splays his hands. 'Except you.'

Me?

Me?

Don't I? Well, I suppose I don't. But who is there to impress?

'She's a principled woman,' he says, subdued. Back against that wall. 'A woman of very strong faith.'

Oh, all this talk of faith. As if it's enough. What about *behaving* as a Christian? 'She didn't plead for them, did she.' I say it to the pile of peach slices, perhaps because I don't quite want to say it. Perhaps because if he doesn't want to hear me say it, then he needn't. 'Maybe she didn't want those men to be ripped up at Tyburn, but she didn't plead for them.'

'How do we know? Maybe she did. She probably did.'

'What about that priest?' I can't leave it; and, worse, turn to confront him again. 'That priest she was asked to plead for –'

'Which priest?'

'And she refused, said, "There are enough priests already".' I don't know which priest; Richard told me. 'What kind of woman could say that?'

'A misquoted one.' He folds his arms, but suddenly he unfolds them and is coming towards me. 'Do you really think *anyone* would say that?'

Suddenly, I feel stupid.

'*Lucy* . . .' like a confidence, 'have you ever met her?' He rests lightly against my workbench but inclines towards me, looks closely at me. I do some savage work on a peach, but give him his response, a shake of my head.

'Well, she's . . . full of life. She says things, yes; doesn't stop to think. But that's just it: she's not calculating. Those Tyburn men . . .' The mere mention of the word, Tyburn, brings in its wake a respectful pause. 'Those men were of no consequence to her. She already has what she wants. They didn't like it, but that doesn't matter to her. She wouldn't *need* them butchered.' He dips to try to catch my eye; I glimpse a strained smile. 'Remember that motto of hers? *Ainsi sera, groigne qui groigne*?'

Yes. It caused quite a stir. Or so Richard told me.

He translates: '"It's going to happen, whether they like it or not." Or –' his tone warmer still, '"Tough", you might say.'

What I want to say is, I hate it, Mark; I hate what's happening. Life used to be good, or at least nothing much, but now look. It's frightening, it's vicious.

He's saying, 'She bears grudges, yes: we all know that, we've all seen that.' He's thinking of Cardinal Wolsey; he was a member of the cardinal's household and he's seen what Anne Boleyn can do to a man she dislikes. 'She ... sees people off. But not like that.' Not like Tyburn. 'That's not her style. She's, well, she's hot-headed, not cold-hearted.' He's pleased with that one: there's a grace-note of satisfaction to it.

And it's a good place to stop this. We do need to stop. Why did we ever start? What has it – *she* – to do with us? His grave little face, so obliging. He's too nice, that's his problem; that'll be his problem, if he's not careful.

'You put up a good defence of her.' I'm not being snide; he knows I mean it. 'You really like her, don't you.'

'Like her?' It's the only time today when I've seen him thrown. He's amused, though, too. 'Yes, I do.'

'Well, on that, we can agree to differ.' I hand him a knife. If he's staying, he can make himself useful.

This time, I've sent him away; had to. I have ten spice plates to load. 'Later?' I suggested; an explanatory sweep of my hand over the stacked plates, the sacks of spices.

He winced. 'Can't. Playing.'

Of course: playing at the banquet for which we're preparing. Of course he won't be around, later, because he'll be there.

Richard's unhelpful comment was, 'Oh, they'll be pretty early to bed, judging by what she's loading onto those plates.' Neither Mark nor I gave any indication of having heard. Figs, almonds, aniseed: they warm the blood, I'd been taught; and warm blood it had remained, for me, until Richard took it upon himself to elaborate. I rather wish he hadn't.

'Tomorrow,' was all Mark said, bowing out, with his smile.

Tomorrow, then. Lately, he's been coming by every few days. What does the Sergeant Porter think, on his rounds? Seeing Mark loping across the yard or bounding up our stairs; hearing the laughter from our window, sometimes hearing the lute. The Sergeant Porter, checking that all's well. Well, it is. Why shouldn't we have music? It's summer. We're working hard. The Sergeant Porter – and anyone else, for that matter – can think what he likes. Mark and I have fun, and fun's important, or so everyone's always saying, here. Not that we have their kind of fun, the kind that's suspiciously keen to declare itself as such. Ours is quieter and all our own. Better, I'll bet. Genuine. Mark is good company; I love his company, and he does seem to like mine. We understand each other, he and I. There've been no more disagreements; the air is well and truly cleared.

I'm tired. Choosing to work late is an option – avoiding the heat of these last few days by napping for a couple of hours, or, once, retreating with Mark to the shade of the riverbank trees – but there's no slack in the mornings. Sir Alexander is on rota as our Chief Clerk of the Spicery – four weeks down, two to go – and he's a particularly early bird, here before eight every day so that he can be over at the Greencloth Office well before nine, presenting his figures. This morning felt particularly chaotic. Him, quibbling over whether it was three cinnamon quills or four that we used, yesterday. The little groom from the chandlery, also early, ferreting around for our candle stubs and having the cheek to say to Stephen, 'We're not *made* of tallow, you know'. And Kit turning up with apologies for being unwell – it was a hangover, clearly – then leaving again before I had a chance to ask more. It's left me with a headache.

Richard's keeping his own hours, too. No complaints from me, even though I've had to vouch for him on a couple of occasions when the Clerks have come checking on attendance. He works very hard; but then he's gone, and it's for four, five, six hours at a stretch before he joins me again. Who knows what he's up to. Last night, when I went down into the yard for some air and to look up into the hazy sky – a dab of moon, a floury thumbprint of a moon – I spotted Stephen sitting with his kitchen-lad friends on some steps, playing cards. A year ago, it'd have been Richard I'd have seen. Now, he seems to have moved on, somewhere. He looks thinner, if that's possible, but very well. His cheekbones are gilded, even faintly freckled. He has some new clothes.

'New doublet?' I said, the other day, when he dropped by on his way to wherever he goes.

He twirled, then allowed, 'Well . . .'

Secondhand, then. Whatever. I didn't actually mean new; whoever has *new* clothes? But still.

'Aren't I gorgeous?' he asked, and we laughed, he and I, but it was true; is.

I asked, 'Where's the money coming from?' although it wasn't really a question; more of an exclamation.

His response was an airy, 'Oh, who needs money.' Then he said, '*You* should treat yourself, you know.'

He used to get on at me about my clothes – or lack of them – but hadn't said much for a while. He used to tell me that Cardinal Wolsey's cook wore silk and velvet damask; obviously he'd heard this, once, and it'd made quite an impression on him. I used to say, So? The cardinal's cook was a man; men make more fuss about their dress.

This time, I said, 'I don't need any new clothes. No one ever sees me.'

'Well, they *should*.' He was grinning. 'You're so *pretty*, Lucy!' He sounded delighted.

'Are you drunk?'

'Drunk!' Derisively, although happily. 'You need some lace. What if the galleon trip happens again?'

The invitation to the Venetian galleon, sugar-loaded, confectionery-loaded, in the Southampton docks. An evening of tastings, in the company of the king. 'I have my nice gown.'

'It's old,' he said.

'*I'm* old,' I laughed.

'You don't look a day over twenty-five. Your pockets crammed with acorns.'

I hadn't heard that one for years: an acorn in the pocket to keep a woman looking young. 'I'm eleven years over twenty-five, Richard.' And I'm *not* pretty. My sisters were pretty. My half-sisters. I don't know what my mother looked like, but my sisters looked like theirs.

This has been a summer of banquets. More so than usual. None of them unmanageable, though. Nothing like the one at Greenwich, in my first year here, in honour of the French ambassador, for which I had to load sixty spice plates. Sixty! Plates of syrup-doused ginger, of sugar-coated almonds, of marchepane-filled dates. A banqueting house had been erected by the river, the guests to be invited there for confectionery after the main feast. I saw inside it. Sir Henry Guildford – who was responsible for organizing it all, being Master of Revels – took me to it while it was being built. He was probably aiming to impress upon me what efforts would be required of me. He succeeded. The building had been designed by Mr Holbein. The ceiling was painted and gilded with the constellations and zodiac signs. The floor was covered in dark green silk embroidered with gold lilies. In the middle of the room was a white marble fountain. To flank that fountain I made a sugar hawthorn tree, to represent England, and a mulberry to represent France. For the tables I made sugar chessboards and pieces, sugar cheeseboards and cheeses.

Quite by coincidence, and of course unknown at the time to

any of us, the banquet took place on the evening of the sack of Rome. While our king and his guests were relaxing on the bank of the moonlit Thames, renegade Spanish soldiers were rampaging through Rome, hacking at its citizens, committing acts of barbarism on people as they lay dying. Never had the world heard anything like it. I lost heart for big events, after that. Celebrations seem to allow disaster to crash in, somewhere, unchecked.

And this summer, what is there to celebrate? Apart from these last few days, the weather has been dreadful, the coming harvest ruined and plague taking hold. The king has been excommunicated. And Sir Thomas More has been executed. We were at Hanworth when the execution happened. Richard came into the kitchen and said, 'Well, More's for the chop about now.'

I asked him, in no uncertain terms, not to be so disrespectful. How could he talk like that about a man who had served his country as chancellor for so many years?

His answer – who on earth had he been listening to? – was that Sir Thomas had imprisoned a lot of men for heresy, in his time, and burned six of them.

I despaired. 'If he did – *if* he did – he didn't do it personally, did he. That was the *law*.'

He shrugged. 'And this, now? This is the law, now. He's the heretic, now.' Then, softening, he said, 'Listen: this is the last of it, I'm sure. This is the ringleader going.'

The evening of Sir Thomas's death, the spice plate came back untouched, delivered by the usher of the king's chamber, no waiting for Stephen to fetch it in the morning. The usher looked grave. The king was tired from hunting, he told us; he'd been hunting all day and didn't want to eat.

I know that the king never doesn't want to eat.

'And by the way,' he said, 'we're moving, tomorrow.'

'*Tomorrow?*' Richard protested. 'You're joking, aren't you?' We'd only just arrived, and were due to stay another three days. 'To *where?*'

The usher shrugged.

'Tell me this,' said Richard. 'Is the queen's household moving, too?'

The usher looked at the floor. 'No.'

Last week, I was introduced to Anne Boleyn. The king sent for me. He does, sometimes. I don't know why. No doubt he regrets it when I appear, dowdy and tongue-tied. Not that he shows it. On the contrary, and I wish I could reciprocate. I envy those who are at ease with him. Richard once told me that Mr

Hill, my counterpart in the wine cellars, often spends evenings playing cards with him.

My summons, as usual, came via an usher: 'His Majesty wishes to see you.' This usher was an impeccably-dressed young man. He leaned against the lintel, crossed his long legs at the ankle. Folded his arms.

'Now?'

He said nothing.

I untied my apron and rushed to my room. And there was Hettie on her pallet-bed, pulled from beneath my own bed. 'Hettie!' Sick?

She was struggling up, flustered and sleep-damp.

'Hettie?'

'It's nothing,' she said: 'headache.'

I knelt to get a good look at her. She looked back at me, clear-eyed. A headache, she said again, sounding disappointed: she's prone to them; they dog her. I stood, ruffling her hair; she was almost certainly right, was my instinct. It was almost certainly nothing worse than a headache. I'd make a paste of rose-petals for her, as soon as I could; press it to her forehead. 'The king's sent for me.'

'*Now?*'

'Steady,' I said, 'I can get it.'

But she was already there, at the chest, extracting my gown.

Arriving back downstairs in the confectionery, I detected some tension between Richard and the usher; they both seemed absurdly glad at my reappearance. The usher immediately remembered himself, and affected nonchalance. Richard left his sugar-sculpture – an archer, as big as a child – and hurried towards me. I opened my arms in invitation for him to circle. When he was behind me, he swiped my bonnet; my hair dropped unfastened down my back.

'Richard!'

'Trust me.'

'No,' I said. 'No, no, no.' I simply couldn't go cavorting to the king like some girl. I'm unmarried, yes, but the point is that I'll never be married. I'm not some young, unmarried girl, whatever Richard thinks to the contrary.

'*Trust* me,' he said, the bonnet held behind his back. 'He'll like it.'

I glared at him but his eyes didn't meet mine, he was too busy arranging my hair over my shoulders.

'There,' he announced; and touched my forehead with his lips. I began following the usher, and realized that I didn't know where we were heading: which chamber? My guess was the Presence Chamber: hardly the hubbub, but not as intimate as the king's own rooms. And it wasn't just where we were heading that I didn't know; I didn't even know where we were. Fifty yards from my kitchen and I was lost. How had that happened? This boy was adept at finding deserted corridors and passageways. Judging from the retreating clamour, he'd somehow slipped us past the whole main kitchen. I'd been assuming this was for my benefit – to avoid a parade in front of a couple of hundred men – but now I wondered if it could be for his. Perhaps he didn't particularly want to be seen with a middle-aged working woman.

I scuttled along behind him with a familiar dread. It's not the king I mind: of course not; far from it. It's the retinue; the retinue was what I was dreading as I rushed along behind the usher. A roomful of nobility, and their attendants. So many people; their scrutiny. And me with my hair down. Silently, I cursed Richard. Then, to be fair, I cursed myself for allowing him to hold such sway over me. And Mark: would Mark be there, too? Would he be one of them, in there? How would I look, to him, there? Just as I look to the rest of them. Tongue-tied, bare-headed and loose-haired in my dowdy gown.

In the end, everything happened before there was time to think about it. The king was on his feet the instant I was in the doorway: up and out of his chair, striding towards me. The smile. The sheer height of him. His clothes: made of gold; solid gold, thread-thin and made into cloth. His shoes: down in my curtsey I focused on the square-toed purple velvet shoes, and the carpet beneath them. There was music; strings. Mark?

'Lucy,' the king said, 'Lucy,' a hand on my arm to draw me up, guiding me towards a fireplace which was unlit, cavernous and cool . . . We'd turned our backs on the throng. My back: my hair hanging down it. I can never believe that he calls me *Lucy* until I hear it. I love it. 'How *are* you?' he was asking me. He'd caught the sun: there hadn't been much of it, but what there'd been, he'd caught. He looked younger than when I'd last seen him. And those eyes: those small, intensely blue, unflinching eyes.

'You're looking wonderful,' he was saying. 'And you've been doing marvellously, lately – the midsummer subtleties in particular; they were stunning – and we're all very grateful to you . . .'

And I was saying the usual: Oh, no, Your Majesty; Oh, yes, Your Majesty; Thank you, Your Majesty; Your Majesty is too kind.

He asked some detailed questions about what I was working on, and so we began talking about the consecration of the three new bishops in six weeks' time: the celebratory feast planned for Winchester. 'This one's important,' he stressed. 'No, really. It's . . .' his glittery eyes to the ceiling, 'what I mean, Lucy, is that I want this summer to go out with a bang.'

Down in the household, the fear is that the summer is about to go out with quite a different kind of bang: there's a lot of talk of the threat of war with Spain. Those of us who rely on shipped supplies have our own particular concerns.

'This has been such a good summer, and we should finish it in style.'

A good summer? With everything that's happened? My heart dropped away from my smile. Is he mad? He didn't *look* mad. He looked entirely sure of himself. There *was* something else, though, when I looked closer; I could see what might be tiredness beneath that touch of sun.

Then he said, 'Come with me,' and suddenly there was a blur of people, all standing. Fabrics, head-dresses sparkling. A haze of perfumes. Everyone was looking at us. No, at *him*, of course; the murmured conversations had stopped and everyone was looking at him. A rasp of that cloth-of-gold, beside me, and he'd made whatever gesture they were waiting for, because they re-settled onto stools and floor cushions. But they hadn't *all* been standing; I now realized that they hadn't all stood; someone had been sitting. I knew who, too: I knew, despite not having dared look. I knew from the fact of her sitting, and from the colour of her gown. A sitting, purple-clad woman: a queen. This queen had no ladies around her; no queen's ladies. Just two men. These two men were now re-taking their seats. One of them was looking at me, his look so direct that I jumped as if he'd whispered in my ear. He was so dark that he could be an ambassador from Spain, but no ambassador would dare look at an Englishwoman in such a manner. Then it occurred to me: *the brother*; he was her brother. Mark had told me how she usually sits after dinner with her brother and one or more of her favourites, debating religion and politics.

Unfortunately, we seemed to be heading for this trio. 'Anne,' the king called, 'let me introduce Mrs Cornwallis, who keeps us all sweet: our confectioner.'

I made my curtsey deep and slow, ducking to avoid her gaze. The sheen of her skirt captivated me. She made one comment, to my lowered head: 'Your midsummer dancers were beautiful.'

'Yes,' the king said, 'I told her,' and then we were away again, pacing the room while he talked more of the Winchester feast. Tapestries hung on every wall, ceiling to floor: a biblical story, would be my guess, told in many scenes; there was no time for a proper look. A clock stood on a writing desk: a clock small enough to stand on a writing desk. Many-wicked candles everywhere. Most of my attention, though, was homed to the music, the mix of fingertips and strings, trying to identify which might be Mark's. The musicians – perhaps four, six – occupied a corner, and I kept my eyes averted.

I was reeling from my encounter with Anne Boleyn. The look she'd given me was similar to her brother's in its directness. Not detached or hard, as I'd expected. Nor arrogant, there was none of the fabled arrogance, although she did hold her head high on that long, slender neck of hers. She'd regarded me with weary, sympathetic amusement. Her eyes had said something like, *Well, hello, there*. Something like, *Well, here we all are*. And what I'd actually felt, against all the odds, was a rush of concern for her. Two years ago, I'd seen her on that canopied barge bound for the Tower, before her coronation, and she'd been a girl in white, her loose black hair ablaze with sunshine. Now, despite the elaborate riches of her gown, her head-dress and jewellery, she looked sallow and scrawny. True, she'd never been the type who could expect to age well; she'd had no bloom. But this decline was shocking. The fragile skin of her throat and around those famously-huge eyes was dry, lined, darkened. Healthy face, healthy soul: that's what people say. What had struck me loud and clear when I'd looked into her face was that she's running out of time. She's choleric, if not already melancholic. She'll need help if she's ever to have another child. Which she must. Debating is all very well, but that's not what she's for, any more. Not the sharpness of her wit, the depth and breadth of her learning. Sugar, I thought. *Cucharum*. Warms the blood, brings a flush to the skin. Healthy for anyone, any time, any place: that's what I was taught. Every other food trails an interminable list of qualities and qualifiers with which we who practise the art of cookery are supposed to be acquainted: warm in the first degree, dry in the second, good for old people with damp temperaments if eaten during spring. But sugar is unequivocal. White and dry, it runs sparkling around a body.

The other day, in the shade of the riverbank trees, Mark asked me how long I've been making confectionery. 'Forever', I said, before remembering myself: 'but probably not as long as you've been singing.' I've been working in kitchens since I was twelve. As a child, I knew nothing of confectionery and my fascination was for tiles. We had a neighbour who was a tilemaker. He'd tiled the floors of churches – our own, in the village – and other religious houses such as Lewes Priory, as well as wealthy people's homes. Sometimes he went away to supervise the laying; other times, he sent crates by packhorse and barge. His tiles were red-brown with honey-coloured designs: a fleur de lys, perhaps, or rosette, or shield. Near our chalky land was a weald of clay which he dug during the winter. In the summer, he'd hammer the drying clay into hand-sized square moulds and then, into each, he'd tap down a wooden stencil. The indents – a lion, deer, boar, bird, fish – he filled with slip. His kiln, below ground and brushwood-burning, took a week to load, fire, cool and unload.

At twelve years old, I went to the local manor house to work in the kitchens. Some of the floors, in that house, were tiled. Dark green tiles. I'd come from the biggest house in our village – my father was a yeoman farmer – but this manor was brick-built, glazed, slate-roofed. My father's house was half-timbered and thatched, open windows hung with sacking. The manor had kitchens, with fireplaces and chimneys. At home, our cooking had been done on an open fire in the middle of the one main room, the smoke finding its way to a vent in the roof.

The mistress of my new home was nineteen. Alice. The master's second wife. No children of her own; just the two stepchildren. She was keen on confectionery and I worked alongside her, learning. Once, she flung sugar syrup at a rosebush and we watched it dry on the petals. Ingenious: real sugar roses; sugar real roses. We picked the crisp, glowing petals for storage, allowing ourselves to sample a few. I've never dared do it, myself: that flinging of sugar, that gloriously haphazard sugaring. And it's not quite what I have in mind, now; I don't want to preserve a real rose in sugar, to sugar a rose. What I want to do is make something like a real rose from sugar. As like a real rose as I can. A rose made of sugar, but with very little that's sugary about it. It's easy with other fruits and plants such as oranges and lemons, nuts and berries: solid, they lend themselves to sugar sculpture. But roses, folded in on themselves, are hard to capture.

I adored Alice. Everyone did. She loved to entertain, and one day the Nevilles came to dine. We struggled to produce a spread lavish enough. They declared themselves very impressed with the confectionery, and the master of the household suggested they take me to work for them. It was the Nevilles who, eventually, in turn, sent me to work for the king. Before I left, I visited my sisters. They told me that Alice had died of sweating sickness.

'It was like it always is,' said Kate, ruefully. 'She was fine at lunchtime, dead by dark.'

Mark asked me if I like what I do.

'Working in a kitchen?' I asked him, 'or making confectionery?'

'Either,' he said. 'Both.'

'I like getting things right,' I decided. The royal kitchens are as good a place as any to do that. 'I like working in kitchens if I'm the head. And I like working with Richard, if you can believe that.'

He laughed.

'He's my sharpest critic, but I trained him.' That's something else I've liked: training Richard. 'And I'm lucky,' I said, 'working for someone who appreciates what I do and encourages me, no expense spared.' I asked him, 'And you? Do you like being a musician?'

He simply said, 'Yes.' He said it immediately, but there seemed something uncertain about it. No, not uncertain, it was certain enough: flat, was what it was. He said, 'I didn't really appreciate it, at the time, but I was very lucky to make that transition. It could've all stopped for me when I was twelve. But instead of just a broken voice, I got a new one. Otherwise, I'd be teaching music, somewhere, I suppose; that would've been the best I could've hoped for.' Then he said, 'All that "sings like an angel" business; I was completely unaware of it, at the time. To me, life was a series of difficult choirmasters and a bit of bullying from the other boys; and it was always cold, and the hours were long.' He shrugged. 'It was hard, but I suppose any childhood's hard, isn't it.'

I didn't say, Not my own; not really. I wanted to say that Richard was a foundling, but that's for Richard to tell people, if he wishes. Sometimes he does: *And me, a poor little foundling!* Mark asked me where I come from.

'Sussex,' I said. 'You?'

'Here.' That same flatness. 'London.'

For no particular reason – perhaps the heat, the river – I said, 'We weren't that far from the sea.'

'We?' Gentle and shy, as if he very much wanted to know something but was wary that the answer could be difficult for one or both of us. He wanted to know about my family, I presumed.

'My sisters and me.'

He asked me how many sisters.

Two, I told him: Ellie and Kate. It'd take all morning, that walk to the sea. Some of the afternoon, too, when the girls were small. On the odd day when we were released from chores. We'd walk from village to village, and past the yew that people said was a thousand years old. Thank goodness for the yew, it kept us going: there for us on the way there and the way back. We'd sit on it, in it, and think about who could have been there a thousand years ago: princesses, pirates, wizards. The walk must have been worth it for the pleasure of paddling, but the lovely sting of the water isn't what I remember. What I remember is the look of it. The gloss on it. Everyone always talked about the cruel sea, the depth of it, the immensity. And yet there it was, at my feet, flexing beneath a supple, shiny skin. He asked me where my sisters are now.

'Married,' I said.

He wanted to know, do I have nieces and nephews?

Do I have nieces and nephews! It was nice to have an opportunity to say their names: John, Matthew, Christopher, Ed, Lizzie, Izzie, Cecily, Mary, little Mary, and a Lucy. I didn't mention Ralph, Henry, and Maudie: it felt wrong not to have mentioned them, but to have mentioned them would have felt more wrong. They're still there, though, and more permanently so than their siblings: their little greenstick bones settling into the earth. Beside my brother's; Eddie's. I told Mark about my brothers: twins, George and Eddie, born when I was eleven.

What I didn't tell him about the boys – it's nothing, and, anyway, I've only just remembered – was how, once, when they were sitting in my stepmother's lap, I noticed something about them. 'Look,' I said to Ellie, and raised my hands in front of them, putting them palm to palm as if praying and then opening them like a book 'See? They're two halves.' The mole beside Eddie's left eye was there on George, but beside the right eye. 'Isn't that something?' I said, but Ellie merely looked at me.

I told Mark that I did visit, had visited.

He said, 'It's not easy, is it: being a visitor.'

No. My sisters tried. For which, of course, I was very grateful. And the boys – well, they were young; they were as they always were. For which I was also very grateful. But I don't know which was worse: my sisters, actuely aware of me, or the boys, barely.

Mark asked me if I'd like to go back, one day.

'To live, you mean?'

He nodded: to live.

I shrugged. *Go back.* I can't. No one's there, to go back to; or not as they were. The children are no longer children, my sisters no longer the girls they were, the girls with whom I walked to the sea. Perhaps none of them are there at all, now: would I know otherwise? For a long time, I didn't even know that Maudie had even been expected, let alone that she'd died: she'd come and gone before I knew. They were stunning children, the children of my sisters: sleek and sure-footed, a fierce clarity to everything they did and said. It was us, the adults, who were gawky, awkward. Of course the landscape remains, unchanged; the landscape of my childhood. What I remember of it isn't what I expect to remember: not the details; not the click and give of the latch on our gate, nor the bites of the bridleway stones to my soles. Perhaps it isn't a landscape for details: what was striking, to me, even then, was its flatness. As if it were rolling over, stretching out and giving itself up to the sun, the sea. My memory of it claims me like a dream, pulls on me like a dream; unfinished.

'You?' I asked Mark.

'Me?'

'Brothers and sisters?'

'No,' he said, quietly. 'Just me.'

To cheer him up, I used that expression: 'He broke the mould when He made you.'

'Yes,' he said; and he did seem rather comforted by that. 'Yes, I suppose He did.'

Of my planned sugar rose, it's no longer the shape that's concerning me. I can manage, mould-less, I'm sure. What's preoccupying me, now, is the colour. Red isn't easy. Or not rose-red, anyway. Or not the kind of rose-red I'm aiming to make. Other colours – yellow, green, blue, brown, orange, pink, violet – are easy. Or if not, if they're not quite right, there are ways of making them better, as long as the sugar isn't then for eating. In the Neville kitchens, I learned to conjure a kind of gold from arsenic, ground quartz and saffron.

But red. Sandalwood is too brown for this rose of mine. Brazil wood, too pink. I need a blood-red rose. Blood? Dries too dark and too dull. The confectioner's mainstay for red is rose-petals; but as we work with them, mixing them into gum, they weep some of their colour away. Even the reddest lose themselves a little to become, in our hands, something else. Pink. No longer red rose-petals. Which is what I need them to be.

Anne Boleyn

❀❀❀

That year, 1528, it was Greenwich as usual for Christmas; but this time, I was there. Suitably separate, though, from Henry and Catherine. I had my own gorgeous rooms, rich with river-view. Any light in that late-December sky was drawn down to the fat Thames then turned on my windows. The green-and-ochre ceilings glowed, the blood-black walls of panelling gleamed. Everyone liked it, my apartment; it was definitely the place to be, that Christmas. I was tired of playing the retiring maiden, and now the privacy of my own rooms and the season provided the means and excuse for some fun. Dinners and cabaret. On the other side of my door and down a corridor or two, Catherine – still queen, if in name only – put on a brave face and presided over the official celebrations with a gout-disgruntled cardinal for company, and no one much else: the Suffolks and Norfolks, the Poles and Nevilles, all of them exchanging season's greetings and clapping stiffly at the various appalling 'entertainments'. Well, if that was their idea of a good time, they were welcome to it. Poor Henry flitted between the two worlds, doing his best. He'd come to us late in the evenings and we'd have to thaw him through, remind him how to laugh.

It wasn't all fun, though, that Christmas. Court was still reverberating from More's publication of his *Dialogue Concerning Heresies*. He seemed to feel that we in England had our eyes closed to certain dangers at home and in northern Europe. Actually, some of us had our eyes wide open but were glad at what we saw. And it wasn't that I was a heretic; nor were my friends. Far from it: we held the Church's best interests at heart. That's what galled me: More's assumption that it was heresy to question the Church's problems. As far as I was concerned, there were good priests and bad ones, and there had been good Popes and bad ones. It was only the bad ones that bothered me.

Not long after Christmas, I got hold of a copy of Simon Fish's *Supplication for the Beggars*. Fish was interesting on corruption in the clergy, and I lent the book to Henry when I'd finished with it. Lo and behold, within days More was taking Fish to task in *The Supplication of Souls*. He wasn't going to let it go, couldn't let it rest; he was determined to slam down any debate. To *enter* debate, I imagine he'd have said, but I wasn't fooled. People venerated More – especially Henry, who, I suspect, would have preferred him to his own narrow-minded, mean-spirited father – but I had my suspicions. Witty, sarcastic More prided himself on his cool-headedness, and could just as well have prided himself on his warm-heartedness: I had no argument with any of that. He was, I suppose, a likeable man. But it was his denial of his passionate nature – his fury – that worried me. The hypocrisy of that denial. If you loathe Lutherans, come out and say it. Don't pretend you're merely interested in refuting their claims. My own loathing is reserved for hypocrites. Useful, then, isn't it, that I have a talent for smelling them out.

There was something else, something more basic: I didn't like the way More looked at me, either, to tell you the truth. The glint of superiority in his eyes. I'd stare him down, thinking, *You don't know what you're dealing with*. And what was that – not knowing what you're dealing with – if not a kind of stupidity? You can read all the books you like but if you can't read people, you're heading for trouble. Old Mrs Queenie, though, he'd always seemed to have a way with. She lightened up with him. They'd chat like old friends. Which is, I suppose, what they were.

When Henry handed me back the Fish book, he said, 'You know, Angel, I think we might need to be more careful about what we're seen reading.'

I laughed. 'You're *king*, aren't you? Can't you read what you like?'

He managed a smile. 'Probably not in front of the Pope's representative, if I want him to look favourably on me.'

I shrugged. Personally, I felt it might do the cardinal some good to get a glimpse of what was happening in the real world.

The cardinal finally troubled himself to call for the tribunal to start on the last day of May at Blackfriars. Eight months, it had taken him; and for no other reasons, it seemed, than the comings and goings of his ridiculous gout, and a series of ineffective meetings with Her Monstrousness. Another eight months of my young life, gone. Henry and Catherine were informed that they would both be required to appear in person on 18 June. And so began a tense two and a half weeks. Some days, Henry was ablaze with optimism and confidence, his talk all of the future – our wedding, renovations to some of the palaces, a trip to France. But on other days, nothing was right – the weather, my dress, the musicians' efforts – and he couldn't stop sniping at and complaining about various officials and relatives. Worse, I couldn't predict when he'd be with me. Sometimes he didn't turn up when he'd said he would, presumably going hunting instead or bashing a tennis ball about with Harry Norris. Other times, he arrived unexpectedly and wanted supper served when I'd already eaten mine, wanted to play cards when – waiting for him – I'd done nothing else all day.

None of this was helped by the fact that we were seeing summer weather the like of which we hadn't seen for years. Sometimes I imagined the Thames was steaming. Servants were listless and argumentative amongst themselves all day long – and the days were exhaustingly long – then, relieved, were noisy at night. No defeatist, I nevertheless felt a sense of doom. If the tribunal failed to deliver, what then? Hot and tired, I couldn't think. Couldn't think beyond Henry being king and, whatever happened, staying king. For all his carry-on, his situation, compared to mine, didn't seem so bad. Mine was that I wasn't yet his queen and now might never be. And I'd meant what I'd said about not being his mistress. I'd have to give up and marry someone else. My heart wilted at the prospect either of some goodnatured man or someone strutting and full of himself.

Perhaps that was why, when, late one night during that wearying two and a half weeks, Henry said to me, '*Please* let me stay; *just* stay,' I did finally acquiesce.

'*Just* stay,' he'd said, hands up to stop my protest, to surrender. 'Please don't send me away,' he said; 'please don't, Anne.' His eyes were faintly bloodshot, his hair sticking to his sweat-dampened forehead. My every bone ached; I'd had more than enough of a long, pitiless day. It was then that the feeling came over me: for all the people involved in our situation – cardinals, lawyers, nobles, the hundreds of spectators at Blackfriars – we were so very alone.

'*Just* stay,' I allowed. I borrowed a nightshirt from my brother, and Henry did wear it all night.

At the end of the difficult two and a half weeks, when Catherine appeared as requested at the tribunal, it was simply to announce that she regarded the tribunal as having no jurisdiction over her and to ask yet again that her case be referred to Rome. She was told to come back in another three days, when they'd have had time to debate her claim and her request. Those three days were the worst, for us. Henry paced my rooms, our gardens, the riverbank. He wouldn't stay with me at night. He probably didn't go to bed at all. 'Why is she *doing* this to me?' he'd roar, or whine; rage, or anguish, or pique, but always with genuine disbelief, amazement. For once, I chose not to enlighten him; chose to spare him the unpalatable truth that he was married to a stubborn and vindictive old cow. I wasn't going to waste my breath on her. We needed to stay calm. We were simply being asked by the tribunal to wait. Three days, that was all. Patience is no virtue of mine, but I'm realistic. And at that stage – three years into our muddle – I was still quite resilient. I despised her but I don't think I quite yet hated her; didn't want her dead. She was merely some desperate old dear, and I had the fierce, unquenchable love of her husband.

When she took her place at the tribunal it was, George told me, on a gold-brocade-canopied chair slightly lower than but otherwise identical to Henry's. A queen's chair. A king and queen of England had for the first time ever been called into a court. They faced each other across a sea of agog spectators. Henry went first, said his piece. It was the usual, the citing of the verse in Leviticus and the expressions of regret that he couldn't stay married to the wonderful, kind Catherine. Blah blah. Then it was Catherine's turn. She rose but, on the arm of her usher, began to make her way through the crowds towards Henry. I can well imagine his face. He hates trouble – he pays or bullies others to deal with it – but there he was, all eyes upon him, as trouble waddled his way.

When she reached him, the usher stepped back and she knelt at Henry's feet. Embarrassed, he got up from his chair and raised her. But she dropped to her knees again. Again, mortified, he raised her. Then she made her case, but not to the tribunal as she was supposed to do. She spoke calmly to him. Imagine those cool grey eyes and that molasses-dark accent. She said, I've never lied to you. You know that. Never. Not about anything. This is the truth about your brother and I: we never slept together. Tell me, Henry, what it is that I've done to turn you against me. Tell me, please. I have no one but you; I am a foreigner alone here in this country of yours. I have loved you all our married life, and I will love you – devotedly – until I die. We have had children together, Henry, and lost all but one of them. Don't do this to me. Don't throw me away. Then she curtseyed low to him, and signalled to her usher, who stepped forward, took her arm, and together they retreated as they had come.

The Court Crier, belatedly coming to his senses, called to her to return: *Catherine, Queen of England, come back into court!* He called three times, but slowly they progressed, that odd pair, the podgy lady and the nimble boy, to the doors and into the crowd outside. It was a crowd of women, George told me, and they were cheering her.

At the time, I was appalled by the scene that my brother described to me. Yet more Spanish histrionics. As I said to George, the only surprise was that she hadn't taken along that disgusting pet monkey of hers to do a star turn. Now, looking back, I admit that I'm impressed. It was an awesome performance, and although it didn't save her in the end (but what could?), it gained her time and allies. And her gain, on both counts, was my loss.

She never did go back into that court on any occasion, despite being summoned. If she had, she'd have had to sit through various witnesses' memories of what that half-dead boy-husband of hers did or didn't boast on the morning after their wedding night. But their evidence wouldn't have been necessary, in the first place, would it, had she given in gracefully and accepted what everybody else knew: that her marriage to Henry was over.

Anyway, it was all to no avail – the stories, the legalities, the long days in that stifling riverside room – because, at the end of July, in Henry's presence, Campeggio referred the case to Rome; just, in fact, as the Pope recalled it. So, we were back to square one. Well, I say 'we' . . . Wolsey, though, was worse off. Wolsey, in fact, was finished. Henry had trusted him to find a solution; and Wolsey had asked for yet more trust. He'd asked for more time and even more time, and Henry had granted it. And now, when a king and queen had been dragged through the courts, the king defied by the queen, the queen's bedlinen – dirty or otherwise – discussed in public . . . now, nothing. Henry had trusted Wolsey to find a solution and now Wolsey seemed to be saying that there wasn't one.

Not good enough. What was the man paid – vastly – for? I *told* you, I said to Henry; I did tell you, didn't I. He wouldn't reply to that; he wouldn't look at me when I said that. He'd look as if he had a headache: eyes half-closed, a fold between his eyebrows, and slow but shallow breaths. If I placed a hand on his forehead, the worry-line would deepen: a twitch, the smallest kind of flinch. He wasn't quite ready to hear the worst of his old friend and confidant. Nearly ready, but not quite. I had to bide my time, bite my tongue. Something I've never found easy.

Summer had well and truly arrived, so we left London for Waltham Abbey, Windsor, Reading, Langley, letting our various hosts look after us while we put the last few disastrous months behind us. Fat Cath stayed at Greenwich. Praying, probably. That, and sewing. Sewing was what she'd been doing when Wolsey had turned up to ask her, one last time, to appear at Blackfriars; she'd flourished a piece of linen and a threaded needle while he requested and she refused. I'll say this for Catherine: she disliked Wolsey almost as much as I did, although of course for different reasons, hers being the view – not unreasonable, I suppose – that a man who has taken a vow of chastity shouldn't have a mistress and children.

Our summer progress finished at the end of September at Grafton, where the lodge is cutely tiny: room only for us and a select or otherwise vital few, everyone else staying in or camping around a manor house about three miles away. Did I say 'select or otherwise vital'? Which, then, was Wolsey? Because suddenly there was Wolsey, turned up to stay with us. He came with Campeggio; Campeggio had come to say goodbye. There was nowhere for Wolsey to stay. Harry Norris gave up his own bed, and moved into my brother's room. 'What could I do?' he pleaded with me. 'Leave him standing there in the courtyard?' I pointed out that everyone else had been quite happy to do so.

Despite acting the perfect hostess – cream tea, even, in the garden – I made sure my displeasure was clear (when don't I?) and, that very evening, Wolsey announced that he'd be leaving in the morning. (Oh dear, was it something I said?) His excuse was that he had to see to one of his nearby properties; he'd just heard that the roof was in need of attention, and whilst he was over this side of the country, and what with autumn nearly here . . . Henry said that we quite understood, but would be sorry to see him go (whereas I said, under my breath, Good riddance). 'We'll come and wave you off in the morning,' he said. I had a feeling something was up; but although Henry had stopped that headachey look whenever I complained about Wolsey, he still refused to discuss him with me. I remember once wailing, 'What *is* it with you and Wolsey? You never say a bad word about him,' to which he snapped back, 'You say enough for both of us.' It's clear to me now that I was forever implying that Henry had been a fool for befriending the butcher's boy, and no one likes to be called a fool. Something I tend to forget in my rush to speak the truth.

How things had changed, over a few years, between Wolsey and me. When we'd first faced each other, arguing about Harry

Percy, what he'd seen was a petite, sparky newcomer barely into her twenties. Too eye-catchingly dressed, and her head held too high. Lacking in the appropriate deference, to say the least. Rude, to put no finer point on it. Worse: a Boleyn; another Boleyn clawing to heights which weren't intended for Boleyns, this time under the guise of love. For Wolsey, nobody except the king had ever been of any importance, and on this occasion he made it clear that I was merely a tiresome episode before lunch. He addressed me with exaggerated patience, for which I ached to slap him.

When Henry took up with me, Wolsey's hastily swallowed surprise was apparent every time he came across us together. He was keen for me to understand that I remained of no real consequence, so he opted for humouring and a laboured deference. I detected it, even if Henry pretended not to. A couple of years on, now, and he'd had to change his attitude. He was attentive, or tried to be. Not knowing how, he sat forward as if he were giving great consideration to whatever I was saying, and focused on me so hard and long that he'd forget to blink. But for all the bright eyes, there was a weariness to him. That eye-brightness, I noticed, was often a glaze. His broad shoulders sagged. His teeth were now more yellow than his once-famed blond hair, his face scratched with veins. I suppose I should probably stop and think, now, shouldn't I, of what it must have been like for him: little Pope, demi-king, able to travel the length and breadth of England stopping for every meal at a house he owned . . . I should try to think of how it must have been to have had all that – to have had England, basically – and see it taken away by a girl not yet thirty.

On the day of his departure from Grafton, I was up at dawn. 'It's a lovely morning,' I announced to Henry.

He struggled up, his nightshirt twisted, and frowned at the window. 'Is it?' Sceptical. With good cause, as it happens, because it was in fact rather bleak.

'Autumnal,' I enthused.

'Autumnal,' he repeated, just as sceptical.

I sat back on the bed, finger-combing my hair. 'Let's go and get some air. Just you and me.'

His frown, now, was for me: bemusement.

'Before the weather breaks,' I said. 'It's our last few days here. Come on. Just for a half hour or so. As if we were young again.' That did the trick, as I knew it would: he was up in a trice.

Once we were out there, it was easy. The morning was indeed autumnal, but in the right way, far more promising than at first glance. The air had a tang, brewed up in the long, dewy grass and hedgerows. We cantered smack up against it, our breaths and those of our horses firing through it like arrowshots. I led Henry further and further away from the lodge: *To that copse over there! To the river! Along this bridleway, across this pasture, this valley* ... It was a good hour or so before he called to me, 'Shouldn't we go back?' He didn't say, *To see Wolsey off*; but he looked hesitant, guilty. I shrugged: a big, devil-may-care shrug, not surrendering the decision but asking, Why? Henry hates trouble, needs someone to do it for him; and there was me, doing just that. *No going back*, was what this was all about. It was all over, for Wolsey; we both knew it. Well, it was time to let him know, too. Time for him, now, to be the tiresome episode before lunch. When we did return, early afternoon, he'd gone; and Henry never saw him again.

From then on, Wolsey's downfall was a job for the Attorney-General, who, a week later, charged him with exercising the Pope's authority over and above the king's, dismissing him as Lord Chancellor – instating a reluctant More as replacement – and designating his Esher house as his place of imprisonment. Everything else he owned – even his tomb under construction – transferred to Henry.

Back in London, the day after Wolsey was charged, Henry told me I should dress for the barge: 'I've something to show you.' Mum and Harry Norris came with us. The journey took us a couple of hours upriver. The sun in its autumnal throes blasted the willow trees and riverwater, but our breaths made momentary snowfalls. The barge finally glided to a halt along-side the white stone walls of Wolsey's York Place, and Henry didn't have to say it: *This is ours, now.*

We spent hours, that day, exploring its galleries, gardens, halls and suites of rooms, but my falling in love with it had happened almost instantly. As soon, in fact, as I'd realized that this was no royal palace with an apartment for the king and another for the queen, and room to be found somewhere for me. This could be our fresh-start palace: truly *ours*, Henry's and mine. Deserted, sweetly eerie, it did seem to welcome us, its doors opening with gasps, its floorboards singing to our tread. The staff had not long gone. Dust was barely detectable, nestled into the carvings on the chairs and frosting the Venetian glassware. Along the miles of shimmering, silken tapestries, my trailing fingertips found an occasional telltale breadcrumb: the hangings had recently been rubbed clean.

So, we could have moved in, then and there. But why settle

for it as we found it? We made plans, that very day, as we walked around. It all took a year or so to complete, hundreds of builders working around the clock under torchlit canvas. And then gone was a whole suburb of London. In its place was a wing for me and my parents, and a massive riverside sports complex of indoor and outdoor tennis courts and bowling alleys. Our fresh-start palace was honoured with a new name: Whitehall. We were desperate to move in. When we did, the plastered walls were still warm in places where the plasterers had been trying to speed up the drying with braziers.

With Wolsey a nobody, wheezing at his home in Esher, everything was once again possible. And indeed – fortuitous timing – a few days before that first trip of mine to Whitehall, we were visited in Greenwich by a man who had an idea on how to proceed with the divorce. He came along with Henry's secretary, Stephen Gardiner; and although I've never warmed to Stephen – surely no one ever has – I'm well aware how clever he is. This brilliant new find of Stephen's was a widower-turned-clergyman: Thomas Cranmer. Dog-like eyes, is what I recall of him from that first meeting. Oh, and his idea, of course: that the divorce was no matter for canon law, but divine law. There should be no need for the Pope to be involved. Canvass the universities – the theologians – around Europe, he suggested; that's where I'd start, he said, if I were you.

Henry was impressed. He sent for my father, not just because he knew he'd want to hear the latest, but also because he suspected that Dad would take to this studious but straight-talking man. He was right: Dad ended up, that very afternoon, offering Thomas a room in Durham House, which was at that time our family home in London. 'We need a new chaplain,' he decided, and so, suddenly, Thomas was one of us. And so he has stayed.

But if we had a talented newcomer, then so did the other camp: the new Spanish ambassador, Eustace Chapuys, assisted by his hand-picked, English-fluent staff. Forty-ish and – although I hate to say it – wearing well. Well-dressed, well-connected, and well-mannered to everyone but me. Calm in a crisis; and, let's face it, his posting was one long crisis. The very picture of charm. Which was why, unbelievably, Henry liked him. He'd readily admit it. 'He's a very charming man,' he'd laugh.

'Not *to me*,' I'd counter; but Henry would merely stroke my face and coo, 'Oh, *you* . . .'

Yes, *me*, whom that lizard Chapuys never once acknowledged, and whose name, I'm told, he never spoke. If he had to mention me to Henry, I was 'the lady'; to everyone else, I was 'the whore'. When I reported this to Henry, his response was a jovial, 'So? He's loyal. An excellent quality in an ambassador, wouldn't you say? Particularly an ambassador with as difficult a job as his.'

Difficult indeed; and made increasingly so by Catherine, who was missing no opportunity to tell Henry that he knew very well that she was a virgin when they married. Once he made the mistake of whirling round and snapping, 'Yes, all *right*. But this marriage should *still* never have *happened*.' It made no difference; she didn't stop, and duly made no exception for the St Andrew's Day Feast. This feast was one for her; she was to preside in her official capacity, at the king's side. I didn't care. No contest: the din of the Great Hall and the lisps of the Nevilles with unspoken death threats in their smiles; or the ample comfort of my own fireside with a select few good friends. When it came to it, though, I wasn't in the mood even for friends. I was due a period; the blood pooled in me, making me hot and heavy. Any sound chafed, even the clearing of a throat or a collapsing coal. And this was the last day of November, a day of clattering rain which I'd spent indoors with a view of scoured gardens and the sludge that was the Thames. Winter was closing down around me. Another winter.

Henry arrived at my door surprisingly early in the evening. Everyone bolted up, dizzied, but he'd already flapped a hand: *Sit*. In three strides he was with me, slinging himself down to the floor, leaning back against my knees. More heaviness. Franky turned from me to Billy, politely leaving us to it. I laid a hand on Henry's head, more from want of anywhere else to rest it than from affection. *Ask me how I am*, I willed him; *ask me how it's been for me, stuck here while you and that Spanish lump play husband and wife.*

But he said nothing, or not for a moment; and then, when he did speak, it was to complain, 'She excelled herself, this evening.'

I didn't, of course, need to ask who.

More of the same.

He dropped his head back into my lap and spoke to the ceiling. 'If I have to hear *any more* of it!'

Suddenly, my blood was everywhere in me, scalding my heart, flushing down my arms. 'Henry, if *I* hear any more of it!'

He froze.

'It's all I ever hear! Poor you and your difficult situation! What about *me*?'

He swivelled to face me, a hand on my knee.

I batted it away. 'How many more feasts am I going to spend

shut away like this? *Christ*, Henry, just how many years has it *been*?'

He was staring at me, sharp eyes narrowed, mouth hard.

'*Three*. Three years. I was a *girl* – remember?' And I laughed, or it was something like a laugh. 'Remember? And *now* what am I, Henry? Hmm?' I leaned forward, my face close to his. 'I'm *nearly thirty*.'

He recoiled, and sat tall: very clearly no contact.

Fine: I slumped back in my chair. 'I could have married someone else,' I said to no one in particular. Across the room, Francis's one eye – although carefully directed to his hands – shone, wide and amused. Next to him, my brother's eyes were closed and his fingertips held to his temples.

'I could have had children,' I said to Henry. 'I could be having *a proper life*.' Instead of endless fiddling under nightgowns.

My maid Annie's fingers were pressed to her lips, one hand over the other.

'You promised me,' I said to Henry. 'Remember that? You promised. You fucking *promised*.' *Oh, it's no use*: I stood; 'I'm going to bed.'

George, bless him, snapped into action: a couple of claps, and, 'Everybody back to mine, please.'

Rasping fabrics. I was in the thick of them, already halfway to my door, when Henry stepped in front of me, held up his hands: *Stop*. Those small eyes were still glass but then he winced. He made as if to say something but only breaths came, deep and sounding scorched. He shook his head – low, slow swings like a mule's – and his hands swooped on mine, squeezed them, moved them in circles. 'You're right,' he said. The two words I most love to hear. 'You're so right. From now on, everything I ever promised you, it's yours. I'll do it: whatever it is I have to do, I'll do it.'

Kill Catherine? was what flashed into my mind and switched a fingernail down my spine. He pulled on my hands, drew me to him, wrapped himself hard around me. The jewels on his doublet clawed my cheek, my ear. 'Next to you,' he said, 'nothing else matters.'

The very next day, I was on my way to Henry's apartment when a boy I didn't recognize – some groom – whizzed in my direction with, looped over one arm, some shirts that I *did* recognize: Henry's. As far as I knew – and surely I'd know – Mrs Harris, and only Mrs Harris, deals with Henry's clothes. So, what was this? Theft? Of *clothes*, now? The *king's*? I paused only for him to draw alongside me, then swiped a hand from its glove and slapped it onto the linen bounty. He stopped dead in his tracks, eyes down. My hand, on his arm, was the one with the strange little finger, the double nail: perfect for terrifying errant servants. I made the most of it, bestowing a couple of luxuriously slow pats. 'And where are *these* going?'

His eyes, wide, came up to mine. 'For mending.' A bat-squeak of protest.

I nodded in the direction he'd come. 'Mrs Harris has a trunk in there for mending.'

He didn't look; his eyes didn't move from mine. There was too much Adam's apple in his puny throat. '. . . not for Mrs Harris.'

'Oh? Oh, I *see*. There's someone else around here who does the king's mending.'

Nothing, from him. As if I'd made a reasonable remark.

Which unnerved me. '*Is* there?'

He nodded.

I folded my arms.

When it struck him that I was waiting to be told who, he whispered, 'The queen.'

It was my turn to swallow hard. 'Who sent you to her?'

'The king.'

I snatched the shirts, strode to Henry's rooms, and, there, banged through door after door until I found him. He was at his desk with dog-eyed Thomas Cranmer, who was instantly up, off balance, bowing and cringing all at once. 'Good morning, Thomas,' I said, glaring at Henry. 'Please don't leave.' I hurled the shirts onto the desk.

Henry frowned at them. 'These are my shirts.' The frown transferred to me.

'But guess where I found them – on their way to your ex-wife for mending.'

The frown deepened. 'And the problem is . . . ?'

Was this, I wondered, really happening? Did he really, honestly not know? Because if he didn't, I doubted I could make it clear. But I could have a damn good try: '*You're supposed to have left her!*'

That brought him to his feet quick enough. Once there, he didn't seem to know what to do. 'Anne,' he said, sharp, exasperated, 'she *likes* mending my shirts, it gives her something to do.' He gestured at them, 'They're just *shirts* . . .'

'They are *not* just shirts . . .'

Thomas was slipping towards the door. '*Don't* leave,' I called to him, '*don't* spare him showing himself up as the complete fucking idiot that he is.' To Henry, I said, 'Mending your shirts is a wifely duty. Do you understand? What *other* wifely duties does she still perform for you?'

His lips tightened in disgust and embarrassment. 'Anne, *really*.'

'These are *not* just shirts.' I jabbed at them. 'They're a betrayal: yours, of me.'

He glared at me. 'They're a couple of shirts that need a stitch or two. And she *is* still, technically, my wife.'

'And I am ... ?'

With that, I had him. It was a joy to see him squirm: 'You are ... you are ...' Clearly he regretted it, now, this clash. He was in too deep; damage was being done. Suddenly inspiration came: 'You are ... always right.'

He couldn't have done better and he knew it, looking to me, bright-eyed, for praise.

I bit down, begrudging, on a smile. 'Yes, I am.'

He braved his own. 'Yes, you are.'

And so we stood there, chancing smiles at each other. He made the first move, stepping from behind his desk. 'You know, Anne,' he came and took me gently, almost absently, by the shoulders, 'I really didn't think. I'm so sorry. It's just that they've always gone to her. And she ... well, she still *does* them.'

'Of course she does.'

He touched my cheek, and nodded, grave. 'Yes.'

'Things have changed, Henry. And now *everything* has to change.'

'Yes. Yes.' As he dipped to kiss me, I remembered Thomas; stopped the lips with my fingertips and glanced around for Thomas. His awkward smile made all three of us laugh.

That year ended not so badly after all. The new parliament, convened with regulation pomp in November, had immediately had lots to say, all of it negative, on the subject of England's clergy. We had converts, it seemed. There was one dissenting voice, but, belonging to old Bishop Fisher, Catherine's champion, it was irrelevant. The farce of a trial at Blackfriars had folded, and Wolsey had gone. And to top it all, in December Henry made my father Earl of Wiltshire and Ormonde, and, in January, Lord Privy Seal, which meant that George became Viscount Rochford – and was back in the Privy Chamber – and I was Lady Anne.

When he heard the news, Dad, deadly serious as usual, came

to warn George and me that he expected us 'to behave accordingly'. He was barely out of the room before George and I cracked up.

'You *bet* I'll behave accordingly,' said George, 'starting with a visit to my tailor.'

For me, no need: I already had a gown underway for the celebratory banquet. Thanks to Henry, I had quite a collection; but this particular dress was to be different. Purple, no less. I knew what people would say: *Purple? She's pushing her luck, isn't she?* I'd never made any bones about it: luck exists to be pushed. If I dressed like a queen, people treated me like one. That's what I'd been busy learning, that year.

So, it was in purple velvet that I swished to my place with Henry at the head of that laden table. Sitting there, I turned the old order topsy-turvy: down-table from me were the two women who'd fancied themselves the most important behind England's queen, Mrs Norfolk and Mrs Suffolk, my thunder-faced Auntie Liz and Henry's cold-blooded, wet-fish-wedded sister. Henry's sister was not as beautiful as I'd remembered: there were drizzles of white in that orange hair of hers, and her face was pinched. Not only hers, though. From the expressions around that table, I could see that although in their opinion I'd been fine for getting rid of Wolsey, they didn't want me for their queen.

The woman they did want for their queen – who, ridiculously, still was their queen – made the required appearances during the Christmas celebrations, while Henry and I were biding our time and planning our escape in early January to Whitehall. Whenever she postponed her purgings and leechings for long enough to appear in public on Chapuys' arm, she looked awful. Never having been much to look at, she now shone with pallor.

'Catherine's losing hope,' my cousin Nick said to me, one evening, when we were gossiping about the day's events.

'Hope of what?' I asked. What hope had she ever had?

'That he'll get fed up of you.'

I took a moment to take it in. '*Really?*' I couldn't help but laugh. 'You really think she thought that might happen?'

'Oh, yes,' Nick said, cracking a walnut. 'That woman has faith.'

'That woman is mad.' I opened my mouth so that he was obliged to feed me the nut. 'Or stupid. Or both.'

He reached into the bowl for another.

'Don't you think?' I asked him.

A flash of his eyes. 'I don't, actually.'

What?

'But I do think she's blind to what's good for her.'

'Well, that *is* "stupid", isn't it?'

He shrugged.

Other people, I noticed, seemed unsure how they felt about Wolsey now that he was no longer around. Even Henry. When he heard, mid-January, that Wolsey was ill – a bad chest – Henry decided to send a doctor. I found them at the gatehouse.

'Is this really necessary?' Wolsey was never ill; everyone knew that. Wolsey and his six oranges a day.

Neither of them seemed to hear; they were peering at the rain, sizing it up. Then Henry turned to me and asked in all seriousness, 'Have you anything we can send him, Anne?'

'Like what?' Some poison?

Amazingly, he didn't pick up on my tone; his eyes remained a cool, blank blue. 'I don't know, something to cheer him up.'

'Something expensive, then,' I said, sarcastically.

Again, no response; just the two pairs, now, of cool, blank eyes. Rain was darkening my gown. Arguing that Wolsey should have nothing from us would take longer than unpinning my brooch. '*Here*.'

Henry handed it to the doctor and gave him one of his lovely smiles, as if nothing untoward had happened. 'From Anne, tell him, with all best wishes for his recovery.'

He did rally, the old codger, although I doubt it was to do with my 'best wishes', which he'd have known full well were insincere. His miraculous recovery came when Henry pardoned him. 'Let's just pension him off,' Henry had decided, despite my much-voiced disapproval. 'He can't do any more harm.' As it happened, he was wrong about that.

In the meantime, our campaign was progressing. In the spring, we began hearing back from the universities on Thomas's treatise that Henry's marriage was invalid. Some agreed, some didn't. Oxford and Cambridge did; the Spanish universities of course didn't. The Italians didn't seem able to make up their minds, despite ever-increasing donations to their college funds. The next step was a letter to the Pope, drafted by Dad and George, asking him to make a decision soon: for the sake of peace in England, was how they put it. Billy spent a couple of weeks, that summer, taking it around and charming everyone into signing it: bishops, abbots, peers. Just about everyone: if it achieved nothing else, we now knew who was on our side and who wasn't.

Henry spent much of that time, and then the wait for the Pope's response, shut away in his library; I'd find him there in the afternoons. He seemed to believe that if he made his way through enough books, he'd find an answer. There had to be a way around the problem, was his view; a loophole. Diligence, he felt, would pay.

And then one afternoon he wasn't in his library. I turned a corner and he was down a hallway in the midst of a commotion. His mouth, mean; his eyes, popped. Rushing, he was getting nowhere, too busy rounding on people. His exact words, at a distance, were inaudible to me but the tone was unmistakable: furious, accusatory.

I'd almost reached him and still he hadn't seen me. 'Henry? Henry?'

My uncle was there; Stephen Gardiner, too; Billy, and cousin Nick; and the Spanish ambassador, Chapuys.

'Henry?'

Those small, pale eyes shunted, stopped at me. No greeting or acknowledgement; only, 'We have our answer.'

Bad news, then. A clamp of dread on my heart.

'It's an edict,' he barked, again as if it wasn't me he was addressing. 'You should be sent from court.' And in case I hadn't understood: 'I should leave you.'

I laughed; or, a blast of something – high, dizzying – came from me. Because surely it was a joke: some dried-up old bloke in Rome, who never had and never would set foot in England, ruling what the English king could and couldn't do. And me? Oh, but it wasn't about me, was it; I was nothing. The love I had for Henry, the plans I had for England: nothing. A thirty-year-old flesh-and-blood woman: nothing. 'Who does he *think* he *is*?'

Henry, taken off-guard, said, 'The *Pope*.'

'Yes, and what *is* that?'

No one moved, but Chapuys drew himself up to his full – and, frankly, unimpressive – height. The look he gave me was as black as any he might have summoned for the Devil. Then he turned on his heel and strode away. We all turned to watch this extraordinary sight: an ambassador taking Henry's leave without a word. He didn't return for four or five days. Went to friends, apparently, outside London. A pity he didn't stay there.

In those four or five days, rumour was running rife: Wolsey had had something to do with the Pope's outburst. I don't know where it started, but it found an ear with me. It made sense: Wolsey was regaining physical strength and favour, and probably had his eye on a return to power. Which wasn't going to happen while I was around, was it. Strange though it might seem after all he'd done to ruin her life, his best bet now was Catherine.

For Wolsey, things had to go back to how they were. I took it, this rumour, to my uncle: if I was chief Wolsey-hater, he was my loyal deputy. And if there are rumours, he hears them. That's if he hasn't started them.

Oh, yes, he told me, he'd heard; and – one better – was working on someone close to Wolsey.

'"Working on"?' And, 'Who *is* close to Wolsey?'

He grinned. 'Think about it.'

I did.

A clue: 'Lately.'

Still nothing.

'His *doctor*.'

Oh. Yes.

He laughed, his repellent nasal one-note. 'For a bright spark, Anne . . . Anyway, the point is, the doctor's seen rather a lot of our corpulent ex-cardinal, lately.'

Yes, 'And?'

'And give me time. Results take time.' From the doorway he added, 'Steadfast fellows, aren't they, these doctors.'

'Results' took a further day – that was when my uncle took me aside, with a tap to my arm. It was as we'd suspected, he whispered. Wolsey had been writing to the Pope. Urging Henry's excommunication unless he gave me up.

'You've proof of this?'

'I have, now.' That thin smile. 'I have the testimony of his now slightly wealthier doctor.'

As usual, Henry wouldn't discuss it with me. Worse, he actually walked out on me. The next morning, though, it was already done: a warrant for Wolsey's arrest. High treason, Henry informed me. And 'informed me' was what he did, as if it were purely a matter of business and thus his idea. Again, no discussion. I held my tongue – no way was I going to jeopardize this – and was careful to mirror his brisk nonchalance. Really, though, I was jubilant, blood fizzing in my ears. I barely heard him say, 'He's up at Cawood.'

Cawood: Wolsey's palace in Yorkshire. Henry was voicing concern over the practicalities of making an arrest at such a distance.

'Cawood?' Well, how about this for an idea? 'Give the warrant to Harry Percy.'

Henry looked at me; he looked and looked, presumably flummoxed that I'd dare mention my ex- to him. His expression revealed nothing; there *was* no expression.

I brazened it out, shrugged it off. 'He's your nearest earl.'

Northumberland. And if an earl can't be trusted to supervise an arrest . . .

'Oh. Yes.' Henry gave up, rubbed his eyes. Clearly, he hadn't slept well. 'Yes.'

What I was thinking as I sauntered from that room, was, *Harry, this comes from me to you with love: poetic justice.*

Wolsey cheated me, though, even in death: he never did face trial and execution. He dawdled his way down the country until, one November day, he died in his bed at Leicester. He'd certainly made the most of that final journey: people lined the roadsides, I heard, to cheer him. They seemed to have forgotten the decades of his absurd riches; they saw no despot being brought to answer for abuses of privilege. They saw a sick, troubled man, and their hearts went out to him.

Their fickle hearts.

Lucy Cornwallis

❀❀❀

AUTUMN 1535

Making gingerbread always warms me up and keeps me busy. Which is what I want, today, here in The Vyne's draughty old kitchens with nothing much to do except suffer the curiosity of Lord Sandys' own staff. This is exactly what I need: to stir long and hard over a flame, east to west for luck, turning spiced breadcrumbs and a pool of claret into a glossy dough. Breathing the sharp ginger, the rounder, polished smell of aniseed, and rough, woody cinnamon. Usually I'd ask Kit to do it for me – Kit, with his sugar-smashing muscles – and then I step in for the easier tasks of rolling it and pressing it into moulds.

Only one more night here, anyway, and then we leave Hampshire, finally leave the West altogether for good this year, and head back for Windsor. The official end of the summer. A summer already long gone, though. Every time the door gusts open – bang, bang, bang, all day; people careless with a loose latch – I glimpse rain seething among the cobbles. And so it's been for weeks. Not that we didn't know it was coming, because it rained on Ascension Day. All this rain has stopped us going blackberry-picking, and now it's too late: after Michaelmas, bad luck. We've spent the whole summer inching through mud from grand house to grand house, bedraggled. Not the impressive display that was intended.

You'd think that if The Vyne can have a whole new gallery for the king's four-day visit, it'd manage to have one functional latch on the kitchen door. But at least I can work, here. Unlike at Wolf Hall, where I had absolutely nothing to do for a whole week because, at some time prior to our arrival, the Seymours had hired the services of a confectioner. The kitchen was packed with boxes of confectionery and subtleties. I did get a look at some of it, despite a defensive head cook. I asked him who the confectioner was; he named a woman who, he said, lives in Bristol. I made quite a show of appreciation, but actually that wasn't difficult: she'd had her work cut out for her, using the old type of sugar plate for her subtleties. Presumably no one has shown her the alternative. For me, the good news came six or seven years ago via Bartolommeo Scappi, the cook who accompanied Cardinal Campeggio on his extended visit from Rome. I'm quite ashamed to think how what were distressing months for everyone else were so entertaining and enlightening for us in the confectionery.

Looking at those Bristol-made subtleties, though, I was faintly nostalgic for the old art, the casting of figures in liquid, boiling sugar. The rapid turning of the sealed moulds, over and over, to coat the insides, then the insertion of a hot needle to break the vacuum. Rather than what we do now, a mere pressing of paste into carvings or plaster impressions. But the old method has drawbacks: it's difficult to colour translucent sugar solution. Our white paste is ideal for working dyes into, or we can paint onto its dull, dried surface. Lately, I've been grinding rose-petals directly into sugar. More and more petals into the merest sprinkle of sugar. Pushing beyond pink into red, then deeper into red.

Roses are survivors: despite this weather, they're still around. I've been looking for the reddest, picking their petals and putting them into my pockets, taking them to my room to store in a jar. And then, when I know I'll have a little time alone, they're back in my pockets, handful by handful, and down into the kitchen.

The Bristol-woman's moulds were old but beautiful – a set of King Arthur and his knights, intricately detailed; probably an heirloom – and she'd made a good job of gilding the figures. She'd also gilded several marchepanes, an impressive gold bird soaring in the centre of each big disc, although the marchepane itself, underneath, looked a touch oily, yellow, to me; the almonds and sugar beaten a moment too long.

Here, at The Vyne, a couple of days ago, Richard stencilled a perfectly pale marchepane of ours with blue and silver fleur de lys. Cornflowers, two huge bundles of them beneath our table: that's what I saw, to my delight, when I arrived in the kitchen, that morning.

'Blue?' I asked.

'With silver,' he said, barely looking up from his work. 'Don't you think?'

'But where'd you get them, these cornflowers?' I crouched for a close look, because don't cornflowers deserve the closest of looks? Their colour so far into blue that the only way out is purple. I hadn't seen any for a while; we'd used our supply by the end of August, and hadn't been back anywhere to replenish. We'd been making do with red, yellow, green: rose-petals, crocus stamens, and spinach juice.

Richard was squeezing a sludge – petals he'd ground into rose-water – in a cloth, over a bowl. Judging from what had collected in the bowl, he'd been at it for a while. He'd had an early start. Another pleasant surprise, because another of the big difficulties this summer – as if I need more – has been Richard. Making heavy weather of everything. It seems to me that he's spent most of the summer sitting on one stool or another, his arms folded high and heels kicking. Forever asking about the next move and the next, and the next: who'll be there and what we'll be doing. And that's when he's been in the kitchen at all; although, at these smaller houses or lodges, he's usually just outside, pacing the yard. Occasionally, though, for three or four days at a time, he's been as he was with these cornflowers: serene, and energetic.

'Richard?' I prompted. 'Where'd they come from?'

'I placed an order.'

'You what?'

A quick grin. 'I *asked* someone, Lucy. Asked someone to think of me, if he saw any. To bring me some, if he could. They're from Norris-land.'

'Oh.' Via the Silvester-person, presumably. 'Sir Henry's here?'

'Yep. To celebrate.'

Celebrate? Panic: what had I forgotten?

'Love is in the air.' He was looking pleased with himself: a small smile, and briskness with the blue-leaky bag. 'Wedding bells, if rumours are to be believed, and – trust me – they are.'

He'd lost me. 'Who?'

A playful tut. 'Sir *Henry*.'

'*Oh*. Oh.' Nice. Nice Sir Henry: happiness at last for the widower. Good.

'And Meg Shelston.'

'Meg Shelston?'

No response; a tilting of the blue-spattered bowl into candle-light.

'But . . .'

He paused, bowl precarious, and looked at me.

'Wasn't she . . . Didn't you say . . .'

He didn't even blink.

'Meg Shelston,' I said, exasperated, '*and the king.*'

'*Oh*.' He pushed the bowl aside. 'Oh, *that*. That was nothing.

Ages ago.' A conspiratorial grin, although I don't know whom he regarded as his co-conspirator. 'In fact, the king's trying to take credit for bringing them together.' He seemed to consider this. 'Best friend and ex-mistress? He could have a point.'

For some reason, I asked, 'What's she like?'

'Meg? Blonde and bubbly. And kind.' I was waiting for a quip when he repeated, 'Yes, kind,' in all seriousness.

Whenever my grandfather said I had cornflower-blue eyes, my sister Ellie would add, 'And straw-coloured hair.' Both my sisters liked to joke that they were jealous of my being blonde. Is there much grey, now, in their chestnut-brown hair? If there wasn't, before this summer, there probably is, now; because what kind of harvest have they had? I'm so lucky that this endless rain means nothing more to me than some chilly journeys and a muddy hem. Will there still be harvest-home suppers in the village, this autumn? For commiseration, perhaps, rather than celebration. Hard to imagine the usual noisy singing as those last carts trundle back from the fields; the garlanding of each farmer's last sheaf.

It's nearly Hallowtide, Allantide, which has always seemed the very end of the year, to me. The day we spend with the dead; thinking of the dead, hard, all day long and into the evening. It was my favourite festival when I was a child: the one day of the year I was allowed to spend with my mother. Me and me alone, with her. And what a day: the church bells for so long after evensong, singing to the dead across the churchyard and into the blue-black sky. The church humming with candlelight. One year – a particularly good harvest, probably – two ladies from somewhere else in Sussex were booked to come and play their harps. When I'm gone, there'll be no one to remember my mother; no one to pray for her. She was her parents' only child, and I'm hers. I'm not even convinced that my sisters and my brother remember me now, when I'm still alive.

Richard tells me there'll be no candles, this Hallowtide. 'Part of the changes,' was how he put it.

'Candles?' I was aghast. 'What's wrong, now, with *candles*?'

'You really want to know?' We were in my room, a couple of evenings ago, sitting in front of the fire.

'I do, actually; yes.' I felt Hettie's gaze on us; back and forth between us.

'Well, apparently, there's nothing we can do for the dead. They're either good enough to get to Heaven, or they're not. No amount of praying for them can give them a leg-up.'

'And where's Purgatory, in all this?'

Richard laughed, or sort of. 'Where indeed? Haven't you heard? There *is* no Purgatory.'

Ridiculous: 'It was there for all those years, and now it's not?'

He shrugged. 'Or never was.'

I sat back. 'Well, I imagine my parish priest will be rather surprised to hear that.'

'I imagine your parish priest has had quite a few surprises, lately.' Then he said, 'You know the moral of this tale, don't you. Stop thinking of the dead and start thinking of the state of your own soul.'

'Oh, don't worry about that,' I said, eventually. 'There was no one to pray for me, anyway.'

'Nor me.'

Nor Hettie, we were probably both thinking.

Mark said to me, yesterday, 'You're down in the dumps.'

'It shows?'

'It does.' A steady look from beneath that unruly black hair. Concerned.

Back to my criss-crossing, slicing bite-sized diamonds from a big square of marchepane between two layers of hard blue sugar. 'I was being sarcastic, Mark. I imagine it *does* show.' I didn't feel like apologizing. 'Sometimes I just *am*. Down in the dumps.' If that's what he wants to call it.

'*Are* you?'

'Well, *yes*.'

He picked up one of my diamonds, turned it around: white gold inside baby blue.

'Are your hands clean?' The king is so particular about cleanliness. His tasters don't just taste, they also look. I didn't want them seeing fingerprints.

He returned the kissing comfit to the others. Perfect fingers, I noticed. 'And, anyway,' I said, 'aren't *you*?'

Those so-blue, black-fringed eyes. 'Aren't I . . . ?'

'Down in the dumps, sometimes.'

This seemed to amuse him: he tried to hold back a smile, failed. 'Not lately.' He looked away. 'Lucy? What is it about today that's so bad?'

If it's a bad day, reverse your apron: that's what the Nevilles' cooks used to say. 'Nothing. Today's no different from any other day. To be honest with you, perhaps that's it. Summer progress gets me down. Especially when it's in the pouring rain. I'm *tired*.' But how could I be tired, having done so little? *Bone*-tired, then. I want to go home, basically. And I don't know where home is. Or the problem is that I *do*, I *do* know, and it's nowhere. 'I'm *old*.'

That surprised me: my thinking it, let alone my saying it and to him.

But he wasn't having any of it: 'What are you, thirty or something?'

'-six, actually.'

'Oh! You're the same age as the queen.' As if this were some kind of triumph. Thirty-six had meant nothing, to him. Him, male, and young. Good. I probably could have said one hundred and six. Or sixteen. 'And no one'd think of her as "old",' he said, 'would they.'

Well, *I* would. That's one comfort, though: there's no way I look like her, a dark woman who's lost her lustre.

'She's a woman at the height of her powers,' he said.

Not her childbearing ones, though.

I asked him his age. Twenty-seven, was the answer. Just a year or two older than Richard.

'But I've never felt young,' he said. 'Never *been* young, really. I don't know that it's possible to be young – properly young; young at heart – when you grow up at court.'

And I wondered how he'd done it: lived his life at court and remained so true to himself. Grown up in the cut and thrust of court, among the preening men of the Privy Chamber, to be someone who slips by with a shine of black hair and a shadowy glance that is, in fact, on the contrary, should it ever be met, sky-blue. I remembered asking him about George Boleyn. 'Bestial' was the word Richard had used, once, for the Boleyn brother, and followed it with, Lock up your daughters, sons, livestock! Mark had decided on 'lively'. 'And I suspect,' he said, 'that he finds me a bit ... well, contemplative, I suppose.'

That's what I was thinking – him, contemplative – when he said, with some passion, 'Lucy, listen: I hate it that you're down.'

I was touched by that, and suddenly it was me who couldn't help smiling. 'Well, I'll have to make sure that I'm not,' I said, 'won't I.'

When he'd gone, I worked on my rose, sitting quietly in a corner of the kitchen as if doing nothing much at all. Mixing a little of my rose-sugar with gum and shaping a petal. Just one petal. It took me three attempts before the tip was delicate enough to turn translucent near a candle. And holding that petal up to the flame, I realized something: it's Mark's. *This rose is for Mark*.

Did it begin, my making this rose for him, when he took a rose-petal from me on one of his first visits? Or did it begin back at the very beginning, with his coming into the confectionery for the very first time?

His coming wide-eyed into my kitchen has re-opened my own eyes. And soon, he'll see this rose of mine. A sugar rose made of almost no sugar at all. A sugar rose made mostly of rose. Soon, it'll rest in the palm of his hand.

November nastiness, outside. Half-inside, too: gusts down the chimney. And me, cosy in bed but sleepless. It's been a strange day. This morning, a secret I was keeping for someone turned out to be no secret at all. But this afternoon, another seemed to come my way. And this one is mine.

It was Richard who relieved me of the burden of the first. At the time, he was sitting dwarfed by sugar-cast walnuts, a mound of cinnamon-coloured sugar half-shells. 'Well,' he sighed, and stated the obvious: 'these all need sticking together.'

'Each with one of those inside.' I indicated a sheaf of papers. He took the top one, peered at the inky scratches.

Poems, I told him. Waiting to be folded up, I hinted.

'For inside our walnut shells? Poems?' He looked at me, wide-eyed. 'Whose idea was that?'

'Mine.'

'Yours?'

'Yes? And?' *What d'you think?*

He looked at the poem in his hand, as if the answer were written there. 'Well, yes,' he said, eventually. 'It's good. It's a good idea.' Then came something of a laugh: 'What's wrong with comfits, all of a sudden?'

'Nothing's wrong with comfits.' A sugar-coated seed inside each of our sugar-cast shells: the usual filling. 'I just fancied a change. But you think it's a stupid idea.'

'No,' he insisted; although he still seemed, to me, to be somewhat at a loss. 'No. I think it's a *good* idea. I suppose it's just, well, why didn't you tell me?'

I didn't know how to answer that. 'I *am* telling you.' Anyway, 'You probably weren't here. And it was nothing; it was just an idea I had.' Yes, and, 'It's not as if I've never had an idea before, is it.'

His hands raised: *whoa.*

He had me worried, though. 'They do like poetry, don't they?'

'Oh, they do, they do. Don't get me wrong: it's definitely a good idea.' He looked down at the poems and up, again. 'You wrote these?'

My turn to laugh, and properly. 'Well, of course not.'

He was unamused. 'Well, *I* don't know, *do* I. I come into the kitchen and there's a pile of poems. I mean, you made *these*, didn't you?' The shells.

Oh, did I make those! Two whole days of work. Two days when Richard decided it was imperative that he begin work on our subtlety of Greenwich Palace. 'Yes, but I *do make* sugar walnuts; I *don't* write poems.' Or write at all. As he well knows.

'Well, who did?'

'Don't know. I asked our dear ol' Master of Revels if he could get me some. Away he went, and came back with those.'

Richard was sifting. 'Well, he obviously whipped up some enthusiasm. There are *loads*.'

'Hence . . .' I nodded towards the shells; the two days' worth of shells.

'D'you think the king wrote some of them?'

'The king?'

'He does take himself quite seriously as a poet.'

'Does he?'

'*Oh* yes.'

I knew about the music, Mark told me that the king writes songs: not bad, was his verdict; not bad at all, really.

'Mind you,' Richard added, '*she* doesn't.'

She.

'Haven't you heard?' he asks.

Oh, no, here we go. I gave him a look, *the* look: how, exactly, would I have heard, and why would I want to?

But of course he ignored me. 'Oh, there was trouble, the other day; big trouble.' Said, of course, with relish. 'She was reading some of his poetry aloud. I don't know,' he raised our sheaf of poems, 'maybe some of these.'

My heart faltered: already, this wasn't sounding good, and I didn't want to be even faintly implicated.

'Reading his poems in a funny voice. Probably with her hand on her heart: that kind of thing. You can imagine.'

Yes, unfortunately.

'And they were all laughing: Billy Brereton, Franky Weston, all of them, loving it. But *he* was there, too: the king! She was actually doing all this –' he slowed down, for emphasis, '– in front of him. And of course he took it badly. I mean, come on, he's the very last person to take a joke against himself, isn't he: everyone knows that. So it was Glad-you-think-it's-funny, and then he stormed off.' Richard sat back, peculiarly satisfied. 'Not that it seemed to bother her in the least. In fact, it just made her worse, Silvester said. She started on his dancing, if you please.

Criticizing his dancing. Even though everyone was quite embarrassed by now.'

I said, in spite of myself, 'She can't be well.'

'Oh, on the contrary, she's on form. Gale in her tail. She used to argue with him, all the time, in front of everyone, and he absolutely hated that, and now she's taken it further, to ridiculing him. Which is probably what she always wanted to do, and now she's big enough and bold enough to do it.'

'No,' I said. 'That's not the behaviour of a happy woman.' This embarrassing, foolhardy behaviour.

'Ah, yes,' Richard raised his eyebrows, 'but when has she ever been happy?'

Perhaps there had always been a kind of madness in her, for her to have done what she did: destroy the queen. And here it is, again, but more so; so much so that it's turned against her. She's destroying another queen: but, this time, it's herself.

'Silvester says she really has it in for the king, at the moment; she's really pushing her luck. The other week, she told Sir Henry, in front of everyone, how much better dressed he is than the king. *Not* a good idea. The king wasn't there, but I'm not sure that's not worse, because it'll get back to him; and you know how that'll look, it having been said behind his back. She was all over Sir Henry: how he's so elegant. How he's so unlike the king, she said; who, she said, looks like he's *stuffed*.' Richard barked a laugh. 'Which is true, isn't it; he *is* getting that way, isn't he.'

'Richard . . .'

'And yesterday, when the king was telling some anecdote, at dinner, she did an enormous yawn – right before his punchline; impeccable timing – and announced she was off to bed! Wouldn't you love to be able to do that?'

I was unconvinced. 'Yes, but *is* she able to do that?'

He gave me a level look. 'Depends, doesn't it. On how lucky she is.' Then he said, 'Lucy?'

'What?'

'We're coming up to Christmas –'

'We're seven weeks away –'

'And you're making *ginger*bread? *Again*?'

'And lemon succade. I made some lemon succade, earlier.' There were lemons, they needed doing: peeling, and the peel boiling with sugar. It's not all sugar castles, not all the time, however close we are to Christmas: other jobs always need doing. And I'm glad: sweetened lemons, a concoction both so sweet and so sharp; the sharpness untouched, holding the sweetness intact.

Richard said, 'We have twelve days of feasts, coming up. Twelve days of subtleties. Why all the gingerbread?'

What could I say? 'It's warming.'

'Yeah, and it helps with queasiness,' he said. 'The queen's pregnant.'

'*Richard.*'

'How long did you think you could go without telling me?'

'I *haven't* told you.'

He laughed.

'It's a secret,' I protested. 'Isn't it?'

'No,' he said, as if explaining to a small child, 'it isn't.'

'It's been announced?'

'No, it hasn't.'

I knew because Dr Butts had been to see me. *Mrs Cornwallis? I'm Dr Butts, the queen's physician. I was wondering: might I have a discreet word?* He'd asked me if I knew of any spices to help with nausea. Ginger, I told him. He seemed happy to take my word for it. *That's excellent. Let's just say, then, that the queen would greatly appreciate more ginger in her diet for the next couple of months.* And then he went away, just as suddenly as he'd arrived, but with a wink and a forefinger to his lips.

'How do people know?' I asked Richard.

'Everyone knows everything, around here, don't they? Up there, they do; back there. Small world, back there. If the queen's laid up, a lot of people have to loll around with her. If the queen's sick, someone's going to have to clear up after her. And then there's the gingerbread . . .' I must have squirmed, because he chivied, 'Oh, come on! Your gingerbread wasn't the giveaway. She's hardly one for secrecy, is she; hardly one for keeping her mouth shut. Certainly not where this is concerned. There's a lot of patting of her stomach. She's very pleased with herself. After all, this has been a while coming.'

'Telling people so early, though,' I said. 'Anything could happen.' Or *not* happen.

He considered this. 'Yes, but something she's never lacked is confidence.'

Thirty-six, she is. My age. Come to think of it, my own step-mother was around that age – this age – when she had the boys. It's possible. It's perfectly possible. When I was young – a child – I assumed I'd have children. Mine were to be two or three girls – chatterboxes – and a son; that's how I saw it, saw them. Girls, and baby brother. The girls, creamy-skinned and sloe-eyed, nobody's fools; the boy, one of those fiercely grave little blonds, standing his ground. It's obvious to me, these days, that I was seeing a reflection of my own family, my own upbringing; a reflection of my dark-eyed chatterbox sisters and blond baby brothers. How unoriginal of me. Or perhaps I was simply very happy with what I had. Towards the end of my childhood, I remember, the daydream changed: the buttoned-down face of my sleeping newborn, the funny bluish bridge of his or her nose, and the downy temples.

One summer's evening, last year, Richard and I were sitting on a step outside somewhere – the back of some big house, I don't remember which; someone's big house – while Joseph was elsewhere with Kit, Stephen and Hettie, unpacking our provisions. The air had a jellied look to it. Richard said, 'Whatever happened to you?'

I gathered my gaze from the landscape. He was staring at me, but somehow seemed not to see me. 'What?'

This brought him to his senses. Hugging his knees, he looked away.

'No, really: what?'

He didn't speak again for a moment; he was obviously trying to find the words. 'Well … why aren't you … married?'

'Richard!' Wasn't it personal or impertinent or something, to ask? He didn't back down, though, or even apologize, and I ended up answering him: '*I* don't know. It just never happened.'

'Not even … a little?' He wasn't smirking, but frowning, serious.

'Richard …' I sounded a warning; but, again, gave in: 'Not in the least.' Then I tried to explain, as best I could: 'I've always been … working.'

Nothing from him, before a laugh of disbelief. 'You,' he said, and looped a strand of my hair behind my ear. 'How can you *not* be married?'

'Whereas you,' I said, '*you'll* marry, won't you.'

'Oh, Lux,' he said, his smile dreamy, 'you're a gem.'

'Why?' I grinned. 'Because I have faith?'

When Mark turned up, this afternoon, he was very quiet, and it was probably for something to say that I asked him, 'Is it true that everyone knows about the queen?' Even as I spoke, I couldn't quite believe I was saying it. What on earth would I say if the response was, *Knows what?*

But Richard is a reliable source, and, sure enough, Mark didn't miss a beat: 'That she's expecting?'

My hands, palms upwards: *Everyone knows, obviously.*

There was no response, from him; no glimmer. Which was unusual. None of those serious little smiles.

I was cornered into saying, 'Well, what d'you think of that, then?'

He nodded. 'It's good.' Emphatically. Seriously. 'It's good, for her, isn't it.'

There was a small silence in which neither of us said it: *Crucial*. To lighten the mood, I found myself asking him if he ever thinks about the children he'll have. Will they be very musical, I wondered aloud for him.

He made a polite attempt at a smile, buried in a downwards gaze. 'I won't be having any children.'

'You won't? Why won't you?'

His unconvincing smile seemed stuck. He couldn't or didn't want to answer. Eventually he said, 'Oh, I don't know. I mean: who'd have me?' and although he was smiling, he wasn't joking: that was obvious.

'Mark, who *wouldn't*?' I couldn't have him thinking like that; as his friend, I couldn't have him thinking like that. Lovely-looking Mark, the kindest man I've ever met, gloriously talented. Then, of course, I felt embarrassed – me, gushing – so I added, 'All those nice young girls!'

His smile vanished into a cross-sounding sigh. 'You're right.' Although it sounded like agreement or an apology, it didn't look like either: his unblinking gaze was defiant. 'That's how it is, here, isn't it. That's exactly how it is, for all the men, here: a game; nice young girls, one after the other. But, you know, Lucy, not for me: I don't want "those nice young girls". It's just not like that, for me. Not any more; I'm not like that, not now.'

I was looking back into those wide, deep blue eyes. Just looking, not thinking. My heart went out to him: really, it did; a flare against my ribs. 'Well,' I dared, 'that's good, isn't it?'

'Is it?' His gaze still held me, but now there was something of a plea in it.

'Well, yes,' I said. To my surprise, I was smiling in the face of his anguish; nearly laughing. Not at him, of course. Just at everything. 'Yes,' I said, 'It *is*.'

As I'm opening the door, Richard has the cheek to say, 'At last.'

Oh yes? and how long does he take over *his* meals? Gossiping. Gossiping with any of several hundred like-minded gossips in the Great Hall. He's untying his apron, his candle-thrown shadow restless on the wall behind him. And beside him – I see him, now, rising from one of our stools – is Mark.

Mark: a pinch to my heart; a fierce, cheeky pinch.

Richard asks, 'What was it?' The meal, he means.

'Heron.'

And he's going, his spoon in hand.

Mark and I stand stock-still – our shadows bouncing – to allow the flame to settle. *Mark*: I can never quite believe that he's here, even though he stops by every day. It's a wonder that I believe in him at all: a slender, soft-skinned young man who, one day, came looking for me. For me, a woman in an apron, twenty-five years in kitchens; a woman with crystallized eyelashes and caramelized fingertips.

Richard's soles are chipping away up the staircase; Mark's eyes switch in that direction and return widened.

'Leftovers,' I explain, gesturing for Mark to sit back down. Richard has two big meals every day but still finds room for the food – better food – that's sent up for me. 'The kitchen's never got to grips with me. Eating alone in my room.' They seem to send me the usual dinner table serving tray for four. Four men. 'Hettie eats like a bird. Anything Richard leaves, Kit and Stephen can have when they're back from Hall.'

Talking of Stephen: a broom, propped against a workbench. Mark looks perplexed when I replace it so emphatically in its corner. So, I have to explain: 'It's *unlucky*.'

'Is it?'

'*Yes*.' Sometimes I worry for him.

'What is?'

I can't help but laugh. 'To sweep after dark. Don't you men know anything?'

'Evidently not.'

'Problem is,' I concede, 'it's dark, now, halfway through the afternoon. Which Stephen forgets.' I start to pull up a stool; lose my nerve and *half*-pull up a stool, my eyes averted from his. This king's favourite, who came looking for me, and found me, but then kept coming back. This beauty in misfit clothing, this changeling, princeling. He's making a queen of me: I've never walked so tall. Nor stepped so lightly since girlhood; I could swear to it; I catch my own footfalls and marvel at the verve and certainty in them. I'm more of a girl, these days – light-hearted, surefooted – than when I actually was a girl. I wonder if he sees that in me; sees her in me. I do wonder what he does see in me.

You're so sane, Lucy.

Oh, if you knew, Mark. If you only knew how things have changed.

Beyond the window, rain fizzes. Downstairs, the usual shuf-flings and thuds: work being done. I'm taking a little time to digest my meal, that's what I'm doing, sitting here with Mark. I can make up for lost time when the boys come back.

Mark asks, 'If they spoil you like that – sending you all that food – do they treat you to sweet things, too?'

'Tart and fruit?' I shake my head. 'For the clerks, not the cooks. Not even for Mr Bricket and Monsieur Doux, I don't think.'

'Monsieur *who*?'

'Monsieur *Doux*.' If only there was just this, all day, every day: having Mark with me, chatting and laughing. All those people who think happiness is something, when in fact it's just this. 'Monsieur Doux's the king's French cook. Mr Bricket is the king's – well, *English* cook.'

'And what does this Monsieur *Doux do*?'

'Stands around looking French, as far as I can see,' now that I think about it.

'Well, I suppose not everyone can do it.'

My lips to one of his dark, scant eyebrows: that's what I'd like. That's what I'd like to do. *Talk, Lucy: distract yourself.* 'It's Mr Bricket I deal with. Sometimes, just sometimes, I'm called to a meeting to plan the king's menu: Mr Bricket, and one of the king's doctors, and whoever's being Server – Lord Thomas Grey or someone – and *me*.' A quick grin, as a flourish.

'And d'you know what he had today?'

'Nope,' and couldn't care less. Instead, I'm captivated by the hollow behind and below each of his ears: twin indentations tucked away high up on his throat. I'd have to angle my kisses to reach them: to come in sideways, dip in and take him by surprise. I'm surprised, too, though: by desire, something I assumed I'd never feel. It's been a long time coming but now here it is, unannounced. A blessing: I'm blessed. The ease of it, slipped beneath my skin. As easy as breathing. The glorious, intoxicating ease of it.

'Swan, this morning,' he's saying, 'and just now, seal.' He looks pleased with himself, as well he might: Mark of the Privy Chamber, privy to the king's dining. I'm absurdly proud of him for being there. For being so liked that he's there.

What if he hadn't ever come looking for me? Or if I hadn't been there but Richard had; and he'd done as requested, deigned to show him a subtlety or two, *This is how it's done, this is what we do*, before brushing him off, sending him packing. There was the barest breathing-space between what nearly never happened and what did; and we were through it before we realized that it was there. Stepping over it without a backwards glance. And now we're on dry land. The home straight. I want to say to Mark, Do you realize? I want to celebrate. I want us to celebrate.

He's saying, 'Sometimes I go and watch the king's salad gardener at work. Flemish man. Nice man. It's a shame, in a way, that it's so unrecognizable when it ends up on those platters: carrots and cucumbers carved into deer or whatever. Radish roots and turnips cut into –' he shrugs.

'Stars,' would be my guess. 'Knots. Roses.'

'And then half a flower-garden tipped on top.'

'Cowslips,' I'm remembering from other kitchens, in my past; the work of other cooks.

'Violets.'

'Capers, olives.'

'You know –' and I'm telling him just for the sake of it, 'I was in the bakehouse this morning when the men came for the dogs' loaves.'

'Dogs' loaves?'

'One hundred and two loaves every day for those greyhounds.'

He laughs, incredulous. 'Don't tell me it's manchet.'

'You'd think so, wouldn't you. King's horses shod in gold, you'd think, and dogs dining on white bread while we're all picking bits of barley out of our teeth.'

Now, suddenly, there seems nothing more to say. Not that I care. I fold hands in my lap. There *is* something, though: 'How are the motets?' The book of motets that he's writing out for Anne Boleyn.

'Ah, the motets.' He looks faintly embarrassed; but, then, he always does. Looks pleased, too, though, to be asked. 'Coming along, coming along.'

Some of her favourites, he's told me, and some of his own composition. I asked him, is it like writing words? Not dissimilar, was his answer. Richard overheard us talking about this book, the other week; and afterwards, when Mark had gone, he said, 'What's he doing, writing that book for the queen.'

It wasn't a question, but I answered anyway. Said it'd make a nice gesture.

He was gilding a marchepane and didn't even look up when he said, 'Would you write a book of confectionery recipes for the king?'

'Really, Richard, it's hardly the same. The king doesn't cook. *She does* play music.' And I pointed out that people are always giving him gifts; our laden shelves are testament to that.

His irritation soared to match mine. 'Not *fruit*, and not from *unknown* people. I'm talking about a gift you – *you* – have laboured over. Something personal.'

I said that courtiers and ladies do it all the time: get things made, or give something of their own. 'Remember that little dog? For Anne Boleyn? He came from someone. Someone's pet dog: that's personal.'

He paused, brush mid-air. 'But that's them.'

I didn't know what he meant.

'Courtiers. And Mark's not really one of them.'

I said, 'He's a favourite of the queen's.' I'd said it: *the queen*. 'Well, he *thinks* he is.'

Typical Richard. Not worthy of a response.

But now I find myself checking with Mark, 'Do you think she'll appreciate your giving her these? Your motets.'

A sudden, startling shine to his eyes. 'Oh yes. She's a really good musician.'

He's misunderstood me; but I'll not pursue it. No doubt he's right. He's so cautious, courteous, generous; who could possibly be offended – or be anything but delighted – by any gesture of his?

He adds, 'She could do with a little cheering up.'

Richard says that they're not talking, the king and Anne Boleyn, whereas surely they should be really happy now that she's pregnant again. I think I might understand, though. So much – everything – depends on this pregnancy, and isn't it possible that they could hate each other for that?

Mark continues, 'And music's such a solace. It was good to hear the king singing again with Sir Peter Carew, last night. It'd been a while.'

'Mark.' It's only now, as he looks expectantly at me, that I realize: I've begun the conversation that I've been wanting for so long to have with him. And now what? Instinct tells me to be direct. Be gentle, but direct. Just do it; just say it. 'Mark, do you ever think – seriously – of leaving here?'

The surprise is that he looks unsurprised. As if he's been waiting for me to ask. 'Well, you know –' a smile that's not quite a smile, more of a wince, 'lately, I have.'

I nod as if I expected this, but actually I'm thrown by his frankness. And relieved. And exhilarated. It's all I can do to hold back a big smile.

He's obviously reluctant to say more. So, it's down to me, again. I'll start with what I've been wanting to ask: 'Would it be so bad, to be teaching somewhere?'

He's puzzled.

'You once said that it would be the most you could hope for, if you left here.' A nervous laugh. 'You didn't make it sound good.'

'Did I say that?' He's amused. 'Did I really? I tell you, Lucy, sometimes I long for it: a simple life, away from here.'

'A simple, happy life,' I venture.

He nods, dreamily. 'Maybe.' Now, though, he frowns: 'But you, surely not; you wouldn't want to leave all this.'

All what? My laugh isn't nervous at all, this time. And I dare to say it: 'I would.'

'You would?' He brightens.

'*Yes.*'

'You'd leave Richard?'

'Richard? Yes.' Why not? 'Richard's had years of me, he's had all he needs of me.' This strikes me as the truth.

Mark is studying me, now; chin propped on one hand. 'And would you go home? To the place by the sea?'

Home's a long walk from the sea. And it's an odd question. 'That depends, doesn't it.' There isn't only me to consider.

'Yes, of course.' His gaze slips away; pondering.

I'll say it: 'I'm not too old, Mark, to start a family.'

The eyes are back, immediately, to mine. And steady. 'No. No, of course not.'

Oh, my blue-eyed boy. How beautiful any child of yours will be.

Our private joke: 'I'm the same age as the queen.'

He reflects my smile. 'Yes. Yes, you are, aren't you.'

It's me, again, who breaks the pause: 'So, anyway, would it? Would it be so bad, for you? A life away from here.' A normal life. A family life.

He lets go of what must have been a held breath. 'There's a printed book of music, now – Wynkyn de Worde's. There'll be others. If I teach in a household with a library, I can probably keep up. Keep learning.' He smiles, 'Might learn more, because it's still all just Fairfax and Cornish, here: church music. On the other hand . . .' My heart tiptoes. '. . . there's nowhere like the English court for a musician. Which is why we're all here. I mean, the Flems and Italians and Frenchmen, too.' A twinkle in his eyes: 'You know what they say: in France – at court – the choir-master can't read music even when he's sober.'

I muster an appreciative smile.

'Best musicians, best composers, best teachers: all here. And you should see the king's collection of instruments.' Suddenly he's up, at the window, facing the darkness, arms folded. 'But, you know, Lucy, Mr Van Wilder is our Mr Bricket, and one day I'll be the new Mr Van Wilder.' Before I've quite understood, he gives me a rueful smile. 'I know what you're thinking.'

You do?

'You're thinking that'd be good.'

Something like a laugh escapes me; I don't have to worry what he makes of it, because he doesn't seem to hear. He's back on the stool; and his eyes, focused on mine, are huge.

'Mr Van Wilder does everything. Has to. Appoints and organizes all the musicians. Commissions, rehearses all the music. He's been chapel organist for years because we haven't had one since the Italian. And I don't want to do all that. I don't want to do *any* of that. I want to sing and play the lute.'

'And write motets.'

'And write motets.' He smiles, now. Lays his hands on the bench, palms down, fingers splayed; looks at them. 'There's a new organ being built in the workshop at Bridewell; Mr Lewes is building it.' He looks back up at me, his smile fainter. 'That's the good news. The bad news is that I might well be sitting at it for the next forty years.'

I wince: Mark, hunched at a keyboard in the perpetual dusk of chapel. Grey-haired, short-sighted. Put-upon and pedantic. Gone: this velvet-eyed boy. 'Mark, listen to me.' And – *oh, Sweetheart* – he actually cocks his head. I want to cup that open, inclined face in my hands. 'You're lucky. You know why?'

He shuts his eyes. 'Lots of reasons.' But, oddly, he sounds miserable.

Press onwards, Lucy. 'You're lucky because you know what you want. That's what makes you different.'

His eyes are open now, fixed on mine, but they might as well be closed. 'This place is full of people who know what they want,' he says. 'That's why they're here.'

'No –' *listen* – 'they just . . . *want*.' Yes, that's it. 'They *want*. Everything.'

He breathes something that's between a sigh and a laugh; hot, and broken. 'And I want so much more than that. *Christ*, Lucy, what's going to happen to me and how am I going to bear it?' He's on his feet. 'I'm sorry,' he's saying, stepping backwards into shadow, 'you're lovely and understanding but I shouldn't have come here, not when I'm feeling like this; it isn't fair on you. I'm poor company, this evening. I'm hopeless. I'm sorry.'

And before I've even drawn breath, he's gone.

Anne Boleyn

❀❀❀

With Wolsey gone, we faced no further unfavourable papal responses, because Henry banned them. Simple. But Thomas More had something to say about that. Quite a lot, in fact. So much so that Henry nearly sacked him, taking the opportunity to point out that it hadn't gone unnoticed that More's signature had been missing from our papal petition. Billy's charm hadn't been enough. More's line was that he'd never hidden his view on the matter. The unspoken coda was, *And would you really want me to?* Which definitely wasn't what Henry wanted, and More knew it. What Henry wanted was More on his side: his beloved More, along with everyone's respect.

More had his qualities, but he was no Wolsey. With Wolsey gone, there was a gap for a new Wolsey, a mover and shaker. And suddenly there he was, in 1530, in the Privy Council; or *above* it, rising clean up above everyone else. Not clean, I take that back. His attitude being, Whatever it takes. Thomas Cromwell; Tom: once Wolsey's own administrator, he'd learned well under his old boss. Learned well everywhere, doing a bit of everything: mercenary, merchant, moneylender, MP.

Pig-faced Cromwell and hang-dog Cranmer: what a pair. Not that they ever *were* a pair: Thomas, an ideas man; Tom liking to get the bit between his teeth. Not a pair, exactly, then, but a team. What a team.

I did like Tom, yes; of course I did. I can't pretend, now, that I didn't. I like people who get things done, especially for me, and especially that divorce. I'm being disingenuous: in a way, Tom is likeable; he's nothing if not affable and interesting. And sensible, and I've always liked a man who talks sense. Widely-read, well-informed. He might well have been Wolsey's one-time assistant, but he had no time for the clergy. He was a forty-year-old widower when we met. He'd lived life. And happened to be still very much living it. Living it well, in that smart London house of his. No hankering for palaces and pomp, but a love of good company and good food. A man of taste, not opulence. A man of the times.

At the start of 1530, it was as if Tom walked in on us all, clapped his hands three times and demanded, 'What *is* all this nonsense?'

My thoughts entirely.

Piggy-eyed? Bullish.

With Tom behind him, Henry summoned the Convocation of the Clergy from Canterbury to Westminster. He meant business, which didn't suit them one bit. Fussing, they came blinking into the light. Waited on, hand and foot, every step of the way. When they finally shuffled to a halt in London and assembled themselves in their acres of garb, Henry let them know what it was all about: a hundred thousand pounds in compensation, please, for expenses he'd incurred in dealing with Rome. If they were considering refusing him, he added, perhaps they should know that there could also be prosecution for having sided with the traitorous Wolsey. Was that clear?

Very. But in return, could they just have back some clerical privileges that had recently been docked?

Since you ask, said Henry, no. And whilst we're on the subject: I'll be Head of the Church in England.

Inevitably, Bishop Fisher – Catherine's principal ally – raised merry Hell in the Lords. All a-quiver, I can imagine: that skinny, papery old man. Parliament responded, panicking, adding the rider: *so far as the law of God allows*. Fine, because no one knew how far that was.

Back it came to the clergy, who obviously didn't feel that they could say no, but said nothing at all. Silence. In the end, Warham – Archbishop of Canterbury – got to his feet. I think, he said to Henry, that we'll have to take that as a yes.

And so we had it, *we had it!* Yet no one else seemed happy. Not even Henry, really. For all his borrowed bullishness, he couldn't be happy or confident until he had people on his side. King though he was, he wanted their blessing. Especially More's. More was behaving impeccably. He did his job, appearing before parliament and, as required, explaining Henry's reasoning. When someone there demanded his own opinion, he merely said, 'It's well-known.' In the following days, he declined to see his friend Chapuys, to avoid any possible representation from the emperor.

And when Chapuys finally succeeded in tracking him down, I have it on good authority that More backed away from him with, '*Please*, you *must* understand . . .'

Oh, but *I* understood. *I* knew More's little game. He'd wanted to resign – that's what I heard, and I don't doubt it – but had then decided to stay. Why? Well, think about it: he and his many friends probably felt he'd achieve most by working from the inside. By sticking with it. His polite restraint wasn't acquiescence; it was politics. Henry liked and trusted him, despite their growing differences, more than he liked or trusted any other of my detractors. So, if anyone could repair the situation – this is how it must have looked, to my enemies – then More could. Or at least limit the damage. Talk Henry round, to some extent. That, I bet, was their reasoning. What never ceases to amaze me was how much they underestimated me, those supposedly clever, worldly men.

A pity, though, that Bishop Fisher didn't follow More's example of apparent good grace instead of spluttering his outrage. Because someone, somewhere, took exception and, a week or so after Fisher's quivering condemnation to the Lords, his household suffered a catastrophe. Poisoned pottage. Seven dead men. The bishop himself – a poor eater, it seems, at the best of times – had only had a mouthful, and was only very sick.

I know what people say: that I did it. But I say: prove it.

If I *had* been a poisoner, wouldn't there have been people I'd have gone for before Fisher? Catherine, for starters.

At Fisher's, it was the cook who actually did the deed: slipped the powder into the soup. At whose behest remains a mystery. Henry lives in terror of poison; of sickness in general, but particularly from poisoning. It's the ease of it, I suppose; the mercilessness: anyone could do it. And now anyone *had*: a cook, whose purpose in life was to sustain and nurture. I mean, who can you trust if you can't trust your cook? To Henry's mind, no punishment could be adequate. Oh, except perhaps one: he had a flash of inspiration and the cook ended up at Smithfield, shut into a cauldron of oil and cooked to death.

There were people I'd have boiled before Fisher's cook. Several very large pots wouldn't have gone amiss. I suppose it was a consolation that they didn't all just hate *me*, my detractors: most of them hated Tom, too, and some of them also hated each other. Uncle Norfolk and his old pal Charlie for example: those two old women, suddenly at loggerheads. No one could quite fathom their problem; it seemed to be anything and everything. They should never have been given the shared job of running the Council. Best friends too readily make worst enemies.

I've never been naive about blood relations, so it was no huge surprise to me when my cousin Nick began avoiding my company. Especially as I'd spotted that he was spending a lot of time with the Neville lad, Exeter. So, he was aligning himself with the lugubrious old families: the Nevilles, Staffords, Poles. Families for whom the Pope would never be what Henry and I had decided he was: the mere Bishop of Rome. English families who wouldn't dream of stooping to own a book in English.

Well, thank God for the Boleyns, for Harry, Billy, Francis, and Franky; for apricot-haired little Fitz, his best friend Hal and his sister Maria. But no Nick, any more. Did it hurt me, this iciness of my cousin's? It was a shock, but momentary. Almost instantly, I was over it. After all, who was he? Nick Carewe. No one. And I was going to be queen. Of course, I'd have rather that people liked me; if nothing else, it'd have made everything easier. But if they didn't – if they were too stupid to see me for the good thing that I was – then that was their loss and of no consequence to me whatsoever.

That's where Henry and I differed. One of the ways we differed. Still do. He cares what people think, and I don't. There isn't time, is my feeling; and anyway, as I've said, people are fickle. A waste of time, all round, waiting for people to get behind you. Something else: Henry easily feels misunderstood. For me, that's not a problem. If anything, I'm understood all too clearly. It's what I pride myself on: making myself understood.

Take Sir Henry Guildford. Controller of the Household, at this time. One day in the summer of 1530, he and I had the last in our series of rows; I can't even remember what this final set-to was about. It's not important, what it was about. What's important was that he didn't like me and he didn't try to hide it. A smile for everyone else; a sneer for me. Well, I was going to be queen, and very soon. No way could I tolerate insubordination. Let's say this spat was about building noise: it often was; it was the bain of my royal life, building noise. I knew Sir Henry Guildford wasn't responsible for construction; but as controller, he would've known who was. I made my complaint, whatever it was, but his response was – as usual – infuriatingly off-hand. Patronizing, dismissive.

I decided I'd ask him, 'Why are you always like this with me? Don't you get tired of keeping it up?'

He frowned, hard, aggressive, and challenged me: 'Like what?'

I made a show of searching for the word. 'Well, *unhelpful*, shall we say.'

The frown sprang into raised eyebrows. 'If you've a problem

with my work, take it to the king.' He was about to say *or queen*; he definitely was, and he only didn't, I imagine, because I couldn't possibly have taken it to her. For once, she wasn't hanging around but was away visiting that malingering child of hers.

'*Listen*,' I went right up to him, 'as soon as I'm in, you're out.'

He folded his arms, cocked his head. '*You* listen: I'll save you the trouble. I resign now.'

And off he stalked, treating us to a fantastic slam of the door.

Slammed doors were nothing new to me. Auntie Liz specialized in them, Wet-fish Charlie occasionally couldn't help himself, and Uncle Norfolk favoured an unnecessarily firm shutting if he felt I hadn't grasped the importance of what he'd been saying. Norfolks and Suffolks: door-slammers, all of them, with their fraying nerves and centre-stage roles. But *Guildford*? Bloody boring Guildford. A slam from him? A *resignation* from him? That, I hadn't expected. Nor, by the sound of it, had anyone else: the room hummed with what pretended to be embarrassment but was, I knew only too well, excitement.

Play it down, I told myself, and quickly. 'Well, good,' I said. 'Good riddance.' And returned to my chair, sat back, crossed my ankles: job done.

The news would have been with Henry in minutes, but he must have gone to see Guildford first because it was a good half-hour before he came along to me. He arrived with that look on his face, an increasingly common look for him at that time: anxious and tired. It made *me* tired, that look of his. He crouched beside my chair, laid a hand on my arm, whispered, 'Anne, how *could* you.'

No point pretending ignorance; I was no Guildford with his *Like what?* 'Did you hear what he said?'

He lowered his head for a moment, as if he needed time to think. 'Nothing much, by all accounts.'

All accounts? Not mine. But anyway, it was what he *hadn't* said. 'It's his attitude,' I snapped. 'He gives me nothing but trouble.'

'Anne,' still a whisper, 'the fact that some of our peers aren't keen on us marrying isn't news to us, is it? If you can just . . .' He placed his hand over mine, patted it. 'All I'm saying is, it's a difficult time, passions are running high –'

'Yes, they *are*: *mine* are.'

He half-laughed. 'Yes, I know. But if you can perhaps just *avoid* certain people, rather than –'

I turned in my chair to face him. 'Henry, that's condoning it.

It's not going to go away, this pettiness. They've had years to get used to the idea, and nothing's changed. They're better confronted. Shouted down.'

Henry rose, knees cracking.

'And I bet he retracted that petty resignation of his, didn't he, as soon as he had you crawling to him.'

Henry spoke over my head. 'Actually, no; no, he didn't.'

Oh. 'Well, good. He was useless.'

'Yes,' said Henry, without conviction, and with that look. 'Now all that remains for me to do is to find someone else for the job.'

I couldn't understand it, this keenness of Henry's to be seen to be doing the right thing. If he was Head of the Church in England, why couldn't he grant himself the annulment? It was a matter of state, was how he'd put it. 'And not –' anxious smile pretending to be indulgent '– one of your shouting matches.' The situation, he'd tell me, needed to be handled with care. Sometimes he'd say, 'If we can just persuade her to withdraw her appeal to Rome . . .'

But she won't.

Or, 'It'd look so much better if we could just get her to agree to *some*thing . . . *any*thing . . .'

On and on, wasting time. Time I didn't have.

I never regret a showdown nor anything I've ever said about anyone I despise. Not even that I wanted to see Catherine hang and all Spaniards drowned. But there *is* something that's haunting me, now, in these last few days of mine, and it's the smallest aside. It was a joke I made at Billy's expense at a picnic, that spring, in Windsor Great Park. Henry and I had woken to a big wet kiss of a spring morning, a full-on smacking surprise of a day. The bold, glossy sky might have been freshly painted. Indisputably a day for a picnic, so Henry placed the order and by mid-afternoon they were there: four skeletal trestle tables cloaked in blinding tablecloths and laden with silverware that shone daggers at us. Confectionery in shyest pink and moody amber: pearl-like, rose-tinted comfits, and squat, spice-dusted gloops of marmalade. And the bare-faced sugar of a spectacularly bow-necked swan.

Even Tom came along, later on, to join us; all no-rush and a knowing smile, *So, here you are.* Pocketing delicacies in those fat lips and reclining on the grass in a show of having finished a hard day's work. This was the day when I first noticed Mark Smeaton: whenever the musicians took a break, he stayed on, strumming. I don't know why; I don't know who, if anyone, asked him. I remember feeling that he suited the occasion, that he was a good find, a good omen: his newborn blue-white complexion, and sunshine a cream on his dark hair.

We stayed all afternoon in the shade of breeze-streaming oak trees, stayed on until the sun was long gone and the air itself was shining. And it was sometime then, in my contentment, that I allowed myself my habitual lament, a half-sigh and half-wail to Henry: 'Oh, *why* aren't you divorced?'

He gently kissed my nose, and teased me: 'Impatient, aren't you.'

'Thirty, is what I am. And, worse, known all over the world as your "intended": no suitors in line for when you give up on me.'

He moved his kissing into my hair. 'I won't, I won't; you know I won't.'

'Oh,' I continued, 'unless you count Billy.'

Billy – cross-legged at our feet, whittling a stick – glanced up. Of all the boys, Billy – absurdly blond – was the most beautiful. Wide-eyed, he obviously hadn't caught what I'd said, and we laughed, as I'd intended, at his guilelessness. He graced us in return with his smile. People called it wicked, Billy's smile, but he was such an innocent. And I keep seeing him, now, exactly as I saw him then: sun-smashed, ever-obliging Billy, so very alive. And I can't stop wondering: if I hadn't said it – that one, silly remark, that joke at his expense – would he have been spared?

Henry finally did it, that July, five years ago: he walked out on Her Oldbagness. After all that time. For four years, we'd had her trailing along with us but keeping to her own rooms. The queen in residence at court; the wife in her home. Henry would only ever see her to ask her to agree to the annulment, which she never did. Earlier in the year, though, it'd looked for a while as if we might get shot of her of her own accord. That pallid daughter of hers had taken to her bed with another of her imaginary complaints, and Catherine asked Henry if Her Sickliness could join us. Henry's response was, 'Why don't you go to her, and stay there.'

Catherine, they told me, lowered her eyes. 'Oh, no,' she murmured, 'I'd never leave you.' Regrettably, she'd been well-advised: if she went, it could be construed as desertion.

He relented, in March: a compromise, whereby Mary was moved to Richmond and her mother scurried there to nurse her.

In May, Henry went one step further and risked playing happy families: Mary, now well, joined us all at Windsor. Whey-faced, knees prayer-hard, and a head crackling with Latin, that girl was no use to anyone. At least she now knew what was happening. She couldn't be at court and be unaware that the world had changed and she and her mother were finished. No, she didn't like it, of course she didn't; not one bit. But she had to know sometime, didn't she.

Mid-July was when Henry rode away from Catherine for good. We set out early from Windsor for Woodstock, and didn't tell her. As simple as that, in the end. It was done. Word was left that she should vacate Windsor within a month. We only got so far, though, before she was pestering us. She'd sent a messenger speeding behind us; he reached us in the evening. Didn't dare look at me, directed his little speech to Henry: the queen very much regrets not having had a chance to say goodbye, was the gist, so she's sending me with her good wishes. But Henry wasn't having it: 'I don't *want* her good wishes!'

The kid's legs had been shaking with exhaustion as he knelt, and now his bottom lip was going.

Henry didn't let up. 'What *is* it with the woman! I don't want to hear from her. Not ever. It's over. Listen: I never want to see you here again – do you understand?' He flapped a hand in dismissal, but, 'Oh –' as the kid stumbled away, '– and you make sure she's clear about this: she's to be out of there by mid-August.' Uncharacteristic was the order that he bellowed to the yeomen: 'Throw this man out!'

They did make a show of doing so, of course; but, of course, that was all it was: show. They'd have seen that he was given a good meal and a bed. They weren't inhuman.

If Henry was never to see Catherine again, the job of badgering her to drop her case had to fall to other people. Most of whom had already tried, at various times. Everyone from Wolsey onwards had had at least one unenviable audience with Her Stubbornness. My Uncle Norfolk had been in the gaggle of nobles who had visited her, earlier in the year. Afterwards, he'd mused to me, 'It really does have to be seen to be believed. She'd burn, first; really, she would, she'd burn.'

'Rather than give me what I want?' I couldn't believe how ridiculous she was continuing to be.

His eyes clicked into life. 'Rather than concede that she's lived a lie.'

And I saw it: the admiration that had been my cousin Nick's, too, when he'd talked of her 'faith'. No one ever spoke of *my* faith; no one ever spoke in that way of my own lost years. But that Spanish cow's stubbornness, they all saw as faith.

More nobles made an attempt, when she'd left Windsor and settled at Easthampstead. Last ditch. This time, Charlie Brandon drew the short straw and had the task of reporting back to Henry. He made heavy weather of it, of course, flopping down into the offered chair. There was the barest acknowledgement of me, but at least there was the semblance of a truce between us. His wife, for all her royal blood, had been unable to manage that. He said nothing, which was his wet-fish way of telling us that it was bad news. I was unsurprised, of course, but still suffered the inevitable twinge of disappointment. Henry lowered his face into his hands.

It was then that Charlie spoke. 'To be honest,' he said to Henry's hidden face, 'I think she'd obey you in anything, except when it compromises the allegiance she feels she owes to two higher powers.'

Henry looked up, weary: *Don't tell me,* 'The Pope and the emperor.'

Charlie shook his head. 'God and her conscience.'

Henry finalized the separation by moving her to The More, which was a gracious ruin of a place, one of Wolsey's. There she was, comfortably installed with several hundred staff, as the year crawled to a close. In November, she honoured a long-standing arrangement and made her last public appearance as queen, at a banquet in Holborn. Henry was co-host, but was able to keep to a separate hall and never saw her. At Christmas, she sent him a present – an engraved gold cup – but he sent it back.

New Year's Day, 1532, I arrived back at Greenwich from Hever, and finally moved into the rooms vacated by that Spanish dog-in-a-manger. Literally a giddying experience, because of the change of view from the one I'd been accustomed to for the past few years: I was at a slightly different point along the river, and one floor up. I hadn't stood at those windows for years; not since I'd been cooped up as one of Her Holiness's ladies, spending the long days dreaming of Hever or Harry Percy. Catherine had loved Greenwich, not least because of the short walk – waddle, in her case – along the covered walkway to her beloved friars in the Observatory. How I remember that walk – or, more often, avoiding it. Fabricating reasons to be elsewhere. Anything to avoid 'Mass duty', hours of kneeling behind that gibbering Spanish bulk. The Observatory was where she'd planned to end up, buried. Well, tough luck: Greenwich was no longer her home.

That first day, I missed my old apartment. I had happy memories of it. And there were the bad associations of the new place:

it was where *she'd* lived, all those years. But none of that was
the point. Liking or disliking didn't come into it. There was a
job to be done: I needed to get underway with preparations to
be queen. Evidently, Henry agreed: he'd employed a lot more
staff for me; so many new faces that I could never know them
all. That first day at Greenwich, I felt quite at sea.

But Henry came to the rescue: he practically moved in with
me. Within days, my new rooms had become *our* rooms. And
we found that we were tending to keep to just a few of them,
shutting the doors on most of the staff. Suddenly, for the first
time, we had a *home*. Henry was busy – very busy, with Tom,
on legalities – but he chose to work at home, in those rooms of
mine, spreading his papers across tables and floors. Tom wasn't
fussed, he could work anywhere. For Tom, it was the work that
mattered: getting it done. What they were doing was drawing
up legislation to further hamper the Church's relationship with
Rome: no more taxes from new bishops to the Pope. Henry was
learning fast from Tom: he began turning up at Westminster, that
February, and kept doing so until he'd forced the legislation
through.

The first time he returned – early – he walked in on me being
fitted for a dress. I'd taken the opportunity to call in Mr Matte,
to catch up on the business of preparing to be queen. So, in came
Henry, troubled by crucial matters of state, to be faced by the
ultimate frivolity: me being pinned into gold-embroidered velvet.
There was nothing for it: I mock-sighed, mock-complained, 'A
woman's work is never done.'

He liked that; laughed. And complimented the dress. And my
figure inside the dress.

'Anyway, anyway,' I said: *how was Westminster?*

'Uproar.'

On his third trip to Westminster, though, he tried a new tactic,
insisting everyone stand up to be counted: if a yes, walk to one
end of the chamber; if a no, to the other. And hey presto . . .

Which was good news, because Tom was already busy with
something else, something much bigger: could the Church be
trusted, he was asking, to give fair trials in heresy cases? The
answer, as any sane person knew, was no. The Church was probably the very last institution to be trusted with its supposed
dissenters. Only the previous year, a man's will had been judged
heretical because it didn't toe the line in favouring money-
grabbing priests, and his body was dug up for burning. That was
how the Church was going about recapturing the hearts of the
disenchanted English people. The man, William Tracy, had left

a bewildered, frightened son, Richard, whom I invited to Greenwich and for whom I did what I could. My taking an interest in Richard was more than that, though, of course; more than a comforting pat on the head and the handing over of a purse. It was also a clear warning to the Church: *No more barbarism*. And how had the Church responded? By turning a deaf ear. Even while Tom was raising the question about its courts – perhaps *because* Tom was raising the question – the man who had married Simon Fish's widow was burned at Smithfield. People were being burned, now, it seemed, not only for asking questions and reading books, but for whom they knew.

And then, that Easter, the chaos came into the heart of our home, our own chapel at Greenwich. Peto, head of Catherine's adored Observants, dared to preach to us that if Henry persisted with his plans, his fate would be Ahab's, his blood licked up by dogs. We sat through it. What else could we do? It was a *sermon*. We sat through it, carefully expressionless. Me, staring at Peto, daring him to meet my eyes. Of course, he never did. Pathetic little churchman, with his warped ideas about women. Puffed up in his pulpit. As soon as he was down from there, I comforted myself, we'd have him. Oh, how we'd have him.

But we didn't. It was nothing much, was Henry's wishful thinking; nothing but a melodramatic old friar. Take no notice, Henry urged me; give it no credence. And, unusually, I allowed myself to be swayed. Maybe it was the absurdity of it: being called Jezebel to my face in church by everyone's favourite man of God. Maybe, too, the way that Henry phrased the small sanction he'd decided on: 'He can damn well stay at Lambeth Palace until I say otherwise.' It reminded me of my father, when we Boleyn children were small: *Stay there and think about what you've done!*

Suddenly it seemed funny.

And if I was going to look at it in that light, then the following Sunday was no less amusing. One of Peto's friars tried in his sermon to pour oil on troubled waters, but was interrupted – actually interrupted – with a rebuke from one of the others, who had the cheek to make it sound as if he was doing Henry a favour. Succession, he lectured the friar, can't follow from adultery; if you agree to it, you're betraying the king.

'Yes!' came from the pews. We all swivelled to see Essex, stupid Essex. 'You should be sewn into a sack,' spittle spraying in the direction of the friar, 'and lobbed into the Thames!'

The friar, though, didn't appreciate Essex's support. 'No doubt you can frighten your fellow courtiers with threats like that,' he said, 'but may I remind you that we friars will get to Heaven just as easily from a waterlogged sack.'

Behind the scenes, that Easter, Thomas More was trying to drum up support for a stand against Henry, I was informed, by doing as that friar had done: telling people that the king would thank them at a later date. As if Henry didn't know his own mind. More was a snob: his attitude was, Who *were* we? Who were *we*, against a thousand years of papacy? He was irrational, too: did he really think that because of *me*, the way would be paved for the infidel? That civilization would end? He was so immersed in his anti-heretical writings – you should see it, said my informant; he never stops, never sleeps – that he was no longer making much sense.

I passed none of this on to Henry. Confident that there was no need. Thomas More might have been losing his grip, but *I* knew which way the wind was blowing. And sure enough, when parliament came back from the Easter break, it was all over in a matter of days. Over, after all those years, in a matter of days. What Henry did first, George told me, was read aloud the oath that prelates make to the Pope. 'See what I mean?' he challenged parliament: 'they're only half ours.' Well, everyone knows you can't have two masters. Thomas More, sensing that he was about to lose the battle, dropped the subterfuge and voiced his main complaint: Henry simply couldn't be allowed to prevent bishops arresting for heresy. What More really wanted, I swear, was that *he* should be arresting for heresy. Left, right and centre. And probably starting with me. He fancied himself the expert on heresy, to the tune of those hundreds of thousands of words he'd been scribbling at all hours in his room. And suddenly he seemed the very last person to trust to behave. If he had his way, how many bodies would he dig up?

Henry's quiet anger with More detracted from the victory which came only a week later, when the Church finally laid down and rolled over. From that point onwards, all ecclesiastical law required royal assent. There was one master, now; one educated, experienced master: the king, naturally enough. It was as it should be. As it should always have been. That day, More resigned. He came in person to do so. We were at Whitehall. Henry told the usher who announced the arrival that More should find him in the garden. He didn't say a word or even look at me as he left the room. I went to a window and waited. Nothing. Rushed to the adjacent wing, and spotted him. He seemed to be concentrating on a sundial, running a finger around it. More's approach was steady, but Henry didn't acknowledge him until he was there and bowing. More handed him something – the Great Seal, I learned later – and bowed again before turning and walking away. Of course I couldn't have heard any words, but I'm certain there were none.

That wordlessness of Henry's chilled me enough at the time, but now, sitting here in this deathly silence of Henry's making, I look back on it as ominous. Until then, Henry had always been a talker. He'd lived for talk, from gossip and confidences – his own and others' – to debates. There was no one with whom he couldn't or wouldn't talk, at length, animatedly, sympathetically; from Chapuys to the commoners who came to ask him to help with their disputes and misfortunes. He trusted talking to bring a meeting of minds. Look how he'd been, even, with Catherine: trying for years – far too long – to talk it through, to talk her round. Although his conduct towards Catherine infuriated me, I'd otherwise found it rather touching, his faith in talking. Especially considering his upbringing. His father had rarely spoken to him except to put him down or order him about. Not only did Henry survive that upbringing, but he surpassed it. He *tackled* life, didn't sneer at it or back away from it; and he tackled it with a burning faith in people, and a generosity to match.

He and More had long done all the talking possible. I couldn't see the consequences for Henry, then, as I stood there at that window, but still I felt for him. He'd grown used to doing battle with those supposedly closest to him: his ex-wife, up there on the moral high ground with her simpering daughter, his vain sister with her nose in the air, and her cold-blooded husband. But nothing could match this latest loss. More had been his mentor.

We didn't mention it until the evening, and then only in the vaguest terms. While we were watching others dancing, I reached for his hand, covered it with my own, and leaned close to whisper, 'Rare are those who are strong enough to see changes through.' I wasn't crowing. Nor was it flattery. But nor was I quite speaking the truth. Because Henry didn't have that kind of strength; not without Tom and me behind him, he didn't. But he was prepared to do it, to stick at making changes, even when it cost him dear: that's what I'd seen from the window, that day, and it had made me tender towards him. I said, 'I'm sorry,' and touched my lips to his earlobe.

'It's worth it,' was his quiet response.

'You still think so?' I wasn't fishing; it was a genuine question. That sundial scene had shaken me.

He put an arm around me and said into my hair, 'More so

than ever.' I turned to him; our foreheads pressed together. 'We're so nearly there,' he breathed. 'Soon, we can get on with our life together as if none of this ever happened.'

I believed it, of course. We'd talked ourselves into sharing that vision. It wasn't so hard to believe that no one would miss a faintly Spanish, Vatican-bowed England. An England where the God-like monarch was married to a grandma-like last-in-line princess. It was only later that I wondered how we could have been so naive.

At the time, it all seemed so simple: the quicker I became queen, the better. Everyone, then, could start accepting it. No one, surely, would stand at a roadside to yell insults at a queen. People shrieked 'whore' because that was what they believed: a whore was what they thought they were seeing. Because what else could I be, a commoner riding unmarried alongside Henry? The king's whore, being paraded. They understood nothing of the politics, the reasons for the years of delay. It seemed to me that as soon as I was married to him and crowned, I'd no longer be a 'whore'. They'd stop. As I said: naive.

We'd marry as soon as Warham died. The last official obstacle, our old Archbishop of Canterbury, had taken to his bed, that summer, clearly for the last time. No need for poison. Just patience. Hang-dog Thomas stood ready to take his place and to rule Henry's old marriage null and void. But until then, life, for us, was on hold. We abandoned our summer trip, turned tail, because of the trouble we'd been encountering in the villages. I'd prepared well for our annual showing-off to the nobles around the country, but now none of my marvellous dresses were to be seen. *I* wasn't to be seen. And the clothes that my ladies and I had sewn for distribution to the poor were packed back into boxes. We were to spend the summer holed up. That was no hardship. My only complaint was that Henry used the time to see something of that daughter of his. I couldn't understand why he bothered with her.

Then, into my slow, stay-at-home summer came a crisis. One afternoon, at Hanworth, when a group of us was rather ineptly, less than soberly, playing bowls, Uncle Norfolk was suddenly at my side: 'A word, please, Anne.'

He'd come to tell me that Harry Percy's wife was petitioning for divorce.

My immediate, unvoiced response was, *About time, too*. Until he added: 'Naming you.'

'*Me?*'

His sharp little eyes slid from side to side: Voice down, please. 'She's claiming pre-contract.'

So, she was claiming that although Harry and I were never officially married, we'd promised ourselves to each other. Which made us, in law, effectively married. Only a special dispensation could break a pre-contract. A dispensation that, as everyone knew, Harry and I had never had. *Wolsey* had broken our relationship. His word had been enough for everyone, back then.

My stomach shrank. *First things first*: 'And Harry says?'

Uncle Norfolk was trying to read my face; everything was happening in my stomach, but he was searching for clues on my face. 'Percy says no.'

My breath flew from me.

He frowned. 'And the truth is?'

And the truth is known only to Harry and me. But I brazened it out. 'You have to *ask*? You think I'd have gone through all this with Henry, come this close, but failed to mention that I'm married to someone else?' I was doing well. The din from my heart could just as well have been due to indignation. *Henry*: 'Henry knows about this?'

'Not yet.' He snatched at my arm. 'Where d'you think you're going?'

'To tell him.'

'Not in the state you're in.'

I rounded on him. 'And what's that? What "state" is it that I'm in?'

He refrained from 'rattled' or 'terrified'; went for, 'Drunk.'

'And you really think I'm going to sit around sobering up while some ill-informed gloater like you goes to him and breaks the news?'

He didn't flinch: there was too much at stake here. 'Anne, be prudent for once in your life. You need to take some advice on this.'

'No, I don't; I don't need advice. I need to go to him and deny it.'

What Henry said when I told him was, 'I wish you'd told me.'

'I *am* telling you,' I insisted. 'There was nothing to tell, before. Ask Harry.'

He blew a breath. 'Well, we'll have to, I'm afraid. There'll have to be an enquiry.'

'That bitch of a wife of his!'

Henry seemed disappointed. 'Anne, the truth of the matter has to be seen to be found.'

'Oh, it will be,' I said. Praying, *Harry, don't let me down.* And he didn't, even though the price he had to pay was staying married to that witch. He denied a pre-contract between us, and her bitter little petition was discarded. She was stuck with him, he was stuck with her. Both of them stuck up there in Northumberland. My brother had seen him just before his questioning. In all innocence, I asked: how was he? George seemed reluctant to answer.

'George?'

'Pissed.'

'For his *questioning*?'

'Don't worry, he was making sense.'

'*Pissed?*'

'Anne.' George sighed. 'Percy's always pissed.'

I must have looked uncomprehending, because he tried to elaborate: 'And . . .' he shrugged, casting around for a word, '. . . unwashed.'

I was struck cold. That gorgeous dandy of a man.

'Crying,' George added, gently, seeing that I was beginning to understand. 'He's usually crying.'

One morning in late August, Henry turned up while I was dressing. He stopped in the middle of my room, wide-eyed, expectant, and opened, raised, his hands.

I guessed: 'Warham?'

He nodded.

I dashed at him, unlaced; but he stopped me, laughing, and held me at arms' length to look at me. His glittering eyes were on mine and then over my face, my hair, my neck.

'We can get married,' I said, breezily.

'We can get *moving*, certainly.' A twitch of my eyebrows had him rushing to explain: 'There's something we need to do first, quickly.'

It was instinct to glance at the maids, self-conscious.

He laughed, 'Not *that*,' and pulled me close, whispered, 'I'm hoping to take my time over *that*.' Then came the explanation: I was to be made a peer. Then he'd be marrying the Marquess of Pembroke.

Marquess. Not Marchioness. I was to be it, *Pembroke*; I was to be all of it. The title, mine alone. The income, too. *Marquess*. 'Can it be done?' I was doubtful.

'Well, if I say it can, it can.' He laughed. 'Can't it?'

Which made *me* laugh. 'It's a lovely idea, but why bother?'

Because a marriage, a coronation, would take time, he said. Just a little, he added quickly, but time nevertheless. Even in this case. Especially in this case, when he'd waited so long. He wanted to do it properly. The peerage would set me up perfectly, with rank and riches. I'd be equal to anyone. Any man. 'And,' he finished, 'you can go to France as a peer of the realm.'

'France?'

'Oh, didn't I say?' A wicked grin. 'We're going to France. On a state visit. I think Francis should have the chance to meet my future wife and feel very, very jealous.'

Francis: our French ally. A show of strength to the Pope.

I was invested on the first of September in the Presence Chamber at Windsor Castle. It's strange to be invested by one's lover. To kneel before him; to rise, bestowed upon. We stood there, facing each other, with everyone's eyes on us. Me, word-less for once. We did it properly. After so many years of muddling through, making do – a king and his wife who wasn't yet his wife, who couldn't yet be his wife – we were going to do this properly. I didn't so much as smile at him. Not a single knowing look. King and subject, that's what we were. And in a way it was a relief.

Despite everything that was to come – my marriage, my coro-nation – I'm not sure that those few moments in Windsor's Presence Chamber weren't among the very best I've ever had. Perhaps because of it being the first time that Henry and I could do something properly. Also perhaps because I knew I was stun-ning. It's something, to know that, isn't it. Henry's full-length mirror had been brought in to me, that morning, while I was dressing. Onto the polished steel flashed someone running crimson. I turned to that ghostly, bloodied me, and she stared back, white-faced. Me, radiant and jewel-eyed. It was obvious, as soon as I saw it: I was made for crimson; crimson was made for me. We'd found each other, fiercest of dyes and sallow flesh. Bolt after bolt of vividness, and a tough-boned girl. We'd do bril-liantly, together.

So, there I was in the Presence Chamber, staring everyone down without even glancing at them. *Is this what you bargained for? Well, this is what you've got, so make sure you take a good, long look.* But they were nothing, really, all those pairs of eyes. Mere irritations, with their doubts and quibbles. What mattered was Henry. My own eyes were on Henry, in Henry's; and his focused on mine with an intensity that was almost savage. That morning, at the mirror, Annie had moved to pin up my hair, but I'd said no, I'd go to him with my black hair a pelt on the ermine-froth of my shoulders. I'd go to him like a bride. A crimson-clad, mad kind of bride.

The morning we were due to leave for France was dew-rinsed, sparkling. I found it hard to turn away from the blazing, last-chance blue of that sky. Idling at a window, I slid my fingertip through the condensation: two swoops, joined top and bottom to make a heart. My own heart couldn't have felt more different from that flat, frosted one. It'd been so long since I'd felt real, physical excitement. Now I felt as if my life was just about to begin. And what a perfect place for its beginning: *France*. So close, that morning, that I could almost smell it: the fragrance of its beams and timbers; different, I remembered, from England's. A sweeter sap. The herbs, too, hung with clothes and swirled into baths: spicier.

There were problems, though, from the very beginning of that French trip; from *before* the beginning. First, the Spanish dog-in-a-manger had decided to sit tight on the queen's jewels. They weren't hers; they were the queen's, they belonged to the queen of England, to whoever was queen. Not her. Both Henry and I were determined that I should conduct my first state visit in the crown jewels. But when Catherine refused Henry's request to hand them over, he had to order her. And then, of course, everyone raised their eyebrows at the unseemly tussle.

Then, suddenly, it all seemed to have been for nothing. I was ready to go, but we were sent word that no one would receive me. A queen should be received by a queen. Well, we hadn't needed telling that the French queen wouldn't oblige: Francis' wife was Catherine's niece. But even Francis' sister, the Queen of Navarre – and my old friend, from my French days – was also mysteriously unavailable. Then Francis had the gall to suggest his mistress, and Henry had to make it clear: *I don't think you quite understand . . .*

We worked our way around it. It wasn't as if we were unused to hitches. I'd stay in Calais, and Henry would go alone on to French soil to Francis. But before we could even reach Dover, something else cropped up. We'd stopped at Canterbury for the night. Before dinner, Henry and I met up alone in the Abbot's walled garden for a little time to ourselves. The air, silting up with dusk, smelled deliciously of old coins. We gossiped about our travelling companions and had a giggle about the old Abbot. Suddenly, ahead, from rosehip-tasselled bushes, stepped a plainly-dressed woman. God knows where she'd come from, or how much she'd overheard. She approached us with considerable purpose: no stray gardener, this. Henry stopped; and I, on his arm, had to do the same. My heart made its unease felt. The young woman swept low before Henry. Nothing, for me. She was blonde, broad-faced, and expressionless except for a shine in her small, pale blue eyes.

Henry surprised me by saying, 'Elizabeth.' He turned to me with deliberate calmness. 'Anne, this is Elizabeth Barton.' Then he actually introduced me to her, as if we were equals at a social engagement. I didn't notice how he introduced me – *Lady Anne? The Marquess? My soon-to-be-wife?* – because inside my head was a thudding realization: here she was, the so-called Holy Maid of Kent. The woman of whom I'd heard so much. Of whom there was so much to hear. The woman who spoke publicly, loudly, of God's displeasure – confessed to her, in her trances – at the king's impending mistake over me, and the calamity it would bring. The woman otherwise known as The Mad Nun of Kent.

I must have been the very last person to have the dubious pleasure of meeting her. As a matter of necessity, she'd already been granted audiences with Henry and Tom. She'd been welcomed, of course, by Catherine and that waste-of-space daughter. And Bishop Fisher was glad to admit to being impressed. She'd managed, within a couple of months, to make quite a name for herself. As to *which* name, you could, as I say, take your pick: Holy Maid, or Mad Nun.

And now here was Henry, after a long day and in our only few quiet moments, keen to do his duty and give the visionary a kingly ear. Presumably she'd been slipped the all-important key to the garden by one of her merry band of priestly believers. Henry and I should have walked away. It was uncalled-for, this ambush. If she had something to say to us, she should have requested an audience. And if people weren't so curious or afraid to stand up and be sceptical, and those requests of hers were refused, she'd disappear soon enough.

'Elizabeth,' Henry was saying, 'it's good to see you again.'

I marvelled, as always, at his careful good-naturedness with the least-deserving. But not as much as I marvelled at her confidence.

Her refusal to look at me left me free to get a good look at her. For a tormented mystic, she was quite pretty in a well-scrubbed way. Thanks, probably, to all the baths that were being heated for her by bowled-over priests. It was clear to me that she was nothing special: just a girl who'd been sharp enough to realize that the way to a good living was to talk more mumbo-jumbo than the clerics. Once someone's servant, she now had Canterbury fawning over her. Men who were supposed to be learned and scrupulous.

'Your Majesty,' she said, surprisingly business-like, 'I have to tell you that if you go ahead with this supposed marriage, you'll be off your throne within a month.'

Where was the staggering and falling down? Why were we being denied the famed spectacle? Perhaps she saved that for the impressionable.

'Elizabeth,' Henry started, 'a lot of people listen to you –'

'I don't care about "a lot of people",' she said, quick off the mark. 'Just you. It's you who should be listening to me.'

Despite my unease, I almost laughed, because surely only I talked to Henry like that.

Henry merely said, 'Well, yes, thank you. And I have. As you know, I always listen to what you have to say. But I'm afraid this isn't a good time, and you'll have to excuse us ...'

She didn't follow; just raised her voice to reach us. 'In *God's* eyes,' she specified, 'you'll stop being king from the very moment you make your vows.'

Henry sighed.

'And –' back to sounding business-like, 'you'll die a terrible death.'

'No, *you* will,' I muttered. And let me tell you, it didn't take a visionary to foresee that.

For a while, we were free of the Mad Nun. We put the incident behind us, reached France and, from then onwards, away from English soil, everything was fine. In France, Francis obliged us and came back with Henry to Calais. I was ready for him in a gown of gold slashed with crimson, and he took me straight onto the dancefloor. He ended up dancing with me for most of the week.

When he'd gone, we stayed on for a couple more weeks. There, in Calais, I could breathe. We were with friends – only friends, for once – and the best of my family, my brother and sister. No Uncle Norfolk; and my father's faintly disapproving gaze was a sea's distance away. On Calais' shore, autumn was being swept away and winter swept in. Each day made a splash, whether with a sky-load of over-ripe sunshine or lances of rain. And everywhere to the horizon was the sea, flexing, bearing us up on the continent and keeping England at bay.

All those days, I was suffused with the feeling that I'd had at my window the morning of our departure from London. Our long, difficult past was over and miraculously shrunk to nothing, as if it'd never been. My future was made of the love of the one man who mattered. The house where we were staying was perfect for us, not least because our bedchambers were directly connected and no one knew what we were or weren't doing after dark. We, ourselves, hardly knew, dizzy as we were with holiday high-spirit-edness and our success with the all-important Francis. We only weren't married, by that time, because I'd declined Henry's offer of a wedding in France. I'd only declined because I was determined to celebrate my victory where I'd fought so long and hard for it: on English soil.

We arrived back in England as king and queen in all but the most official and – to us – irrelevant sense: only the gloss of the official ceremonies to come. We both felt it, this sea-change. And that very first night back, we slept together as husband and wife. No discussion. I didn't stop him, and I didn't stop myself. I almost didn't notice, perhaps because what had always been noticeable was the stopping, the refraining; it was the curtailing that had always taken the effort. Consummation, by contrast, was, of course, effortless.

Elizabeth, I should have known much earlier – *could* have known – that I was pregnant with you. You probably began your steady unfolding within days of our coming home from France, when we were still sea-legged. You'd been waiting seven years to get started, and now you wasted no time.

A week or so later began the dreams that nowadays would tell me I was in the earliest stage of one of my pregnancies. Undreamlike in their coherence and their focus on real places, but dreamily unpeopled. Instantly recognizable scenes from my childhood, but no Mary, no George. Not a glimpse, even, of Mary's eggshell eyelids as she blanked Dad's displeasure. Certainly none of the whirlwind of George and our dogs on the draw-bridge. In all other respects, though, the deserted dream-Hever was accurate, and seemed to make a point of its accuracy: everything homed-in on; *Look! This was here, wasn't it, but you never noticed.* Of course I hadn't. Life at the real Hever had been for living, not looking at. And who could have remembered all the odds and ends, nooks and crannies, that filled these dreams? A loose thread on the cushion of a neglected windowseat. A hairline crack down a shutter in my parents' bedroom. The commonplace of my childhood, now somehow revealed as wondrous. All of it there, in the hours of sleep, for the taking.

Your father and I married in January, as soon as we knew about you. And I do mean as soon as. 'Let's get married tomorrow,' was what Henry said when I told him. We'd just woken and were sitting up in bed.

'No, really,' he insisted, although he was laughing. 'Why not?'

'Oh, well, now, let's see . . . There's . . .' I ditched the sarcastic breeziness and gave him a look: *Catherine.*

He was ready with an answer. 'Null and void. That was no marriage. I'm not married. I'm free.'

News to me. 'So why the seven years I've had to endure?'

'Because it does need to be done, the divorce; I'm not saying it doesn't. Has to be seen to be done. Properly. On paper. But for us two . . .' He shrugged: *it's irrelevant, isn't it?* 'So, anyway, tomorrow?'

'Henry, I hate to be . . . well, to be a *woman* about this, but I've nothing to wear.' Only a man would assume a wedding could be whipped up in a day.

'Yes, you *do*.'

'*No*, I *don't*.' I think I'd know if I'd been fitted for a wedding gown.

'You *do*.'

'I *don't*.'

He cupped my face. 'Listen: you know what I've always wanted? A crimson bride.'

And so that was what I was, the very next day. My wedding did take place on English soil, but was far from a victory parade. The secrecy, though, proved as useful as Henry had envisaged. Sometimes we claimed we were married on that very first day home from France; so, you were conceived in wedlock. Other times we cited March, which was when Catherine was officially over and done with. Only those who were there at our little ceremony know the truth: one of Henry's chaplains, Dr Lee; Harry Norris, who was best man, and my maid, Annie; and our two witnesses, George and Billy. George knew in advance, of course, as did Harry and Annie. We told them the day before, not long after we'd sat there in bed and made the decision. We stipulated that the ceremony should happen before dawn. I think George and Harry stayed up all night, that night. Just before five, Harry went to wake an unsuspecting Dr Lee, while George came to me.

I was only dozing, and Annie was quick to the hearth. So George said he'd get going, to wake Billy.

'Wait,' I said, 'I'm coming.'

'What for?'

I didn't really know. Perhaps it was that if I was going to have a pre-dawn wedding in a crimson dress, I might as well go the whole hog and be hovering at an unsuspecting witness's bedside as he woke. In other words, if I wasn't going to have my victory parade, I'd make something else, something fun of this strange non-event. Or was it because it was Billy? Perhaps it was too tempting to pass up, an opportunity to have him sweetly at my mercy. I settled on, 'To surprise him.'

'Well, you'll certainly do that.' This wasn't in his plans.

I checked, 'He's alone?'

'Yep.' He'd have made sure of it.

He waited the few moments it took me to be helped into my linen shift and gown, and for Annie to bring the shine to my hair which, the previous evening, we'd rinsed in rosemary. Then off we stole, the two of us, into Whitehall's passageways. Somehow, George had a key to Billy's rooms. Maybe the boys all kept copies of each other's keys. Once inside, he successfully shushed a dazed, wide-eyed groom; a couple of others remained oblivious. Together, we crept up on Billy's bed, before George conceded with a reluctant flourish: *Go on, then, if you're so keen.* With a twinge of trepidation, I parted the hangings and half-tucked myself inside. George stayed close, holding our candle above me. Light from the flame beat around the enclosed space. There was a smell: something like mud or hay, a stable. As my vision adjusted, I couldn't distinguish much of Billy. He was laying on his side, facing away. There was that hair, though: his gold-spun hair. Irresistibly touchable. I ran a feather of it between my fingertips. 'Billy,' I whispered. The ends of my own hair skimmed his bedclothes. He turned slightly, looking over his shoulder, paused, then turned sharply.

'Anne?'

'Billy,' my fingertips on his lips, now, 'it's my wedding day and I want you as my witness.'

Lucy Cornwallis

❀❀❀

WINTER 1535–6

My name, hissed.

And again.

It's Richard.

How long have I been sleeping through this?

A Hettie-sound: scritch of a blanket; she's stirring.

'*Lucy?*' again, from behind the door.

And nearer, from Hettie-darkness: ''s Mr Cornwallis.'

Yes, I *know*. Why does she always call him 'Mr Cornwallis'?

I must have made some sound of assent, because the door separates from its frame; the gap turning the pale, fluid gold of tallow-light. A figure looms and sits – *thud* – on my bed, his face recognizable when he places the flame by his feet. Less recognizable is the man-scent: I know it from Kit and Stephen, but from Richard, and up close, in my own room, at night, it's a small shock. 'Are you drunk?'

'Stone-cold sober.' He sounds it, too.

I've been jammed up against sleep, and now I'm falling away. 'What time is this?'

'Don't know.'

The embers are dead. The air beyond my blankets is freezing; it's pinging tight on my skin. *Greenwich*, I tell myself. *This is my Greenwich room: that, there, is my Greenwich-room window*. Is this night or nearly morning? A dead-of-winter morning, faint-hearted, rousing itself at the last minute. I remember, now, coming to bed exhausted. The day after Twelfth Night, the busiest of our twelve busiest nights of the year. Thirteenth night, this would be. All we did, all day, was clear up. 'Richard –'

'I know. I'm sorry. We're all very tired, aren't we.' He's hunched.

'What's the matter?'

'And they're still partying.'

'Who is? Where?' I can't hear anything. What I hear, when I listen hard, is a nothing made of trees and the river.

'The great and the good,' he says. 'And the less good.' His sigh, despite its heaviness, sounds distant. 'It's such a busy old world, here, isn't it.'

'Yes, and you like that.' *So, stop bothering me and go away.* I turn over, shut him out.

He says, 'I *did* like it.'

I keep my eyes closed. 'Richard, what's the *matter*?'

'Oh, you know,' it's coming, now, in a rush, 'when you haven't seen someone properly for a while and you're really looking forward to seeing them again – just for half an hour at the end of the evening – but then they're busy. Suddenly there's a party, and they're going to be kept busy all night.' He adds, 'But of course you *don't* know, do you,' and in his voice there's a smile that's no smile at all. 'Cool-headed Lucy, untroubled by matters of the heart.'

Oh, go away. 'I might surprise you, one day.'

'Why, what you gonna do? Marry Kit, or something?' Immediately, he's contrite: 'I'm sorry. You're beautiful and wonderful and you're wasted. And that makes two of us.'

He's being impossible; it's best to keep to practicalities – to deal with him; to get this over with – which is why I roll back and ask him, 'Do you need to sleep in here?' Because this might just be what he's after. He did share my room for years, until he was allocated his own, and he was never beyond an occasional nightmare.

'Thank you, but no. I'm all grown-up, now.' A glint in his eyes. 'Unfortunately.'

A glint, too, on his doublet: a brooch, silvery. I reach out and touch it as a kind of question.

'Present,' he answers.

'You can't wear it, Richard. You know you can't.' Silver: for gentlemen. I despair of him; he's heading for a comeuppance.

'Oh, it's only –' he shrugs – 'only sometimes.' And grins. 'Discreetly.'

I give up, turn away.

'No –' his hand on my shoulder, 'I've something to tell you.'

'Well, *what is it*?' Said to my pillow.

'The old queen's dead.'

Which old queen? We don't have an old queen.

'Queen Catherine's died.'

I'm up; cold air on me like a splash. 'What d'you mean?'

Hettie crosses herself; there's a sound and I know it's Hettie crossing herself.

'A messenger came, apparently, this afternoon.'

'She's *dead*? How?'

He shakes his head slowly, as if considering. 'I don't know. She was ill.'

'Was she?'

'I don't know. She was old.'

'She wasn't *that* old, Richard.' How old was she? Fifty?

He bends to pick up the tallow, transforming himself back into shadow-face.

No, 'Wait.'

'I don't know anything else.' He's defensive.

But, 'They should be told, shouldn't they; over there, those partying people. Someone should tell them; they need to know.'

He faces me, full-square, lit up, and frowning. 'They *do* know. That's *why* they're partying.'

But that makes no sense; all I can do is repeat what he's just told me: 'The *queen* is *dead*.'

'The *old* queen,' he says as if he's correcting me: the emphatic gentleness of it.

'The *queen*,' I insist, because it's true. I'm sick of all this pretence. No, furious: that's what I am; two fistfuls of blanket at my chest, my throat. Queen Catherine was crowned queen and she didn't stop being queen because she didn't die.

Until now.

She's gone.

Now there's only Anne Boleyn.

Uneasily, Richard tries to explain: 'People are pleased, I suppose. Because she was in the way.'

Which actually makes me laugh: 'Oh, no, she wasn't.' Quite the opposite. 'She was *shut* away.'

'She was still . . . in the way. I mean, listen to you: "the *queen*". You and a lot of others.'

'But it didn't make any difference, did it.'

'But it might have done,' he whispers. 'Could have done. At any time.'

'But it *didn't*. And now she's dead, and you're telling me that people are actually *celebrating* her death? A lady who did no one any harm – only ever did a lot of good – and ended up abandoned, imprisoned, banned from seeing her daughter?' I see him take a deep breath. 'Yes, come on, you tell me: why would – how could – anyone do that?'

His eyes are either lowered or closed; I can't see which. 'Because the king says so.'

Oh, *really*, Richard. 'Of course he doesn't.'

His eyes, turned towards the window, are coins. 'The king is over there, and he's partying. And *she* is *dancing*.' Slowly, he gets to his feet. 'And will be, too, for a good many more hours, if Silvester's to be believed.'

I didn't try to stop him leaving; and now, across the landing, there's the cough of his own door settling into its frame. I'm at my window; I'm solidly blanket-wrapped but my bare feet have begun to ache. Hettie wants to say something – I can sense it – but I don't want to have to respond. There's no sign of life in the courtyard below, or any of the windows, doorways. This could be the end of the earth: black walls and, somewhere behind them, a vast, restless river.

Just before Christmas of my first year in the household, I was called before the queen. Twelve years ago. I was Richard's age. The queen was the age I am now; which seemed old, to me, then. Her husband had turned thirty, that year. No one knew it, but she – queen for almost two decades – was in her last few trouble-free years.

Her daughter was the reason for my summons: the five-year-old princess was too young to attend the season's feasts, and the queen wanted her to have a preview of the promised highlights, the subtleties made by the newly-appointed confectioner. I was to bring a couple of pieces that were easy to carry; or, rather, bring someone who would carry them. Geoffrey, my then-groom, walked behind me with a box containing two sugar-cast ladies buried for their own safety in flour. I'd become so nervous by the prospect of my first-ever audience with royalty that, oddly, I was angry. I suppose I felt put-upon, cornered. Tricked, even: I was a *confectioner*; I'd come here to do confectionery; why couldn't they just leave me alone to get on with it? I took it out on Geoffrey, giving him the occasional black look. Poor Geoffrey, I doubt he was feeling any better, and he was struggling with that box.

We reached her rooms and, as soon as we were announced, my apprehension dissolved into surprise: the queen was tiny; full-figured, but at least a head shorter than every other woman in the room. And yet when I rose from my curtsey it was as if she were still looking down on me. Kindly, with considerable interest. Perhaps it was the slight incline of her head, or something in her smile. It was quite a smile: despite the matronly figure, she was girlish. The princess was a miniature and slender version, from the same incline of the head down to the relaxed clasp of her hands. Nothing baby-like about her; barely child-like. Girlish, though, yes: that same lively smile. Mother and daughter, like a pair of girls. Could have been sisters. The queen spoke to her little girl in rapid but heavily-accented English – all about sugar, and feasts – but somehow simultaneously there was an undertow of something else, presumably Spanish. Speaking to her daughter in her mother-tongue, she called her *Maria*. I took a while – because of the accent – to recognize it: the 'r' lifted deftly on the tongue as if nicked by a knife. She was *Mary* and *Maria*, and her eyes switched diligently back and forth between her mother's and the subtleties. They were the same as her mother's, those eyes: the colour of an English sky.

It's strange to recall the two dancing ladies that they were admiring; how simple they were. Queen Catherine never saw subtleties of the new type of sugar paste, shining as if built from fresh snow. They belong to the reign of Anne Boleyn. Shining, and built: layers and details, gilded and gaudily-coloured. The modest figures that Queen Catherine showed her daughter had the look of frozen water and had been cast whole, small enough to hold in cupped hands.

What do I know of Spain? Oranges and lemons: the brilliant skins of soft, gnarled leather; a flare of scent from the first finger-nail-puncture. Pomegranates: burnt-looking and packed with jewels. And Queen Catherine: colourless eyes, milky skin, golden hair. Quizzical smile. How strange that she was the Spaniard; not Anne Boleyn, dark as an Arab and as sharp as a boxload of lemons. How strange that our queen is Anne Boleyn, angry-looking daughter of a jumped-up noble; not the princess of Christendom's most royal family. I do know a bit more about Spain than the oranges, lemons, pomegranates; and what I know, I know from Signor Scappi, the cardinal's cook who spent all those months with us while the cardinal investigated the king's claim for a divorce. I very much liked Signor Scappi ('*Bartolommeo*, please.'): he always had a lot to say that was interesting, despite his English initially being poor. He was an endearing mix of gravity and twinkle. Greying temples and nut-brown eyes.

When I first met him – he came to the kitchen to introduce himself to Richard and me – he said with obvious interest, 'You do not like the queen.'

I was aghast: 'I *do*, Signor Scappi!'

He shook his head. 'You, yes. But the English.'

'I *am* English. The English *do*.'

He nodded, gravely. 'But the others, no.'

I tried to explain. 'Everyone . . . *likes* her, Signor. It's just that they – these people, these others – they . . . want . . .' How to describe it? I didn't know, myself, let alone how to put it into basic English. They want favours. Or changes. Or both. For those people – those others – Anne Boleyn means favours, changes. That's all.

He said, 'The queen, she cannot –' he raised a hand, palm down, then lowered it a little: *lie low, give in.* 'You know why? Her mother. Her mother is a queen who marries a king. Together: "the Catholic kings". Together, Aragon and Castile is Spain. Her mother –' the hand again, but this time a swiping motion – 'the Arabs, from Granada.' He raised his eyebrows, looked pleased. 'Her *mother*. Again and again.' More swipings, and some approving nods. 'Strong.' A grin. 'Strong with the husband, also.' A shrug: 'You know – men.'

Richard gave me an amused glance.

Signor Scappi said, 'The queen knows of husbands. It is nothing. Some girl? Nothing. But a marriage? Everything. A country: everything.'

In time, I learned the whole story according to Signor Scappi. The queen's royal upbringing as youngest in a big, happy family. Her achievements and accomplishments: scripture, languages, music. How she was sent from her family at sixteen to England to be married; and widowed six months later. Widowed in a sleet-sodden castle on the border with Wales. Not taken back, nor taken in. No money: her father claiming he'd sent it, her father-in-law claiming it as dues. Seven years in an old house on an overgrown bank of the Thames. Strongly-worded begging letters – *My ladies are hungry* – and food parcels. And in all that time, a single new dress; black, said Signor Scappi, being all she could afford.

What Signor Scappi didn't have to tell me was how she must have felt when her dashing, eighteen-year-old brother-in-law's first act as king was to ask her to be his queen. *All happy, all good*, Signor Scappi might have said in his days of tentative English. The phrase that comes to my mind is, Knight in shining armour.

There were new dresses, suddenly, for her; lots of them. New palaces for both of them. They'd both grown up in the shadow of that wily, miserly old king; but now they were free, together. This was their new England, and it sparkled.

Signor Scappi once said of them to me, 'They are good friends.'

'Were,' I had to say . . .

He was foxed: '"War"?'

'Were.' I explained: 'Not now.'

He did understand; smiled sadly and revised, '*She* is a good friend.'

They *were* good friends, it's said, in the old days: giggling and gossiping, and talking things over until all hours. And then, when it was all over, even though she was angry with him (furious on behalf of their daughter), and even though she defied him (wouldn't send her jewels – he had to send someone to take them – nor the royal christening gown which had come with her from Spain), she *did* remain his friend, never stopping loving him or fearing for him. So people say. Well, she certainly had cause to fear for him when he fell in with hard-faced, hard-hearted Anne Boleyn, her disreputable brother and their boisterous male friends.

I simply can't imagine how she must have felt when her knight in shining armour turned tail, sending her back to a castle with no family and few comforts. Richard heard from Mr Hill, Sergeant of the cellars, that she'd requested some wine – she was back to having to write begging letters again, but this time to the man she loved – and the instruction from the king to Mr Hill was to send *new* wine. Not *no* wine. The wine would indeed arrive, but would be unpalatable.

I wanted to know, 'Why would he *do* that?'

Richard said, 'Because she's making it difficult for him.'

'But wouldn't *you*?'

He laughed. 'Of course I would.' Then he said, 'I do wonder, though, if she hasn't made her point. Now might be the time to give in gracefully and go for the nunnery.'

'She's a *wife*,' I said; not a nun. 'She's a *queen*.' Like her mother: wife and queen. And like her mother, a fighter. I should have said, This isn't about making a point, Richard; she's fighting for her life.

And now it's all over. All over, just like that, on a dreary thirteenth night. I wish Mark were here. *Why aren't you here? You're so nearly here; mere walls away. Walls, doors, gates. A whole palace away. I won't see you until tomorrow. You're hours and hours away. But who's to say that this silence isn't coming from one of your fingerpads pressed to a length of catgut? I can tell myself that's what I'm hearing: you, not playing.* I need to talk to him, but he won't talk to me. 'I've come to apologize,' was what he said, the day after his outburst. He didn't look at Richard. Richard looked at me.

'I've come to apologize,' Mark announced again.

Richard dropped his rabbit's-tail brush onto the workbench and walked from the room.

'There's no need,' I said to Mark. I didn't need an apology. For what?

He lowered his gaze and stepped up to my bench; rested a hand on it, between us. 'There's every need,' he said, quietly. 'Lucy, I swore at you.'

Christ, Lucy.

I kept my spatula moving in my bowl. 'I pushed you.'

He shook his head. 'I'm not making excuses ... Well, I *am* –' a quick, helpless smile, absurdly lovely – 'but I haven't been sleeping. I've been doing a lot of thinking.'

'What's there to think about?' *Don't think, Mark. Just do.*

'The fool I'm making of myself: that's mostly what I end up thinking about.'

'You're not. Making a fool of yourself.' I paused the spatula. 'You're no fool, Mark.'

He stepped away, began pacing the room. 'It's generous of you to say so.'

His politeness gets me down, sometimes. 'No,' I said, 'it's the truth.'

That was when he put it to me: 'You remember how I used to come here and we'd just talk about nothing?'

Did we? I suppose we did.

'Well, this might sound strange,' a ghost of that smile, 'but I long for that; at the moment, I long for it. Not that I'd ... go back. To where we were.' He leaned against the wall, folded his arms. He looked thin, and tired. 'But I long to be here and just ... well, just to be here.'

Oh, Mark, it's all I want –

And yet it was exactly what I didn't want: us, facing each other across the kitchen; him, thin and tired; me, late with some marchepane, my own rose still unfinished, unassembled in its box. And Richard, probably, outside on the staircase.

It could be worse, I suppose. Could be even colder. Windy. Pouring. As it is, the boar hides lying over our luggage are slick but the moisture's settled in the air, not falling. And a mere breeze raises the river's hackles. Nevertheless, February's no time of year to be heading onto water. I'm curling my toes to keep them awake but they're so frozen that they feel breakable. Not that a journey by road would be any more comfortable. If this move were from Whitehall to Hampton Court, not Greenwich to Whitehall, we'd have the haul through London and then along the King's Road: mud and mobs, as Richard says, although surely even he wouldn't joke after this year-solid of rain that we've had. No joke, now, the mobs that are out there in that mud.

Why move at all? Why move, now, at this time of year? What's wrong with Greenwich? Beautiful Greenwich: even on a hopeless day like today, this brickwork is jewel-red and the big bay windows velvety. The same age as I am, this palace, but, unlike me, still new. Not as magical, perhaps, as the old palace at Richmond with its twirls of turrets and weathervanes. More elegant, though, than brash Hampton Court, and more stylish than sprawling Whitehall.

Whitehall.

If we do have to go – if we really do have to – can't we get moving? This isn't the weather for sitting around in a barge.

Richard, where ARE you? How long can it take you? All these men on the riverbank, and none of them, as far as I can see, is Richard. Nor a musician; any musician: that's my guess. Not that I'd know what a musician looks like, I don't suppose. Not an off-duty one, dressed for Thames-travel. Certainly none of them looks in the least like Mark. But, then, who does?

I can already feel the feeling that I'll have when I see him, if I see him. It's here, in bud, in my stomach.

Mr Browne, pacing our barge, claps and blows on his hands, gives me a pained look. I like him, our heraldic painter. A smile of recognition, from me, albeit fleeting and rueful, for his hand-blowing. His response is to halt and look at the throng on the bank; and his looking is pointed, so that unless I turn away, I have to join him in it. Together, we take it all in. One of the king's dogs has escaped from the kennels – again; don't I recognize this one? And streaks through the crowds, grinning. Mr Browne resumes his pacing. 'Still no Richard?' He's cheerful, making conversation; we're obviously nowhere near leaving, Richard's in no danger of missing us.

I feign a helpless look. 'Busy. Such short notice, this time.' My turn to be pointed: I want him to agree with me; I want it recognized, this shortage of time for preparation; I'm cross about it.

He raises his eyebrows, allows it. But only just. 'Joseph's done a good job for you.' He nods at Joseph, who's sitting morosely in front of Hettie and me, his back to us; job done. Well, yes. 'Yes.' My precious rose is just one more subtlety, to Joseph. A tiny one, at that; untroublesome. Eased in amongst the others, somewhere in these trunks. A ruffle of blood-red petals waiting for its finishing touch, a final petal or two.

Mr Browne nods at Hettie. 'Young 'un, here: not too good, today.'

'No.'

Poor Hettie, she should be in bed, she's choked with a cold. *Look at you*: all nose; swollen, leaky nose. Her face is white where it should be pink and red where it should be pale. Not a day for being stared at. But stared at, we are. Any Royal Waterman new to the job is baffled by us: two women who aren't ladies but aren't the other kind, either; the hangers-on plying trade until the Sergeant Porter catches on and resorts to strong-arm tactics. That's definitely not us, with our downcast eyes and drab cloaks.

The swans have bustled away into the fog, most of them; put-upon. Just a few keeping watch, disdainful of all the activity, their beaks in the air and a nasty gleam in their eyes. Even swans look stooped and dull, this morning. *Come on, Richard.* How much longer? We're to travel ahead of the king; we're supposed to be at work before he arrives. And it's not as if we don't have work to do: Shrovetide, soon. Behind us, moored empty at the Privy Steps, is the king's gorgeous painted barge. Up on the steps, the flourish of stone beasts standing guard, mid-snarl, have raindrops hanging from their muzzles. Winter is everywhere like smoke. I wonder who, if anyone, is peering from the royal apartments at us settling ourselves down, wrapping ourselves up.

Richard: a flash of finery in the crowd. Hurrying towards us, but somehow also sauntering. How does he do that? Carefree, that's it, that's what he is; takes my breath away to see it, that carefreeness, and also the fact that he's not wearing a cloak. And I can see that brooch on him. Let's just hope no one else notices. He clomps onto the barge, sweeps past Hettie and me; sits down on the other side of me.

I can't ask what I want to ask, not immediately, so I say, 'You'll freeze.' It sounds like an accusation, rather than sympathy.

He won't have it; gives me a sceptical look, shakes his head. Slots his hands into his armpits.

'I mean it.' As if I'm the one to freeze him.

Earlier, back in our kitchen, I'd asked him if he'd do something for me, and he found that funny, because when – in his opinion – does he ever do anything else?

Well, that's a laugh. But, then, he was in a good mood. Which was why I felt I could ask.

We'd been told that we'd be moving to Whitehall. The official royal residence, which was probably why I'd assumed that everyone would be going. Not some hunting lodge. This wasn't a weekend away for a select gathering. Then, when Richard reappeared in buoyant spirits after a brief, unexplained absence and I remarked on his mood, he said, 'Silvester's coming; he's on the move with us.'

Silvester. That page of Sir Henry Norris's. Richard's friend.

But wasn't everyone coming?

Mark.

I asked, 'Isn't everyone coming?'

Only the king, Richard said; the king's household. Not the queen's. She's not well, he said.

I was thinking: is Mark the king's, or the queen's? I asked: could Richard find out for me if Mark was coming?

And he laughed.

And the laugh made me feel as if I were standing there naked. 'What?'

'You and Smeaton,' he mused.

My stomach nipped: *he knows.*

Oh yes? And what do you know, Richard? Tell me, what is it, exactly, that you know about love?

He said, 'You're such an odd pair, aren't you.'

And something in his manner had me wondering anew: *does he know?* All at once I felt victorious and desolate.

'Are we?' I was gentle, now; humouring him, teasing it from him.

'In your own little world,' he said, with the same fondness.

He doesn't know, I realized. Reprieve: not Mark, me, and Richard; just Mark and me, for now.

In our own little world.

Well, yes, good, because there's nowhere else I'd rather be.

Richard objected, 'Just how am I supposed to do this finding-out?'

Well, how would I know? 'You have contacts, don't you?'

He shrugged, begrudgingly, unconvinced. 'Suppose so.'

It's taken him most of the morning, but now he's here. 'Not easy,' he starts, without me prompting him. 'Not everyone is privy to Master Smeaton's movements. Correction: no one is. I had to hang around, in the end, until I saw him.'

'You *what*?' I can't have Richard hanging around the palace after men.

He's dismissive. 'Chapel.'

Oh. Hanging around chapel probably doesn't count. Couldn't he just have asked someone, though, if the musicians were coming?

Or which musicians were coming? That's what I'd envisaged: Richard asking, in conversation. Not that he'd have that kind of conversation, I suppose: a conversation about musicians. But not everyone's to know that, are they.

'And then what did you say?' *When you found him.*

He gives me a look, incredulous. 'I *said*, Lucy wants to know if you're coming to Whitehall.'

Oh, no, 'You *didn't*.'

He's round-eyed with impatience. 'But you *do*. Want to know. Don't you?'

It's said in all innocence. What I need to know is the answer; that's what's important, here.

'And he said, I've asked if I can stay.'

'"Asked if I can stay"?'

'That's what he said.'

But, 'Why?'

'Don't ask *me*.'

'You didn't ask *him*?'

'Look: he was a bit "off". Well, no, not "off"; but ... in a hurry. God knows why – I mean, *he*'s not packing, is he; it's *me* who's haring about all over the place.'

Richard, ambushing him: a mistake. My mistake. 'Did you say we were going?'

He stops to think. 'Probably not. As such. But I did say "coming", didn't I: are you *coming* to Whitehall. Wouldn't that imply that we were going?'

'And did he say anything?'

'Anything?'

'Just, anything?'

Again, he needs to stop, to think. 'No, that was it, more or less. You know – "bye". That was it.' He looks bored, now: looks around at the crowds on the bank.

'Richard, is he sick, d'you think? Did he look ill?' Because that must be it, the reason.

Richard turns back to me, his attention snagged on the river-bank; he takes a second to focus. 'It's the queen,' he says, calmly, 'who's sick. Smeaton probably thinks he can do her some good. He's one of the faithful, isn't he; rallying round.' There's no sneer; he's purely matter-of-fact. 'But I doubt anyone can help her, now. And you know what else I think?'

This barge, the other barges, the king's barge, and our packing cases: we're leaving her, I understand suddenly. That's what we're doing. This is what this is. And just as suddenly I understand why: the promised baby has melted away – her last-chance princeling – and so are we, too, now, all of us; we're moving upriver away from her.

Richard speaks into my ear. 'I think it won't do him any good at all to stay associated with her. The best thing he could do would be to move, with us; the worst thing, to stay.'

'Richard,' stop; start again; please, *please*. 'When did this happen?'

'Ten days ago.' Whispered.

'Why didn't you tell me?' I'm quieter, even, than he is.

'I did. This morning. Said she was sick.'

Sick? Sick. It sounds different when it's whispered. Heavier. Ten days ago was Queen Catherine's funeral.

He looks down as if he's not speaking at all. 'The first I knew was this morning, when we were told to pack. And, actually, "sick" is all I know. But . . .'

But this barge, these barges, the king and his household on the move. The king wouldn't be leaving, would he, if she were sick, just sick; he'd stay, help, wait.

It's over, isn't it.

Richard says, 'I don't think anyone knew, before that. If Silvester didn't know, then no one knew. Of the men, I mean. She's been in her rooms for ten days, and the women weren't saying much. Just "sick".'

A baby dropped away; as soft as butter but deadly red. Where is it, now? Where do they go, lost babies? Are they kept? Shrouded and buried. Under wraps. Or what? burned? Who does it, takes a lost baby away to lose it all over again? I've heard it said that Anne Boleyn poisoned Queen Catherine. I couldn't help but hear it; everyone says it. This, I do know: while the queen lay dead, the king was knocked cold by a fall from his horse for two days until – like a fairytale princess – he woke. Now he limps, groans, rages, nothing like a princess and not much like a king, certainly not the king that he was. And the day the queen is slid into her tomb, her usurper's baby turns to slush.

What does she make of all that, Anne Boleyn? Anne Boleyn, emptied, somewhere behind the blind, unflinching stare of her windows. Even if she isn't watching us, she'll feel the ripple of floorboards, the eddies of doors. People packing and leaving.

Mark is in there with her; she has him in there with her.

Anne Boleyn

❀❀❀

I've never been good at keeping secrets, Elizabeth; they feel too much like lies. You, though, in those earliest months, tucked away, invisible, had no choice. No one but me could know, really, about you. But for someone so tiny, you were big news – the biggest possible news – and nonchalance has never been very me. Optimism was, though, in those days, before my subsequent pregnancies turned me cautious. I didn't seriously doubt you'd survive. Hardly surprising, then, all in all, that I did drop the odd hint. The odd comet-tail of a hint.

It was another three months, though, before I could make my first victory parade of a kind. And then, marvellously, it coincided with the first parade of your own. I first recognized your somersaults for what they were, just before I walked into the world to be publicly acknowledged at last as Henry's pregnant wife and queen-to-be. George had been sent to France to gauge Francis's opinion on the matter, and he'd come back with good news. So then everything had been announced, in one go: that Henry and I were married, that I was pregnant, and my coronation was to follow. For now, though, it was the eve of Easter Sunday, and I was going to Mass. My dress alone, a month in the making, could have done the job of making me the biggest star that England had ever seen, but I'd also added diamonds. And only diamonds, for once. Diamonds swinging in my hair and scattered along my collarbones, with a beauty at the base of my throat. Diamonds ringing my wrists, cresting my fingers, clustered over my heart and roped around my waist. Annie was helping with the fastening and hooking, and it was while I was sitting very still, her hands fluttering at the back of my neck, that I first realized you were moving.

At my intake of breath, Annie said, absently, 'Sorry, did I catch you?'

When you and I stepped out of my rooms for our walk to Mass, Elizabeth, we made quite a show. Trumpeters ahead, and sixty maids of honour behind. And all around, slack-jawed nobles. No one, it seemed, had quite expected this, or perhaps not all at once: the marriage, done; the pregnancy, underway; the coronation to come in six weeks' time. As I approached, some of those faces shaped up, turned bit-lipped and bright-eyed. But others, of course, didn't. When Henry had made his announcement, he'd suggested that they all come to me after Mass with their congratulations. So, they had to; every one of them. Some seemed giddied; others, strained and careful. It could have been fun, I suppose, but by that time I was exhausted. Sickness was no longer a problem, but my wonderful dress was dismayingly tight and I was desperate to strip off and sink into a bath.

I took a lie-in, the following morning, to recover. Claimed I was fighting off a cold. Henry seemed unbothered but my mother was soon at my bedside, clucking that I should be feeding a cold and starving a fever. At her request came a special delivery from the Privy Kitchen. When I'd got rid of her, I put the tray aside. But then it was George's turn to barge in and sit on my bed, in his case attempting to perk me up with gossip. I had to confess that this was just a lie-in.

Give me an hour, I said.

And then I lay there and imagined I could hear beyond the clamour of my own household. Beyond the distant chatter of the women who waited on me and the girls who were my wards. Beyond the murmurings, somewhere, of my chaplains and physician; the clattering of cooks below and stablehands outside. A whole, huge household, up and running around me. I listened beyond them, listened hard into an England-sized, England-shaped silence. *Was* it silence? Or was it full of the prayers that Henry had decreed be said for me – for 'Queen Anne' – in every church, that morning? Did people out there in England even know who I was? Were there some – lots, perhaps, away from London and our usual routes – who were turning to their neighbours at that very moment and whispering, *Is Queen Catherine dead, then?*

My Uncle Norfolk and his old partner in crime, Charlie, had been sent three days previously to break the news to Catherine that Henry and I were married and expecting a baby at the end of the summer. They told her that she was back to being what she'd been, all those years ago, when Henry's brother had died: 'Princess Dowager'. Her reaction? She wasn't the king's subject, she informed the perpetually embarrassed Norfolk and Suffolk, but his wife; she wasn't subject to his rulings. Until the Pope ruled otherwise, she was still Queen of England, which was how her staff would continue to address her. To me, at the time, this little stand of hers seemed laughable: as if it mattered what they called her, her staff banished up there in Bedfordshire.

Now, of course, I understand it. The stand was made for her daughter. If Catherine accepted that the royal marriage had in fact been no marriage, then the princess was a bastard. No prim new prefix of 'Lady' could hide that. Despite her much-vaunted faith, Catherine must have known for a long time that, in her own case, the game was up: Henry would never again love her, nor, probably, even see her; and her all-powerful but busy nephew had less and less time for an ageing aunt he'd never known, whose casting aside had happened years back. She had no future: that, for herself, I suspect, she could accept. Not, though, for her daughter.

The divorce hearing, in the end, was deliberately low-key, despite the presence of the archbishop and various notable, amenable clergy. It took place in Dunstable, local to Catherine; near enough for her to come with no ceremony when she was sent for. But she refused, of course, to attend. She was still appealing to Rome: a tactic now forbidden, in law, for any subject of the king, but we know her views on that. In the last week of May, Thomas returned from Dunstable to make his announcement in Lambeth Palace: the divorce was done.

And I was ready to go. The very next day, I sailed in the queen's barge to the Tower, because tradition demanded that we spend a couple of days celebrating there before the procession back through London to Westminster and my coronation. Jostling for position alongside my barge were all the barges of the City Guilds draped with awnings and carpets, and crammed with musicians. It was no easier on land, I learned later: the crowded streets were crunchy with broken glass because no window could withstand the unrelenting, celebratory cannon-fire. Out there on the water, I couldn't even hear myself laughing.

Henry was already at the Tower, poised for a very public greeting. When he'd helped me ashore, he placed his big hands gently on my bump. We were home and dry, and, for all that laughing out there on the water, I was secretly relieved.

The Tower, previously so damp and dingy, had been transformed by the year's-worth of work we'd had done in readiness. The next day, our festivities continued with a round of knightings, as if this were the coronation of no mere consort but of a true regent. The message from Henry, unbelievable though it now seems, was loud and clear: he and I were partners.

The day I left the Tower, the day of my ceremonial return to London, started badly for me with a barely contained clash with Dad. Mum was in my parents' room, dressing. For no reason that I could fathom, Dad had come into my suite, which was unusual for him – he's a man who keeps his distance – and he was pacing. In an adjoining room, I was still being dressed, my white-gold gown with its extra panel being fitted over my bump. I have to admit: I hated the drastic change in my shape. I was busy making my feelings known when Dad barked through the open doorway, 'You should think yourself lucky.'

It was the tone: it was vicious.

Luck. As if it had all fallen into my lap. But luck had had nothing to do with it. I *hadn't* been lucky: seven years and a break with Rome, just to marry the man I loved? I'd denied myself seven years, working long and hard for this coronation and for this first pregnancy of mine to be legitimate. How *dare* he stand there and put me down as if I were some giddy girl like my sister. As if I should be grateful. Well, I wasn't grateful. If anything, I was furious. Even on that day of celebration, I was furious, underneath, at all those bastards. Of whom, I was beginning to see, my own father was one.

I yanked myself free of Annie and stalked to the doorway, the better to let fly my accusation. 'You actually resent this, don't you.' *My success.*

He deflected it with an elaborate roll of his eyes; those black-flash Boleyn eyes. 'Don't start.'

'You started it.'

Behind me, George sounded a warning, 'Anne . . .'

Nice try, George, but he's asking for it.

Dad lobbed his next barb over my shoulder: 'And *you* . . .'

The vehemence in it took me with it, turned me around: *George.* Then I was back, quick, to Dad. 'Him, *what*?'

Suddenly, Dad looked sheepish. I saw that he didn't know: he didn't know *what*. He just didn't like us: that's what I saw.

George reached around me and closed the door; closed it, didn't slam it. 'Now's not the time,' was all he said.

I whirled, wounded, but he was gently emphatic: 'I don't want to hear it. Not now. Forget it. Leave the old sod to stew.' His smile was sad, but affectionate. He indicated my unfastened gown. 'Come on, get dressed.'

True: it was the dress that people would come to see; I was under no illusions about that. On the brink of queenship, I needed to seem both girl and goddess. A white-gold dress, but with a jewel-wild bodice. And on my still-uncrowned head, a soft circlet of jewels. Around my neck, pearls, but each as big and luminous as a blind iris. And dropping down from that single string, a rosebud of a diamond. I had no worries that I'd fail to live up to expectations – to surpass them – as I was borne through the crowds: the centrepiece in a half-mile procession of just about every knight, bishop and ambassador, of anyone who was anyone, in England.

And indeed the people of London did look and look. But it was all they did: gawp, bug-eyed and open-mouthed. Not, themselves, a pretty sight. Great stretches of them between the various displays at crossroads and City gates: the pageants, oratories, and child-choirs at which – despite my ferociously nagging bladder – I had to stop and respond appropriately, acting gracious and delighted. Between those distractions, the only sound beyond our horses was the tinkling of my canopy's tiny silver bells. Once, the king's fool could contain himself no longer and hollered into the crowd, 'What's up with you lot? Scurvy heads?' And then a few caps were removed, but reluctantly.

It seemed to take all day to get to Westminster Hall, to Henry, and I've never been so glad of a cuddle, some sugary tit-bits and a glass of mulled wine. And oh the joy of changing from that dress before being spirited away through a back door and onto the river for a secret journey to Whitehall and bed. I could hardly speak, by then, for weariness.

The next day was the big one, and this time I was on foot, walking from Westminster Hall to the Abbey in the company of a different crowd: England's abbots, Greenwich's monks, and the choir of the Chapel Royal. The smallest boys were the most grave, and I noticed Mark Smeaton keeping an anxious eye on them. Following me, this time, was just one elderly lady: my grandmother carried my crimson train. Yes, the doughty Dowager Duchess herself stepped forward from what was becoming a fragmented family to show England just what the Norfolks could be made of. Her stepson, my uncle, had claimed he had to be in France on business; and, as ever, his ex-wife, Liz, was somewhere else, stewing in her own bitter juices. (That woman will refuse to attend her own funeral.) But their wonderful son came: Hal, back from Paris, especially. I'm not sure it wasn't the best moment of my day: catching sight of a so very grown-up Hal, blowing him a kiss and getting a gorgeous shy smile in return.

Pregnant and velvet-heavy, I was thankful for Grandma's slow pace. I even turned quite dreamy in the warmth and glow of our cloth-of-gold canopy. We followed the red carpet into the Abbey and all the way up to the ceremonial chair where dutiful Thomas held the crown. And then, with that too-big crown on my head – my bespoke one wasn't ready – I had to concentrate on sitting straight and stock-still through the Te Deum.

The celebratory banquet was back at Westminster Hall. No fun for me, alone at a table on a dais with a good view of everyone else enjoying themselves. I watched my brother begin telling jokes: mischievously conspiratorial, then basking in the boys' appreciative roars. Meg Shelton looked sweetly uncertain how to respond, flushed with a daring that she couldn't quite indulge. Harry Norris swooped to her rescue, drawing her into conversation. I was without my own Henry, because a king never attends his queen's coronation. Because it's hers. But I knew he'd be watching – probably with Tom Cromwell – from above, in one of the hall's screened galleries. The two of them surveying us and congratulating themselves on their hard-won success. Granted: this victory was theirs at least as much as it was mine.

I did my duty, did my best to sample most of the dishes, swallowing into heartburn. Eventually, I wanted nothing but to rest my elbows on the table and my head in my hands. I'd never been so glad to detect the final flourish, the bringing out of the subtleties. That was, until I saw them. The problem was that, for the briefest moment, I didn't know what to make of them. They were ships, and there were so many of them. In my exhausted but heightened state, I was baffled as to what the confectioner might mean by it. How would the coming reign of Anna Regina – which was to be prosperous and stable – be associated with any such fleet, with such a show of nautical strength? Did those ships represent Catherine's threatened Armada?

No one else seemed worried. Everyone looked enchanted by the vast, glittering display. All the more glittering because the confectioner had left them uncoloured. Unmanned, too, despite being fabulously detailed. Their ghostly pallor and the vacancy of them somehow made them more breathtaking than if they had been perfect replicas. People reached to touch them, to test them. I glimpsed a tiny white barrel rolling beneath Meg's fingertip along an iced deck. A lattice of rigging rang to the tapping fingernail of the French Ambassador.

Having suffered through the formal ceremonies, I made sure of plenty of my own-style celebrations. This was to be my summer, before my confinement in August. So, in June and July, at

Whitehall and Greenwich, we partied. Strictly no clergy. One day came news which threatened to spoil our fun. Henry's sister had died. It wasn't entirely unexpected news: she'd been ill for quite some time, no one being able to fathom the cause. Charlie had agreed to do the honours at my coronation, acting as High Constable of England for the day and heading the procession, but that very evening he'd returned to Suffolk, to her bedside, and we hadn't seen him or heard from him since.

We sent our respects by return, but then it wasn't hard for me to persuade Henry that there was nothing to be gained from cancelling our picnic. No one else demurred. Henry's sister, not much older than me, had become someone in her latter years who belonged to a previous era.

With her death, the ranks of my enemies were reduced by one, which is never a bad thing. She'd been the least of my troubles, though. She hadn't liked me, was all. There'd been no rallying of troops behind her. Unlike, if rumours were to be believed, the Mad Nun. Not 'troops', exactly, in the Mad Nun's case, either, but the Exeters. And who knew where the Exeters might lead. They'd been conspicuously absent from my coronation. For the Mad Nun to froth at the mouth in Canterbury was one thing. It was quite another for her to pal up with the Exeters, who were suspected with good reason of traitorous views as to their place in the line of succession. That first glorious summer when I was queen, I had a feeling that wasn't so much unease as irritation. I meant to start as I wanted to go on: with attention to detail. I didn't want to slip up.

So, I had a conversation with Tom Cromwell about the Mad Nun. Caught up with him one day in the Privy Gallery and asked him if I should be worried about her. I should have known better, because his response was typical, verging on the smug. 'If anyone does need to worry about her, it'll be me.'

'Well, all right,' I quelled my impatience, 'but do you? Are you?'

A vigorous shake of that big head, jowls a-quiver. 'No.' Dismissive, again. Amused.

I recounted what I'd heard.

He was almost bursting with his own weird kind of pleasure, his eyes and lips shiny. 'You think I haven't heard all that? That, and a lot more, besides.'

Well, what?

He flapped a hand. 'It's all under control.' Then more bonhomie: 'What d'you think I do all day?' From his pile of papers, he drew a pamphlet. 'See this?'

'What is it?' He knew very well that I wouldn't be able to read the Latin.

'This,' he said, 'is our own dear Father Peto, now in Amsterdam, preaching the validity of the king's first marriage.' He raised a finger, to halt me. 'No need to get outraged. You've already heard the man call you Jezebel.' Remembering himself, he added, 'If you don't mind me bringing it up.'

Which, for some reason, made me laugh.

'We know what the man thinks, and we know we won't change his mind. You're not going to tell me that terror over what Father Peto is saying is keeping you awake at night?'

Again, it was ridiculous, and I had to laugh.

'The man's a lunatic, agreed? What *is* interesting, though, is who's funding him. Who's putting the money where Peto's mouth is.' He flicked at the pamphlet. 'Who, in other words, paid for this?'

'Well, who *did*?'

Now it was as if I'd said something funny. 'Give me time,' he said, sliding the pamphlet back into the pile. 'This only came this morning.' Then, just when I'd assumed he'd finished, he added, 'It might be Thomas More.'

'More?' It made sense. His views were well-known, of course, despite his reticence, and then there'd been his absence from my coronation.

Tom raised the finger again. '*Might* be, I said. Whoever it turns out to be, what's important is that it isn't ever about just one person: one mad woman, or one principled man. You, Anne, take things personally. But it's never about just one person. They all have their place in a network. It's the whole network I want.' And then he was on his way again.

Elizabeth, little Virgo, you were born just two weeks into my confinement. You and I denied them the satisfaction of keeping us weighed down, cooped up, in that Greenwich room for a month. You, like me, I suspect, aren't one to sit back while life goes on elsewhere. I imagine their intentions were fair enough, to make a place where I'd feel rested and safe. And perhaps other women do feel like that about their confinements; but, then, I'm not other women, am I. Despite its luxury, I hated it: the heavy curtains, remaining drawn on midwives' orders; the ever-burning brazier, again on midwives' orders. But what I hated most about it was who was in it with me. Women. Only women. I don't enjoy the unmitigated company of women. And especially not of one woman in particular: my brother's wife. I was denied my brother's presence, but Jane Parker was there, all day every day. The wife he didn't want, a woman no one much wanted, yet I – at my most vulnerable – was lumped with her. And didn't she know it. Forever sitting herself down on my bed. Presumptuous and insinuating, muscling in and laying claim to her supposed privilege: sister-in-law. She was all eyes: whenever I opened or moved mine, there were hers, pooled with whatever little light there was in that gloomy room. It was such a thrill to her: our enforced proximity and intimacy, and the coming drama in which she couldn't fail to snatch a part. Worse, she wouldn't stop trying to be chummy with me about George, adopting the manner of the exasperated wife: raised eyebrows and rolled eyes; we two girls against him. Well, I wasn't against him. Never had been and never would be.

But if I missed George and our friends – and oh I did – my separation from Henry was unbearable. We'd not been apart since our marriage, but suddenly, when I needed him most, we couldn't see each other for a month. Yet I knew he was there, close by, in the same building. How odd it was, to have to settle for news of him. News of what he and the boys were up to. Nothing much, but so much more than I was managing. News, perhaps, of a particular meal or tennis game: something quite incidental, but it was detail that I thirsted for. I drank it down, both elated and stung.

And so the boys' lives spun on in lazy but elegant circles as they marked time, waiting for the moment when someone would arrive with the answers to their questions: a live child, or not; a live queen, or not; a prince, or not. That was all they had to do: play, and wait. But me, I was stuck, breathless and swollen, knowing that I'd suddenly be called upon to climb a mountain.

Did Henry miss me? As I missed him? Did he have this faint ache behind his eyes? This weight in his chest? Or was his life busy enough to distract him, in all but the quietest moments? But in those quietest moments, then what? *Did he miss me?* All my moments were quiet, now, despite my women-friends' best efforts. For me, women's chatter was no substitute for George's hard-edged jokes or Harry's wry attentiveness. Even my women-friends' music-making: it was competent, but that was all it was. They'd exercise themselves on the lute and the virginals, make an effort for me; but I'd find myself thinking of Mark Smeaton's singing, the ease and yet the perfection of it, how it would slip inside my mind and take me somewhere with it before I'd realized. My curtained retreat rang mostly, though, with the rasps of my comb: there was little that could be done for me, at this stage, apart from tidying my hair. 'Oh, let *me*,' was my sister-in-law's refrain.

I had even quieter moments, of course, when I feigned dozing or was in fact falling asleep or waking; and then, with the room silenced, I could feel close to Henry. I'd talk to him, under my breath. Take him wandering through conversations. One day, I asked Annie to get me one of his shirts, worn. Later that same afternoon, in it came: one of his tennis shirts, silky-thin linen heavy with his scent. When I held it to my face, it was as if a key turned somewhere inside my head: the instant twin sensations of fit and give. For that instant, everything was all right. The women laughed at me, I know; I couldn't fail to know, because they made so much of it. It was far from secret, that fond laughter of theirs; on the contrary, a kind of celebration: I was human, after all.

Elizabeth, about you not being a boy: don't believe what people might tell you. It's easy to assume that your father and I were devastated. That the birth of a girl was a great disgrace, a tremendous blow. Not at all. We were disappointed, yes, but only because if you'd been a boy, you'd have solved a lot of our problems. Your being a girl didn't create any.

So, the news for the country was: not a prince, this time; but a healthy girl. Nothing had gone wrong, and the future remained . . . well, remained the future, close by and no less bright than it had ever been. In the meantime, Henry couldn't help himself: he was stupid over you, his pearl-nosed piece of perfection. It was he who chose your name: his mother's, which also happened to be my mother's.

And me? I was aware of everyone's surprise at how I was, but theirs was nothing compared to mine. I'd never considered myself maternal, and had feared myself the opposite. But there I was, smitten. You drew me into your dense blue searches of my face. Touching you was like skimming a fingertip over warm milk. Your trust in me was spellbinding as you slept curled towards my heartbeat. You slept for me like you'd sleep for no one else; none of those know-it-all busybodies. They were nothing to you; you wanted your mother. You *knew* me.

I didn't want you wet-nursed: yes, *me*, for whom pregnancy had been tedious and repugnant. But above all, I'm practical, and *I* had milk. No one would hear of it. They didn't say, at the time – how could they, to a woman who'd just gone through her first labour? But, I suppose, their minds were already on the next pregnancy, the possible prince. In their eyes, my job with you was done.

At three days old, you were taken in your great-grandmother's arms to your christening. Bundled in ermine and purple velvet, you went through the garden down the gallery once so beloved of Catherine to the Observant Friars. And there, especially for you, was a font of solid silver. I'd been distracted, fussing no end, as you were taken; so it's your return that I remember. My grandmother is a woman who knows how to make an entrance. Her presence is undiminished – perhaps enhanced – by age. I'd have liked to have lived as long as she has, to have had the chance to continue her legacy of fearless, fearsome Norfolk women. Now it's down to you, alone, little one. It didn't matter in the least to Grandma that you were a girl: that's what I saw, in her face, when she handed you back to me. Well, *she*'d been a girl, hadn't she? Hers is a face that'll disappear when she dies; there are no portraits of her. It's her weaselly-faced stepson, my uncle, who'll stare grimly down the generations, representative of the Norfolks. But she's the one who's made this family. Looking into her eyes, I could see that we were agreed: a tough woman is worth several men. And even then, you looked likely to be a tough woman. Yes, her expression said to me, boys had to be had; but they'd come.

I did come round to the idea of another baby, and quickly. If it'd mean a brother for you, I'd do it. You'd be more secure. In December, in the lull before Christmas, the lovely cradleful of you was whisked away from me, in Margaret Bryan's experienced hands. To Hatfield, into your own household. Time for you to stop being my baby and start being England's princess. Henry sent your half-sister along to learn her place, which was behind you, looking after you. I made sure to send someone to look after *her*: My aunt, Anne Shelton, who loathed her, and whom she loathed. By Christmas, I was Hever-dreaming again, which I put down to the lurch of separation from my firstborn and perhaps to the eddies of festivities. But, in fact, just three months after you'd been born, I was already pregnant again.

It would've been nice to be able to take it easy; but the old Spanish sow, with her instinct for bad timing, chose to start making life difficult again. Heaven forbid that Henry should forget her during the coming festive season. She sent word that

Buckden – damp, chilly Buckden – was doing her health no good at all; and now that winter was slamming in, she needed to be moved. She wouldn't have guessed that Buckden was *meant* to be doing her health no good at all. Henry read her letter aloud, as I'd asked. He remained expressionless as he read. With a feeling somewhere between sinking and flaring, I assumed I'd have to do it yet again: cajole him to be tough with her. But as soon as he'd finished, he crumpled it and said, 'Well, she's asked to move; so, move, she shall.' There was almost no consideration before he decided, 'Somersham.' Even I was surprised. I've never visited Somersham Castle – why on earth would I? But I know where it is. Near Ely. Soaking up the North Sea. Henry was certainly getting the idea.

Problem was, Chapuys got it, too. Somehow – as ever – he heard very quickly of the plan, and requested an audience with Henry. Henry alone, was his idea of an audience; but that wasn't part of the deal. Henry and I were partners, and especially in this matter. We were talking about a woman who was claiming my queenship. Nevertheless, I decided that dignified silence from me would be appropriate. Intimidating, even. So, I sat there, and he – as ever – ignored me.

'No,' he said, as soon as Henry confirmed for him the Somersham plan. 'She's ill, she's frail, and that place is worse than Buckden. If you do go ahead with this latest proposed banishment, we'll look upon it very, very badly.' A dark look, from him; a hilariously Spanish look.

I wanted to slap him, to bring him to his senses. What business of his, of Spain's, was it? The woman hadn't been in Spain since she was a child, and now she was an old woman. She was England's problem, and required the English solution of a freezing, dripping castle. To my amazement, Henry didn't sigh, didn't sulk or bluster, but gave the impression that Chapuys' objection was nothing to him. He shrugged, unconcerned. 'Fotheringhay, then.' He hadn't skipped a beat.

I held my breath, and fixed on Chapuys.

Chapuys, head cocked; Chapuys – foreigner – disoriented. 'Where it is?'

'Northamptonshire,' Henry breezed, and I marvelled at how he'd managed to make the word sound warm, comforting.

Chapuys wouldn't know, *couldn't* know what that place was like; because how could a Spaniard even begin to imagine?

Catherine, though, had lived here long enough and travelled here sufficiently to know that the offer of Northamptonshire wasn't the helping hand she'd hoped for, but a nasty twist of the forearm. And she responded how she always responded: refusal. You'd have thought I'd have been used to it – and, of course, in a way, I was – but I had less and less patience for it. We were years and years on, now, and I'd become Henry's wife, England's queen, the mother of the heir and mother-to-be of another. The Catherine situation was supposed to be over. Everything that could be done – and plenty that couldn't – *had* been done, to resolve it. And yet there she was, trying to hold back or even turn back time. And she was taking others with her. There were people – many, many of them – who still called her queen; people who believed that England had another queen, another princess. It was as if there was a separate, second kingdom.

Henry said I was being ridiculous. '*You* are queen,' he'd say. 'We've put all that behind us.'

And I'd say, 'That's exactly where she is, right behind us. Dogging us, haunting us.'

It was time for her to be visited by someone: someone who'd make her do as she was told. Who else, but Charlie? It was always Charlie's job. And just because he was a newlywed, that December, was no reason for him to be excused. On the contrary, it was reason enough for him to be volunteered. Three months bereaved of the ex-starlet, he'd remarried. But – wait – that's not it, or not all of it: his new bride was his own son's fourteen-year-old fiancée.

His typically po-faced response to raised eyebrows was, She's very mature for her age. Actually, he was right: she was. Where he was wrong was in thinking Kate Willoughby was the one we were all concerned for. She's canny, clever; very. In many ways, her marrying him was a Godsend. She makes him think, which doesn't come naturally to him. She's made something of him, and this late in his life, which is no mean achievement but just one of her many. He's a better man for having married her, and it's done her no harm; she flourishes as was always clear that she would.

Nor was it as if I was touchy about the memory of the ex-starlet. Charlie's boy was the one I felt for. We all did. He was already unwell by then, but his father's betrayal and the sudden loss of Kate clearly took their toll. He was around the same age as Fitz, and they seemed to have the same sickness. That same awful, bloodied cough. Henry and I found it excruciating to witness the state of Fitz. No way could we ever have done anything to distress him. Our sole aim was to ensure as much pleasure for him as possible in his remaining years. As it happened, that autumn he'd come home to us from Paris, accompanied by his beloved boyhood friend, Hal; and we'd married him to Maria, my darling cousin and Hal's little sister. In that way, we layered family around him, and kept alive his prospect of a future. Charlie's boy, though, had had his family pull away and his future swiped from him.

Henry called for Charlie and gave him the job.

'Now?' was all Charlie asked, incredulous. No doubt an entire pre-Christmas drinks season was flashing before his eyes.

'Now,' Henry confirmed, buoyant, his enthusiasm implying that this was a crucial expedition being entrusted to his trustiest noble.

And so off Charlie had to go, riding out into December, towards what must have felt like the ends of the earth and a reception that he knew would be, to say the least, chilly. Not something to which Charlie was accustomed: a woman displeased to see him. If you don't count me, that is.

We heard nothing of him for almost a week. It was as if he'd been swallowed up somewhere between the beacon of our Christmassy court and that distant, stony castle. Kate looked dazed. Going through the motions. No longer a single girl, but having to go through the most sociable weeks of the year with no husband nor any news of him. By contrast, her ex-, her new stepson, was putting his heart and soul into the season; and, probably, in consequence, a fair bit of his blood into his hand-kerchief. On the solstice, word came.

Henry scanned the letter, giving me the gist. 'She's locked herself in,' he said, grimly.

I had no idea what he meant. 'In where?' I visualized a draw-bridge, drawn.

He glanced up at me. 'Her rooms.'

I was still confused. 'Where's Charlie?'

Laying the letter in his lap, he said, emphatically, 'On the other side of the door.'

I half-laughed. 'Can't he break it down?'

He sighed, irritated. 'And how would that look?'

'A lot better than standing on the other side of it,' I snapped back. 'What's he *doing* there?'

'Talking to her.' Curt; back to the letter.

'Yes, but is she listening to him?'

Henry said nothing.

I grabbed the letter. 'He's dismissed most of her servants,' I read. The drawbridge again, this time with Catherine's servants dejectedly trooping across it.

Henry wondered aloud, 'Why do that?'

'Because they bolster her, Henry. Addressing her as queen. Without them, she's –' I was going to say 'nothing', but clearly that wasn't true, 'less.' I handed him back the letter, and asked, 'What will you tell him?'

'To keep trying.' He pursed his lips. 'I want her out of there.'

I went to find Kate, to check that she'd also had a letter. She had. She asked me, 'Will he be back for Christmas, do you think?'

All I could do was shrug.

Christmas Day came and went: no Charlie. Actually, I'd forgotten about him; but then I remembered, spotting Kate sitting with some other girls in a corner of the Presence Chamber, glasses in hands, listening to Mark Smeaton's virginals-playing. I wondered if there was mulled wine for Charlie in that servant-depleted castle.

Three days later, we received another missive. Not only had there been no mulled wine for Charlie, but there'd been trouble. The dismissed servants had trooped across that drawbridge and, inevitably, into the nearest village, where they'd told their tale of woe. Which then spread, as tales of woe do, to other villages. By dusk on Christmas Day, scores of villagers had gathered at the moat to protect the woman they thought of as their queen, perhaps still *knew* as their queen. (Who – up there – would have told them differently? Priests were supposed to; but priests, of course, tell people whatever they choose to tell them.) And there they remained.

'This is *ridiculous*,' I protested to Henry: Charlie, trapped between vigilante villagers and a locked door. I might not have liked Charlie, but nor did I relish the prospect of half of Bedfordshire threatening a lone nobleman. Not just any nobleman, but the Duke of Suffolk. And, anyway, their brute loyalty annoyed me. That they imagined her a sick woman, wronged and harried. That there could be no such feeling for me, who was flush with success and love and pregnancy.

Henry merely laughed, although not particularly happily. 'Poor Charlie,' he said, and paused before adding, 'I think he should just come home.'

And finally, on the thirty-first, he did. Those smooth looks of his, ruffled. His eyes as shadowed as those of his son.

For Charlie, it'd been a rough Christmas, but now it was all over. Whereas for me and Henry, as ever, it continued. The Spaniard wouldn't last all that much longer, but then there was that daughter of hers. Mary was every inch her mother's daughter: intent on carrying the dispute into the next generation. Believe me: I'd tried, with Mary. I'd tried being nice, when I married her father and was crowned. I'd sent her a long letter: only accept the situation, I said, only accept me, and bygones can be bygones. A clean slate seemed the only way forward, to me. And it seemed, if I might say so, a generous offer. Not so, apparently, to Mary's mind. Her reported response was, shall we say, robust.

So, we'd switched tactics. To tough. Henry informed her that unless she accepted the situation, she wouldn't be allowed to see her mother, and she wouldn't have her father's love. Back came a typically tight-lipped response: although it pained her more than she could ever say, she regretted that she had no choice.

Henry's response was mixed. On the one hand, I could see, even though he tried to hide it, he was shocked. He was naive, believing anyone and everyone would come around. Even her. On the other hand, he was learning, and I suspect he'd half-expected this high-handed brush-off. Certainly it was no news to him that she was as stubborn as her mother. Not that it made it any easier for him to read that letter. Which, incidentally, he didn't let me read for myself.

I needed to act quickly. I insisted he take her at her word. Send her to Hatfield, I said, to take second place to Elizabeth, and don't – *don't*, whatever you do – see her. Don't give in. Don't pander to these histrionics. I told him: she says she's made her choice; now let her feel the consequences. Let her see how she likes it. Then we'll see. He said nothing. Dead-eyed. Flinching from me. As if it were my fault. Listen, I said: she can't be any daughter of yours unless she accepts the life you now have. The family you now have, was what I meant. Unless she accepts your authority, I added: a deft but belated switch into a language he'd understand. And he did suddenly sit a bit taller. If you meet her halfway on this, I said, you're making a bed to lie in. A rod for your own back. All those tired words, but all of them true.

'Yes, yes,' he allowed, in the end, as if he were granting me something. When all I'd been doing was thinking of him.

I'd concentrated on sounding as if I were reasoning my way through a problem, but actually I could have killed her. I'm practical, remember, and her death was beginning to seem the most practical solution. It was her own fault: she was leaving me precious few options.

Around this time, after one of his rides out to Hatfield, Henry didn't come to me on his return. When word reached me that he was back, I had to go as far as his bathroom to find him. Harry Norris was attending him; he rose from the low tiled wall on which he'd been hunkered. Behind him, Henry was in the sunken bath. And he was oddly blank-faced. Panic flushed me.

'What is it?' I demanded, from the doorway. 'What's wrong with Elizabeth?'

Henry pursed his lips. '*Nothing's* wrong with Elizabeth.' There was a nastiness in how he said it: viciously dismissive; a put-down, a slap down. Declining to meet my eyes, he moved away in the water: an infuriating swanning.

Which didn't stop me. 'You're sure? *Henry?* You wouldn't just not tell me?'

He had his back to me. 'Nothing's *wrong* with *Elizabeth*.'

Ah: Mary. Of course: *Mary*. I'd forgotten her. 'Something wrong with Mary, then,' I ventured.

He glanced back at me, but only to shake his head and mutter, 'Nothing that's not normally wrong with Mary.' Reluctant to let me in on it.

I made my way across the steam-slick tiles to the top of the bath's steps. 'I *told* you: *don't* let Mary muck you about.'

His gaze slunk up to mine, eyes dense with distrust. 'She *didn't*. *I* didn't.' Then, hands in his hair, slicking it back from his damp forehead, he came clean: 'I . . . saw her.' The eyes changed, a little. 'She'd been watching me, Anne.' Pleading: that was what it was, in his eyes. 'From a balcony in the yard. Watching me getting ready to go. She was kneeling. Stayed there, on her knees. Head bowed. And I had to turn from her and go.'

'And *did* you?' I whirled to Harry. '*Did* he?'

Harry simultaneously froze and nodded.

If Henry hadn't been out there in the water, I'd have slapped him. Stupid man. Typical man. Is it so very hard to kneel, to bow a silly little head? To hold the pose for a few moments while it had the desired effect? And Henry, of course, had fallen for it.

Nothing, *nothing*, can convey how furious I felt, not at that one coy display – she could kneel all she liked – but at the whole, relentless situation. I should have been getting on with relaxing into my second pregnancy, but instead I was . . . *clenched*. Imagine having found your soulmate – the luck of it, the joy of it – and, against gargantuan odds, having married him. Then comes a stunning baby, plus a second on the way. Imagine being at the same time at the very top, doing the job you always knew you'd do better than anyone else. Now imagine a mad old woman claiming that none of it was ever yours to have: it's all hers. And, unbelievably, she has the ear of the people, and their hearts; she has them under a spell that you, for all your cleverness, can't break.

It was so nearly there, that perfect life of mine; *so* nearly. Yet 'nearly there' meant it wasn't there. I felt cheated of the life I could be having, if it weren't for the Spaniard and her daughter. Thumping like a heartbeat in me was, *If not for them, if not for them*. I was feeling bereft of that life I could have had. It should never have happened like this: my prince coming to me with an old bride and a charmless child dragging behind him. If only he'd never married her. If only he hadn't been so keen to prove himself, to make the grand gesture, at seventeen, by marrying her.

Sometimes I got so low that I'd have to remind myself: the Spaniard and her daughter were just people. Bodies. If the worst came to the worst, two bodies wouldn't be so hard to get out of the way.

Lucy Cornwallis

❖❖❖

SPRING 1536

This is mine; or for now, it is. A step that I like to sit on, in a passageway no one seems to know. One of the forgotten corners of Whitehall. Funny, that: the busier the palace, the more chance of finding backwaters like this. If I lean forwards, I can glimpse the Thames. It looks still but of course it's slipping by, soundless, on its way down to Greenwich. Often carrying the king's barge. Even in my occasional few minutes, here, on my even rarer leanings-forward, I've seen the blur of colours that's his barge. Now that we're all here at Whitehall, the whole royal household, the king seems always to be down at Greenwich. With box-loads of my confectionery. The orders are passed down to me, *A banquet for ten, please, Mrs Cornwallis, packed for the barge.*

Banquet for twelve.

Eight.

Small banquets, these, but almost daily. It's hard to keep up. Eventually, in my innocence, I asked Richard, 'What's all this, with Greenwich?'

He told me: the king has Jane Seymour at Greenwich. He made Cromwell give up his apartment for her and her family.

Her family? I didn't understand.

Visits are chaperoned, Richard said. 'Which is how you know this is serious. This is no mistress.'

Again, I didn't understand, I needed to ask, So, what is she, then? But already he was protesting, 'Have you *seen* Jane Seymour? I know, I know, I know what you're going to say, "looks aren't everything", and I quite agree, or half-agree – but fish-face Seymour! I mean, it has to be said, the queen's no beauty but –' But suddenly he was asking, 'What?'

157

Which made me jump. 'What?' I fired back.

'You look . . . Are you all right?'

'Oh,' I said. 'I'm . . . tired. This –' I slammed down my spatula, disgusted with it, helpless. Everything is trickier to do, lately. Impossible to do. I'm losing my touch.

He headed over to me, and there was a cautiousness in his approach that made me wary. 'It's perfect,' he said.

'But it won't –' *Look! – stick.*'

'It's sticking, Lucy,' he said, easily. 'Look,' he soothed. 'Look, look,' and in his hands it was fine.

I looked away, across the muddle of the kitchen. 'It's not easy, all this.'

'It's Lent.' There was an exasperated smile in his voice. 'It's our quietest time of year. Go.' A watchful, indulgent smile. 'Out. Take some time to yourself. You're . . . tired.'

And that was the day I found this step of mine. Yesterday, I ventured further, went to see the queen's Privy Cook; found my way to the twin Privy Kitchens and went into the queen's. I walked in there, directly beneath her apartment. He was busy admonishing some boy, '. . . and I don't want to have to tell you twice.' I interrupted, and, predictably, he was surprised to see me. I'd come, I explained, to ask if the queen would like any confectionery. Seeing as the two households – king's and queen's – seem to be separate, now. Not that I said so. Nor did I spell it out: I'm getting my orders from the king's kitchen, but not the queen's. He frowned at the floor, as if he were thinking; but when he looked up, he seemed to have forgotten what I'd asked.

'So, does she?' I prompted. 'Does she need any confectionery?' I decided to say it: 'Because at the moment, it's all going to Greenwich.'

'Well.' He looked worried. 'She's not very sweet-toothed, is she?'

How would *I* know? *He's* her chief cook.

He sighed. 'Maybe something for the ladies.'

'Anything in particular?' Any feasts or banquets planned? I doubted it, but I had to ask; I had to.

He shook his head. 'Just . . . whatever you usually do.'

The other day, Mark and I were talking about it, the situation with Anne Boleyn, and suddenly Mark asked me whether he should tell her.

'Tell her what?' I asked.

He was bashful. 'You know: how I feel about her.' He bit his lip.

Openly declare his support? The prospect horrified me. No,

not a good idea. That's what I'd have said, but his lip sprang back, toothmarked, and he was saying, half-smiling, 'Who knows, though, how you tell a queen you're desperately in love with her. It's not something I've had any practice at.'

My instinct – unacted upon – was to laugh: what was this latest funny little turn of Mark's? Desperately in love with Anne Boleyn? I was about to say, *Oh yeah? Since when?* But in the same instant I realized: since always.

It's her.

She's the one.

Not me.

Slammed up against the realization, my heart came to a brief dead stop. The physical shock of it banging shut nearly made me cry out. My face must have been smacked with dismay. And there was Mark, looking at me. Sitting beside me, opened up to me and unsuspecting. Asking for my advice. I saw it, then; I saw it all: to him, I was a confidante. That's what I'd been, for him, this past year. That's all I'd been. And here he was, waiting for advice, wide-eyed and trusting.

His face, those eyes: I kept on looking at him as if looking away would cause him to disappear. Would I never touch that skin, that hair? No, never; I'd never touch him, now. Not so much as a touch. None of it would happen: everything I'd dreamt of. Nothing would ever happen. It was me who was going to disappear as soon as I looked away. And even though it hadn't yet happened, I knew how that would feel. It was close by, that feeling; I could sense the breath of it, the brush of it. It was waiting until I was alone. Biding its time. It could afford to. It had singled me out and was about to claim me for the rest of my life.

In the meantime, though, there was Mark, waiting for my advice. I had to come up with some advice. Good advice. Because he deserved good advice, didn't he? Because – *be fair, Lucy, be fair* – none of this was his fault. He'd been true to his feelings. He'd been discreet. He'd been brave. I couldn't fault him. The misunderstanding was mine. How had it happened? How had I managed to make such a stupid mistake? How had I – supposedly sane and sensible – come to believe he could have such feelings for me? Why *would* he? Me: an ageing woman who's never looked further than the four walls of her kitchens, who knows nothing and has nothing to say for herself.

To him, though, I was his confidante. And it occurred to me, suddenly, that to be his confidante was better than nothing. As his confidante, I could still have his respect or fondness or whatever it was that he felt for me. I could hang on to that. I had to hang on to that. It was that or nothing.

If I was to hang on to that, then everything should seem to be exactly as it had been. Nothing else should show. If I didn't want my pain to show, then I couldn't feel it. At least not until I was alone. So, I slammed it down into a nub of surprise and there it settled, a hard and heavy presence but somehow also nothing, a bubble, as if I were in a cart bumping over the brow of a hill. It sang like a numbness, but, inside, I sang louder, to drown it out: *You're doing it, Lucy; see? You're already doing it. It's do-able. You're surviving. This is survivable. At least for now.*

And then, unexpectedly, surfaced one small hope: it was Mark who was making the mistake; it *was* Mark who was making the mistake. Or a mistake, certainly: a different one from mine, but a mistake nonetheless. Because he's nothing to her, is he. Not really. He's had his head turned. It's understandable: she's dazzling, and he's favoured. But surely he's no one, to her. And he'll realize, soon enough. And then what? Where will he turn? Perhaps he'll realize, then, what love is or can be, and where it's been, all along.

And for me? Would it be so very hard to be second-best to a queen? Will it be so very hard to wait and see? It's not as if I'm any stranger to waiting. It'll happen sooner or later that he'll realize. Sooner, probably. Sooner would be better.

He'd asked me: should he tell her? 'Yes,' was what I decided to say. 'Yes, of course. You should. You should declare yourself to her. And better still,' I reached around to a shelf for the rose, muslin-wrapped, that was ready for me to give to him, 'give her this.' And there it was, suddenly, at last: my rose in the palm of his hand. I nodded – *Unwrap it* – and watched as white folds dropped away from fiercely red blades. He touched a fingertip to one petal-edge and his breath came back in a rush, close to a laugh, incredulous and delighted.

Then, looking at me, he was serious. 'I can't,' he said, and meant it. 'I can't give her this.'

'Oh yes you can,' I said.

Richard said it as he came into the doorway and saw me: 'You don't know, do you.' He spoke quickly and quietly, not really to me. Buying time, if only a heartbeat of it. Steeling himself. Expressionless – lips, white; hair, flat like a child's – he lacked composure, and I'd never seen him like that. His eyes flickered, took in that Kit and Stephen were in the room. He came in, pulled me by the arm. I was holding a spoon; sugar fluttered, streaked my skirt, sparkled on the floor.

Outside, at the top of the stairs, we faced each other. His eyes, on mine, were so wide they were animal. He said, 'Smeaton's been arrested.'

'*Arrested?*' As if it were a foreign word; I couldn't think what it might mean, not in relation to Mark. I didn't even ask what for; there was nothing that Mark could be arrested for. This was nothing to do with him in particular but a natural, arbitrary calamity, a lightning strike.

'And not just him. All of them.'

All of whom? The musicians? Even less to do with Mark, then. Some kind of crackdown. Debts, or a fight, or something.

'Norris, Brereton, and – *God, Jesus* – even her own *brother.*' Even though he was whispering, it came as a kind of shout: 'It's for *adultery*, Lucy, with the *queen.*'

'But you said, *her brother*. You can't . . . with a brother.'

He was staring at me.

'Can you?' Then I remembered: this was about *Mark*. Her brother was irrelevant: *forget the brother*. This was about *Mark*. 'Mark?'

He didn't flinch.

It came from me as a wail: 'But Mark never –'

He waved it away, didn't want to hear it. 'It's treason.' That's what he wanted me to understand.

Treason. Tyburn. Oh, no: no, this is ridiculous; someone needs to take control, here. 'Richard,' *We must keep calm*, 'this isn't true. Someone's having you on.'

He shook his head.

'But –'

'Think,' he urged, 'of the enemies they have.'

'Mark doesn't –'

'Mark's nothing, it's not about Mark, he's just there to make it worse.'

Worse? It needs to be worse than her own brother? I could only stare at him, incredulous. Those animal eyes. He was making me face it, all of it.

But surely the charge won't stick. 'He'll just say . . . she'll just say –'

'He's admitted it.'

In a flash I saw Mark going from here to the queen and the queen kissing him, leading him into her bedroom, closing the door. No. No chance. 'It's not true. Why would he admit it?'

Richard's lips parted but he realized his mistake and held his breath.

'Oh,' I said, lightly, as the implication became clear: under torture. Then, a crack in my chest. 'Oh no, no, no. Richard, no. Richard, no.' Mark's perfect fingers, the knuckles like pearls. His long back, its nubs of angel's-wings. His silvery skin. He's squeamish, I remembered.

'I don't know,' Richard whispered, uneasy. 'I don't know that they'd dare.'

'If they dared with anyone, it'd be Mark. There's no one to speak up for him.'

'Where are you going?'

I was already several stairs down. 'Cromwell.'

He actually laughed, or squealed; slapped a hand over his mouth. 'What are you going to do?'

'Kill him.' My own laugh was a furious, hot breath. Then I was serious: 'Reason with him.'

'Lucy, this is all reason; it's nothing but. That's the problem.'

'Well, then,' I shouted up the stairwell, suddenly feeling quite sure of myself, 'I'll plead.'

I had an idea of where to aim, and a trail of Cromwell-liveried servants to follow. And I walked as if I knew the way, avoiding everyone's eyes. A lot of eyes. I didn't think: not at all. Just walked, fast. Passageways, stairways, doors. And soon, I was there: a corridor lined with Cromwell-liveried yeomen. I strode down the middle, my skirt beating a rhythm around my legs.

A man stepped in front of the closed door. 'You have an appointment?'

'Yes, I do.' And before he could ask, 'Mrs Cornwallis, the king's confectioner.'

He was back in the time it took me to look down at my clogs and remember the sugar I'd trodden on. Wordless, he opened the door for me. Inside, was a man at a desk. Cromwell. Heavy-featured. He, in return, looked at me. I was aproned, capped, besplattered and sticky. He didn't look so good himself, for all his finery. Plum-dark shadows beneath his eyes.

He said, 'We have an appointment?' Meaning that we didn't. Curiosity, though, had got the better of him, hadn't it.

I said, 'Mark Smeaton, the musician, is innocent –'

'I can't discuss this.' He raised a meaty hand. Nodded to an attendant.

'*No, wait,*' I barked at the attendant, and, of course, it worked. I said to Cromwell, 'What if I told you something?'

He didn't respond immediately. 'Well, that would depend on what it is.'

Quite. I didn't know. I went for, 'He's spent every night with me, in – I don't know how long – months, nearly a year. Ask my servant. Ask my assistant.' My insides turned cold: I was asking them to perjure themselves. 'Ask the Sergeant Proctor.' I could almost hear what the Sergeant Proctor would say: *Oh, him? he was always there.* 'Every night,' I said again, to make sure; tilted my chin, to look sure. 'We never missed a night.'

Cromwell stared at me, no doubt thinking, So, this is the woman who makes my sugar plate when she manages to cover herself up and drag herself away from being pleasured. Comes to the kitchen every morning soaked in a man's juices and puts her sticky fingers into my gingerbread.

Looking away, I caught the glitter of an attendant's interested gaze. The dimple of another's clamped-down smirk. What had I done? My reputation: it was gone, irretrievably. Slashed from me, by my own doing. Word would travel. It would travel, too, to Mark: *We hear you've a taste for sugar.*

That's if they believed me. I was asking these men to believe that a boy like Mark would love a woman like me.

And he didn't, did he.

I shut my eyes. Anticipating Cromwell's laughter. There was merely a smile in his voice, though, when he said, 'He's been a very busy man, hasn't he, our Smeaton.'

I opened my eyes and there it was, that smile, faint and small-eyed.

You pig.

'I'm sorry to have to break it to you, Mrs Cornwallis, but it's possible – if one has the energy – to commit adultery in the daytime.'

So, I wouldn't be enough, in his opinion. Me: red-nosed, sugar-caked. Her: book-clean hands, bodice rough with jewels. I said, 'Tell me the days.'

'I beg your pardon?'

'Tell me which days – I'm sure you have them documented –' I nodded at the papers on his oh-so-important desk, 'and I'll tell you where we were.'

He said, 'You are a member of the king's household, and he is – or certainly has been, latterly – a member of the queen's. I don't need to tell you that the two households have, recently, spent considerable time apart.'

I said, 'There's a river out there.'

He frowned, lost.

'People travel. It's not impossible. People who –' *say it* – 'are in love, they travel. To be together.'

He raised his voice: 'And they also spend time in the queen's bedchamber. Now, I don't need to discuss any of this with you, but I will tell you something in the hope that we can put paid to all this. Your young man was overheard declaring his –' he sighed – 'passion for the queen.'

It shot through me: I'd sent him to do that, hadn't I. 'Overheard?'

'Servants,' he said, 'they get everywhere, don't they.'

'I told him to do it. To declare himself to her.'

For the first time, Cromwell looked surprised. 'You told him to do that?' The smile crept back. 'What strange arrangements you young people have, these days.'

'"Passion",' I said, 'isn't adultery.'

'Mrs Cornwallis,' he was acting bored, now, 'he has confessed to everything.'

'Under torture.'

He reached casually for some papers. 'That's a very serious allegation. Torture is, as I'm sure you're aware, illegal.'

'Oh, yes,' I said, 'I'm aware of that.'

His gaze snapped up. 'You must think we live back in the dark ages. You probably think so, don't you,' *kitchen maid*. 'Smeaton seemed convinced enough of his own guilt. There will be trials, Mrs Cornwallis, properly conducted in accordance with the law. Open to the public – you're welcome to attend. In the meantime, it only remains for me to thank you for your help: I shall make sure that the jury is informed of Mr Smeaton's considerable appetites and dubious moral character.'

I stepped forward; he jerked back. 'Take the confession,' I urged, 'take whatever you need from him, then let him go. Banish him. He's nothing, to you. He's nothing.' Suddenly both my hands – fists – were at my mouth, one around the other, holding down my broken, noisy breaths. 'Listen. You listen to me. We were going to go away. Move away. Marry, have children. If you can believe that.'

He hadn't moved, not a muscle, not even to blink.

'When you've finished with him, whatever state he's in, give him back to me, let me take him away.'

He opened his mouth, and then he spoke. 'Pleas should go to the king –'

'I'll go to the king.'

'No –' He was up, and around the desk. Stopping in front of me, he glanced down at his shoes; looking up again, he seemed even more tired than when I'd first seen him. He spoke gently. 'I'm going to be honest with you. It's important that you listen. Can you do that?' He paused until I nodded. 'All this, that you planned with Smeaton: it's not going to happen, and you'll have to accept that, *but* … there is something I can do.' It was he who nodded, now, a couple of times, to himself. 'Don't go to the king: that's my honest advice. The king is a very, very angry man. He doesn't want anything to do with any of this; he doesn't want even to have to think about it. He certainly doesn't want to think of these men … having lives. Having wives. Not after what they did to his. That'd make him even angrier.'

'He believes it?' My voice sounded small.

'Of course he believes it. But what I can do for you – all I can do for you, but believe you me it's worth something – is get Smeaton a commuted sentence. Not a traitor's death. For the others, that'll happen anyway: they're nobles; they won't be hung, drawn, quartered, will they; it'll be the axe. Smeaton, though …' He shrugged with his mouth. 'But I can get the sentence commuted. The king won't let him live, I'm telling you that for certain. The commuted sentence is the best you'll get. But I can get it. I promise.'

'Thank you,' I said.

I was determined not to cry until I was alone but, somewhere back down that long line of yeomen, I began to fail in spectacular fashion. At least they hadn't yet heard the story.

That was Smeaton's lay, you know.

If you can believe it.

I cried all the way through the palace, and couldn't care less. The louder, the better. Because people should know. They should know this is a Godless place.

I went to my step and stayed there; stayed there all day and all night. I didn't mean to; just didn't move. Over the hours, the palace settled and its rhythms became mine. A slam of a door, the stroke of blood in my ears. A trip of footsteps, a flurry of stomach juices. The slosh of a pot, a sigh. At sunrise, I was so stiff that I wondered if I'd ever move again.

I did, though, of course.

I headed for the kitchen.

Anne Boleyn

❀❀❀

What with your departure to Hatfield, Elizabeth, and the continuing mess with Catherine and Mary as well as the strains of early pregnancy, I badly needed cheering up in the earliest and darkest days of January. Unexpectedly, salvation came via my cousin Francis. I was surprised to see him: he'd been in France for a while, and, anyway, I didn't seem to see much of him any more. Typically, he made a big entrance, kicking open my door, although on this occasion it was because he was carrying a box. He gave me the usual roguish smile, but I spotted a double-take, and in that instant, I saw myself in his one uncovered eye as not, quite, myself. Older, I suppose. Wearier, perhaps. We exclaimed our greetings, and he deposited the box at my feet, gesturing for me to lift the lid. 'From Lady Lisle,' he said.

I half-laughed, half-groaned: *not more.* Honor Lisle, over in Calais, was very keen to secure places with me for her daughters, but crate-loads of gifts couldn't change the fact that there were no vacancies.

I crouched beside the box; and, opening it, suffered a stab of shock. Cowering in a corner was a furry little creature, no bigger than a man's fist.

'It's actually a *dog*,' Francis said, over my shoulder, both helpful and derisive.

'A *dog*?' It was nothing like any dog I'd ever had.

A collective intake of breath from my ladies.

I extended a finger, touched the silky brown fur. It quivered. And so did I. 'Oh, *Francis*, you should have *carried* him.' I checked: 'Him?'

He nodded.

'He's *terrified*, in here.'

'Oh, he'll get over it.'

I lifted him as gently as I could, to a low chorus of sighs, and he braved a look at me, shiny-conker eyes in a tiny face. 'Pixie-face,' I said to him. 'Pixie.'

Spring dispelled the stagnancy of winter in more than the natural sense. Tom hadn't been hibernating, he'd been busy, and now his capable hands delivered us the Act of Succession. Our children – Henry's and mine – were to be the heirs to the throne. No mention of Mary: a touch I loved. Something else that I appreciated: a coda to the effect that any denial of the Act – anything said or anything written against it – was high treason. Truly a laying down of the law.

First of all, it was the end for the Mad Nun: Tom had the go-ahead, now, to take action against her. A bit of frothing at the mouth had had to be seen to be respected, at least until we knew what we were – or weren't – dealing with. But she'd gone on to make friends in high places, and then, in prison, had admitted the 'visions' were fabrications. Presumably she'd guessed the game was up. Something else she must have known: she'd have to die as she'd lived. She'd made herself notorious. That'd been her aim. I was assured her death was suitably spectacular. She and the four clerics who'd been her mainstays were dragged behind horses to Tyburn and hanged before being cut down, rope-strafed and retching, eyes blood-burst, for their beheadings. I can't say I felt for her. She'd revolted me: the cynicism of her preying on people's fears and peddling them lies. She might have looked milky-sweet, but she'd had about her the foetid air of the old, superstitious England.

Was a mad nun one thing, but a respected bishop another? Fisher was open about his opinion of the Act of Succession, but was merely dispatched to the Tower to occupy a suite of rooms and reflect on his foolishness. The surprise for me was that he was still alive. Tough old gristle, Fisher. The Pope made a little stand on his behalf, declaring him a cardinal and sending the requisite red hat. 'If he's not careful,' Henry said to me, 'he won't have anywhere to wear it.'

'And More?' Because that *had* surprised me: Henry following Fisher with Thomas More.

'Oh,' he looked downcast, with something like embarrassment, 'that's just to frighten him.' Then he looked up and made an effort to smile. 'He'll come round.'

Rumour had had it that Catherine was forever begging the Pope not to carry out his threat to excommunicate Henry, just as she was forever begging Spain not to declare war on England.

Well, I could believe that. Rumour had also had it that whenever anyone said a word against me in her presence, she'd ask them to pray for me instead. She claimed I'd need their prayers, one day. Two years ago, the Pope finally stopped heeding her: he excommunicated Henry. And ordered him to abandon his new wife and child and to return to the old ones. And ordered him to pay costs for the hearing of the case. I won't need to describe Henry's response. Catherine, though ... Apparently, she believed he'd do as he was told. She packed up her rooms and waited for his arrival to reclaim her. That, I can't begin to understand. At least I know when something's over, when someone's decision is made. You won't find my bags by the door tonight.

My second baby was due in September; a second consecutive September baby. One day in early July, I began having contractions. Faint, and infrequent. It was a quiet day, nothing in particular going on: easy for me to plead a headache and retreat with Annie to my rooms. I told no one the truth. It'll pass, was my reasoning; it has to pass. I paced, sat, lay; sat, paced, lay. Finding it hard to keep Pixie with me. Usually he'd be curled in my lap or next to me on my bed, but I couldn't stay still. Picking him up, putting him down; reaching for him, putting him aside. I was grateful for his presence, though; for that steady, sympathetic gaze, and warm fur. As the day went on, I wasn't sure if I was imagining an increase in the frequency and strength of the contractions. Perhaps, I reasoned, it's reaching a peak before it can settle down. Sit it out, I told myself. Stay in there, I told the baby; pocketed away, where you're safe. Before long, Annie was having to ask me if I was all right. 'Mmmm,' I'd manage. Obviously I wasn't, but I didn't want to speak it because that'd make it real, something to be dealt with. If I could just sit it out ...

By evening, it was clear that I was in trouble. Not only was my bump pulled tight, but my bedroom door, too. Annie had summoned my mother, my sister, and Meg (and not, thank God, my sister-in-law). To everyone else, including the midwife, I was firmly unavailable. My mother said to me, 'It might be nothing. It might still be nothing.' And that's what I felt, too. I was wondering: could I have my dates wrong? Because why else would the baby be coming? I talked it over with Meg, but I don't remember what we concluded. Privately, I was wondering: could a baby be born at seven months – eight, perhaps – and survive?

Could it be ready, early? Because why else would it be coming? Perhaps healthy baby princes were exceptional, ready early; perhaps that was it.

It wasn't 'nothing': by midnight, it was labour. My feeling, then, was of disbelief. Genuine disbelief, holding no place for anger. I was a wide-eyed spectator: could this really be happening? To me? Much the same with despair: there was no time for it. I had something, now, to deal with; something big. I had something to survive, and I could sense myself – my body – rising to it, determined to be a match for it.

Henry, though, I did feel for; or there were moments when I did. Into my pain-dark mind would come a sense of him, like a sunburst: glorious colours – his hair, face – and the heat of his optimism, his good faith, his delight at the prospect of another baby. It was appalling to think of that being extinguished.

In a different way, I was bothered by Pixie's absence. Not that I wanted him there; of course I didn't. But his absence was ... well, it was *there*. Sometimes I meant to ask where he was, where they'd put him, if anyone was with him; but the questions slipped away from me as if in water. Labour was taking me over, as it does; I gave myself up to it, marvelled at the pain. There was no baby-cry when they finally got the body free from me and took it from the bed. Only creaks of the floorboards as my sister – something in her arms – turned and moved away.

It – she – was a girl: my mother told me, after I'd asked and asked. Something else my mother said, when I pressed her: the little girl looked – would have been – perfect.

I did as my mother told me, and slept. There was no point in being awake. I don't know who broke the news to Henry, but, when I woke, he was there, sitting beside my bed. His expression didn't change when he saw that I was awake; but it was no expression at all. Like that, we looked at each other. Eventually, he spoke; he said, 'It happens.' Well, yes, he'd know all about that, wouldn't he. It had happened to *her*. I wanted to say, Not to me, it doesn't. But it had, hadn't it. It had happened to her and it had happened to me. England's two unlucky queens: in the same boat, under the same curse.

No announcement was ever made. People had to draw their own conclusions, and I looked them straight in the eyes as they did so. I had no obligation to explain myself. I'd come back into court life as soon as I could – a week or so later – and although I was hardly cheerful, my sense of doom was beginning to disperse. Disasters happen, I reminded myself. They were as likely to happen to me as to her. They happened to all kinds of women.

One disaster means nothing. It was the future that mattered. That'd always been my view.

Henry's view, I didn't know; I didn't see much of him. He was considerate and jovial whenever we were in each other's company; but, as if I were still heavily pregnant or had just had a baby, I was left with the women while he sought the company of others. Not merely of the boys, though, this time. As the summer wore on, it became apparent – not only to me, probably to me last of all – that the close company of a certain girl was particularly dear to him. One of the girls in my household, she was nothing special. A watchful seventeen-year-old; nothing much to say for herself. I can't even guess at what attracted him to her; but attracted, he did seem to be. Stupid man. They spent days riding alone together, I heard; and I saw for myself how they spent the evenings. 'You rest, Angel,' he'd say to me, smiling, getting up from the table and heading across the dancefloor, making a beeline for her. What was I to do? Get up and clamber after him, tap him on the shoulder and tell him I was fine after all and fancied a dance?

I couldn't believe it, I simply couldn't believe any of it. I couldn't believe it was *her*, a nothing seventeen-year-old. And I couldn't believe he'd behave in such a way. He had *me* as his *wife*; he had his *lover*, now, as his wife. Wasn't that what the past seven years had been about? Didn't he have what he wanted, now? Why, suddenly, would he need someone else? Especially a colourless little nobody. Actually, we weren't lovers, Henry and I, at the time: that's true. We were sleeping separately, but only because I was tired.

With this girl, he was like a silly boy. Full of himself, pleased with himself. With me, he was dismissive: 'I'm not discussing it with you,' or, 'Can't you let a man have some fun?' Fun? We'd just lost a child. This silly overgrown boy was someone I didn't know. And not only didn't I know him, but I couldn't bear him. I wanted to hit him, to knock away this pretender, to knock back into place the man I knew, the man I was missing so much.

Once, he even said, '*Catherine* never complained.'

'Which is why,' I yelled back at him, 'she's locked up at Kimbolton.'

No one else took it seriously, either; everyone looked put-upon when I raised it. The usual response was barely a response at all: '. . . Anne . . .' Usually accompanied by a shrug. Meaning, I presume, *That's how it is.* And this, not only from the old ones but my friends, too, and family, even my brother. 'It's nothing,' George said to me, 'it's the life of Henry's queen.' Adding, 'And it's the life of a woman, really, isn't it.'

Not this queen. Not this woman.

Then, help came from an unexpected corner. It was unexpected that I took it; not unexpected that it was offered. Think about it: who would take the opportunity to sidle up to me and coo, *I understand*? My sister-in-law, Jane Parker. She was the only person who did, though, and I took what sympathy I could. She listened, wide-eyed, nodding vigorously, then said all the right things to bolster my case, before feeding me titbits of the minx's indiscretions, which I lapped up to stoke my outrage. She once said something like, 'I've a good mind to tell her what I think of her,' and my response was something like, 'Well, don't let me stop you.'

Exactly what she did say to that vacant seventeen-year-old, in the end, I don't know; but whatever it was, it got back to Henry. His little girl had gone running to him with her tale of woe. And he dropped his infuriating off-handness to come and blast me about Jane having dared to say anything at all. Progress: Henry talking to me, even if it was at quite a volume.

I launched an equally noisy defence, claiming that Jane Parker – as he knew full well – was nothing to do with me. I couldn't resist adding, though, that I was impressed she'd had the courage to say what everyone else was thinking. I'd barely paused for breath, and already he was back at the door. Which wasn't what was supposed to happen. Later, it occurred to me: perhaps I didn't look quite so good, nowadays, when I was yelling. I'd used to; I'd used to look my best, blazing. Perhaps I didn't look too good in any circumstances, now, being older and having just had two pregnancies in two years. I was permanently flushed, and my hair seemed to have lost its shine, no longer dropping around me like silk.

And so I understood that I was going to have to do as everybody said: sit it out. Like so much else that had happened, that year. It was more than Jane Parker got to do, though: Henry sent her from court. I could have been very angry – *he*'d sent one of *my* women from court – but of course he'd done me a favour. My brother told me that she was blaming me. She was bitter that I'd let him send her away, when she'd only been speaking up on my behalf. George smirked when he said, 'I don't think you'll be over-burdened with offers of sisterly friendship from her again. I suspect we're both free of her.' He looked relieved yet still tense when he said, 'One less thing to worry about.'

Only a year and a half before, I'd chosen as my motto, 'The Happiest'. And now here I was, grateful for one less thing to worry about. Concentrate, I chided myself, on what matters. I had a job to do – one job, as queen – and I'd found, to my dismay, that I wasn't all that good at it. Not bad – two pregnancies in two years, one lovely child – but not as good as I would have to be. My health had taken a knock-back, and I was no longer young. I made a decision: I'd rest. No getting myself upset over Henry. And as it happened, that minx had indeed been a summer's distraction for him. When autumn came, she faded.

Henry was busy. In October, on his orders and Tom's instructions, the Observant Friars were dissolved. Yes: Catherine's favourite friars, dismissed. The chapel in which the royal heir had been christened, just a year beforehand, was turned into a mill. When I looked from my windows, whenever I glanced over the gardens and saw that covered walkway leading nowhere, I'd feel disoriented, as if waking from a long sleep into a changed world. Two pregnancies in the two years since my marriage: I'd been weighed down, my attention turned inwards; one confinement, then one convalescence. I'd been missing what was going on.

Something else I seemed to have missed: the Admiral of France's visit to London, in November, was referred to by Tom as a patching up of Anglo-French relations. I didn't say so, but I was quite unaware that any patching up was necessary. My uncle and Charlie were the hosts, along the river at Bridewell. They enjoyed it; I heard it was going well. What troubled me was that de Brion hadn't come to see me. Hadn't come to pay his respects. Then – worse – Chapuys, I heard, had been invited over there for an evening. *Chapuys?* Not so much a changed world, then, as a world going mad.

There was worse to come. Henry turned up at my rooms, late one afternoon, pre-dinner, which was unusual enough, at that time, to get me wondering. He looked sheepish, too.

'What?' I wanted to know, immediately.

He frowned, 'Nothing,' but he took me by the arm, guided me to privacy, to a window seat.

I stayed standing. '*What?*'

'Well, no,' he glanced, unseeing, through the window, 'it's just that . . .'

And it was *just* that de Brion was seeking a betrothal between the pasty-faced bastard-child, Mary, and the Dauphin.

I said, 'It's a joke.'

I said, 'Isn't it?'

He didn't answer; said that if Mary were unavailable, France's second choice was the emperor's daughter. And the Spanish had intimated that they'd be pleased to accept.

What on earth was going on? Henry was affecting helplessness, which I hated. He was always doing it, I'd had nearly a decade of it: helplessness about the divorce, about Catherine, about how people were treating me. Helpless: the most powerful man in England, if not the world.

Me, I was stubborn. No affectation about it. I couldn't win an argument with France if France was refusing to have an argument with me; but I could refuse to think about Mary, let alone discuss her. More of a stand had to be made, though. This was a snub too important to leave be.

I said to Henry, 'Suggest a betrothal between Elizabeth and their little one, Charles.'

He went to speak: *But what about Mary?*

I put up a hand, turned and walked away: No discussion.

While the proposal was on its way to France's Francis, via his Admiral, I had to more or less forget about it, distracted as I was by a more immediate, domestic crisis. One dank December afternoon, on which Hal, Fitz and Maria had dropped by, George slipped into my room. It was definitely a slipping in: he leaned back against the door, closing it softly behind him, making no move to step further into the room. His eyes were on mine. Something was up. My heart rate, for one thing. Was I so easily shaken? Weary: that was what I was. I felt unable to rise to it, whatever it was.

But rise, I did – at least, physically – and, excusing myself, leaving the little circle to close behind me, I went to George. His half-smile was mere reflex, a greeting. Under cover of Mark Smeaton's singing strings, he whispered, 'It's Mary.' Our sister, he meant. *It's Mary*, said ominously, always meant our sister. 'She's back.'

'And?' True, it didn't sound good – she'd come to court for the birth of my second baby, and was supposed to be gone again – but Mary has always been a law unto herself. I couldn't guess at the reason for this unscheduled return.

'Married,' he said, 'and pregnant.'

Pregnant. My happy-go-lucky sister, in no need of more children. In need of no more children. My own sister. 'Married?' I said, quickly. She was a widow. I'd heard of no plans-making; and I'd have heard. There would be a marriage to be made for Mary, at some time in the future; but it hadn't been, yet.

'To William Stafford,' George said from the corner of a smile that he sent across the room. The recipient of the smile was Maria. Her anxious little face lit up in return.

'A Stafford?' I couldn't fail to recognize the name, of course, although I wished I had. The family name of the Duke of Buckingham: well over a decade dead, but his disgrace still raw. Henry didn't execute nobles, he simply wouldn't do that; but Stafford had been a pretender, and it'd had to be done. 'Who *is* this William Stafford?'

'Some soldier.'

Some *nobody*. 'But she's the queen's sister!'

'Keep your voice down.' His smile flicked over Mark Smeaton, to keep the peace.

'She *can't* be married to him.' Surely she couldn't have done this. *Why* did she do these things? Did she do them on purpose, or was it all as blithe as it looked?

The smile was still stuck there when he said to me, 'Well, I hope she is, because she's very pregnant.'

The eldest Boleyn child flouncing into court, confirming everyone's suspicions of the Boleyns: that we were out of control, unable or unwilling to control our appetites; which, to put it bluntly, were base. 'Where is she?'

'With Mum.'

'How's Mum taking it?'

'She's got her hands full, keeping Dad at bay.'

Dad and his temper. And how furious he'd be: we children and our dubious marriages. Mary, left destitute by her first husband; then my own, protracted mess, still continuing; and George's nasty little wife banished by the king. Now this: Mary rolling up, having made her own marriage to a commoner, as if nothing mattered; as if she'd never learned anything. Mary – I could see it – laughing at everything and everyone, as she does. And then crying, as she does. But Dad, with his temper, would only make more of a spectacle of us.

I said, 'We need to get her away from here. What does she want?'

'I don't know. I don't think *she* knows.'

No, of course not: that wasn't the way Mary worked. 'We have to get rid of her. Preferably before Dad gets his hands on her. Get rid of her, George. Give her whatever it takes.' And I added, just to make it clear, 'I won't see her.'

I assumed Mary was the reason for Henry turning up at my apartment a couple of evenings later. I was getting ready for bed. Annie showed him in to my bedroom. I stayed sitting on the bed;

he stopped by the door. It was instantly clear that this had nothing to do with my sister: Henry's face looked small. Panic leapt into my throat. 'Is it Elizabeth?'

He shook his head, but his expression didn't change and he didn't say, *It's nothing.* 'Anne . . .'

My scalp tightened.

'It's Pixie.'

Pixie's absence slammed up against me. I wanted to say, *But he's here*, even though I knew, I *knew* he wasn't. I hadn't seen him for an hour or so. I'd *known* he wasn't here. Without knowing it, I'd known. What had I been thinking? Nothing, in my tiredness. Or, perhaps, that Annie would bring him in, later. Henry stayed there by the door, looking utterly miserable, while he told me: earlier, outside my rooms, Pixie had got under someone's feet – a groom's – and then fallen from a gallery.

I waited for him to say that he'd survived. When he didn't, all I could say was, 'I should have been there.' Because no one should have to die alone, away from loved ones. Who knows what pain and terror that little dog felt in his final moments. And where was I? Where was the one person he'd have wanted? 'Why didn't they call me?'

'They were –' he bit his lip, 'scared.' And I saw it, I saw why Henry was here: they'd asked him to break the news.

Pixie was *so small. So* small; and so *young.* A baby. I covered my face with my hands and cried. Henry came over, held me, rocked me. After a while, he spoke into my hair: 'Shall I stay?'

There was something too rigid in the way he held me. I pulled away from him, drying my eyes, wiping my nose, to say I'd be fine.

I suppose it was inevitable: by February, he had a new woman. That it was Meg was supposed to soften the blow. My brother had had a hand in this: pushing Meg forwards, getting her noticed, making her available. Keeping her sweet. He regarded it as a smart move; I was obliged to be grateful. Better the devil you know, was the reasoning.

Certainly I knew Meg, and knew she was no kind of devil. Anything but. More importantly, she was on our side. Even more importantly, she was in love, I suspected, with Harry Norris. She was discreet, too. Which helped. Problem was, not everyone was so decorous. Franky Weston, for instance: suddenly, he was all over her. He's young, I reminded myself. Didn't have to remind myself, it was so obvious. I comforted myself, He has a lot to learn.

Franky's deference to Meg was only the start of it. I soon found I couldn't be as accommodating as I'd hoped. I hated the set-up. Couldn't stop myself hating it. And was that so unreasonable? Henry should have been repairing our relationship, shouldn't he? I knew I was being difficult – George was always saying, *He can't get near you* – but it wouldn't have killed him to try, would it? To try harder. To make the first move, or meet me halfway or even a little over halfway. Instead of spending his afternoons in bed with my cousin.

De Brion's secretary paid us a visit, around this time, but there was still no word in response to my proposal. I badgered Henry to push the issue, but he seemed unbothered. I began to feel as if, in his eyes, I didn't exist. And in everyone else's, I did and I didn't. I was watched – I was sure of it – but avoided. Soon, it was that way even with myself: I seemed both invisible and too visible; my skin, ghostly – I was sleeping poorly, hearing the chimes of two, three, four – but my eyes and lips prominent, swollen, fissured.

My respite was you, Elizabeth; my visiting you. Because I *could*, for a change: I wasn't pregnant; the journey wasn't difficult. I lived for those visits, that winter. Do you remember being held up in Lady Bryan's arms as I arrived? Do you remember the muffled protests of snow beneath our boots, out in the gardens? Will you remember? I bet you remember Pixie.

Sometimes I'd think of Henry asking. 'Where's Anne?' and getting the answer, 'With your daughter.'

Your daughter: remember?

Your wife, with your daughter.

He paid his own visits to you, of course, amid a lot of show. Above all, he's good at show. Lady Bryan told me that when he brought the Venetian ambassador to see you, he stripped you. Literally showed you off: *My perfect little girl, the image of her father*.

Unlike the other one. Mary, apparently, was wasting away. Her mother wrote twice to Henry, pleading to be allowed to go to her, to nurse her. Twice, she was refused. Henry's way of saying, *See? I, too, can be stubborn*.

That spring, Tom was busy making arrangements for the audit of every single religious establishment. No more piecemeal investigations: they'd all be under scrutiny, now, as to what they believed and practised, and how they supported themselves. And if they didn't support themselves . . . well, that'd be it, for them. Tom had the bit between his teeth; he relished this new task. I was less sure, which led to a few quarrels. I'm a reformer, I want people to see the error of their ways. To educate them, not eradicate them.

It's not that I'm a soft touch. It was on my orders that Hailes Abbey's phial of blood – supposedly Christ's, miraculously liquid – was opened and examined, that summer, and found to be duck's blood, presumably regularly replenished by the monks. It was me who went to Syon Abbey, later that year, to talk tough to the nuns. How could they recite prayers in a language incomprehensible to them? That's what I wanted to know. How could that be communication with God? How could it not matter to them what they were saying? Ranks of sour-faced nuns. It'd been much the same with the Hailes Abbey blood: was I thanked for exposing the scam? No, I was ignored; the phial re-filled, the pilgrims' visits resumed. Before I left Syon Abbey, I gave every nun a copy of the prayer book in English. Learn what it is that you're saying, I told them. Or don't say it at all.

Some people, though, are uneducable because they're determined to be so. For them, I have less than no time. In May, time was up – and believe me, they'd had more than enough of it – for Houghton, who was Prior of the London Charterhouse, and four of the most outspoken Carthusian monks. It wasn't their beliefs they died for. No one has died for his or her beliefs while I've been queen. This wasn't about God. It was about me; Henry and me. They were vocal in their denial of Henry's supremacy: he wasn't the Head of the Church, and I wasn't his wife. These men set themselves above Henry, denying his word. Who were they, to do that? Were they kings? This wasn't religion; this was politics. And dirty tricks. One of them announced that Henry had had an affair with my mother. For that, and the rest of their bad-mouthing and frenzy-whipping, they died at Tyburn. Tom arranged the full whack: they were dragged there, strung up, cut down, revived to watch their own castration, these non-men. Disembowelled, they were cut into quarters, the more pieces to display around London.

Dad, George and my uncle went along to watch, and took Fitz with them. I suspect Fitz didn't feel able to say no: he, who already wasn't much of a man. I suspect he went because he couldn't do much by that time and he was doing what felt like his duty: witnessing his father's detractors die. I only found out when I noticed Maria looking even more worried than usual.

'Fitz is really poorly,' she said, when I questioned her. 'I think it was a long day for him, the other day.'

'The other day?'

She lowered her gaze. 'Tyburn.'

As soon as I'd established how he'd come to be there, I went to take issue with one of the guilty party. The first culprit I came across was my uncle. I hailed him down a passageway with, 'Don't you ever *think*?'

He stopped, turned, and raised one eyebrow.

'Taking Fitz to Tyburn!'

He walked slowly towards me. Up close, he went for a sarcastic, 'That's something you'd rather people didn't see?'

'*Fitz* is *delicate*. Didn't you think what you were putting him through?'

He made a small show of stepping back, folding his arms, inclining his head. Regarding me with his usual unpleasant smile. 'What's this sudden concern for one of the king's other children?' The smile sharpened. 'What are *you* putting *Mary* through?'

It surprised me – this sudden, apparent loyalty to the po-faced bastard-daughter – but it didn't throw me. 'Not enough,' I said, immediately. 'Not nearly enough. I'd send that little martyr to Tyburn, if I could.'

He laughed to himself, shook his head. 'You *are* wicked, aren't you.'

'No,' I said, 'I'm human. I'm not a hypocrite. Whereas *you*: *you*'d have any of us up there on the end of a rope if it suited you. *Any* of us. We're all just pieces of meat to you. You've no loyalty. No heart, no soul. It's *you* who's the piece of meat. Bred to – well, to *what*? – to walk around these corridors, doing whatever it is that you do. What *is* it that you do? What *is* the *point* of you?' I said, 'It won't be me who meets the sticky end, will it. Because I'm queen. *You*, though: you should remember what happened to Stafford. No one's above Henry's wrath. Especially not an arrogant little prick like you.' And with that, I was off.

From the way in which Henry strode into my Privy Chamber, a few hours later, I could see I was in trouble. But then again, when wasn't I?

He launched in, without preliminaries and in front of everyone. 'Did you call Norfolk an arrogant little prick?'

I fought the urge to smirk; it was wonderful to hear it said by a purple-faced king. 'Well, he *is*,' I said. I knew very well that my brother, turned aside, was smirking.

'*No*, he *isn't*. He's a respected elder nobleman.'

'He's a weaselly old bastard,' I protested, 'and, anyway, *I'm* queen. Why are you defending my uncle before me?'

Henry stood there, hands on hips, and yelled, 'You don't *behave* like a queen.'

'You mean I don't simper? *Listen*,' I bellowed back, 'you knew

I wasn't meek and mild when you married me. And you *liked* it that way, if I remember rightly.'

'Well, those days are well and truly over.'

That stung.

'I *assumed*,' he went on, 'that you'd learn to be queenly. When you got what you wanted. When you got where you wanted. I *assumed* you'd calm down and grow up. You were a clever girl, Anne; you know? Such a clever girl. I *lived* to hear what you had to say; did you know that? But now? Well, you've nothing to say, have you, that isn't some carping-on about someone.'

I stood, now; leapt from my chair. 'That's *not true*. *You* don't *listen* to me. When do you *ever* listen to me, nowadays?' I heard an intake of breath from my brother, or someone.

'Perhaps,' he said, 'that's because I have to spend all my time listening to complaints about you.'

'*No*, you *don't*. That's the point: you *don't* have to listen to them. Why don't you just tell them to fuck off? Have you ever considered that *you* don't behave much like a *king*?'

I knew, even as I said it, that I was going too far. There was a silence, in which he glared at me. I doubt he was lost for words; I suspect he simply wanted me to feel the full heat of that glare. Then, before turning and going, he briefly closed his eyes; and murmured, as if to himself, but of course loudly enough for me and everyone else to hear, 'When will this ever end?'

He did still listen to me on some subjects. On some people. Fisher, for one: Bishop Fisher. For how much longer, I was always asking, could Fisher reside in the Tower at our expense? It was obvious that he wasn't going to recant, to accept the situation. Red hat or no red hat, he fancied himself as the Pope's representative over here. I had no sympathy for him. Why should I? He'd see *me* dead.

He went to trial, that June, while Henry and I were at Hanworth. The verdict was guilty. There was nothing Henry could do, then, even if he'd wanted to. Oh, except spare him hanging, drawing, quartering, for the axe. No Tyburn for Fisher. Instead, the more decorous Tower Hill. For all our differences, we've come to the same end, Fisher and I, and not even a year apart. He wore his Sunday best, I was told. Ready to meet his maker. The biggest excitement of his seventy-plus pious years. He'd have died anyway, within a year or so; he was merely helped on his way. Me, though: how many years will I be missing?

Fisher had no daughter to leave, did he. None of them did, those men.

Well, I only hope God was impressed by Fisher's dapper attire. That evening, I did some dressing up of my own, because I attended a Mass for his soul. It was important to show the proper attitude towards a poor, misguided soul. At least I did it. He wouldn't have been going to a Mass for me, tonight, if he'd lived. Not that there'll be a Mass for me.

Anyway, Fisher was lucky: there were far slower, messier deaths. Three Carthusian monks were chained, standing, to stakes: no food or water, no washing, no relief of any kind until they died. Remember, though: all these men were traitors. They'd admitted to it. *I'm* no traitor. Nor did I do what Tom says I did. My coming death is a mere convenience so that Henry can marry someone else and make peace with Spain. And to think he never did it for me, however much I asked: never put the previous queen to death. Too scared of Spain. There's no country to stick up for me. This *is* my country. How would it have been, if Catherine had died years ago? Without a big fat poisonous Spanish fly in the ointment, would Henry and I have settled and been happy? People say I poisoned her, but I say that, in a way, she poisoned me.

All the righteous indignation around when Fisher died was nothing compared to when More went to the block. But guess whose voice joined in, this time? Henry's. Suddenly, it was me who'd made him do it. How did I do that? Guide his hand towards the warrant? I hadn't been near enough to him for a long time to hold his hand. Henry, helpless again. Of course, he didn't *say* as much. Didn't say much at all. Just moved house and refused to see me, for two days. *Gone hawking*, I'd be told. Or, *Retired early*. Then, eventually, he'd see me – had to – but not look at me; not really. I was invisible. Well, maybe. If he tried hard enough. But inaudible? Oh, no, not a chance.

Loathing things unsaid, I decided to tackle him. The day I chose, he'd been hawking: up and gone again before I was up at all. I was well and truly ready for his return. He didn't arrive back in his rooms with the others, though. But Harry Norris was there, with Meg. Often the case, now, I'd noticed: Harry and Meg. Either Henry had tired of her, or – who knows? – he'd been magnanimous enough to recognize the truth of the situation and leave her and his best friend to follow their hearts.

'Where's Henry?' I asked Harry.

He glanced around; he'd been preoccupied with Meg. 'Oh –' embarrassed – 'he must still be down at the stables.' His smile was a wince of apology. 'Sorry.'

I flapped the apology aside. It was better for my purposes, of course, that Henry was in the stables. There was a possibility of privacy.

I found him coming across the stableyard, and launched in. 'Stop blaming me for More's death.'

'Anne,' he knocked a shock of sweat-damp hair from his forehead, 'I've had a long day.' He didn't slow up.

So, I was behind him. My voice carries, though. 'Very convenient for you, isn't it, if More's death is my fault.'

Now, he did stop. Turned, even. 'I *don't* blame you.' Blankeyed. Mud-caked.

'Oh, so, his death was nothing to do with me?'

This drew something from him: he sighed a laugh, humourless and exasperated. 'Well, *of course* it was *something* to do with you.'

Here it came: the truth of how he felt. 'How, exactly, is that?'

He actually took a step towards me. 'If it weren't for you, none of this'd be happening.'

I walked right up to him and said into his face, 'If it weren't for me, you'd still be in a marriage that was no marriage at all.'

A skywards flick of those colourless little eyes, and he strode away. Hampered by my dress, I couldn't give chase. I circled the yard, struggling to keep my temper.

Oddly, when relations between us reached their worst, we then had a period of respite. Perhaps we both knew we'd reached the brink, and, at that stage, the only imaginable way was backwards. No doubt it helped that we were away, on progress. The weather was abysmal, but we were cosseted by our various hosts. Mindful of More's execution, I suspect, they were falling over themselves to impress Henry. I'd never seen so many portraits of him. Excellent business, suddenly, for painters.

We began to sleep together again, perhaps because we were away from home. With everyone at such close quarters, our separate beds had become so much more noticeable. And then, thrown together, we found that we could. The relief was dizzying. When George arrived back from France with the news that the answer to my proposal was no, I didn't care. In fact, I partied. Because who needed the French? They were cowards.

More bad news, though: Spain had, at last, taken Tunis. The Emperor was on a roll, and an unstoppable Spaniard wasn't a good prospect for England. I didn't say it to Henry, I wouldn't have dared, but it was as if he heard me anyway: *Don't think about it*. Because this was summertime, even if it felt more like January. We were on holiday. We didn't have to think about anything, not until we were home.

Tom visited, from time to time, and gave the impression of enjoying himself. It seems that he was never off-duty, though. From an unguarded comment from Meg, via Harry, I learned that Tom was considering reinstating pasty-faced Mary as heir.

What?

France's betrayal? Their loss.

Spain's war-mongering? Only to be expected.

But Tom's latest scheme? What on earth was he playing at?

There was only one way to find out. Even though it was late, I rushed to the guest room he'd been allocated. I wouldn't have been able to rely on Henry for a straight answer. Tom was sitting up in bed, paperwork spread over the blankets. He didn't seem in the least put out, as I'd known he wouldn't be. Business is business, whatever the hour. Even as I was still closing the door behind me, I was confronting him with what I'd heard.

'Anne,' he said, evenly, 'you're a pragmatist. Elizabeth's not even two years old. Marriage, for her, is a long way off. I need something I can work with *now*. There's interest in Mary, whether you like it or not.' He raised a hand, to halt me. '*Forget* liking it or not liking it: there *is* interest in Mary. I'm only working with what I've got.'

I didn't say, *It's the principle*. His word, *pragmatist*, stopped me. Because he was right, of course he was right; there was no argument: me, arch-pragmatist. But somehow he was also wrong. Very, very wrong. I just said, '*No*.' Exploded: '*No!*' Stalked across the rickety floorboards to grab him by the shoulders. 'How can you do this?' Because what was happening? Why was everything slipping away from me, again? 'This is my life you're playing with!'

'I'm not *playing*,' he said, over-patiently. 'I'm doing the job I'm paid to do.'

He wasn't a pleasant sight, close up. I let go, paced, but picked up a jug and threw it at a wall. 'You do this,' I shouted over the smash, 'and – you know what? – I'll see you're executed for it.'

He said, 'Don't threaten me.' He was managing to look half-amused.

'I'm not "threatening" you,' I said, at the door, 'I'm telling you. You do this, you die for it.'

'You can't touch me,' he said, and what struck me as odd

even then was that he said it almost sadly. Did he know, even then? Did he have an inkling?

One person I did expect trouble from was my sister-in-law, and, that summer, I got it; albeit at a distance. Back at Greenwich, there was a demonstration by some of the women who'd stayed, along with wives of some prominent city men, in favour of the old Spaniard and her sickly bastard. Reports as to who was involved were hazy – perhaps deliberately so – by the time they reached us, but something everyone agreed upon was that Jane Parker had been one of the ringleaders. So, she'd switched allegiance. Well, she was no loss to me. Indeed, I rather liked the thought of her hitching up her skirts and hammering on Thomas's door, or whatever it was they'd done: it amused me. Made a welcome change, to be amused by Jane. But of course it wouldn't do. So, Henry sent her to the Tower, to cool down.

I continued to make light of it. 'You really do have an awful wife,' I said to my brother.

Game, he leaned to whisper in my ear, 'And I'm not so sure about your husband.'

It was intended to make me laugh, of course. And it did, in that I obliged. But actually his playful little aside had brought a lump to my throat.

I knew, then, didn't I. I knew *something*. Knew trouble was coming; just didn't know where from. I'd have never guessed at the Seymours. The Seymour boys seemed to be loyal courtiers. They'd become favourites of Tom's. And I assumed Tom could be trusted. I trusted his judgement. There *had* been Seymour-trouble, but only amongst themselves. What trouble, though. For what seemed like a nice, quiet family, they'd done spectacularly well for scandal. Five years previously, one of the boys had discovered that his wife had had a long affair with his father. The two children he'd assumed were his own looked likely to be his father's. The wife was dispatched to a nunnery, the two little boys disowned. Then, father and son set about patching up Seymour family relations. And made a good job of it. Five years on, no one ever mentioned the scandal. No one except me, that is. As we rode up to their house, that summer, I was recapping for George, who'd been abroad for the worst of it.

Henry, though, made clear he was having none of it. 'Anne!' A pained look.

'What?'

'Well.' He lowered his voice to say, 'Don't you think they've suffered enough? Let them put it behind them.'

Admirable sentiments indeed. I raised my eyebrows at George, and no more was said. Or not in Henry's company.

The Seymour family was relatively new to money, and everyone knew that there wasn't much of it. Their house, Wolf Hall, was old – three hundred years – but Sir John had had an extension built especially for our stay there. Our five or six days there were lovely: I wish I could say otherwise, now, but I'd be lying. I liked Sir John: he reminded me of my own dad, but seemed – well – *nicer*. Cousin Francis, who was with us, was a close friend of the brothers. And Jane? I barely noticed her. I knew her from her time at court, but she'd made no impression on me then and made even less when we stayed with her family. A dim, plain spinster, I'd have said if you'd asked me at the time. I still say so. I said it to Henry, I remember, while we were there, when she came up in conversation.

He shook his head. 'She's nice,' he said, his voice rising in surprise. Then, lower, more decided: 'She's nice.'

Lucy Cornwallis

❀ ❀ ❀

SUMMER 1536

When my fears hammer in the small hours, I give up trying to do anything but work. I creep, wick-led, to the kitchen to smooth sugar-crusts and lay acres of goldleaf. Then, sometimes, morning is up and running before I've quite noticed, and I wonder if I have, somehow, slept. Richard is careful to follow my cue and talk about nothing but work. Not difficult: there's so much of it; the kitchen is padded, barricaded, with it. Moulds, jars, pans, braziers, stacks of sugar-shapes. And, fittingly, in the middle, emerging, soaring above it all, our centrepiece. This is a royal wedding banquet, no less, in preparation. 'Nothing clever,' we've been instructed, 'just plenty of old-fashioned favourites.'

No one added, *Not like for –*

But of course we never did a wedding banquet for *her*. No, for the wedding that changed the world, we made not a single pea-sized comfit. For the coronation, later, yes: sugar hardened by the tens of pound, towering and shimmering under the torches. But the wedding was secret. One dawn, I'm told, in the king's private chapel at Whitehall. Anne Boleyn in red, I'm told. Isn't it unlucky, to marry in red? We'd have been close by, Richard and I, but oblivious, asleep. (Those were the days – nights – when I slept.) Our services not required. William Brereton, though, knew all about it and his services *were* required; he was a witness. And when he married, a year or so ago, the king wanted us to make a subtlety for the feast. He summoned me. 'Billy's more of a romantic than he looks,' he said.

Which meant nothing to me, I didn't know how he looked. They all look the same, to me.

'So,' the king asked me, 'what will you make?'

I was at a loss; I wasn't any kind of romantic. 'A galleon,' I tried.

'A galleon?' He seemed to like the idea; or, it amused him.

And I tried to explain. I told him how I used to stand on a cliff-top, with chalk-matted grass between my toes and the sea slipped everywhere under the sky. 'And then, sometimes, there'd be a galleon . . .'

'Well, a galleon it is, then,' he said. 'Or three.' He grinned at me. 'Three, please, Lucy. Because never forget: safety in numbers. Sea-faring is treacherous.'

I don't know what it is that frightens me. Everything. Everything and nothing. A door closing, somewhere over in the main kitchens: that's enough to make my heart sit up and listen. But silence is just as bad, perhaps worse. Silence seems like a trick; I have to listen hard and deep into it, trying to catch it out before it catches me out. And then a torch extinguished across the courtyard will signal some unspecified danger; but, later, the appearance of another will be just as unsettling, as inexplicable. Why am I frightened? It's not for me that I'm frightened; it can't be; I don't care about me.

For this coming wedding, I've had a specific instruction. Not that I was told, at that stage, about the wedding. Just given the instruction. So, I started it in all innocence – just another project – and it was what I was working on when Richard came in, that awful day, and pulled me from the room.

Every day, the subtlety seems bigger. I'm building it bigger, of course I am, but it seems to be bigger still whenever I return to it. Or perhaps it's me who's smaller. I spend a lot of time standing up on the workbench. Have to, to reach. Most days, I'm up there. Most nights. Free of my clogs, nudging the grain with the balls of my feet. I have to be alone, up there; there's no room for anyone else. Daytimes, I listen to the boys. I hear differently, up here. Or just hear, perhaps, for a change. The tapping of Kit's pestle. Stephen's rhythmic, absent-minded puffing, *pa-pa-pa*.

When the Master of Revels showed me the drawings of the subtlety that was required, my response was that it was impossible. Having any kind of response was a surprise to me, the way I've been feeling, but I suppose it was inevitable. Because there I was, the king's confectioner, being consulted by the Master of Revels, and what else could I have done? Crouched on the floor with my hands over my ears? So, there I was, the king's confectioner, and the king's confectioner is never pleased to be given specific instructions. The king's confectioner is the king's subtlety-maker. Was I suddenly not capable of coming up with designs of my own?

The required timescale wasn't the problem, it seemed to me, as I did my job and took those drawings from the Master of Revels, leafed through them. The difficulty was the subtlety itself: its shape. Looking at the drawings – and failing, initially, to appreciate the scale – I'd said, 'We can work with the falcon, I suppose,' the falcon mould, Anne Boleyn's heraldic falcon. I'd said it more to myself than to the Master of Revels; but he insisted: 'Not the falcon. It isn't a falcon.'

'Look,' I said, 'we've no mould for this; and with the deadline you're giving me, we can't commission one.'

His reply was, 'Can't you just . . . *model* it?'

I really don't know what they think sugar is. Or what they think *I* am.

I'm improvising, though, and, actually, I'm making it work. Cobbling together and coaxing it. Working around each problem as I reach it. Shapes are just shapes, after all, and they're everywhere. I'm using the moulds we do have, bits and pieces of them turned this way and that. Feathers from our swans, and the beak from our falcon. There's a fair amount of the falcon in there, put to good use. Its nasty, open beak pushed shut and turned small on this new, giant bird.

I suspect that Richard sees me working and thinks that my being busy is a blessing. He doesn't know that no matter what I do, the memory of Mark reaches back and tears at me. And I'm glad of it, too. Because not to think of Mark would be to betray him. Which is what everyone else has done. They thought nothing of him beyond how he could be useful to them. Now he's gone, they don't think of him at all. As if he was never here.

But he was, he was. And now, some days, nights, all I can think is that he isn't. *He's not here, he's not here, he's not here*: the absurdity of it beats around me. Because how can it be? That he was here and now he isn't. I could go anywhere, everywhere – chapel, gardens, riverbank, royal apartments – and he wouldn't be there, because he's nowhere, and how can I make sense of that? How can he be nowhere?

When there was still time, did he think I'd come for him? That somehow I'd use my royal favour to his advantage?

What, then, did he think when I didn't?

Visitors to the kitchen are banned, these days, by order of the Master of Revels himself. In the interests of secrecy.

Good: peace and quiet.

And anyway there's no room here for visitors.

Visitors, that is, who aren't the Master of Revels. He's checking up on me, which is something he's never done. It's not a problem, because he seems appreciative: *Well, look at that!* I don't know that anyone would know what the subtlety is, anyway. I didn't, at first. Perhaps I wouldn't ever have done, had Richard not told me.

Richard explained it to me, that morning I arrived back from the step. When he first saw me, he took a deep breath, but all I had to say was, 'No,' to make clear I didn't want to tell him anything of my conversation with Cromwell. So, what he said instead, after a silence, in a change of subject, was, 'You were making a subtlety.' He indicated the mess I'd left.

I shrugged: *so what?*

He asked me what it was for.

I shrugged again. *Some banquet.* I was so very, very tired.

'It's a kind of castle,' he said. Because that was the mould I'd been preparing: a castle.

Oh, really, Richard, does it matter? I shook my head. 'That's just the base. And it has to be burning, that castle; needs flames. And a giant bird coming out of it. The castle's the easy bit.' I'm not doing it, anyway, I told myself; not now. Richard can do it. Seeing as he's so interested.

'Someone asked you to do this?'

I considered saying, No, it's for my own supper; but I raised my head and nodded towards the drawings.

Richard fetched them, unrolled them. 'Mr Holbein,' he remarked, seeing the signature.

I said, 'A great big bird coming out of a burning castle, as seen from a number of angles. And I quote: *To help you in your task.*'

Richard rolled them up again. 'Do you know what this is?'

'It's an insane amount of work.' *So* tired.

'It's the Seymour coat of arms.'

'Is it?' So, the Seymours have something to celebrate. Well, hip, hip, hooray.

'It's a phoenix rising from a castle.'

'A phoenix, is it. Well, we've no mould for a phoenix.'

Richard gave me a look, a Richard-look. 'We've a mould for a duck; we should go for a duck waddling from a burning castle.' Then he wanted to know when it was for.

I told him.

He gave a low whistle; then said, '*I'll* do it.'

No, I said. I didn't say, It's not as if I've anything else to do.

'A wedding,' he said, 'so soon.'

I didn't want to think about time; the days out there, rolling in. Nor did I want to hear about weddings.

'He's going to marry her.' He turned his green eyes to me. 'The king's getting a new wife.'

Oh, will you ever stop your rumour-mongering? 'The king's already married, Richard.'

He shrugged, and stayed shrugging; hugged himself. 'Presumably he won't be, by then.'

I was tired of this nonsense. 'I doubt even the king can get himself a divorce so quickly. The last time he tried, he couldn't.'

Richard said, 'This won't be a divorce.' He looked over at me, unblinking, until I understood.

I didn't quite believe him, though. '*A queen?*' A king can't kill his queen, can he? No one can kill a queen.

The other day, he said, 'Roses. Shouldn't we have roses? For this wedding.' He was looking up at the phoenix, frowning, as if to say, *This is all very well, but* . . . 'We don't have roses, Lucy.'

I said, 'You know where the moulds are.'

There's something I've been thinking of making. I can't quite stop thinking about making it. Gold. A kind of gold. The kind made with arsenic. I think about mixing up the powders, making the paste and painting it onto the feathery wings of the phoenix. And gilding Richard's little round roses. Could I do it so that no one would notice any difference from goldleaf? If anyone could do it, it'd be me: king's confectioner. Perhaps I should experiment, on one of my sleepless nights. Just one night, just an experiment. Perhaps I should gild just one special celebration treat each – a manus christi – for Cromwell and the king.

It'd be difficult to suspect gold: the brash shine of it; the clear gleam. No hint of subterfuge; nothing underhand. So unlike a suspicious green. I wonder if it'd be the very last suspect of all. And me? Am I right to think that it would be almost as hard to suspect *me*? And, anyway, what if anyone did? I don't care. I don't care what happens to me.

One day a couple of weeks ago, returning from his morning meal, Richard was a shadow in here, indecisive and soundless. So, I realized: it had happened. But he felt he couldn't say. I climbed down from the workbench and began boiling sugar; I was making manus christi. Back to good old-fashioned sugar-boiling. I tracked the boiling sugar through its various changes, up and up in temperature, stickier and stickier, and then, when at last it was on the brink, poised for its noisy plunge into the basin of water, I said, quickly, to Richard, 'There *is* something you can tell me.'

In the corner of my eye, he folded his arms high, dropped his head: listening.

'Cromwell made me a promise,' I said, 'that the sentence – Mark's – would be commuted. Just tell me, yes or no: did he keep that promise?'

'Yes,' he said.

The wedding feast is over and done with. We now have our kitchen back as it was, thanks to Stephen's good job of cleaning up. It was a whole day's work, for him, yesterday, to clear. We all helped, of course. Even Richard. And now, this morning, I'm sitting below orderly shelves, among the bare bones of my kitchen.

I had a visitor, earlier: the Master of Revels came to tell me that the king is very pleased with how I rose to the challenge of preparing for the celebrations at such short notice. 'Rumour has it,' he said, with a smile, 'that he's acting very generously. I'm quite sure he'll be showing you his appreciation.'

I smiled back, because that was what seemed to be required. I can't imagine what the king could give me that I'd want. He's already taken everything from me without even knowing it. He wouldn't even want to know.

I'm sitting here in this bare-boned kitchen because I don't know where else to go. There's nowhere else I'd rather be; this is as good a place as any. And I'm alone, which is what I want. I've sent Richard, Stephen and Kit away, given them a day's rest. Perhaps I should be outside, on the riverbank or in the gardens, but the prospect exhausts me: even just the clear blue of the sky to have to acknowledge.

What would Mark think, to see me like this? Not much, perhaps. There have been far more drastic changes around here than what's happened to me. There's far more to think about, for anyone given to thinking.

And for those not given to thinking, it seems, the past few years are suddenly understood to have been a kind of bewitchment. The king, I've heard, is tearful with gratitude. Regards himself as having woken in the nick of time; saved himself, his family, his kingdom.

Me, I'm sleepwalking: that's how it feels. I don't know how

I'll carry on, but I do know that it'll happen. Regardless of me. I'll go on making confectionery. Making it for a christening, probably, in the not too distant future. Before that, there's the summer progress. The various festivals.

The door's opening. It's Richard. He's lingering in the doorway; his reluctance frightens me. He's saying my name; and now, 'I've something to tell you.' He shakes his head, 'Nothing –' *Nothing awful.*

My anxiety drops a notch. But only a notch.

He takes a step or two forward but his heart isn't in it. It peters out, his approach. 'Lucy,' he says, quietly, 'I'm going.'

I shrug. Fine by me. He can see there's nothing to do, here, today. And didn't I tell him that he could have a free day?

He frowns, 'No . . .' and tries again, 'I'm leaving.' He's still over by the door. 'Silvester's leaving, and I'm . . .'

Leaving with him. Silvester: the page, his friend. What does he mean, leaving?

'For London,' he says, his gaze holding mine. 'We're going to London.'

'Today?' A long trip, for one day.

'To *live*, Lucy.'

But that's impossible. What would he – they – do in London? 'Richard –' It comes as an exasperated half-laugh. They live *here*, the two of them. They *work* here.

He comes closer, now, by a step or two. 'I'll find work.' He adds, 'I'm sorry, Lucy,' and sounds it.

'But you *have* work. *Here*.' That laugh, again, from me. 'What work would you find, in London?'

He doesn't take offence; comes to my bench, rests on it, leans across it towards me with a wan little smile. 'I'm a dab hand at confectionery.'

Yes, and who taught you that? I don't say it, I don't. Instead, I say, 'You can't,' and the way he cocks his head, trying to take me seriously, makes me realize how forcefully I must have said it; how confidently, definitely. And because that's not how I feel, I say it again, but even more so. 'You can't go.' Because I have to keep him here with me. I can't lose him, too. I can't lose him. 'This is your home, Richard. This is *our* home. You *come* from here.' And isn't that true? He could almost have been bubbled up, here in the kitchens, by mistake, in some pot: funny little fish. Baked tough, over the years, at the mouths of the ovens, and grown on royal scraps. Then drawn by his nose to the confectionery.

'Yes, but now it's time –' He places a hand over one of mine.

I snatch mine away. '*London?*' What will people make of him, in London? Him and Silvester. I've never met Silvester, but I'm quite sure he's unusual; Richard wouldn't take up with someone who wasn't.

'Lucy,' he says, pained. 'Lucy, listen.' That hand of his, free of mine, rises, emphatic, before dropping back gently onto the benchtop. 'With what's happened to Sir Henry –' Sir Henry, Henry Norris, the nice widower, Silvester's employer. '– We don't want to stay here.'

We used to be 'we', didn't we? Richard and me. *We* were always 'we'.

'Don't cry,' he whispers before I realize that's what I'm doing. 'Don't, Lucy; don't cry.' He runs his fingertips through my tears; they're slick with my tears, they're sliding on them. He keeps saying it – *Don't cry, don't cry* – but he doesn't mean it; he means, *Cry, cry*. So, I do. I stand there in front of him, just crying, not even dealing with the mess of my own tears but leaving them to him. I want to say, *Take me with you*, but I don't mean it, not really. I can't mean it, I can't go with him. He's going with someone else. Just as I would have done. And anyway, he came to me, all those years ago. I can't now go with him. That's not how it works. And I wouldn't want to; that's not what I'd want.

I must have stopped crying because he cups my face in his hands. 'I'll come back and visit,' he says. He assumes I'll be here. And I suppose I will, won't I. 'High days and holy days,' he says.

That, I can take him to task for. 'I'm busy, high days and holy days.' Confectioners' busy days: high days and holy days.

He allows it, with a smile. 'Well, I can come and lend a hand.'

'But if *you're* a confectioner, *you'll* be busy.'

'Listen: I'll visit.'

That's the best I'm going to get. It's better than nothing. He's back to smiling in that nervous way – tentative, appeasing – and he glances around the kitchen. 'Anyway, just think,' he chivies, 'All this to yourself, without me to distract you.'

I can't help but say it: 'Richard, I don't know what I'll do without you.'

His smile lessens a little, settles a little. 'Oh, you don't need me,' he says, misunderstanding.

The last of him to go is one hand, the hand that closes the door. And as it does, I realize one thing for certain: I won't ever replace him.

Anne Boleyn

❀❀❀

Although it took a while to be sure, by the time we were home again from the summer progress last year, I suspected I was pregnant again. I should've been pleased, shouldn't I, but all I remember is misery. Because it could all go wrong. Could already *be* wrong. This pregnancy felt like my last chance, and there was nothing I could do about it. Alongside everything I could make happen – have the vision for, argue for, insist upon – was something about which I could do nothing. I found it intolerable that something so close to me – inside my own body – was down to sheer chance. Nothing to do with me. Everything and nothing to do with me.

What didn't help was that I was so sick with this one. And tired: more tired than I'd ever been. I fell asleep at night dreading the morning – the morning already weighing on me – because then I'd feel so exhausted all over again. And this wasn't like my previous pregnancies: no one was pleased for me. They simply expected it of me. They'd been expecting it for a while. That was Henry's attitude: of course he was relieved, but his attitude towards me was an only faintly cheerful, *Get on with it*. The transparency of it was what I found so difficult to take. I suppose I'd known it all along: that this was the deal. Well, I had, hadn't I? If I hadn't, quite, I certainly did, now.

The dim Seymour spinster had come back to court, and Henry was spending a lot of time with her. I used to wonder: what does he *do* with her? Embroidery? Because as far as I could see, that was all she could do. He insists upon seeing her as a good woman. The truth is, she's a *thick* woman. And Henry's a stupid man. The Seymour spinster's much-vaunted goodness made me badder than ever. If she was the angel, I was the devil. The role had been left to me, so I might as well embrace it. I was too sick to want to drink the boys under the table but – trust me – if I could've, I would've.

It was easy for Jane Seymour, wasn't it. Walks in the gardens are a pleasure if you're not chafe-nippled, and it's easy to smile serenely when you don't have dried sick on your lips.

My fear had always been that Catherine would be the death of me, but when she finally died, just after Christmas, my situation only changed for the worse. Henry broke the news to me by saying, 'We're safe.' He'd rushed into my Privy Chamber. I was resting by the fire, my stockinged feet in Billy's lap for massaging. Billy dropped them, and stood.

'We're safe,' Henry said, his face lit up. 'Catherine's dead.'

'She's dead,' I repeated. I had to say it aloud to stand any chance of believing it. And although I hadn't spoken it as a question, I suppose I did mean *how? Where? When?* She'd been sick for ages, but I thought she'd never die unless I killed her. 'She's *dead?*'

I looked at Billy, who broke with a laugh: a single, brief note of sheer relief. Mark Smeaton had suddenly stopped playing for us; the sounds were of people, their gasps and shufflings and Billy's one note.

I didn't know my own response. It wouldn't come. It just wouldn't come.

Henry had his back to me; he was pacing, excitedly.

Gone, I said to myself. Gone, the woman who would have taken everything from me, if she could. Taken *him* from me.

Henry whirled to me. 'Safe from Spain,' he said.

Spain. Spain wouldn't bother to attack, now. The emperor had had no heart for it for years and now there wasn't even any face-saving to be done. England, safe from Spain: that's what Catherine's death meant to Henry. And of course it did: he was thinking – feeling – like a king. But if Catherine's death had happened when it should have done, or even only a year or so ago, we'd have – what? Hugged each other? Something, anyway. Something physical. Something *loving*. Her death would have been good news *for us.* Now, nothing was good news for us. There was Henry, pacing; and me, here, sitting. Suddenly, everything – the years and years – felt such a waste of time.

'I'm going to fetch Elizabeth,' he said, more to the room than specifically to me. 'Let's have a party.' He flashed us a boyish grin. 'We're safe!'

I did dress up, that evening; I did celebrate with the rest of them – *We're safe!* But all I could think, by then, was, *You're* safe, all of you.

England's safe.

But me? Me, whom the Spanish would always loathe? French-educated, French-speaking me? If Spain was becoming our new friend – and I'd seen how well Chapuys had been received by Henry and Tom, at Christmas – and France was in the cold, where did that leave me?

There was worse to come, and it started almost immediately. One afternoon, only a week or so later, I was reading by the fireside when Harry Norris rushed in, unannounced, boots brutal on the carpets. I stood so fast that my blood failed to keep up. He caught me, steadied me.

'Sit,' he said, pressing me into my chair. 'Sit.' He was dishevelled, smelling of dried sweat and damp outdoors.

'What is it?'

'It's Henry.' Crouching in front of me, he looked up into my face; his own, blank. 'He's had a fall from his horse. We've brought him in. He's not conscious.'

'Not conscious?' I couldn't take it in.

'Not conscious.'

I went to stand. 'I'll go to him.'

He pressed me back down. 'No. Not –' he touched his free hand briefly to my stomach '– in your condition.' And then he said it: 'Not yet.'

'Harry –' A plea.

'No. Listen. We'll call you.' *If we need to.* 'Rest. Rest. Please.' He was on the verge of tears.

I touched his face; he closed his eyes, exhausted. My stomach rose and I felt as if I were falling. I whispered, 'I don't know what I'll do.' *If he dies.* 'I just don't know what I'll do.'

Henry.

'He's strong,' Harry said with such certainty that I recognized the opposite as the truth. We'd been kidding ourselves for a while now. Henry was no longer the man he'd been; he was nearing fifty, and turning from muscle to bulk. He could easily be felled.

I sat all night, waiting to be called. Marooned in a palace, listening for the sounds that would tell me that their king was dead although I didn't know what those sounds would be. With every distant shutting of a door, I crept to my own, listening hard for something else. And every time, there'd be nothing. I couldn't cry, for fear of blotting that silence, but my throat was full of the loss that I'd already endured. Why didn't Henry and I love each other any more? How had we come to this, and so quickly?

If he survived – *please, God* – could we make it work? But if he didn't survive? I'd be a queen without a king. A kingless and – as yet – princeless queen. A queen no one believed in, and her little girl.

When finally I was called, it was because Henry had started to come round. It was Harry, again, who came for me. With less urgency, though, this time. But still unwashed. 'Well,' he said, 'he's back with us.' Gave me a weary smile. 'From time to time.' He took my hand into his own startlingly cool one and led the way.

For the next day, Henry didn't make much sense; he was sleepy, and gloomy. My presence at his bedside seemed irrelevant to him; he directed his numerous complaints past me to Harry and the physicians. It was only when he was up, the following day, that I came in for my share. Harry's warning glances at me said all the right things: principally, *Give him time*.

Catherine's funeral followed at the end of that week, at Peterborough Cathedral. Neither of us attended. By the time it happened, it felt like no victory at all. I'd been as irritable as Henry, all week. On the actual day, I spent the morning sewing and took a walk in the afternoon with George. In the evening, when Henry went to a Mass for Catherine, I went to bed. I was still sitting on my bed when Annie reappeared and stood there, at the foot of it, apparently dumbstruck. When I asked her what was the matter, she proffered a linen bundle that looked as if it were one of my shifts – presumably the one I'd just taken off and handed to her – and unfolded it to reveal a blotch of wet blood. Coin-sized. Flower-sized: a single bloom. Mine? I'd felt nothing. It'd crept from me. Panic churned me. *I'm going to miscarry.* I looked from the blood to Annie; she looked away. I lay back down, and curled up.

She spoke, but barely: 'Shall I call someone?'
Who?
'No,' I said. 'It might not happen.' I didn't move. I knew she was standing there, behind me, but I couldn't think of what to do with her. I couldn't think of anyone or anything. Just, *Not this. Please, not this.*

Eventually, Annie stepped forward and tried to help me into bed, but I curled tighter, making myself impossible to move. She wanted to help but I wanted none of it; nothing.

I did miscarry, although there was scant blood for a further few days before the worst of it came. It happened at night. I knelt on my bed, rocking through the pain, glad I was alone, focusing on getting it over. When I told Henry – days later – I said it straight. Kept my chin up.

Fact: *I've miscarried.*

His response mirrored mine; he gave nothing away.

I added, 'I think it was the worry.'

'Of?'

'Your fall.'

He made a show of nods, as if giving serious consideration to my explanation but somehow clearly doing the opposite. The bastard.

'Oh,' I added, 'and of your carrying-on with that dim Seymour cow.'

He got up and left the room.

He left the palace, a few days later. Still without having spoken to me. I let him go; wouldn't stoop to following him. It was almost a relief that he was gone. And, anyway, I was still bleeding: not usually more than staining, but an occasional difficult, messy hour or two so that I couldn't yet contemplate the river-journey to Whitehall. I stayed, convalescing. Or that's what I told myself.

What was I thinking, back in those February-dark days, just three months ago? I don't know. I'm not sure I was thinking at all, in those Greenwich-bound days. Something I *felt*: I felt unrelated to the thirty-two-year-old woman who, a couple of years ago, had become Henry's queen and given birth to England's princess. That woman had been strong, proud, gorgeous, and had had everything to live for.

I did spend time musing on how Henry was wrapped up in the dim spinster. I doubted it'd last. Because what could they possibly find to talk about? I supposed she was making soothing noises and giving him understanding looks. Well, a monkey could do that. More importantly, what was *Henry* doing? Making a point, I suspected. The point being that he was tired of spirited women, and hankered for the good, old-fashioned kind. Well, guess what: I didn't have much regard for self-pitying, narrow-minded middle-aged men.

Within a fortnight, I was back to the job of being queen and Henry's wife. Back to the hubbub. At Whitehall. My only problem was, that was where *she* was: the Seymour spinster. And her following: because, predictably, an entourage had gathered. Including my cousin Francis, the one-eyed turncoat. There the Seymour spinster was, in the middle of it all, looking sanctimonious. Sitting around, pudding-like; her dim little eyes forever seeking those brothers of hers, awaiting instructions. I'd have loved to send that country bumpkin back where she belonged, to spend her remaining tedious years sewing kneeling cushions for her local church, but Henry would've over-ruled me and how would that have looked? *Sit it out*, I told myself.

On one of my first days back, when I hadn't yet learned to absent myself from her scintillating company, she was sitting there in the corner of my room, clicking open and shut a locket. This, accompanied by the appreciative murmurs of various pea-brained, easily impressed ladies, told me that it was a gift. No wonder she was spellbound: I doubt anyone had ever given her anything, before. And now her fat neck was graced by the king's gold. *Click, click, click*.

'Oh, for fuck's sake, stop that!' I stalked over and yanked it. Managed it, too, but only by having the chain bite hard into the fold of my index finger. I dropped the locket to cradle my bleeding hand. Annie had to dress it for me.

I might not be able to beat her and her po-faced retinue, but I certainly wouldn't join them. It was a relief to spend time with my own friends. They might have been fewer, but at least they were genuine. What was *happening* at court? Fun had become a dirty word. *I* could still enjoy myself, though: me and my friends, we'd still have fun. *More* of it, even, at the po-faced retinue's expense. And more of everything else, at Henry's expense. I was determined there should be no let up on being queen. I had my bed canopied with Florentine cloth of gold and hung with Venetian gold tassels. *My* bed, a bed better enjoyed at that time with no Henry in it. And myself: my new passions were a tawny velvet and a russet silk. Mr Matte was busier than ever, dressing a queen and her little princess.

Strategy, was what George called it. He was buoyant, he was everywhere. Determined, I suppose, that there'd be no let up in being a Boleyn. He was down every passageway and around every corner; in every room, in the thick of every conversation. Being George to the utmost: the man with the quickest wit, the sharpest eye, the biggest laugh. Beside him, the Seymour brothers were shown up in their true, insipid colours.

It was Boleyn strategy. We weren't to be put off our stride by a passing fancy for the Seymours. And we'd follow the way the wind was blowing, turning our backs on France and looking instead to Spain. Tom had become very keen on Spain; and Tom *was* policy, policy *was* Tom. His change of tactic was clear from the attention he was paying to Chapuys, if nothing else. There *was* something else, though: his panderings to the bastard half-Spaniard, Mary. He returned one of her mother's crosses to her, I was told. It was something she'd been asking for but had previously been denied.

George's opinion was that we couldn't beat Tom. So, after Tom's lengthy tête-à-tête with Chapuys on the last day of March, news of which spread like wildfire, my brother began lying in wait. Within a couple of days, his chance came: he waylaid Chapuys coming into the palace and accompanied him to Mass, issuing an invitation to supper afterwards. Chapuys was caught off-guard, but he's nothing if not polite. As they walked into Chapel, I was ready, I was *there*. George stopped and bowed to me. Flustered, Chapuys copied. I was acknowledged, at last. Bowed to, no less. There was a collective intake of breath behind me: Seymours and Mary-supporters, seriously displeased. Chapuys flinched, a spasm of self-disgust. Chapuys, compromised. Well, good. About time.

Actually, no: to tell the truth, this wasn't what I felt. I'd love to say I did, but the truth is that I was impressed. Touched, almost. Worried and weary as I was, I needed to believe in that nervous bow from the ambassador. I imagined there might be an understanding between us, now that Catherine was dead.

But I still didn't really like it; not really; of course I didn't. I'd been momentarily bowled over by Chapuys's unexpected, apparently gracious greeting. The rest of it, I didn't trust: Tom's being kind to Mary, being chummy with Chapuys. Tom, in short: it was *him* I didn't trust. Because I didn't know what he was up to. Repairing relations with Spain, yes; but where, in those plans, was I? Was I to be irrelevant? Friendship with Spain, if there had to be: I'd go along with that, I'd do my duty for England. But I wouldn't let it happen at any price. Not at the price of Spain completely disregarding England's queen.

Tom hadn't been doing much to inspire my confidence. I discovered he'd swapped apartments at Greenwich with the Seymours, so that they could enjoy the benefits of the interconnecting door with Henry's apartment.

I was incredulous. 'What did you do that for?'

He shrugged, unconcerned. 'Because Henry asked me.'

It dawned on me that all I'd been, for Tom, was something he could do for Henry. He'd made me queen for Henry, not because he was my supporter. I'd always known he didn't really like my friends. They, in turn, didn't really like him. Two different worlds, often in the same room, at the same table, but two different worlds. To him, they were good for nothing; to them, he was a bit of a bore. But we all needed each other. He socialized with us just enough to keep in with the in-crowd; and we welcomed him because he oiled the wheels.

But Tom didn't like Mary's lot any more than he liked us. Less, in fact. He was personally committed to reforming the Church and Mary's lot would turn it all back. He'd lose everything he'd worked for. So, there he was, between a rock and a hard place. He didn't seem a happy man, which could have cheered me but didn't. Because Tom, unhappy, was dangerous. Cornered, he was, I knew, capable of anything.

Exactly a month ago, a month ago to this very day, Henry was shouting at Chapuys, insisting on one condition: a written apology from the emperor for how he'd treated me over the years. Insisting on official Spanish recognition of me. Not that I was there, to hear it. Because that wouldn't have been dignified, would it. Anyway, I didn't *have* to be there; I'd already said my bit, to Henry. For once, it hadn't been hard to make him listen. I'd appealed to his pride. I'd asked him, How will it look? The emperor decides you're wonderful, after all, with the exception of everything you've spent the past decade working for; everything you stand for. I had the usual response, from him: the non-response, the pursed lips. I was taking a chance. Did I have anything to lose, though? And, anyway, I'm at my best when I'm up against it. And I was good; oh, I was very good. I demanded, Is that what you want? Is that what you'll settle for? And he went off, not having said a word. Nothing new in that.

I knew when the meeting with Chapuys was scheduled for: 18 April, the soonest day after Easter; Easter Tuesday. And I knew it wouldn't be difficult to get it reported back to me. It was Franky Weston who obliged. He was there, witnessed it: Henry, apoplectic; Tom, ashen.

Tom, scuppered. Tom, daring to interrupt, desperate to salvage the negotiations. And getting shouted down, in turn, for his pains. Tom, leaving.

He didn't return for a few days; claimed he was sick. I was thrilled by Franky's account of that scene in the Presence Chamber. And of course I was. I'd won, hadn't I. I'd proved what I needed to prove. All I could think was, Let people doubt it, now, then: Henry's commitment to me.

My little victory: Henry, outraged on my behalf. Except that it was on his *own* behalf that he'd been outraged, wasn't it. How did I lose sight of that? It was what I'd banked on. What I'd encouraged. Perhaps I was a touch dizzy on my apparent success. Or relieved, certainly. Guard down. Resting on my laurels.

A lull of nearly two weeks followed the Chapuys storm. A Calais trip, planned for the day after May Day, to look forward to. Life, back to normal, more or less, it seemed; which meant, for Henry and me, that we tended to keep out of each other's way. Tom seemed to be keeping out of everyone's way. I should have guessed he wasn't licking his wounds, or not only licking his wounds. He was thinking. Planning. I should have known, because does he ever give up? Those few days in bed helped him; gave him the time to think. To stop, and start again. To stop thinking of me as queen. He couldn't get at me, as queen; I'd done nothing wrong as queen. The trick was to think of me as a woman.

Stop thinking 'queen', it's over-complicated. Think 'woman'. Think 'woman surrounded by men', and there you have it. The bonus was that they were men he didn't like; men he'd love to see go.

The same, for Henry: stop thinking 'king'. A king's life is complicated by strategies, responsibilities, loyalties. Think 'man'. 'Cuckolded man'. There's only one possible response to that, isn't there.

Mark Smeaton was the first to be arrested. *Mark*: how pitiless is that? Such easy prey. None of us realized he was gone. Not least because he was often somewhere else: wandering minstrel Mark. Working in the chapel, or on one of his mysterious Mark-quests, visiting the gardeners or whatever else it was that he used to like to do. Tom probably even knew that; knew he could get a head start with Mark by taking him unnoticed and keeping him for twenty-four hours, extracting a 'confession' to start the ball rolling. He'd probably made it his business to know quite a bit about Mark.

But here's something else: the truth about Mark and me. Just the day before his arrest, I spotted him standing at a window, looking miserable. Morale among the boys was low, I was well-aware. Despite Henry's apparent turnaround, our little crowd was, understandably, still tense.

I asked him, 'What's up?'

He turned to me, hugging himself, gave me a rueful smile, and said, 'Nothing that a mere look from you can't cure.' And that was all he said – turning back to the window – but it was enough. The way it was said, it was clearly meant to mean something.

There was something, here, to be dealt with. And at a time when I could barely deal with getting up in the mornings.

You do pick your timing, don't you.

I touched his arm, but turned away. Burdened, now, with his vulnerability. Fighting an urge to fling it back at him: *You're not meant to mean it, you know.*

But he didn't know, did he, and probably no amount of being told would ever make it clear to him. Because that was Mark: serious-minded; heartfelt. Why had we ever taken him on, I wondered; taken him in, welcomed him into our little circle. Lovely though he was, he was also, it seemed to me, a liability.

I was unsettled, all day, after that. Angry, even. I wanted everything back to how it had been; I wanted everything to be fun again. Perhaps that's why I said what I did to Harry Norris, that evening. It happened when I goaded, 'When are you going to make an honest woman of Meg?' and he looked suitably bashful.

'Ah,' I said, 'I know what it is. You're waiting for me, aren't you. Waiting for something to happen to Henry.'

He looked aghast; I seemed to have overstepped the mark. True, it probably wasn't the time for such jokes. Which is probably why I'd said it.

I was surprised at Harry's humourlessness. 'Oh, *really*, Harry.'

'Anne –' He held up his hands and I knew what was coming: *If I've ever given you any such impression* . . .

'Harry!' I was furious. 'Don't flatter yourself.'

And he sat there, tightlipped.

'It was a *joke*.' I gave up on him and glanced around at everyone else, at stoney faces. 'A *joke*? Remember those?'

The funny thing is, none of us knew, then, just how serious it was about to get.

It was later that evening, at about eleven o'clock, when I'd given up on company and was alone, thinking about getting ready for bed, that some lackey turned up at my door with a message from Henry. Calais was cancelled.

'Why?' I wanted to know.

He said he didn't know.

His manner was, I felt, insolent.

He said that the message was that we weren't going to Calais, the day after tomorrow; that was all he knew.

So, I decided to go to the person who *would* be able to tell me. But not alone.

I came to your rooms, first, Elizabeth. You were still with us, at Greenwich; you'd been with us for Easter. Margaret Bryan was still up, sewing. 'But she's asleep,' she said of you, and I almost laughed in her face because it seemed to me that a little missed sleep, a surprise waking, was neither here nor there, now; not with what I was beginning to suspect was at stake.

I came into your bedroom and you were indeed asleep. I stood for a while, similarly spellbound, beside your bed. Wondering at you, at the wonder of your sleep, at the abandon with which you were able to sleep. Had I ever slept like that? Would you ever sleep like that again? Well, if I had anything to do with it, you would; you'd always sleep like that. Princess.

And then I did what I had to do, what I'd come to do. I gathered you up. You came easily, too sleepy to protest, but I soothed you nonetheless: 'It's me, it's Mummy.' You'd been baking in your blankets: you were fragrant, sticky, endearingly criss-crossed where you'd been pressed onto rumpled bedlinen. You are such a big girl, now: a proper *girl*. I had no idea how I'd carry you. But I had to. So, I did.

We headed for your father's rooms. Your eyes, when open, had a sheen, reflections of the flares bracketed along the walls. You were so good, so quiet, while I blundered down that passageway with the whop-whop-whop of blood inside my ears. Eventually, trailing the studied unresponsiveness of the yeomen, we made it to where I'd guessed your father would be. And suddenly there he was, facing us, stock-still, standing his ground. I don't remember who else was there. People. The usuals. The Venetian ambassador.

Your father was sheer bulk, yet every feature was small and becoming smaller in retreat from us: lidded eyes, tightened lips, his blood rising to the tips of his ears.

I spoke first. 'What's going on?' I asked. 'I know something's going on.'

He found his tongue. 'Anne,' he said, sharply, 'why is she up with you at this hour?'

Indignant father. Chaotic mother.

I knew why I'd taken you there, but now I didn't know how to put it into words. I made a start, though. 'Your daughter.' It sounded like an accusation. I unfolded you a little, and you obliged, lifting your head to look at him, sweetly sleep-blurred. 'See? Your daughter.' Then I said, 'Something's going on, I know it is. You're up to something. But don't you *ever* forget who else is involved in this. Whatever you think of me, don't you take it out on her.'

'She shouldn't be up.' For all his apparent concern for you, you weren't the focus of his attention. It was splayed across the room. Other people: that's who mattered to him. He was embarrassed.

I said it in a rush, like a curse: 'Yes, that's right, start behaving like a father. It's a pity you can't behave like a husband, too.' And I asked him, 'Why have you cancelled Calais?'

The reply, if you could call it that, was almost inaudible: 'I don't have to answer to you.' Then, clearly: 'Please go, Anne. Take Elizabeth back to her room.'

I'd get no further. I'd get no answer about Calais. I suppose I'd always known that. Certainly since turning up with you, like that, I'd known it. I'd made my point, though. I do think I had.

The May Day jousts, the following day, seemed to be going ahead as planned; no one had heard anything to the contrary. So, we all turned up at the Greenwich tiltyard like in the old days, determined to make the best of it. Even Fitz came along, bright-eyed, pleased to be out. Henry and I took up our places in our separate boxes: a tradition for which, on this occasion, I imagine we were both grateful. And you came along, briefly, Elizabeth; do you remember? To see the horses. To stay for the first joust, George and Harry. Just the one, so you didn't become bored. Your father lifted you so you could pat your Uncle George's horse's nose. Do you remember? I remember your delighted squeal when it nudged your tiny hand.

Harry's horse was nowhere near us spectators; Harry was having trouble with him. As your father gave you back to Lady Bryan, he was calling for one of his own horses to be fetched for Harry as a substitute. Your father doesn't joust any more – he's had one fall too many, and it's a young man's sport – but he hasn't relinquished his best jousters.

'Are you *sure*?' Harry was asking. Because of course it's personal: horses.

'Yes! Take him!'

I laughed to see them back to how they'd always been with each other, Henry and Harry. Henry, expansive in the face of Harry's reticence. I sparked with renewed affection for them: my boys. It seemed such a shame that they hadn't been spending as much time together, lately, as usual.

Harry rose to the challenge of an unfamiliar horse, to win. George was the graceful loser. All goodnatured, as usual. This'll go on and on, I felt, watching them: us, being the stars here. Me and the boys. It simply couldn't be any other way. We'd made this court our own: we were the court, and it was us. This is a bad patch, I told myself, but we'll weather it.

That afternoon, Henry seemed to tire earlier than he should

have: by chance, I spotted him leaving his box. George was sitting with me. I tapped his arm, nodded in Henry's direction. 'Where's he going?'

George craned to see.

'D'you think he's all right?'

He shrugged. 'Looks fine to me.'

By then, Henry'd gone.

That was the last time I ever saw him.

Not until George went to find Harry, later, to travel back with him, did he discover that Harry had left with Henry. Just the two of them, and a groom each, riding to Whitehall. A sudden departure, a very small party. Still, he didn't think anything of it. Not enough, even, to remark on it to me. And if I thought about it all, which I'm not sure I did, Harry's absence that evening was entirely understandable. After a day of high jinks, he'd probably decided on a quiet evening with Meg.

The truth came, a day later, from Harry's groom, who'd heard some of the conversation of the two riders ahead of him. Henry had asked Harry about Mark Smeaton and me. The groom overheard Henry asking, 'Did you *know*?' And again, and again: '*Did you know*?'

And Harry's denials, of course. Poor Harry, he didn't even know there was nothing to know.

Henry was unplacated, disbelieving. According to the groom, he said to Harry, 'Makes me wonder what else you keep from me.'

Harry protested, incredulous.

Henry said, 'You're very close to Anne, aren't you,' and Harry answered, 'She's an old *friend*; you *know* that.'

Then the groom heard no more, Henry and Harry descending into fierce whispering. That was when they spoke at all: there were lots of silences. I can see it, now: Henry brooding, like only Henry knows how; and Harry at a loss. I feel for Harry, having to hear it from Henry himself, yet also I envy him. I wish I could ask him: how did he seem, to you? Is he ill? Has he gone mad? Does he believe it, really, do you think? Who, exactly, really, is he angry with? When they arrived at the Whitehall stables, Henry swept down from his horse and stalked away. Harry hung around, chatting to the groom, seemingly unsure what else to do, where else to go.

None of this we knew, not until he'd already been taken to the Tower on the following morning. I didn't know until I, myself, was called for questioning. My summons came at midday: Uncle Norfolk wanted to see me in the Council Chamber. Admittedly, it was an odd venue for a tête-à-tête; formal. I remember thinking, What's the old goat up to? 'I'll be along,' I said, 'when I've eaten. Tell him.'

It was the messenger from two evenings ago, the crier of the Calais cancellation. He treated me again to his absurd, clipped little bow.

When I went into the Council Chamber, I realized at once that this was to be no swapping of gossip. There certainly was something going on, and this was it: it was here. My uncle wasn't alone; with him were William Paulet and William Fitzwilliam. The Williams were sitting; my uncle was standing, pacing, assuming authority. He had his official face on. I nodded to the Williams; they nodded back.

My uncle said, 'Sit down,' gesturing at a chair.

Startled, I did so.

'Now,' he said, and I suppose I was expecting some preamble but he simply said it: 'Sir Henry Norris and a man called –' he consulted some notes '– Mark Smeaton have been arrested on charges of having committed adultery with you.'

'*What?*' I sprang up.

'Sit down, please, Anne.' He said it as if bored.

My intake of breath came back as a bleat. 'You *are* joking.'

'Sit *down*,' he said, now stern.

No. *Oh* no. No *way*. I walked up to him: that ridiculous, pinch-faced little man. 'Tell me you're joking,' I said, like a threat.

'I'm *telling* you what I*'ve* been *told*.' He flapped a piece of paper.

I said, 'But it's not true, is it. *Who* told you?'

He lowered his voice: 'They *have* been arrested, Anne, on those charges. Now, will you *please sit down*.'

'I need to see Henry.' This, I said to the Williams.

But it was my uncle who replied: 'That wouldn't do you any good.'

'I'll be the judge of that.'

'No, *I* will.'

Suddenly, I couldn't breathe.

'Sit down.' He placed a hand on my shoulder, pressed me down.

What happened then was that I was questioned. I gave straight answers; the questions didn't merit protest. This was to be gone through, it seemed. *Fine, then: let's go through it.* Did I have sex with Harry, Mark, on such and such a date, at Greenwich, Hampton Court, Bridewell, Whitehall, Eltham?

No, I didn't. No, no, no.

Only once did I lose my temper. A particular date struck a chord: a September day, a couple of years ago. 'That'd have been a week after Elizabeth was born. What are you suggesting? That he came sauntering into a roomful of women and charmed them all into looking the other way while he snuck into my bed, onto the bloodied bedlinen, for some fun?' He did flinch, I saw it; I saw, too, the distaste with which he'd always regarded me. *Good, you foul little man; why should I be nice for you?*

'I'm suggesting nothing,' he said. 'I'm asking you a question.'

'And the answer's no, isn't it.'

'Is it?' Official, checking: *in your own words.*

'The answer's no.'

In the end, he said, 'Right.'

My blood prickled: *Yes, but what happens now? What is this really about?*

He answered my unspoken question immediately. 'I shall need you to accompany me to the Tower.'

'The Tower?' Actually, it was the last thing I'd expected. 'But I've just *told* you: none of it's true.'

'Nevertheless,' he said, shuffling papers, declining to look at me, 'you're under arrest and will have to reside at the Tower.'

'Oh, this is absurd,' I said. 'I need to see Henry. *NOW*.'

'It would benefit you,' this was emphatic, as if I were a child, 'to come without fuss.'

Oh, and you'd know, would you? How much do you know? How much of this, then, is your doing?

He added, lightly and crisply, as if being helpful: 'Don't pack. Just come with us. We'll send along whatever you request.'

My turn to say, 'Right.' *Have it your way.* I stood. 'Let's go.' I'd let him see that I couldn't be intimidated.

The two Williams sloped off. Only my uncle came with me to the river, and, on the way, he dropped his officious manner, shaking his head and tutting as if to say, *Well, well, well, what a business.* As if I – rather than him and other liars – were somehow at fault. I asked him where my father was.

'Keeping his head down,' he said.

I should've known. I asked him where Harry was. In the Tower, was the answer.

I wondered if I'd see him, there. I supposed not. 'And Mark, too?'

He nodded.

I hadn't seen them go. No one had, as far as I knew. Perhaps no one was seeing my departure, either. I hoped not. It wasn't my own barge that was waiting for me; the queen's barge, which had been the Spaniard's before I'd had her emblems knocked from it and replaced with mine. For that, I remembered, Henry had ticked me off: *Couldn't you have waited?* I'd done so much waiting, by then, though, hadn't I.

This one, to take me to the Tower, was an anonymous royal barge, at the royal steps. And there, on those steps, was Tom. He'd dared to show up, to show his miserable face. Actually, it *was* a miserable face: he was affecting an expression of world-weariness, as if he were the one with the problems. As if this was all very regretful. *Hurts me more than it hurts you.* In truth, though, he must have been delighted. I said, while walking past him down the steps, 'You've certainly exercised your imagination with this one, haven't you.'

He said nothing.

At the bottom of the steps I turned and spoke up to him. 'It's all a bit obvious, though, isn't it? I must admit I'm surprised at you. A bit *easy*. My husband's best friend? And some gullible little hanger-on?' Settled in the barge, I added, 'Needs must, though, I suppose. You need something on me, and you can't find anything else.'

The barge seemed to buckle as he stepped aboard.

'Your problem,' I continued, 'will be making it stand up in court. You must have thought about that. It must be worrying you. I mean, you might like to believe in all this bed-hopping; but it's quite possible, isn't it, that no one else will. A jury might just see right through it. And then what? This could be your one big mistake, couldn't it.' I checked, 'I presume I *will* be going to court?'

His tone matched his face. 'Yes, Anne.'

I smiled at him. 'A fair trial?'

'All the king's subjects get a fair trial.'

'Oh, yes,' I laughed. 'Yes, of course.'

I ignored them, Tom and my uncle, throughout the journey. I'd nothing more to say to them. They chatted to each other: nothing much; business. I shut it out, their mundane conversation. In its place were the oars, clipping the river-surface then rising from it and raining droplets. My mind was empty. I was exhausted. I did think, at one point, *Harry, I'm coming*: just like that, a clear cry but unsounded. Harry, in the Tower: he was where I was going; I was going somewhere he was. And any place where Harry was couldn't be all that bad. Even if I didn't get to see him. Mark's music: maybe I'd hear that, in the distance, while I was there. I could listen for it. We'd come through this, the three of us, I told myself. No one would believe what was being said of us.

Henry, though: where was Henry?

Henry, I couldn't sense at all; not his whereabouts, nor, indeed, anything else about him. Especially not his state of mind.

To my relief, we disembarked via the royal steps and not at Traitors' Gate. Mr Kingston, the Tower's superintendent, was there; he helped me ashore. Smiled, even, although seriously. A nice man, Mr Kingston. Before, I'd have said he was in the wrong job; now I know it's the *right* job. Thank goodness for Mr Kingston, at the Tower. I asked him if I'd be going to a dungeon.

'No, no, no, no, no,' he said: I'd be going to my apartment.

My *apartment*! I'd forgotten its existence, I hadn't been back there since my coronation. Suddenly, I started crying: relief, I suppose, along with weariness and self-pity. 'Oh, my lovely apartment,' I burbled, stupidly.

'Yes, that's right,' he soothed, taking my arm, leading the way.

I could make this my home, I realized. Hole up here, and think everything through. Explore my options. Explain myself. Get help.

What wasn't anywhere near so lovely as my apartment, though, was who was in it. Whoever had chosen my attendants had chosen carefully to give me maximum discomfort. My lady jailers gathered at the door to greet me. First, Auntie Liz. My heart seized up. She sniffed, up that long nose of hers. That was her greeting. Beside her, was Meg's mum. She, I know, considers that I've led Meg astray. She looked at me with a peculiar mix of suspicion and satisfaction. Ready for me. Then there was Mrs Cosyn, wife of my own Master-of-Horse, my head of stables. I trusted Cosyn with my horses because he was extraordinarily dedicated. One of the reasons for his dedication, everyone knew, was that he preferred the stables to home. Who wouldn't, if he was married to Mrs Cosyn. Silly bitch. Given to intrigues. Fancying herself as someone. Her eyes lit up when she saw me. She was as overdressed as ever. Last, but by no means least, was Mr Kingston's wife. She's nothing like him. Takes the job to heart, relishes the job in hand.

But then also, hanging back, two others. Tommy Wyatt's sister, Marg. '*Marg!*' My childhood friend. She smiled, shyly, embarrassed: difficult circumstances in which to meet again after so long. It was both wonderful to see her, and sad. She looked done-down, somehow. Me, too, though, I suppose. Age. And, 'Mrs Orchard!' My old nanny. And she really *is* old.

Was it a trick, these two being here? Were they going to go, now? I pushed past the horrible four to be welcomed by Mrs Orchard's hug and, 'Well, well, well,' which, unlike my uncle's wasn't disapproving. I knew she wanted to finish with *Haven't you grown* but was restraining herself. *She'd* shrunk. She and Marg seemed self-conscious in the company of the four; but I was here, now, wasn't I, and if we didn't quite match them in numbers, we were certainly a match for them in other ways. Mrs Orchard was saying. 'Come on, we've something for you to eat. You must be starving, after that trip.' And, actually, I suddenly was; I was.

That evening, Mr Kingston came by to see if I had everything I needed.

'Oh, she's fine,' his wife answered before I could speak. She was playing cards with her three fellow-spies. Ostensibly playing cards, but also, clearly, listening to my conversations with Marg and Mrs Orchard; with Marg, mostly, because Mrs Orchard was dozing.

'I'm fine, yes, thank you,' I told Mr Kingston, and invited him to stay a while. Unconventional, probably, but this was hardly a conventional incarceration. And, anyway, some male company seemed like a good idea.

'Oh, well . . .' *If you're asking.* Ill at ease, yet obviously gratified, he settled himself down.

'This is particularly good,' I said of some pie.

'Oh.' Interested, he accepted a slice. He didn't stop eyeing me, though; seemed wary of me. Probably he felt I should be crying. Well, sometimes I *had* been; but I couldn't cry all the time. Or so I thought.

As soon as he asked, 'You're bearing up, then?' and I nodded, about to say that I was well-fed, warm, in good company, my throat closed and the tears began again.

He looked mortified, of course.

I reached over and reassured him with a hand on his arm. 'It's just the *injustice* of these charges,' I managed. 'You know? You've heard?' Surely he had.

He nodded, looking at his shoes.

'I mean,' I despaired, 'I've been thinking: I remember Franky – Weston – once saying he loved me. Declaring it in front of everyone. Like they do, these boys. And now I think, Oh, so, are they going to get him, too?'

And that's exactly what happened. The very next day.

Franky.

And Billy, too, for good measure.

George: what happened with George was that he went from Greenwich to Whitehall as soon as he heard I'd been arrested, to see Henry. Presumably to find out what was happening, and to try to sort it out. He was arrested when he arrived, not having set eyes on Henry. The charges were the same as for his friends.

The same charges?

It was Mrs Cosyn who told me. The news had a physical effect on me: I stood and paced as if letting a pain die down. Then I turned to her and burst out laughing. 'I'm not *that* stupid,' I laughed. 'Any woman who sleeps with George deserves what she gets.'

George and I were arrested last Tuesday. On Friday, the boys – minus George – went to trial: Harry, Franky, Billy, and Mark. My brother, as a peer of the realm, was due a trial by his fellow-peers. The boys' trial was in Westminster Hall. The axe man would have been in attendance, his axe turned away from them until the verdict came. It didn't take much to imagine the jury-rigging that would have been done to ensure the required verdict, but Mr Kingston told me, anyway. 'Top notch,' was how he put it. 'Knights, all of them.' All of them enemies of the boys.

'Who was foreman?'

'Ed Willoughby.' He was just as impressed.

'Oh, well, that was Billy done for, regardless,' I said. 'Ed Willoughby owes Billy a lot of money.'

Mr Kingston looked crestfallen. He'd been happy to believe in the system.

Some system: the boys probably weren't even informed of the charges against them, and there'd have been no one to speak for them. They'd gone there to be judged guilty, as simple as that. To be seen to be judged guilty. The axe man turning his blade towards them. All they could have hoped for was that Henry would have a change of heart. Would have a heart.

On Saturday, my household – at Greenwich, where I'd left it – was dissolved. Anyone in my service was let go and absolved of any association with me. Which implied I wouldn't be going back.

So, my trial – coming, on the Monday – was a formality. And yet it wasn't: it was my one chance to be heard. That was if Henry didn't step in, first, to stop it all. To send me away some-where. Abroad, or a nunnery. And he would, wouldn't he? That was what I was still hoping, on Sunday.

Because he didn't hate me *that* much, did he?

George's trial was to follow mine. We were treated to the Great Hall here at the Tower, a much bigger venue, because of the numbers of spectators expected. Two thousand, Mr Kingston later told me, impressed. His wife accompanied me into the hall, and settled me in the appointed chair. And there I was, facing my uncle again. He was Lord Steward. What pained me for an instant was that Hal was beside him: his son, deputizing as Earl Marshal. Hal didn't look at me; not once, that I was aware of. I was grateful for that; it would have been more than I could bear. As it was, I sat calm, ready. Took a moment to look around. There was Tom, chewing his lower lip. We looked at each other, across that hall. *You or me.* Because there was the faintest chance, wasn't there? All those people: not all of them could be in his pocket or owe him a favour. Would someone stand up and say something? Could there be a kind of riot?

And then it began: my uncle's listing of alleged incident after alleged incident. I'd heard it all before, of course, but the magnitude was still striking. Me, who'd refrained from sex with my married lover for almost seven years. Perhaps it was supposed to be that once I'd started, I couldn't stop. Got a taste for it. Made up for lost time. So that even my own brother would do. Even when I was pregnant, recovering from a birth, a stillbirth, a miscarriage. Perhaps I did it to take my mind off all that.

My uncle's tedious litany gave me time to continue looking around, and there was Harry Percy. One of the jury. Poor Harry, dragged down from Northumberland to do his duty. I couldn't see how he looked – couldn't see if what people said was true – because he was sitting with one elbow on the bench in front of him and his forehead resting in that hand. And then it was time for me to answer as charged.

Watch, Harry. Listen. This is how to do it, this is how to be a man.

No, I had not slept with those named men on those dates or any other. No, I hadn't promised to marry Harry Norris if Henry died. I hadn't hoped for Henry's death. Hadn't poisoned Catherine, nor planned to poison Mary (I didn't add, *Although I wish I had*). Yes, I'd given money to Franky Weston (who hadn't?), but I gave money to a lot of people. I had money, they didn't. I was queen, they needed looking after, or treating. It was expected. A pointed glare at my uncle: *As you well know.*

There was no case to answer, surely. I'd done well, I knew I had. I'd kept my cool. But it was time for the jurors to give their verdicts, each of them, from the most junior upwards, and they all knew which verdict was expected of them. And so it came, a string of carefully expressionless guilties. Harry Percy didn't lift his head even to give his verdict. Mrs Orchard wailed; I recognized the voice, its fragility. When everyone was quiet, we all turned to my uncle: *Let's hear it.*

And – can you believe it – he was snivelling. Leaking. Red-eyed, red-nosed.

Well, it was a bit late for that.

I'd have loved to have leant across and given him something to *really* cry about.

He pronounced sentence: death by burning or beheading. He didn't have to add, dependent on Henry's goodwill.

Henry's goodwill.

Then it was time for my say. I knew I could say whatever I liked, but bear in mind that I was keen on Henry's goodwill. I was understandably keen on that.

I said that what I regretted was that so many men were to die on my behalf. As for Henry, I said, I realized that I hadn't been the ideal wife – and a king does need an ideal wife – but it seemed, after all, regrettably, that I wasn't wife-material. I'd done him no greater wrong than that, though, I finished.

And sat down.

Harry Percy stood up. And fell down. The kerfuffle of a dead-weight body on wood, and of his fellow jurors galvanized. He was helped from the room. I still didn't see his face, just the stooped back of him, and his feet dragging.

The spectators and jury stayed sitting for George's trial. I was taken back to my rooms, to pick at some lunch. The details of George's trial, I later extracted from Marg. I don't understand why she was reluctant. George put in a sterling performance. I'm proud of him. But, then, I always have been. I wouldn't have expected any less of him. We're Boleyns, after all. We don't mess around.

He gave straight, calm denials to every charge, refusing to rise to the bait. The only hitch came when, finally, he was handed a piece of paper on which was written something he was supposed to have said; something of a delicate material, unsayable in public. The question, from our uncle, was, Had he or hadn't he said it?

Quite properly, George wasn't standing for such pussy-footing. He simply read it aloud: 'The king is incapable of making love to his wife because he has neither the skill nor the virility.' I imagine him enjoying it; carefully straight-faced but realizing he had nothing left to lose, and enjoying it.

Unlike Marg, who clearly hated having to tell me, to say it; she's lived a rather sheltered life. If she was at all worried about *my* sensibilities, she shouldn't have been. I laughed. It was *me* who'd said it, to George.

When the hushed uproar had died down, George handed the

slip of paper back to our uncle. 'No,' he said, bored, 'I never said it. Who says I did?'

Uncle Norfolk was so flustered by the direct question that he answered, kind of: 'A lady at court.'

'Ah,' said George. 'The only lady at court I know of who'd wish me this much ill is my own dear lady wife. Am I right?' Turning his smile from our uncle to the jury, he said, 'For any of you who aren't aware, we're not on the best of terms.'

Our uncle, of course, wouldn't reply.

For the record, George is wrong about Jane being the only woman wishing him ill – although, George being George, he probably doesn't realize it – but I suspect he's right about the informant having been Jane.

The jury returned their guilty verdicts and my uncle passed sentence: Tyburn; not needing to add, pending the goodwill of the king. Time for George's last words, and apparently these concerned his debts. That's what was worrying him: the people he owed money. He apologized. 'I would have paid up,' he said, 'you know I would. I just –' and here, he smiled, helpless, and shrugged – 'didn't see this coming.'

Yesterday, Thomas was allowed to visit me. As my confessor. To hear my last confession. 'I've been trying and trying to get to see you,' he said, and I believed him: that small, earnest face of his. 'How *are* you?'

'Much better since they sent my minders away.' After my trial, they'd gone, the four of them; their task – spying – done. I wouldn't mind being here for the rest of my days, I told him: it's quite cosy. There are worse ways to end one's days. And then I asked him, I said, 'Tell me, straight: is there any hope?' I meant a nunnery, abroad.

He knew what I meant. But he looked downcast.

'There was talk of a nunnery for *her*,' I protested: *Catherine*. Even as I said it, I knew it was unlikely to be considered suitable for me. But still I argued, 'I've more sense than she ever had. I'm no martyr, I'm a pragmatist. I'd go quietly.' He looked up, and I read his mind: I've never done anything quietly. I gave him a rueful smile. 'There's always a first time. I'm a fast learner.'

How come Catherine was banished to various draughty castles to live out her remaining years, but I'm held fast here in the heart of London under sentence of death? Am I really more dangerous than she was? Catherine, with her twenty years of having been on the throne; the loyalty that that inspired. Catherine, whose unthroning risked war with Spain, and civil war. Whereas me: with the exception of godly Thomas, there's no one on my side.

Thomas told me: it was Tom who'd given permission for this final visit. Get her reconciled, was what he'd said. To her end, he'd meant.

Yes, I wanted to say, but that's Tom. Where's my husband, in all this? But I knew, didn't I; I knew where he was. I'd gleaned it, from others' asides and silences: Henry was spending all his time with the dim spinster. He had no time to think of me.

I changed tack, asked after the boys; Thomas had been allowed to see the boys, too. 'Are their rooms all right?' I asked. 'Is someone making their beds for them?'

He laughed, in disbelief.

'No, really,' I said, although I was laughing, too, 'you've no idea. They're *hopeless*.'

The beds looked fine, he reassured me: the boys looked fine, and their beds looked fine. 'To be honest, though,' he added, and my heart stilled in readiness, 'your brother seems very worried about his debts.'

I said I knew.

'The debts he's leaving,' he reiterated, and I felt that he looked particularly firmly at me when he said 'leaving'.

Get her reconciled.

I didn't flinch.

'And I don't know if he's being over-anxious . . .'

'I shouldn't think so. He's always enjoyed the high-life, hasn't he. Way above our means.'

'Well,' Thomas said, 'Mr Kingston's talking to Henry, to see if the debts can't be honoured. And it seems that he's having some success.'

'Oh. Good.' Magnanimous Henry, all of a sudden. Or, more likely, when it comes to money, there can't be any loose ends; no grudges against Henry, who's the cause of all this.

Thomas was looking pensive. So, I probed, and he admitted, 'That chap Mark isn't doing so well.'

'Mark? Why not? What's happened to him?' I realized I hadn't been thinking much about Mark. Hardly surprising: I hardly knew him.

'They have him in irons.'

Now I *did* flinch. 'That seems a little unnecessary.'

Thomas raised his eyebrows in agreement. 'No privileges.'

And it struck me what a privileged lot we were, the rest of us, sitting out our last days by firesides, with pies and the kindly attentions of Mr Kingston. But even Mark, thank God, had been granted one privilege along with the rest of the boys, or so I'd heard: no Tyburn, no gallows; but the block at Tower Hill, instead.

And me, ex-queen, one better: not an axe, even, but a sword; a super-sharp sword, wielded by an expert executioner from Calais. Apparently, I won't feel a thing.

Magnanimous Henry.

Thomas was saying of Mark, 'He's not helping his case. He's saying he's guilty.'

'Still?' I knew he had, but I'd assumed he'd been promised something; his freedom in exile, perhaps. A promise that'd obviously been gone back on. 'But why *is* he saying it? He's *not* guilty! And – let's face it – I'd *know*.'

Thomas looked embarrassed, but recovered himself: 'All I can think is that he *feels* guilty. About *something*.'

About his 'feelings' for me. As if anyone gives a damn. 'He's not helping any of us.'

Thomas nodded, vacantly.

'Oh, I know, I know: nothing – no one – would, could. But still.' Impatience flared. 'I mean, what did he say? To you. What did he actually say?'

'Just that. That he's guilty.'

'Of what, though? Did you ask him? Did you say, Of sleeping with the queen?'

Thomas winced. 'No.'

'Well, you should've,' I grumbled. We sat in silence for a moment, and then, in much the same tone, I said, 'Meg's never going to marry Harry, now.'

Thomas nodded.

'And he has a lovely little boy, Harry does. A really lovely little boy.' Thomas opened his mouth to speak but I said, 'Billy. Billy has a wife, you know.' But of course he knew.

He said, 'You have a daughter.' Said it softly, a gentle reminder of why he'd come here. I swallowed hard, looked away, gathering myself for what I knew I had to do: talk.

Not long after Thomas had gone, my brother and the other boys were executed. George, Harry, Billy, Franky and Mark. Mark last, kneeling in all that blood. No fuss from any of them, or so Mr Kingston told me. No admissions of guilt, either; although otherwise, it seems, they said all the right things to keep Henry sweet for their families' sake. There's quite an art to it, seeming contrite without actually confessing.

Oh, except Mark; I forgot Mark. He said he was going to the death he deserved. Liars go to Hell, don't they. That poor boy doesn't stand a chance.

Tomorrow, my turn. I've chosen a crimson gown. The Calais man is a day late, the weather in the Channel very bad. I hope it reaches England, that weather, and I hope it's worse by then and that it never gets any better. I hope it drenches this miserable country. Drowns it.

I have a day longer for people to rally to my cause. You never know. The bishops, say; the bishops I supported, whose jobs I got for them. Whose Church I changed for them. My own father, even, perhaps. That'd be nice. No word, though, so far. Or my husband. Yet tomorrow, I'm told, when I'm stripped of my gown and the two pieces of me are stuffed beneath the floor of St Peter's Chapel, here, unmarked, my husband will announce his forthcoming engagement.

Out with the old, in with the new. Not very old, in my case.

I seem to have been a stepping stone, that's all. For him to step from his stale, useless marriage with an ageing Spaniard to a marriage with a docile English spinster. No one will remember me, a brief three years in the middle of those marriages. Me, who did all the work.

What Henry thinks, what he really thinks, I'll never know. I suspect he doesn't; doesn't think. I suspect he's stopped thinking.

And you, Elizabeth? At best, you'll be pensioned off. That's what I'm hoping. A life in obscurity. Perhaps you'll be passed off as someone else's daughter; because you're young enough, still, not to know. Except that you *will* know, won't you. As long as Marg manages to smuggle this away from here, you *will* know.

I should take this opportunity to pass down some motherly wisdom, shouldn't I. I know what I should say: if you want to keep your head, keep it down. But my guess is that you – Tudor, Boleyn – will run the risk of losing it anyway, one day, so I say this: be your mother's daughter and hold it high.

Epilogue

Anne Boleyn's remains were buried beneath the altar pavement in the chapel royal of St Peter ad Vincula in the Tower on 19 May 1536. The cloak she was wearing at the time of her death is rumoured to be in the private collection of one of the families who had been so opposed to her.

Henry married Jane Seymour on 30 May 1536; their son, Edward, was born in October 1537, but Jane died twelve days later. Henry famously married a further three times. His fifth wife, the teenaged Catherine Howard, was Anne Boleyn's cousin and the only other of his wives to be put to death by him (after a marriage lasting less than two years). Her remains, like her cousin's, were buried beneath the altar pavement in the chapel royal of St Peter ad Vincula within the Tower.

Henry outlived Anne by just over a decade, dying in 1547. His nine-year-old son succeeded him. Following Edward's death in 1553, his half-sister Mary ('Bloody Mary') succeeded to the throne; and upon her death in 1558, Anne Boleyn's daughter began her long reign. Elizabeth was recorded as only ever having mentioned her mother three times during her life, but she clearly favoured courtiers whose families had links to the old Boleyn family.

Henry had Thomas Cromwell executed in 1540. Thomas Cranmer survived into old age but was then burned at the stake for his religious beliefs during Mary's reign.

Anne Boleyn's parents lived quietly after their children's executions, but only survived them by a couple of years. Her father's tomb, in the parish church at Hever in Kent, has an impressive brass. The longest-lived of Anne's immediate family was her sister, Mary, who lived for another decade; and both her children were long-lived.

Anne's sister-in-law, Jane Parker, was executed for her alleged role in facilitating Catherine Howard's adulteries.

Anne's uncle, the third Duke of Norfolk, was condemned to death but Henry died the day before the scheduled execution and he was reprieved. He lived into old age.

Henry Fitzroy, Henry's illegitimate son, died within a year of Anne. He is buried at the Norfolk family's mausoleum in St Michael's Church at Framlingham in Suffolk. His wife, Lady Mary Howard, who survived him by twenty-one years, is buried beside him. Mary's brother, Henry, Earl of Surrey, was executed in Henry's final year, 1547. A tomb was later built at St Michael's for his remains.

Sir Henry Percy died less than a year after Anne. Sir Francis Bryan lived until 1550.

Select Bibliography

Ackroyd, Peter — *The Life of Thomas More* (Chatto and Windus, 1998)

Brears, Peter — *All the King's Cooks, The Tudor Kitchens of King Henry VIII at Hampton Court* (Souvenir Press, 1999)

Fraser, Antonia — *The Six Wives of Henry VIII* (Weidenfeld and Nicolson, 1992)

Ives, Eric — *Anne Boleyn* (Basil Blackwell, 1986)

Sim, Alison — *Food and Feast in Tudor England* (Sutton Publishing, 1997)

Thurley, Simon J — *The Royal Palaces of Tudor England: Architecture and Court Life, 1460–1547* (Yale University Press, 1993)

Weir, Alison — *The Six Wives of Henry VIII* (The Bodley Head, 1991)

Weir, Alison — *Henry VIII, King and Court* (Jonathan Cape, 2001)

Acknowledgements

❀❀❀

Thanks – profuse, and first and foremost – to Martyn Bedford for covering my sabbatical and then my maternity leave with – as ever – stunning efficiency and endless good cheer.

To Gale Owen-Crocker and Jackie Pearson at Manchester University, too, for allowing me the sabbatical, and David Denison before them for re-organising my job so that writing became possible again; and to Ian McGuire and Bill Broady for covering some of my teaching there.

Thanks so much to my parents for the lend of the apartment in Spain where most of this novel was written.

Thanks – more than I can say – to Antony Topping, my agent, for the work that he's done on my behalf, and for all the time, advice, encouragement, reassurance and laughs he's given me.

Thanks to Philip Gwyn Jones at Flamingo for his faith in the novel and his work on it, and the title, to Jon Butler for all his patient editorial help at what was a difficult time for me, and to Mandy Kirkby for volunteering to read the manuscript in her last week at Flamingo.

Thanks to David Supple for such thorough ante-natal care whilst the novel was being written.

And to David Kendall for all kinds of reasons.